彩圖

中級英文文法
Let's See! 四版

U0033920

Verbs Followed by Infinitives
要接不定詞的動詞

Don't attempt to persuade me to get rid of my favorite armchair.

看圖解學英文文法，
立即搞懂文法重點，
輕鬆扎根文法素養！

大量彩圖圖解，
學文法不再艱澀抽象！

主題式條列文法條目，
分量適中有助學習！

精編文法素養練習題，
幫助熟悉與活用！

Unreal Present Conditionals
與現在事實相反的條件句

If his travel agent offered tourist trips to the moon, Jim would book tickets right away.

Relative Clauses With Prepositions
搭配介系詞的關係子句

This is my pet mouse's favorite book, at which she can look for hours.

The Passive
被動語態

The coffee is brewed fresh every morning.

作者 Alex Rath Ph.D.　　譯者 羅竹君／丁宥榆
審訂 Dennis Le Boeuf & Liming Jing

Contents

Part 9   Verbs: Essential Usages 動詞的一些重要用法

Part 10   Infinitives and -ing Forms 不定詞與動名詞

Part 11   Phrasal Verbs 片語動詞

Part 12   Modal Verbs (1) 情態動詞（1）

Part 13　Modal Verbs (2) 情態動詞（2）

Part 14　Adjectives 形容詞

Part 15　Adverbs 副詞

Part 16　Linking Words 連接語

Part 1 Nouns 名詞

Unit 1

Singular and Plural Nouns: Regular
單數與複數名詞：規則名詞

> 單數名詞要用**單數**動詞，
> 複數名詞要用**複數**動詞。
> - That book **is** on the shelf.
>   那本書在架子上。
> - Those books **are** on the shelves.
>   那些書在架子上。

1 可數名詞具有單數與複數形態。大多數**規則名詞**直接加上 s，即構成**複數名詞**。

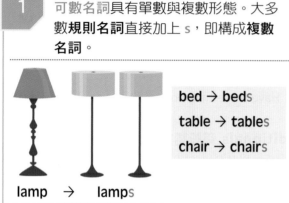

bed → bed**s**
table → table**s**
chair → chair**s**

lamp → lamp**s**

2 字尾是 ch、sh、s、x、z 的名詞，要加上 es。

crutch → crutch**es**
flush → flush**es**
kiss → kiss**es**
box → box**es**
buzz → buzz**es**

> 例外
> 這兩個字尾的 **ch** 都發 /k/ 的音，只加 s。
> - stomach → stomach**s**
> - monarch → monarch**s**

3 特殊字尾的名詞：

y
- 子音 + y → 去 y 加 **ies**
  - baby → bab**ies**
  - lady → lad**ies**
- 母音 + y → 加 s
  - key → key**s**
  - holiday → holiday**s**

> 例外
> 「子音 + **o**」只加 s
> - cello → cello**s**
> - piano → piano**s**
> - photo → photo**s**

o
- 子音 + o → 加 **es**
  - tomato → tomato**es**
  - potato → potato**es**
- 母音 + o → 加 s
  - radio → radio**s**
  - kangaroo → kangaroo
    → kangaroo**s**
  有兩種複數形式，加 -s 或與單數同形 ↵

> 例外
> 兩種拼寫都有
> - buffalo → buffalo**s**/buffalo**es**
> - volcano → volcano**s**/volcano**es**
> - mosquito → mosquito**s**/mosquito**es**

f
- 字尾 f/fe → 去 f/fe 加 **ves**
  - leaf → lea**ves**
  - thief → thie**ves**
  - wife → wi**ves**
- 字尾 ff → 加 s
  - cliff → cliff**s**
  - sheriff → sheriff**s**

> 例外
> 兩種拼寫都有
> - hoof → hoof**s**/hoo**ves**
> - scarf → scarf**s**/scar**ves**
> - dwarf → dwarf**s**/dwar**ves**

> 例外
> 字尾 **f/fe** 只加 s
> - giraffe → giraffe**s**
> - belief → belief**s**
> - safe → safe**s**
> - roof → roof**s**
> - chief → chief**s**

Practice

1

請將括弧內的名詞以「複數形態」填空，完成句子。

1. Eliot saw dozens of _____ (frog) in the pond.
2. Since I cooked, you need to wash the _____ (dish).
3. Real life _____ (hero) are much better than those in comic books.
4. Our company has _____ (factory) all over the world.
5. Gary sharpens his _____ (knife) with a wet stone.
6. There are six _____ (galley) on this cruise ship.
7. Laura rented two _____ (safe) for storing her jewelry.
8. We need three _____ (loaf) of bread and two _____ (carton) of milk.
9. The government caught two _____ (spy) last week and will bring them to trial.
10. *Hamlet* and *Macbeth* are Shakespeare's famous _____ (play).

2

請勾選正確的答案。

1. I visited many ☐ churchs ☐ churches during my trip around Europe.
2. A man cannot have two ☐ wives ☐ wifes at the same time in Taiwan.
3. Electric ☐ toothbrushes ☐ toothbrushs can clean your teeth better.
4. Do you know a story about a poor girl selling ☐ matches ☐ matchs on the street?
5. If I had had two ☐ stomachs ☐ stomaches, I could have eaten more cake.
6. Most ☐ babies ☐ babys start to say simple words by the time they are 12 ☐ months ☐ monthes old.
7. Keith told me he put the ☐ keies ☐ keys on the washing machine.
8. I can get you some more ☐ boxs ☐ boxes from the supermarket if you need them.

3

o 與 f 是兩個麻煩的字尾，字尾是 o 或 f 的名詞，其複數形態的構成方式經常不只一種。請試著將左欄的名詞改寫為「複數形態」，填入右欄正確的空格內（可參考字典）。

1	子音 + o		-es	-s	-s/-es
mango	hero	zero			*mangos/mangoes*
cargo	potato	memo			
kilo	solo	tomato			

2	-f/-fe/-ff		-ves	-s
puff	knife	brief		
half	roof	gulf		
chief	calf	tariff		

Part 1 Nouns 名詞

Unit 2

Singular and Plural Nouns: Irregular
單數與複數名詞：不規則名詞

1 不規則名詞的複數形態，構成方式雖然沒有規則，某些依然有跡可循。第一種方法是變換其中的「**母音**」。

a → e	ou → i
man → men	mouse → mice
woman → women	louse → lice

oo → ee	
foot → feet	
tooth → teeth	
goose → geese	

2 第二種不規則名詞是字尾加上 en 或 ren。

child → children   ox → oxen

3 第三種不規則名詞是「**單複數同形**」，不論數量多少都不變化形式。

 sheep   reindeer

 bison   moose

deer   aircraft

- species
- series

4 源自**希臘文**或**拉丁文**的名詞，其複數形態也沿用希臘文或拉丁文之拼法。

-us → -i
alumnus → alumni 校友
stimulus → stimuli 刺激物
radius → radii 半徑
syllabus → syllabi 教學大綱
fungus → fungi 菌類

-on → -a
phenomenon → phenomena 現象
criterion → criteria 標準

-is → es
analysis → analyses 分析
crisis → crises 危機
basis → bases 基礎
oasis → oases 綠洲
thesis → theses 論點

-x → -ces（或規則）
index → indices/indexes 索引
appendix → appendices/appendixes 附錄

-um → -a（或規則）
memorandum → memoranda/memorandums 備忘錄
referendum → referenda/referendums 公投

5 關於魚類名詞的複數形：
1. 如果指「**同類魚**」或「**泛指魚**」，不論幾隻都是單複數同形，**不加 s/es**；
2. 如果指「**不同類**」的好幾隻，可以加 s/es 也可以不加 s/es，但**以不加較常見**；
3. 當它們指「**魚肉**」時，則為**不可數名詞**，不能加 s/es。

I bought <u>three</u> salmon. 我買了三隻鮭魚。
↳ 三隻一樣品種的鮭魚

Scientists are working hard to protect <u>many types of</u> salmon from extinction.
科學家致力於保護許多種類的鮭魚，以免牠們絕種。

I love to eat fried cod. 我愛吃煎鱈魚。
↳ 鱈魚肉

Practice

1

請將括弧內的名詞以正確的「單複數形態」填空，完成句子。

1. The dentist insisted that I floss my _____ (tooth) every day.

2. There are 22 _____ (child) in each class.

3. There are many _____ (species) of waterfowls in the USA.

4. A shepherd dog can manage hundreds of _____ (sheep) alone.

5. On Christmas Eve, Santa Claus will ride a sleigh pulled by eight _____ (reindeer) to give out gifts.

6. Frontline Plus is used to kill _____ (louse) that bite dogs and cats.

7. _____ (bison) are large animals that live on the plains in North America and Europe.

8. Molds and mushrooms are considered two members of the _____ (fungus) family.

9. Auroras are special atmospheric _____ (phenomenon) occurring in the polar regions.

10. Marvel's *Spiderman* comic book _____ (series) is the source of several movies.

11. The government has called on every citizen to work together to get through this economic _____ (crisis).

2

請從圖片中選出符合說明的詞彙，並以適當的「複數形態」填空，完成句子。

1. _____ are born in fresh water. They grow up in the ocean but swim back up the rivers to lay their eggs in the breeding season.

2. _____ is low fat and nutritious. It is a common source of fish fillets.

3. Goldfish and koi are two famous ornamental _____. They are popular aquarium and pond fish.

4. Clams, mussels, and shrimp are all described as _____.

cod

salmon

carp

shellfish

Unit 3

Countable and Uncountable Nouns
可數與不可數名詞

1 名詞可分為可數名詞和不可數名詞。可數名詞的數量可以計算，並且有**單複數之分**。

可數	不可數
spoon	rice
spoons	rice
湯匙	米

one bowl	two bowls	碗
one highchair	two highchairs	兒童用餐椅
one child	two children	小孩

2 可數名詞的前面，通常會加不定冠詞 a/an 或「數量」，不能完全不加修飾詞單獨使用。

a stove 一個火爐
an icebox 一台冰箱
two washing machines 兩台洗衣機

3 可數名詞可以搭配單數或複數動詞。**單數名詞用單數動詞，複數名詞用複數動詞**。

This tree is **beautiful**. 這棵樹很美。
These trees are **beautiful**. 這些樹很美。
That flower is **fragrant**. 那朵花很香。
Those flowers are **fragrant**. 那些花很香。

4 不可數名詞的數量不可以計算，並且**沒有複數形態**。

milk 牛奶

beer 啤酒

5 不可數名詞前面，通常不能加**不定冠詞 a 或 an**，也不會直接用**數字**來計算。

✗ Dolphins show signs of a cognition and language use.

✓ Dolphins show signs of cognition and language use.
跡象顯示海豚有認知與使用語言的能力。

比較

在某些情況下，不可數名詞之前可以加 a/an 和「數量」，例如在咖啡館、酒吧或餐廳「點飲料」時。

• We would like one wine, one beer, and one coffee.
我們要一瓶葡萄酒、一瓶啤酒和一杯咖啡。

6 不可數名詞沒有複數形態，只能搭配**單數動詞**使用。
（常見的不可數名詞，請見 Unit 4。）

✗ Accurate informations are **hard to find**.
✓ Accurate information is **hard to find**.
精確的訊息不容易找到。
✗ Intuitions are **the basis of a guess**.
✓ Intuition is **the basis of a guess**.
「直覺」是猜測的基礎。

7 可數名詞和不可數名詞都可以用 some 或 any 來修飾。

→ **some** 用於肯定句
I'm going to cook some peas **tonight**.
我今晚要來煮一些豆子。
I'd like to have some fried rice.
我想吃一些炒飯。

→ **any** 用於疑問句和否定句
Is there any green tea **in the refrigerator**?
冰箱裡還有沒有綠茶？
I don't have any coins **in my pocket**.
我的口袋裡沒有零錢。

Practice

1 請從框內選出正確的名詞填空，並註明其為 C（可數）或 U（不可數）。

cherry
typhoon
sugar
lamp
anger
soda
block
soup

soda   U/C

2

請將句子中的錯誤劃去，並寫出正確的用語。

1. Sandy and Trent went to ~~store~~ to buy new home furnishings.
   a store

2. They bought sofa, four dining chair, and a nightstands for their new apartment.

3. Trent isn't satisfied with the sofa. The sofa are too dark.

4. There is not enough dining chairs, because Trent always invites his friends and relatives to their house.

5. The nightstand do not fit their bedroom decor, either.

6. They had argument over the newly bought furnitures.

7. Trent thought Sandy should take an advice or two from him.

8. But Sandy doesn't like any of Trent's opinion.

9. Now, Trent has convinced himself that the dark sofa are easy to maintain. He has stopped inviting so many friends and relatives to their house, and he repainted the bedroom to match the nightstand.

Unit 4

List of Common Uncountable Nouns
常見不可數名詞表

> 有些名詞同時具有**可數**和**不可數**的形態，但是**兩者的意義不同**。

glass		
C 杯子	a glass of water 一杯水
U 玻璃	stained glass 彩繪玻璃

hair		
C 一根一根的毛髮	a hair in my soup 我的湯裡的一根頭髮
U 毛髮的總稱	red hair 紅頭髮

paper		
C 報紙	a paper 一份報紙
U 紙張	some paper 一些紙

iron		
C 熨斗	an iron 一台熨斗
U 鐵	the Iron Age 鐵器時代

potato		
C 一顆顆的馬鈴薯	two potatoes 兩顆馬鈴薯
U 食用的一份	some potato 一些馬鈴薯

事物的整體

baggage
clothing
equipment
food
furniture
fruit
garbage
jewelry
luggage
machinery
mail
money
scenery
silverware
traffic

抽象名詞

advice	intelligence
anger	knowledge
attention	love
beauty	music
confidence	patience
courage	peace
education	progress
evidence	recreation
happiness	sadness
health	significance
honesty	truth
importance	violence
information	wealth

氣體

air
ammonia
carbon dioxide
hydrogen
nitrogen
oxygen
pollution
smog
smoke
steam

顆粒

corn	rice
dirt	salt
dust	sand
chalk	sugar
flour	wheat
pepper	

軟物

bacon	meat
beef	mud
bread	pork
butter	seafood
chocolate	skin
cheese	toast
cream	tofu
jam	toothpaste
jelly	

液體

beer	perfume
blood	sauce
coffee	shampoo
cologne	soda
gasoline	soup
juice	syrup
ketchup	tea
milk	vinegar
oil	water
paint	wine

固體

aluminum	plastic
copper	silver
cotton	steel
glass	tin
gold	wax
ice	wood
iron	wool

語言

Arabic	German
Chinese	Japanese
English	Russian
French	Spanish

學科

biology
chemistry
geography
geometry
history
literature
mathematics
physics
psychology
science

自然

electricity
fire
fog
hail
heat
lightning
rain
snow
sunshine
thunder
weather
wind

oxygen

1

請將各個名詞與對應的圖片連起來。

- jewelry
- pepper
- perfume
- wheat
- cheese
- copper
- hail
- mud

2

請依據題意與提示，以正確的「不可數名詞」填空，完成句子。

1. Tony speaks C_____e and F_____h. He is a professional interpreter.

2. Living things cannot survive without w_____ and o_____.

3. Artificial i_____e will greatly improve human life in the near future.

4. I had b_____n, t_____t, and hot c_____e for breakfast this morning.

5. Ada studied b_____y and c_____y in college. After graduation, she worked in the research department at a biotechnology company.

6. The eruption of the volcano released many types of toxic g_____s and heavy s_____e. If you breathe them, they will endanger your health.

7. Louis lacks c_____e in himself. He doesn't believe he can achieve anything.

8. This coin is made of c_____r and tin.

Unit 5

Nouns Always in Plural Forms
只以複數形態出現的名詞

1 有些名詞永遠只以**複數**形態出現。其中有一種是具有「**成雙、成對**」的特性，要搭配**複數動詞**來使用。在計算的時候，可以使用 a pair of、two pairs of 等來修飾。

Your new trousers are fashionable.
你的新褲子真時髦。
Where are my glasses?
我的眼鏡呢？
Please pass a pair of chopsticks to me.
請拿一雙筷子給我。

2 某些學科類的名詞永遠以**複數**形態出現，但它們的意義其實是「**單數**」的，要搭配**單數動詞**來使用。

The news is shocking. 這則新聞震驚社會。
I studied economics and politics in college.
我大學時修了經濟學與政治學。

- news 新聞
- politics 政治學
- economics 經濟學
- physics 物理學
- mathematics 數學
- statistics 統計學
- optics 光學
- athletics 體育
- gymnastics 體操
- civics 公民學

比較

statistics 指「**統計數字**」時，則是**複數意義**，要搭配**複數動詞**。

Our company's statistics are promising.
我們公司的經營數據顯示前景看好。

politics 這類的詞指「**觀念**」時，也是**複數意義**。

We differ in our politics.
我們的政治立場不同。

glasses

trousers/pants

shorts

jeans

scissors

socks

underpants

chopsticks

3 某些表示「疾病」的名詞，也都以**複數**形態出現，但它們卻也是「**單數意義**」，要搭配**單數動詞**來使用。

- rabies 狂犬病
- measles 麻疹
- mumps 腮腺炎

Rabies is a dangerous disease.
狂犬病是一種很危險的疾病。

gloves

briefs

panties

1

請勾選正確的答案。

1. The newspaper ☐ is ☐ are on the sofa. Today's news ☐ is ☐ are so bad that I don't want to read the newspaper.

2. Are you looking for your ☐ sunglass ☐ sunglasses?
☐ It is ☐ They are on your desk.

3. I'm looking for ☐ a pair of ☐ a piece of gloves. Do you sell gloves?

4. Mumps ☐ is ☐ are a common disease among children.

5. Statistics ☐ indicate ☐ indicates that the crime rate is decreasing.

6. Billiards ☐ is ☐ are one of my favorite games.

7. What ☐ is ☐ are your monthly earnings?

8. I'd like to express my special ☐ thank ☐ thanks to Mr. John Hogan for his support.

2

請從框內選出正確的名詞填空,完成句子。

shoes
ruins
pajamas
gymnastics
shears
tights

We will see the Roman _____ on the trip.

Father is pruning the bushes with a pair of _____.

Lisa has practiced _____ since childhood.

Mary loves pink _____.

Judy got a new pair of ballet _____.

Tutus and _____ are important for ballet dancers.

Unit **6**

Counting Uncountable Nouns
不可數名詞的計算

1 計算不可數名詞，很常見的一種方法是使用量詞（quantifier）。

可數名詞也適用於這種 of 片語。

a bottle of

water   beer   wine

a jar of

honey   tomatoes   jam

a can of

soda   sardines   beer

a slice of

pizza   lime   ham

a bowl of

rice   soup   porridge

a piece of

cake   broccoli   bread

a package/packet of

crackers   nuts

a carton of

milk   juice

a bar of

chocolate   soap

a tube of

toothpaste   hand cream

a pot of

coffee   tea

a box of

macaroons   chocolate

2 另一種計算不可數名詞的方法，是以同義的可數名詞來代替。

a slice of bread	a roll 一條麵包捲
a piece of bread →	a bun 一個圓麵包
a loaf of bread	a loaf 一條麵包
a sum of money	a coin 一枚硬幣
an amount of money →	a 50-dollar bill 一張 50 美元的鈔票
	a 10-pound note 一張 10 英鎊的鈔票

Practice

1 請將各項物品名稱搭配適當的「量詞」，以「of 片語」填入空格中。

1 mustard 2 cheese 3 luggage
4 melon 5 toast 6 mussels 7 soap
8 liquor 9 bath salt 13 shower gel
10 cookies 11 tea 12 spices 14 peach lotion

1.	*a jar of mustard*	8.	
2.		9.	
3.		10.	
4.		11.	
5.		12.	
6.		13.	
7.		14.	

Proper Nouns and Collective Nouns
專有名詞與集合名詞

1 專有名詞用來指一個特定的人、事物或地點，字首要大寫。

Abraham Lincoln

Madrid

the Bible   the Mediterranean

2 大部分的專有名詞都不需要加 **the**。

Uncle Lee has gone to Cairo on vacation.
李叔叔去開羅度假了。
Halloween **falls on the 31st of October.**
10 月 31 日是萬聖節。
Mt. Fuji **is the highest mountain in** Japan.
富士山是日本第一高山。

3 集合名詞用來指「一個整體」或「一個團體」，屬於可數名詞。

- family
- company
- audience
- class
- army
- committee
- crowd
- mob
- team
- police

4 集合名詞可以搭配單數動詞，也可以搭配複數動詞。

1 當它指「整體」時，要用**單數動詞**；
2 如果指「組成這個整體的一個個成員」，就用**複數動詞**；
3 美式英語的集合名詞要用**單數動詞**搭配。如果要強調**成員**，美式英語用 members 與**複數動詞**搭配。

英式 My family are **from Canada.**
美式 My family is **from Canada.**
我的家人來自加拿大。
Family is **the bedrock of community.**
家庭是社群的基石。
英式 The government are **taxing the poor and giving the rich tax breaks.**
美式 The government is **taxing the poor and giving the rich tax breaks.**
政府對窮人課稅，卻給予富人賦稅優惠。
Government is **the main provider of social services for the poor.**
政府是為窮人提供社會福利的主要來源。

5 「特定的數量」、「數目的總和」也屬於集合名詞，但這時要搭配**單數動詞**。

Thirty thousand tons is **a lot of food aid. That is a lot of rice and wheat.** 三萬噸是為數不小的糧食援助，有大量的稻米和小麥。
Six thousand dollars is **not a great amount of money.** 六千塊美金不是太可觀的數目。
The United States is **going to take part in the G20 conference.**
美國將出席二十國高峰會。

6 集合名詞 people、police 和 cattle 則要使用**複數動詞**。

When people act **like cattle, we describe that behavior as the herd instinct.**
當人類的行為像牛群一樣時，我們描述這種行為是一種「群起效尤」的本能。
Like everybody else, police are **only human.**
就像其他人一樣，警察也只是凡人。

Practice

1 請勾選正確的答案。如果句子的美式用法和英式用法不同，請以美式用法為準。

1. One hundred thousand yen ☐ **is** ☐ **are** a lot of money for tuition.

2. Family ☐ **is** ☐ **are** more important than school in shaping values.

3. People ☐ **needs** ☐ **need** jobs to pay for daily necessities.

4. The cattle ☐ **is** ☐ **are** eating grass on the meadow.

5. Has Kenny already gone to ☐ **the Beijing** ☐ **Beijing**?

6. The whole class ☐ **was** ☐ **were** fascinated by his loud and clear voice.

7. His concert had ☐ **a large audience** ☐ **large audience**.

8. The crowd in front of the city hall ☐ **was** ☐ **were** dispersed by the police.

9. The army ☐ **is** ☐ **are** essential for a country's self-defense.

10. The mob ☐ **has** ☐ **have** occupied the airport for over three weeks.

11. The police said ☐ **they were** ☐ **it was** coming in five minutes.

2 請將句中的「專有名詞」標上 P（**proper**），「集合名詞」標上 C（**collective**）。

1. My <u>class</u> elected <u>Mark</u> to be the class leader.
          C   P

2. An army of five thousand men assembled at the border of India.

3. The criminal ran into the crowd in Federation Square.

4. *La Traviata* attracted an audience of thousands to the City Theater.

5. Half of the staff of KPMG International Limited got a pay raise.

6. The mob occupied hospitals and airports, causing chaos and wreaking havoc.

7. Football teams from 32 countries gathered in Russia to compete in the 2018 World Cup.

8. The government has come up with several solutions to prevent the unemployment level from getting worse.

Unit 8

Compound Nouns
複合名詞

1 複合名詞是由**兩個或兩個以上的名詞**組成的**一個或一組名詞**。

bathroom 浴室
keyboard 鍵盤
jet fuel 噴射推進飛行器專用之航空燃油
sheep dog 牧羊犬
low fat milk 低脂牛奶

2 複合名詞中，第一個名詞往往被視為**修飾語**，用來修飾第二個名詞。因此，不管整個複合名詞是單數還是複數，**第一個名詞通常只作單數形態**，不隨之變化。

a plastic bag 一個塑膠袋
two apple pies 兩個蘋果派
the town hall 鎮公所
 ↳ 修飾語

比較

有些名詞因為本來就固定用**複數形**，因此當作**複**合名詞裡的修飾語時，也採用**複數形態**。
- a sports team 一支運動隊伍
- the clothes closet 衣櫥

3 複合名詞的構成方式有三種，第一種是由**兩個或兩個以上的名詞組成的詞組**，是分開的兩個或三個單字。

ice cream 冰淇淋
music store 唱片行
oxygen mask 氧氣罩
key card 鑰匙卡
vacuum cleaner 吸塵器
tomato salad 番茄沙拉
chicken soup 雞湯

bus stop 公車站

4 複合名詞的第二種構成方式，是**將兩個名詞連在一起變成一個字**，中間**沒有連字號**。

shoeshine 鞋油
newspaper 報紙
wastebasket 廢紙簍
rainbow 彩虹
earthquake 地震
bedroom 房間
baseball 棒球
lifestyle 生活方式
battleground 戰場

armchair 扶手椅

5 複合名詞的第三種構成方式，是**將兩個或三個名詞連在一起**，中間**有連字號**。

mother-in-law 岳母；婆婆
runner-up 亞軍

6 複合名詞的複數形，通常是把「**最後一個字**」變成**複數形**。

computer virus → computer viruses
電腦病毒
cruise ship → cruise ships 遊輪
bookstore → bookstores 書店
weekend → weekends 週末

7 也有許多複合名詞的複數形並不是把最後一個字變成複數。因此比較標準的說法，是把複合名詞中的「**主要名詞**」改成**複數**。

father-in-law → fathers-in-law 岳父；公公
passer-by → passers-by 路人
attorney general → attorneys general
首席檢察官
editor-in-chief → editors-in-chief 主編

Practice

1 圖中物品名稱為何？請分別從 A 框和 B 框內選出適當的名詞，組成「複合名詞」，來說明圖中的物品名稱。注意要用正確的格式（可參考字典）。

A

coffee	fax
screw	star
cotton	drug
camp	

B

fire	abuse
grinder	fruit
machine	driver
field	

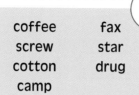
<u>fax machine</u>

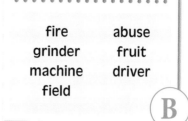

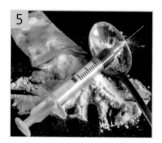

2 請從框內選出適當的「複合名詞」，以正確的「單複數形態」填空，完成句子。

- tissue paper
- coffee milk
- brother-in-law
- passer-by
- animal right
- football
- tool box
- rock music

1. When Dave has the flu, he uses a lot of <u>tissue paper</u> to blow his nose.

2. Some pet owners have strong opinions about ＿＿＿＿＿＿＿＿.

3. Geraldine doesn't like to listen to ＿＿＿＿＿＿＿.

4. Archie likes to kick the ＿＿＿＿＿＿＿ around the field.

5. My extended family includes three ＿＿＿＿＿＿＿.

6. When Denny was being pushed around by three gangsters, the ＿＿＿＿＿＿＿ did nothing to help him.

7. Chester has two ＿＿＿＿＿＿＿ full of hammers, wrenches, and screwdrivers.

8. I feel like having a cheeseburger and some ＿＿＿＿＿＿＿ for breakfast today.

Unit 9

Possessive 's: Forms
所有格「's」的形式

1 用來表示名詞所有格的符號是「's」。

Hal's map 海爾的地圖
Vicky's AI watch 薇琪的人工智慧手錶

Form 形式

2 單數名詞 +「's」→ 所有格

Amy's recording contract
艾美的錄音合約
my little sister's favorite stuffed animal
我妹妹最喜歡的動物填充娃娃
the teacher's glasses 老師的眼鏡

3 字尾是 s 的複數名詞 +「'」→ 所有格

my parents' house 我父母的房子
states' rights
州權（美國憲法所賦予各州的權利）
birds' nest 鳥巢

4 字尾非 s 的不規則複數名詞 +「's」
→ 所有格

men's room 男廁
children's play area 兒童遊戲區
people's imagination 人的想像力

5 字尾是 s 的單數人名，經常要加「's」
成為所有格，也有人主張只加「'」。

Levi Strauss's original blue jeans
= Levi Strauss' original blue jeans
李維・史特勞斯原創的牛仔褲
Santa Claus's sleigh and reindeer
= Santa Claus' sleigh and reindeer
聖誕老人的雪橇和馴鹿

6 用 and 連接的兩個名詞，如果共同擁
有某物，則在**最後一個名詞**加上所有
格即可。

Ben and Jenny's
ice cream
班和珍妮的冰淇淋

7 用 and 連接的兩個名詞，如果分別都
擁有某物，則**兩個名詞**都要加上所有
格。

Jane's bicycle and Joe's bicycle
珍的腳踏車和喬的腳踏車
Stephanie's lunch box and Susie's lunch
box
史蒂芬妮的午餐盒和蘇西的午餐盒

比較

Sam and Chris's house
↳ 兩人共同擁有的房子
山姆和克里斯的房子

Sam's and Chris's houses
↳ 兩人各自擁有的房子
山姆的房子和克里斯的房子

Practice

1

請將 A 欄的詞彙與 B 欄的詞彙配對，以「所有格's」的形式，寫出它們的關係。

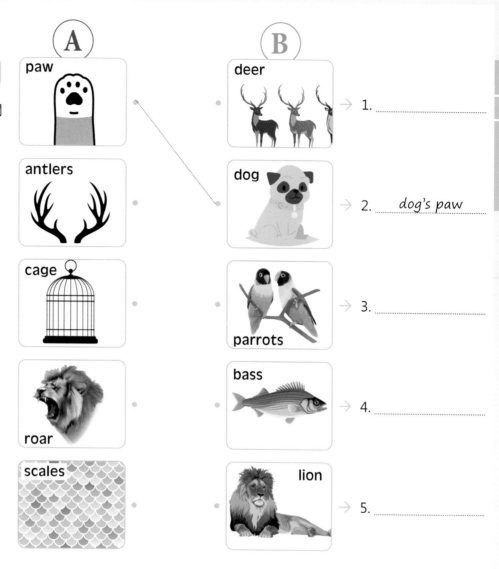

A
- paw
- antlers
- cage
- roar
- scales

B
- deer → 1. _____
- dog → 2. *dog's paw*
- parrots → 3. _____
- bass → 4. _____
- lion → 5. _____

2 請依圖示，寫出表示「共同擁有」或「分別擁有」的所有格。

1
John
Amy
apartment

John and Amy's apartment

2
Edward
Betty
kitchen

_____

3
Selina
Christine
teddy bears

_____

4
Ken
Lynn
laptops

_____

1 所有格「's」通常用於「人」。

Sam's wallet
山姆的皮夾
Melissa's purse
梅莉莎的皮包

Amanda's suitcase
亞曼達的皮箱

2 所有格「's」可以用於「人」,也可以用於「動物」、「地點」、「時間」或「度量」。

動物

the horse's bridle　　a cow's bell
馬匹的籠頭　　　　　牛鈴

地點 Brazil's soccer team
巴西的足球隊

the concert hall's sound system
↳ 不常用

= the sound system of the concert hall
↳ 常用

音樂廳的音響系統

時間 yesterday's dishes 昨天的菜
next month's program 下個月的節目

度量 an hour's walk 一小時的步行
ten dollars' worth 10 元美金的價值

3 所有格後面的**名詞**如果在前面已經提過,在聽者可以清楚判斷的情況下,經常**可以省略**。

I have my sandwich. Where is Bart's?
= Bart's sandwich ↵
我自己有三明治,巴特的呢?

Claire's compact car is red, and Claudia's is blue. = Claudia's compact car ↵
克萊兒的小車是紅色的,克勞蒂亞的則是藍色的。

4 所有格**省略名詞**的用法,經常拿來表示「**商店**」、「**工作地點**」。

I went to McDonald's for lunch.
我到麥當勞吃午餐。
I'm going to the dentist's this afternoon.
我今天下午要去看牙醫。
Can you go to the baker's and get me some bread?
你去麵包店幫我買一些麵包好嗎?

5 所有格**省略名詞**的用法,也常拿來指「**某人的家**」。

How about going to Janet's this weekend?
↳ = Janet's house/home
這個週末去珍妮家好不好?
I was at David's yesterday.
↳ = David's house/home
我昨天在大衛家。

Practice

1 請依圖示，從框內選出適當的名詞，以「the + 所有格」的形式填空，完成句子。

dentist

barber

doctor

hairdresser

baker

1

I am going to have a perm at ___the hairdresser's___ .

2

Father usually gets his hair cut at _____ .

3

Gill went to _____ yesterday.

4

Jacky often needs to go to _____ .

5

I love to buy cinnamon rolls at _____ .

2

請將括弧內的詞彙以「所有格」的形式填空，完成句子。

1. This is the spare tire from ___Paul's car___ (Paul / car).

2. I was walking down Third Street and I found _____ (someone / keys).

3. Put the _____ (dog / bone) back on his bed.

4. The _____ (company / office) is closed after 5 p.m.

5. I am going to the newsstand to buy _____ (today / newspaper) so I can read the sports section.

6. After a _____ (week / vacation), I am ready to get back to work.

7. These are my _____ (grandparents / bicycles), but we can ride them.

8. These are _____ (Mick and Jeri / wedding photos) and shots of their honeymoon.

9. You must get a _____ (driver / license) before you borrow my car.

Unit 11

"The . . . Of . . ." for Possession
「The . . . Of . . .」表示「所有權」的用法

1 「無生物」的所有格，通常不用「's」，而要用「the . . . of . . .」的形式。

the **door** of **the house**
房子的門

the **time** of **the party** 派對的時間

2 「無生物」中，除了 Unit 10 所提到的「地點」、「時間」、「度量」常用「's」而不用「the . . . of . . .」之外，「擬人化」的用法也可用「's」來構成所有格。

the **moon**'s **halo** 月暈
for **heaven**'s **sake** 天呀
the **company**'s **crisis** 公司的危機

3 「the . . . of . . .」常用於**較長的句子**裡。

✗ I met the Japanese distributor who handles our product line's director.

✓ I met the **director** of the **Japanese distributor** who handles our product line.
我遇見管理我們日本生產線的經銷商主管。

4 太複雜的「**複合名詞**」，也適合用「the . . . of . . .」來表示所有格，避免拗口。

the **opinions** of **the editors-in-chief**
= the **editors-in-chief**'s **opinions**
主編們的意見
the **daughters-in-law** of **the boss**
= the **boss**'s **daughters-in-law**
老闆的眾媳婦

5 在雙重所有格中，有時可以用「the . . . of . . .」，使句子更順暢。

Peter's father's hat
= the **hat** of Peter's father
彼得的父親的帽子
Sally's dog's beautiful hair
= the **beautiful hair** of Sally's dog
莎莉的狗的一身漂亮狗毛

6 「the . . . of . . .」的用法也可用於「**生物**」，例如「**人**」或「**動物**」。

a cat's life = the **life** of **a cat**
貓的一生
Jude and Mary's marriage
= the **marriage** of Jude and Mary
裘德和瑪麗的婚姻

7 有時，我們常用複合名詞來表示兩物的「**附屬關係**」，而不用**所有格**。

the **bathroom window** 廁所的窗戶
the **dog house** 狗屋

比較

- **Tony**'s **juice** 東尼的果汁
  ↳ 人的所有格用「's」。
- the **juice** of **these watermelon**
  ↳ 物的所有格用「the . . . of . . .」。
  這些西瓜的榨汁
- **watermelon juice** 西瓜汁
  ↳ 用複合名詞不強調所有權

Practice

1

請將括弧內的詞彙以最適當的「所有格」（「's」或「the . . . of . . .」）填空，完成句子。

1. There is going to be a performance at _____Nelly's school_____ (Nelly / school).

2. What is the _____ (name / ballet) they will perform?

3. _____ (Nancy / dance teacher) is Tracy Deville.

4. The _____ (address / theater) where the show will be performed is on the tickets.

5. The _____ (price / the tickets) is low.

6. _____ (Norma / part) in the ballet is small.

7. The bereaved were comforted by the _____ (jury / judgment).

8. Jeff joined the _____ (workers / movement) to demand higher salaries.

9. Do you think I can borrow _____ (Veasna / VIP card) to shop in this store?

10. The _____ (building / facade) is spectacular.

2

請用「the . . . of . . .」的句型改寫句子。

1. The lotion's cap is missing.
   → _The cap of the lotion is missing._

2. The United Electric Company's vice president will visit our new factory next week.
   → _____

3. Audrey and Lucas's grocery store is going to open next month.
   → _____

4. The Empire Hotel's Chinese restaurant's waiters are well trained.
   → _____

5. My mother-in-law's birthday is coming soon.
   → _____

Unit **12**

A, An
不定冠詞 A、An

1 a 和 an 是不定冠詞，意指「**一個**」。**非特指的單數可數名詞**前面要加 a 或 an。

a raincoat 一件雨衣
a basketball 一顆籃球
an umbrella 一把雨傘
an ear ring 一只耳環

不定冠詞 a/an 不能用來修飾**複數可數名詞**和**不可數名詞**。
✗ a trucks   ✓ two trucks 兩輛卡車
✗ an employees   ✓ some employees 一些員工
✗ a snow   ✓ lots of snow 很多白雪

2 一個字的發音若是「**子音**」開頭，則用 a。

a buffalo
一頭水牛

a notebook
一本筆記本

3 一個字的發音若是「**母音**」開頭（通常是字母 a、e、i、o、u），則用 an。

an oral practice class
一堂口語練習課

an elephant
一頭大象

4 有些字看起來像是母音開頭，實際發音卻是「**子音**」，此時也要用 a。

a university [ˌjunəˋvɝsətɪ] 一所大學
a Euro [ˋjuro] 一塊歐元
a unique [juˋnik] design 獨一無二的設計

5 有些字看起來像是子音開頭，實際上**開頭的子音卻不發音**，實際發音是「**母音**」開頭，此時則要用 an。

an hour [aʊr] 一個小時
    ↳ h 不發音
an honest [ˋɑnɪst] man 一個誠實的人
an heir [ɛr] 一名繼承人

6 以 f、h、l、m、n、r、s、x 為字首的縮寫詞，都是「**母音**」發音開頭，前面要用 an。

an FBI [ˌɛf bi ˋaɪ] agent 一名 FBI 探員
an RNA [ˌɑr ɛn ˋe] molecule 一個 RNA 分子

an LED [ˌɛl i ˋdi] light bulb
一顆 LED 燈泡

7 通常當讀者或聽者**不需要清楚知道**所指的是哪一個人或物時，就用 a/an 作限定詞。

There is a truck in the parking lot.
    ↳ 我們只知道裡面有一輛卡車，但不需要知道是哪一輛。
停車場有一輛卡車。

She has a grandchild.
    ↳ 我們不知道她有沒有其他孫子，或這個孫子是誰。
她有一個孫子。

Practice

1

請依圖示，從框內選出對應的名詞，並加上 **a** 或 **an**，填入空格中。

UFO
SUV
astronaut
one-way road
eagle
volleyball
onion
heir
whale
meatball
first-aid kit
idea

1. _____
2. _____
3. _____
4. _____
5. _____
6. _____

7. _____
8. _____
9. _____
10. _____
11. _____
12. _____

2

請在框內填上 **a** 或 **an**，完成下列「非特指某個人或物」的句子。

1. I went to _____ bakery downtown and bought these buns.

2. Jack's father gave him _____ unicycle on his birthday.

3. I saw _____ lioness at a distance when we drove through the zoo.

4. Is he filling in _____ online application form?

5. There is _____ backpack on the floor. Whose is it?

6. I'm meeting _____ sales rep from the Bobson Company.

7. It's going to rain in any minute. Did you bring _____ umbrella?

8. Are you _____ early bird or do you often sleep late?

9. I'm writing _____ email to my teacher.

Unit 13

The
定冠詞 The

1 the 是定冠詞，可修飾**單複數的可數名詞**，也可修飾**不可數名詞**。

the trash bag 這個垃圾袋
↳ 單數可數名詞

the cans and bottles 這些瓶瓶罐罐
↳ 複數可數名詞

the recycling of paper products
↳ 不可數名詞

紙類產品資源回收

2 「特定的人、事物」前面，要用 the 來修飾，我們稱這種用法為「**特指**」的用法。

Is this the bag of old clothes that needs to be taken to the church's drop-off box?

這是要拿到回收箱的那袋舊衣服嗎？

Do you see the black hairy dog in front of the fire hydrant? What breed is it?

你有看到消防栓前面那隻毛茸茸的黑狗嗎？
牠是什麼品種？

3 「再次提及某個人或事物」時，也要用 the。

There is only one restaurant around here. The restaurant is near the highway.

這附近只有一間餐廳，那間餐廳離高速公路不遠。

4 當「對方清楚知道你講的是哪個人或事物」時，則可以用 the 來修飾。

The pickup of recyclable material is on Tuesdays. At 3:30 p.m., the truck parks where Brownstone Alley meets Third Street.
↳ 我們都知道 the truck 就是回收車。

資源回收日是星期二，回收車會在下午 3 點 30 分停在布朗史東巷和第三大街的交叉口。

What time is it? It's time to take out the recyclable material.
↳ 我們都知道回收物指的是一袋瓶瓶罐罐。

現在幾點了？
應該把回收物拿出去了吧！

I handed the bag to the guy by the truck. The guy told me that they didn't accept cartons used for beverages.
↳ 我們知道 the guy 就是指垃圾車旁的人。

我把袋子交給垃圾車旁的那個人，他跟我說他們不收飲料紙盒。

5 of 的介系詞片語也一定要搭配 the 來使用，句型為「the . . . of . . .」。

the music of Franz Schubert
舒伯特的音樂

the war of words 唇槍舌戰；筆戰

the player of the year 年度最佳球員

Practice

1　請用 **a**、**an** 或 **the** 填空，完成句子。若該句不需要加冠詞，
則在空格內劃上「/」。

1. Ken went to the store to buy ＿＿＿＿ book to read on his trip.

2. His wife asked if she could read ＿＿＿＿ book when he finished it.

3. Do you have ＿＿＿＿ information on the new policy?

4. I saw two houses, but I didn't like ＿＿＿＿ second one very much.

5. Did you see ＿＿＿＿ metal box I put on the coffee table?

6. Please pass me ＿＿＿＿ napkin.

7. Colin wants to be ＿＿＿＿ epidemiologist in the future.

8. ＿＿＿＿ king and queen live in the palace.

9. Lindsay is ＿＿＿＿ athlete.

10. ＿＿＿＿ man at the door is Mr. Robertson.

11. Since it's so hot in here, I will turn on ＿＿＿＿ air conditioner.

12. His latest album has won ＿＿＿＿ album of the year.

13. Can you hear ＿＿＿＿ words they're whispering?

14. Do you like ＿＿＿＿ paintings by Johannes Vermeer?

15. How about going to ＿＿＿＿ newly-opened tea shop across the street and have a glass of lemon tea?

16. Good idea! But I think I'll have ＿＿＿＿ milk tea instead.

Part 2 Articles 冠詞

Unit 14

Talking in General
「泛指」的用法

1 通常，我們會以不加 the 的複數可數名詞或不可數名詞，來泛指「一般的人或事物」。

Chili peppers **come in many shapes and sizes.** ↳ 一般通稱的辣椒

辣椒有很多種形狀和大小。

Salsa **is always hot and spicy.**
↳ 一般的莎莎醬

莎莎醬都很辣，味道又重。

2 「a/an + 單數可數名詞」也常用來泛指「一般的人或事物」，通常意味著該人或事物的「大部分、任一、全部」是如此。

An Airedale **is a large black terrier with a wiry, tan coat.**
↳ 這種類型的所有萬能梗犬

萬能梗是一種有著又硬又黑毛髮的大型犬種。

3 而「the + 名詞」則用來指「特定的人或事物」，是特指的用法。

The chili peppers **from your garden are**
↳ 指特定的辣椒
mild and sweet.

你花園裡種的辣椒味道很溫和，還有甜味呢。

The salsa **at this restaurant will burn your**
↳ 特定的莎莎醬
mouth.

這家餐廳的莎莎醬會讓你的嘴巴冒火。

4 「the + 單數可數名詞」經常用來泛指「一般的事物」。動物、花卉、植物名稱經常以這種形式出現。

The hawk **has the keenest eyesight of all birds.** ↳ 泛指所有的老鷹

在所有鳥類中，老鷹的視覺最銳利。

The sparrow hawk **is the smallest member of the hawk family.**
↳ 泛指所有的松雀鷹

松雀鷹的體型在所有老鷹之中最嬌小。

5 「the + 形容詞」經常用來泛指「某一類型的人」。

the poor 窮人
the middle class 中產階級
the rich 富人
the middle aged 中年人
the old 老人
the blind 盲人
the deaf 聾人
the young 年輕人

Tax cuts help the rich and hurt the poor
↳ = the rich people   ↳ = the poor people
and the middle class.
↳ = the middle class people

節稅的作法對富人有益，卻損及窮人和中產階級。

6 「the + 國家名稱／民族名稱」可泛指該國或該民族的「人民」。

The Hmong **are people living in highland areas of Southeast Asia.**

蒙族人是住在東南亞山區的人民。

The Amish **don't believe in using electricity or cars.** 門諾教派信徒不用電也不開車。

Practice

1

在要加 **the** 的空格內填上 the，不需要加 **the** 的空格內劃「／」。

1. Elle likes to drink _____ coffee.

2. Richard asked his wife where she had put _____ coffee.

3. _____ Coffee is grown all over the world.

4. There are the three brands of _____ coffee I like to drink.

5. Arlene only buys _____ French roast coffee.

6. Raymond says _____ Italian roast coffee at this café is superb.

7. _____ Penguins are birds that can't fly.

8. _____ vulture is a bird that will eat dead animals.

9. _____ blind are people that can't see.

10. _____ rich can afford gas no matter what the price is.

11. _____ Lebanese live in a country with a Mediterranean climate.

12. People from the ancient empire located in what is now Italy were called _____ Romans.

13. The largest mammal in the world is _____ blue whale.

14. My son is in first grade and is learning how to play _____ recorder.

2

請將下列使用「形容詞 + 名詞」的句子，改寫為使用「the + 形容詞」來泛指的句子。

1. The poor people need national health insurance more than the middle class people and the rich people.

   → *The poor need national health insurance more than the middle class and the rich.*

2. The city council has approved several proposals for the welfare of the elderly people.

   → _____

   _____

3. The excavation of these sites has revealed the life and culture of the Maya people.

   → _____

   _____

4. Opportunities go to the strong people, not the weak people.

   → _____

Unit 15

Expressions With "The" (1)
要加 The 的情況（I）

the sun

1 獨一無二的事物，要加 the。

Even angels in Heaven love to use the Internet.
連天使都愛用網路。

the earth

the stars

the President

the world

2 彈奏樂器，要加 the。

J. S. Bach played several musical instruments, including the harpsichord.
巴哈會演奏好幾種樂器，包括大鍵琴。

the piano

the harmonica

the guitar

3 一般性地點，要加 the。

Frank is going to spend the weekend at the shore.
法蘭克將到海邊度週末。

the suburbs

the countryside

the ocean/sea

the mountain

the city

4 政府、政治機構，要加 the。

- the FBI 聯邦調查局
- the Ministry of Finance 財政部
- the White House 白宮

5 發明物，要加 the。

Leo Fender invented the electric guitar.
李奧・凡德發明了電吉他。
Several people, including Alexander Graham Bell and Antonio Meucci, were credited for the invention of the telephone. 包含貝爾和穆齊等幾個人，被認為是電話的發明者。

1

請從框內選出適當的名詞，加上 the 填空，完成句子。

Moon

mayor

airplane

cello

President

lion

countryside

beach

stars

king

city

1. Let's go for a trip in _____ and get some fresh air this weekend. I'm tired of _____ .

2. Katherine is going to play _____ at the National Concert Hall next month.

3. _____ of the city will show up at the opening of the exhibition on Friday morning.

4. Liz is building sand castles on _____ .

5. _____ is going to build a golden palace as a birthday present for the queen.

6. There are many impact craters on the near side and the far side of _____ .

7. _____ of Guatemala is going to visit us in June.

8. The Wright brothers are credited with the invention of _____ .

9. _____ is the king of the beasts.

10. Nothing makes you feel smaller than looking into the night sky and seeing _____ .

2

請將 A 欄與 B 欄的用語搭配，造出具有意義的句子。

A
· Bill is climbing
· Lee commutes between his downtown office and
· Larry is working for
· In 1990, NASA launched
· John is swimming laps in
· Caterina learned to play

B
· the pool.
· the Hubble Telescope into orbit.
· his home in the suburbs.
· the flute when she was 12.
· the Ministry of Education.
· the mountain.

1. _Bill is climbing the mountain._

2. _____

3. _____

4. _____

5. _____

6. _____

Unit 16

Expressions With "The" (2)
要加 The 的情況（2）

1 報刊名稱，要加 the。

- *the **China Post*** 中國郵報
- *the **New York Times*** 紐約時報
- *the **Washington Post*** 華盛頓郵報

2 某些時間慣用語，要加 the。

- in the **morning**
- in the **afternoon**
- in the **evening**

3 某特定時刻的**天氣狀況**，要加 the。

The **typhoon** has passed the island.
颱風已經通過小島。

the **hurricane**

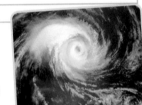

the **rain**

the **snow**

the **wind**

the **tornado**

4 娛樂活動或場所，要加 the 或 a。

Lorna is going to the movie theater tonight.
蘿娜今晚要去電影院（看電影）。

the **movies**

the **concert**

the **circus**

the **fair**

the **theater**

the **symphony**

the **performance**

the **fashion show**

Practice

1

請用 the、a 或 an 填空，完成句子。

1. The weather forecast said there will be _____ big storm coming this weekend.

2. The traffic was held up by _____ heavy snow.

3. Can I clip _____ article from the front page of _____ *Washington Post* after you finish reading it?

4. Can you buy me _____ *Time* magazine on your way to the office?

5. _____ book exhibition is held annually in February.

6. Are you going to sell these chickens at _____ fair?

7. I'd rather go to _____ symphony than listen to CDs at home.

8. His dream is to play in _____ concert at the National Concert Hall.

9. _____ wind is blowing hard outside.

10. I usually read newspapers in _____ morning.

11. Cinema International Inc. is planning to build _____ IMAX theater in the neighborhood.

12. Stanley has gone to _____ movies with his friends.

13. Did you think _____ fashion show in the Crystal Hall last week was a big success?

2

請勾選正確的答案。

1. ☐ Snow ☐ The snow is formed when the temperature drops below zero and the humidity is high.

2. ☐ Tornadoes ☐ The tornadoes are violent natural phenomena. They often cause great damage along their path.

3. Even though I had an umbrella with me, I got all wet when I walked home in ☐ rain ☐ the rain.

4. I've got two tickets to ☐ circuses ☐ the circus. Are you going with me? You'll love ☐ performance ☐ the performance.

5. I watch soap operas in ☐ the evening ☐ an evening after I finish eating dinner and washing dishes.

6. Every time I lit a match ☐ the wind ☐ a wind blew it out, so I waited until I found an alley between two buildings.

7. Harry reads ☐ *the Taipei Times* ☐ *Taipei Times* every morning before going to work.

Unit 17

Expressions Without "The" (1)
不加 The 的情況（I）

1 星期幾不加 the。但是「週末」要加 the。

Phil goes to the gym on Saturdays.
菲爾每星期六上健身房。

- on the weekend 在週末

MONDAY
TUESDAY
WEDNESDAY
THURSDAY
FRIDAY
SATURDAY
SUNDAY

2 月分不加 the。

The exhibition will take place in June.
這場展覽將於 6 月展開。

Months of the Year

January	February	March
April	May	June
July	August	September
October	November	December

3 某些時間慣用語，不加 the。

Jerry went home at midnight.
傑瑞半夜才回家。

- at night
- by night
- at noon
- by day

4 季節不加 the。「秋天」如果用 the fall，就一定要加 the。

spring

summer

autumn / the fall

winter

5 節日不加 the，但如果和 festival 連用，則通常會加 the。

New Year's Eve

Christmas Day

Halloween

Thanksgiving

- the Mid-Autumn Festival 中秋節
- the Dragon Boat Festival 端午節

Practice

1 請從圖片中選出適當的詞彙，並視情況加上 the 或 s 等填空，完成句子。

night   noon   summer   autumn

Dragon Boat Festival   Valentine's Day   Father's Day   Songkran Festival

Saturday   Sunday   February   June

1. _____ falls on the fifth day of the fifth lunar month.

2. Typhoons usually hit Taiwan during _____ and _____.

3. _____ is a unique festival in northern Thailand. People celebrate it by splashing water on one another.

4. Jim was born on the third of _____, so he is a Gemini.

5. Where does your family plan to take your father on _____?

6. I have to finish this project by _____, because I'm taking this afternoon off.

7. Would you like to go out with me on _____? I know a romantic French restaurant.

8. The weekend includes _____ and _____.

9. I go to work from 9 a.m. to 6 p.m. I don't work at _____.

Unit 18

Expressions Without "The" (2)
不加 The 的情況（2）

1 學科名稱，不加 the。

I am good at geography.
地理是我擅長的科目。

- math
- music
- physics
- history
- chemistry
- literature

2 工作地點、家，不加 the。

Lester said he was going to work.
萊斯特說他要去上班了。
I called Toby's house and he was not at home. 我打電話到托比家，但是他不在家。

3 體育活動，不加 the。

I love playing soccer. 我喜歡踢足球。
He is playing badminton. 他正在打羽毛球。

play basketball

play baseball

play football

play golf

play tennis

4 「**by + 交通工具**」及 **on foot** 片語，不加 the。

Are you going by bus? 你要搭公車去嗎？
We are traveling by train.
我們要坐火車旅行。

by car

by plane

by motorcycle

by bicycle

on foot

5 社會機構、學術單位，不加 the。

Phillip's cousin is not at school today.
菲利普的表哥今天沒有來上學。
Myna goes to college. 米娜去唸大學了。

go to church

go to jail

go to school

go to court

這些社會機構、學術單位，如果指的是建築物本身，則可以加 the。
請見 Unit 20 說明。

Practice

1 請仔細分辨下列句子是否屬於前述「不需要加 the」的狀況。
在空格內填上 the、a、an，或劃上「/」表示不需要冠詞。

1. My daughter rides her bicycle to _____ school.

2. Irene wants to study accounting at _____ university.

3. My son just started _____ school.

4. There's a small fountain in front of _____ school.

5. It is much more pleasant to see the garden on _____ foot than by _____ car.

6. Are you going to travel by _____ plane or _____ train?

7. Put this box in _____ car that is parked in the driveway.

8. Everyone got off _____ bus to take photos of the beautiful canyon.

9. Randy had a friend that almost went to _____ prison.

10. Lacking evidence, the police released Joe from _____ jail last week.

11. He kept complaining about food in _____ prison cafeteria.

12. After we had gathered enough evidence, we finally brought this case to _____ court.

13. Elaine didn't go to _____ work today, but she was not at _____ home, either. Where did she go?

14. Johnny stayed in _____ office until midnight.

15. _____ Math is my favorite subject.

16. I studied _____ literature at college.

17. Susie loves to read stories about _____ history of China.

18. Rebecca has no idea how to compete in _____ bobsleigh races.

19. Team members on _____ bobsleigh have to be well-trained, or it could be extremely dangerous.

20. Who left _____ baseball bat on the floor? Someone could trip over it.

Unit **19**

Place Names With or Without "The"
專有地名加 **The** 或不加 **The**

要加 the 的專有地名

1 | 海洋名，要加 the。 | • the **Pacific Ocean** 太平洋 | • the **Red Sea** 紅海
| | • the **Indian Ocean** 印度洋 | • the **Mediterranean** 地中海

2 | 河川、流域、海灣名，要加 the。 | • the **Danube** 多瑙河 | • the **Amazon Basin** 亞馬遜河流域
| | • the **Seine** 塞納河 | • the **Persian Gulf** 波斯灣

3 | 運河、海峽名，要加 the。 | • the **Panama Canal** 巴拿馬運河 | • the **Victoria Strait** 維多利亞海峽
| | • the **Intracoastal Waterway** 海灣沿岸航道 |

4 | 群島名，要加 the。 | • the **San Juans** 聖胡安群島
| | • the **Florida Keys** 佛羅里達礁島群 | ↳ 參看後面「獨立島嶼名，不加 the」。
| | • the **West Indies** 西印度群島

5 | 山脈名，要加 the。 | • the **Himalayas** 喜馬拉雅山脈
| | • the **Alps** 阿爾卑斯山脈 | ↳ 參看後面「獨立山岳名，不加 the」。
| | • the **Rocky Mountains** 落磯山脈

6 | 沙漠名，要加 the。 | • the **Gobi Desert** 戈壁沙漠
| | • the **Sahara** 撒哈拉沙漠

7 | 各種大型建築物、公設，要加 the。

the **Statue of Liberty**
自由女神像

the **Taj Mahal**
泰姬瑪哈陵

the **Great Wall**
萬里長城

the **Milan Cathedral**
米蘭大教堂

the **London Eye**
倫敦眼

8	橋樑、塔名，要加 the。	• the Tower Bridge 倫敦塔橋
		• the Golden Gate Bridge 金門大橋
		• the Great Pyramid of Giza 吉薩大金字塔
		• the Eiffel Tower 艾菲爾鐵塔

| 9 | 博物館、紀念館、畫廊，要加 the。 | • the Andy Warhol Museum 安迪・沃荷博物館 |
| | | • the Lincoln Memorial 林肯紀念館 |

| 10 | 電影院、劇院名，要加 the。 | • the Central City Opera House 中央城歌劇院 |
| | | • the Carré Theater 卡列劇院 |

11	飯店、餐廳、酒吧、俱樂部，要加 the。以「人名所有格」構成的地名、建築名，都不加 the。	• the Hotel Royal 老爺酒店	• Jack O'Sullivan's Tavern 傑克蘇利文酒館
		• the Deer Path Inn 迪爾佩斯餐廳	• McDonald's 麥當勞
		• the Brass Monkey 銅猴子酒吧	• St. Paul's Cathedral 聖保羅大教堂

不加 the 的專有地名

1	洲名，不加 the。	• Asia 亞洲
		• Europe 歐洲
	但是一些大區域名稱，則慣用 the。	• Africa 非洲
		• Australia 澳洲
	• the Middle East 中東 • the West 西方	

2	國家名，不加 the。	• Mexico 墨西哥
		• Canada 加拿大
	國家名稱中若含 kingdom、republic、states 等「可數名詞」，則要加 the。	• Korea 韓國
		• Malaysia 馬來西亞

• the Netherlands 荷蘭　• the Philippines 菲律賓
• the United Kingdom 英國
• the Republic of Congo 剛果共和國
• the United States of America 美利堅合眾國

| 3 | 州名、省名，不加 the。 | • California 加州 |
| | | • Ontario 安大略省 |

4	鄉村、城鎮名，不加 the。	• Florence 佛羅倫斯
		• Canterbury 坎特伯里
		• Nagasaki 長崎

| 5 | 湖泊名，不加 the。 |

Sun Moon Lake 日月潭

Lake Victoria 維多利亞湖

45

6 獨立島嶼名，不加 **the**。

Orchid Island 蘭嶼

Santorini 聖托里尼島

↳ 參看前面「群島名，要加 the」。

7 獨立山岳名，不加 **the**。

K2 喬戈里峰

Mount Jade 玉山

↳ 參看前面「山脈名，要加 the」。

8 街道名、廣場名，不加 **the**。

- **Elm Street**
  艾姆街
- **Davis Street**
  戴維斯街
- **Times Square**
  時代廣場
- **Trafalgar Square**
  特拉法加廣場

- the **Gulf** of **Mexico**
  墨西哥灣
- the **Statue** of **Liberty**
  自由女神像
- the **Rock** of **Gibraltar**
  直布羅陀巨岩
- the **University** of **California**
  加州大學

但是任何以 of 片語構成的**地名**、**建築名**，都要加 the。

9 公園名、學校名，不加 **the**。

- **Central Park** 中央公園
- **Seattle University** 西雅圖大學

10 機場名，不加 **the**。

- **Taiwan Taoyuan International Airport** 臺灣桃園國際機場
- **JFK International Airport** 甘迺迪國際機場

1

請勾選正確的答案。

1. Ukraine is located in ☐ **Europe** ☐ **the Europe**.

2. Northern Ireland is a part of ☐ **the United Kingdom** ☐ **United Kingdom**.

3. Manila is the capital of ☐ **Philippines** ☐ **the Philippines**.

4. The longest river in Africa is ☐ **the Nile** ☐ **Nile**.

5. ☐ **The Colosseum** ☐ **Colosseum** is an ancient amphitheater in the center of Rome.

6. ☐ **Metropolitan Museum of Art** ☐ **The Metropolitan Museum of Art** has the largest collection of European art in New York.

7. The trees on ☐ **Ridge Street** ☐ **the Ridge Street** are beautiful this time of year.

2

請在需要 **the** 的空格內填上 **the**，不需要的則劃「/」。

1. .... St. Basil's Cathedral is located on .... Red Square in .... Moscow.

2. .... Tikal National Park in .... Guatemala has preserved many sites of the Mayan civilization.

3. After we finished lunch, we walked along .... Victoria Harbor back to our hotel.

4. .... Mont Blanc is the highest mountain in France and Italy.

5. I stayed in .... Hotel Nikko when I was vacationing in .... Guam.

6. What is playing at .... National Theater tonight?

Expressions With or Without "The"
With Different Meanings
加 **The** 或不加 **The** 意義不同的用語

三餐

1 三餐通常不加**冠詞**。

Let's meet for breakfast in the hotel dining room at 8:00. 我們 8 點在飯店的餐廳見面，一起吃早餐吧！

Do you want to have dinner in the Rooftop Restaurant?

想要一起到屋頂餐廳吃晚餐嗎？

2 指「**特定的一餐**」，則要加上冠詞 the。比如，表示三餐的單字後面如果有**介系詞片語**、**分詞片語**或**形容詞子句**修飾，則需要加 the。

The lunch provided during the conference wasn't too bad.

會議上提供的午餐其實不算太糟。

3 breakfast、lunch、dinner 前面如果還有**形容詞**，則需要加 a/an。

They gave us a quick lunch and hurried us onto the bus. 他們讓我們匆匆地吃了午餐，接著就催我們上巴士。

4 meal 這個字可加 a 或 the。

A meal is included in the trip.

旅遊行程中會提供一餐。

地點

5 ① 一些**地點**名稱若表示「功能、目的」，則**不加** the；

② 若單純表示「**地點**」、「**建築物**」，則**要加** the。

Adrian went to school.
　　↳ go to school 指的是「學校的功能」、「去學校的目的」。

亞德里安去上學了。

This morning Wilfred went to the school to talk to the principal.
↳ the school 指學校「這個地點」、「這棟建築物」。

今天早上威爾福前往學校找校長說話。

Vivian had to go to church.
　　　　↳ 目的是去做禮拜。

薇薇安得上教堂。

Nicole is applying for a job at the church.
↳ the church 指「工作的地點」、「這棟建築物」。

妮可在應徵那座教堂裡的一份工作。

It's time to go to bed.
　　　　↳ 目的是上床去睡覺。

該去睡覺了。

Mom laid out your clothes on the bed.
　　　the bed 指衣服放置的「地點」。↵
媽媽把你的衣服放在床上。

lying on the bed

Practice

1 請在空格內填上 the、a 或 an，如果不需要冠詞，請劃上「/」。

1. Did you eat _____ breakfast offered by the hotel?
2. We had _____ breakfast at a local coffee shop.
3. After Carl drops his wife at work, he has _____ breakfast at a café.

4. Please tell your sister _____ dinner is served.
5. _____ dinner in that French restaurant is famous.
6. Grandma made _____ delicious dinner for Lisa and me.

7. We went for _____ meal after shopping.
8. Does this price include _____ meals?
9. We went to the fishing harbor for _____ fish meal yesterday.

2 請在空格內填上 the、a 或 an，如果不需要冠詞，請劃上「/」。

1. I am tired and I am going to _____ bed.
2. Who left the books, toys, dolls, and pajamas on _____ bed in my room?
3. Your slippers are under _____ bed.

4. Is there _____ church nearby?
5. Dad should be out of _____ church in a few minutes.
6. When I arrived at _____ church, he had already left.

7. Is that _____ nursing home where Mrs. Finch stayed after her stroke?
8. Although Grandpa has retired, he is never at _____ home in the morning.

Part 3 Pronouns 代名詞

Unit 21

Personal Pronouns:
Subject and Object Pronouns
人稱代名詞：
「主格代名詞」與「受格代名詞」

one thing
I like it.

many things
I like them.

1 人稱代名詞可分為三類：主格代名詞、受格代名詞和所有格代名詞。

		主格代名詞	受格代名詞	所有格代名詞
第一人稱	單數	I	me	mine
	複數	we	us	ours
第二人稱	單數	you	you	yours
	複數	you	you	yours
第三人稱	單數	he/she/it	him/her/it	his/hers/its
	複數	they	them	theirs

2 主格代名詞用來當作句子中**主要動詞**的「**主詞**」。

Where is Dad? He is in the garage.
爸爸在哪裡？他在車庫裡。

Mom didn't take us to school.
She is in New York.
媽媽沒有送我們到學校，她目前人在紐約。

3 受格代名詞用來作為句子中**動詞**或介系詞的「**受詞**」。

Can you call me tomorrow?
你可以明天打電話給我嗎？

Please ask him to help us.
請他幫忙我們。

I'll talk to him.
我會跟他談談。

Call and ask for him.
打電話找他。

I will ask him all about it.
我會向他問清楚一切。

4 be 動詞的後面，要接主格代名詞。但在電話用語中，**第一人稱**通常用 me。

Don't you recognize my voice? It's me.
你聽不出我的聲音嗎？是我啊！

It is I, your beloved King.
是我，你深愛的國王。

It was I who broke the window.
打破窗戶的是我。

5 「比較的句型」中，as 和 than 的後面經常接受格代名詞。
但如果在正式用語裡，as 和 than 後面還是以「主格代名詞 + 動詞」的形式為佳。

She is taller than him.
= She is taller than he is.
她比他高。

I am as short as him.
= I am as short as he is.
我和他一樣矮。

6 口語中，受格代名詞可以在**簡答句**中代替**主詞**。

Peter: I'm very thirsty.
Sam: Me too. / I am, too.
彼德：我的口好渴。
山姆：我也是。

Practice

1

請勾選正確的答案。

1. Wally called to say ☐ he ☐ him is coming soon.

2. Charlotte has a great sense of humor. I like ☐ her ☐ she very much.

3. Your grandparents gave you a nice gift, but you have not said "thank you" to ☐ they ☐ them.

4. ☐ They ☐ Them are giving out tickets for speeding.

5. Why don't ☐ us ☐ we go to the night market together?

6. Marian didn't go to her office. ☐ She ☐ Her stayed at home.

7. Would you help ☐ me ☐ I doing the housework this afternoon?

8. Ivan's girlfriend is in Puerto Rico. He says he has called ☐ her ☐ she several times.

9. A boy and a girl compared their heights. He was taller than ☐ she ☐ her.

10. You are smarter than ☐ I ☐ I am.

11. Betty can't climb a tree. ☐ I ☐ I can't, either.

12. It is ☐ us ☐ we that cleaned the house before our guests arrived.

2

請以正確的「人稱代名詞」填空，完成句子。

1. Jenny got up early this morning. _____ practiced the piano after breakfast.

2. James got up too early today. _____ felt sleepy when playing baseball with his friends.

3. Sandy is not in the office. Do you know where _____ is?

4. I don't know how to sing. Can you teach _____?

5. Maybe that snake is sick or dead. _____ is not moving.

6. I saw Sam sneaking out of the room. It must be _____ who took the diamond ring.

7. Lisa and Helen are free tomorrow. You can ask _____ to help you move to your new apartment.

8. We're going to the beach this Sunday. Would you like to go with _____?

9. Nick has broken his ankle. Can you help carry _____ to the health center?

10. Aren't you having a meeting tomorrow morning? Shall I give _____ a wake-up call?

Part 3 Pronouns 代名詞

Unit 22

Common Usages of Subject Pronouns and Pronoun "It"

「主格代名詞」與代名詞 It 的常見用法

1 主格代名詞 we 有時**包含聽者**，有時**不包含**，視說話的情況而定。

Why don't we go to the Indian
↳ we 包括說話者和聽者。
restaurant tonight?

今晚我們何不去印度餐廳吃飯？

We are going out on the town tonight. Do you want to join us?
↳ We 包括說話者，但不包括聽者。

我們今晚要到城裡，你要和我們一起去嗎？

2 主格代名詞 you 可拿來指「**包含你我的所有人**」。這種情況在非常正式的用語中須用 one。

You can waste a lot of time staring into space.

你大可以浪費很多時間發呆。

You can send emails around the world almost instantly.

你幾乎可以瞬間將電子郵件傳到世界各地。

One must support one's country.

一個人必須支持自己的國家。

3 主格代名詞 they 也可拿來指「包含你我的所有人」。

They say 1.5 million people ride the transit system each day.

據說每天有一百五十萬人搭乘運輸系統。

4 主格代名詞 they 經常拿來指「**政府或權威人士**」。

They have new laws to allow them to spy on you. 政府制訂了新法，讓他們可以監視你。

They are watching you at this very moment.
此時此刻他們正在監視著你。

5 代名詞 it 也可以指「**人**」，尤其在「**詢問或告知身分**」的時候。

Who is on the phone? Ask who it is.
是誰打電話來？問問到底是誰。

Who is it? 是誰啊？

It's Ed on the phone. 是艾德打電話來。

6 代名詞 it 在某些句中並沒有特殊的意義，也就是所謂的虛主詞，這種用法常見於說明「**時間**」、「**距離**」、「**天氣**」和「**溫度**」的句型中。

I'd guess it is about 9:00. 我猜現在大概9點左右。

It is about ten kilometers to the town.
這邊離城裡大約 10 公里。

Bring in the laundry because it's going to rain tonight. 把衣服收進來吧，因為今晚會下雨。

It's so hot you could fry an egg on the blacktop.

天氣熱得要命，都可以在柏油路上煎蛋了。

7 代名詞 it 作為虛主詞的時候，後面經常接「**加 to 的不定詞**」或者 **that** 子句。

It is interesting to travel in South America.

= To travel in South America is interesting.

去南美洲旅遊很有趣。

It is a good idea that we avoid the tourist spots.

= That we avoid the tourist spots is a good idea.

避開那些知名景點，是個不錯的主意。

Practice

1

請勾選正確的答案。

1. Who is ☐ him ☐ it at the door?

2. Why don't ☐ we ☐ us stay at home and play the Nintendo Switch games?

3. ☐ We ☐ Us should hang out together sometime.

4. ☐ It ☐ She is Janet on the phone.

5. Have ☐ you ☐ your been to Honolulu before?

6. ☐ They ☐ It say sharks do not attack humans for fun.

7. ☐ Them ☐ They have brought up a proposal of building a community center in every administrative district.

2

請依圖示，從框內選出適當的用語，搭配 it 作為「虛主詞」，填空完成句子。

was cold outside	is 200 meters from here
is going to rain	was 10 p.m.

1

....,
so I put on my jacket.

2

....
when Jake went to bed.

3

....
Let's bring in the laundry.

4

....
to the mountain peak.

3

請用 it 當「虛主詞」，改寫下列句子。

1. To go down a water slide is exciting.

→ ....

2. To drink soy milk every day is good for your health.

→ ....

3. That we follow the traffic rules is important.

→ ....

Unit 23

Possessive Pronouns and Possessive Adjectives

「所有格代名詞」與「所有格形容詞」

1 所有格代名詞和所有格形容詞的形式非常類似，經常在句子中搭配使用。

		所有格代名詞	所有格形容詞
第一人稱	單數	mine	my
	複數	ours	our
第二人稱	單數	yours	your
	複數	yours	your
第三人稱	單數	his/hers/ -	his/her/its
	複數	theirs	their

2 所有格形容詞要接**名詞**，用來說明該名詞的「**所有權**」。

Jack can't buy his new car until next month. 傑克下個月才能買新車。

Andrea traded in her SUV for an electric car. 安德麗把她的休旅車換成了電動車。

3 所有格代名詞要**單獨使用**，後面不需要接名詞。

I thought I saw Wayne's new gas-electric hybrid vehicle, but it wasn't his. 我以為我看到的是韋恩的油電混合車，不過那輛車並不是他的。

Patsy's new electric car takes only three hours to charge, which is better than mine. 佩希的新電動車只要花三小時充電，比我的還要好。

4 my own、your own、his own 這類的用語放在**名詞前面**，用來強調某事物的「**專屬權**」。our own、their own 則是「**共同擁有權**」。

This is my office computer.
這是我辦公室的電腦。

I've got my own computer now. I don't share it with anybody else in my department anymore.
我現在有自己的電腦，不再和部門裡的其他人共用電腦了。

That isn't my email address. That is the general address for customer support.
那不是我的電子郵件，那是開放給一般顧客服務的電子郵件位址。

This is my own email address.
這是我專用的電子郵件位址。

5 my own、your own 這類的用語之前，也**可以加** of。此時 of my own、of your own 等，會放在**名詞後面**。

I use a personalized email address of my own for my side business.
我用私人的信箱接收和副業相關的電子郵件。

6 my own、your own 等用語，也可以用來強調「**某人自己的事，與他人無關**」。

Do your job. 做你的工作。

Do your own job, and stop telling me what to do. 做你自己的工作，別一直指揮我做事。

7 (do something) on my own、on your own 這類的用語，則表示「**獨立從事某件事，不靠外人幫助**」。

I can't solve this problem on my own because it involves another department. 我沒辦法自己解決這個問題，因為這牽涉到其他部門。

Nobody knows what to do, so you are on your own. 沒有人知道該怎麼做，所以你得靠自己了。

Practice

1

請勾選正確的答案。

1. That is ☐ her ☐ hers villa.

2. He drives ☐ him ☐ his car to work.

3. I was eating ☐ my ☐ mine lunch box at that time.

4. They're going to sell ☐ their ☐ theirs refrigerator.

5. ☐ We ☐ Our garden needs weeding.

6. Do you see that apartment? That's ☐ my ☐ mine.

7. Your house is more expensive than ☐ our ☐ ours.

8. This is the first time I have had ☐ my own ☐ on my own house.

9. Louise doesn't have ☐ her own ☐ she own house.

10. I can't do it ☐ on my own ☐ my own, and I need some help.

11. I can't find ☐ my ☐ mine cell phone.

12. Howard has his cell phone, but Amy can't find ☐ her ☐ hers.

13. I used to drive my father's old scooter, but I have a scooter
    ☐ my own ☐ of my own now.

14. It's ☐ his own ☐ on his own idea.

15. This is ☐ mine ☐ my apple pie.

16. He crossed the desert ☐ of his own ☐ on his own.

2

請用正確的「所有格代名詞」填空，完成句子。

1. This is David's computer. This is Helen's computer, too. So, this
   computer is ___*theirs*___.

2. Sonia owns the shop alone. The shop is _____.

3. Your car is an SUV. My car is a compact. _____ is
   smaller than _____.

4. I wanted to borrow Andy's bicycle, but he said the bicycle was
   not _____.

5. We have paid off the mortgage on the apartment. Now the
   apartment is _____.

6. I'm doing my job. You should be doing _____.

Unit 24

Reflexive Pronouns (1)
反身代名詞（I）

I Love myself!

1 反身代名詞用來指涉「自己」。

反身代名詞		
	單數	複數
第一人稱	myself	ourselves
第二人稱	yourself	yourselves
第三人稱	himself herself itself	themselves

2 當句子的**主詞**和**受詞是同一人或同一事物**時，為了避免重複，會使用**反身代名詞**。

I bought myself a bottle of champagne.
我給自己買了一瓶香檳。

The old man trusts nobody but himself.
那位老人家除了他自己，誰也不信任。

3 反身代名詞經常用來「**加強語氣**」，強調是「**某人親自**」做了某事。

Dean drew everything in the comic book himself. 漫畫書是迪恩自己畫的。

Hank and Bernice started selling their games themselves.
漢克和柏尼斯開始自行販賣他們的遊戲。

I myself prefer to work alone, but I will take on a partner if I have to.
我個人是偏好獨力作業，但如果必要，我還是會找個合作夥伴。

4 有時，反身代名詞是用來強調「**獨自**」做了某事，沒有其他任何人介入。

Adam washed, dried, and folded all the laundry himself, even though Marvin was supposed to help him.
原本梅爾文應該要幫忙的，不過亞當卻獨自洗好、烘乾並摺好所有的衣服。

Bobby needs to finish the job himself, and nobody is supposed to help him.
巴比得自己完成工作，別人不應該幫忙他。

5 by myself、by yourself 等是反身代名詞的慣用語，說明「**某事由某人獨力完成，不靠他人幫助**」。

He did the job all by himself.
這項工作完全是由他獨力完成的。

Earl can't keep the comic book store open all day and all night by himself.
只靠厄爾獨自一人，根本不可能讓漫畫店整天營業。

He tried to do it by himself, but he couldn't do it.
他嘗試過自己做，但是沒成功。

6 help yourself、enjoy yourself 等也是反身代名詞的慣用語。

Please help yourself to soft drinks while reading the comics.
看漫畫的時候，請自行取用飲料。

Enjoy yourself at the Game Designers Workshop.
在「遊戲設計家」工作坊裡好好享受吧。

Practice

1

請勾選正確的答案。

1. Harry bought □ herself □ himself a new camera for his birthday.
2. Peter lacks self-confidence. He doesn't believe in □ he □ himself.
3. We sailed across the Strait of Magellan □ myself □ ourselves.
4. I translated the novel □ my own □ by myself.
5. You don't have to do your homework □ all by yourself □ yours.
6. They completed the experiment □ by □ on themselves.
7. Please help □ you □ yourself to the dessert.
8. Johnny bought some wrapping paper and ribbons. He wanted to wrap the present □ him □ himself.
9. Sandy made □ she □ herself a scarf.

2

請用正確的「反身代名詞」填空，完成句子。

I painted the picture
_____.

Lily forgets things all the time, so she often writes _____ a note.

Please help _____ at the salad bar.

Henry assembled the bookshelf by
_____.

Emma traveled around Europe by _____ last month.

Sarah and Jimmy cooked the dinner all by _____.

Unit 25

Reflexive Pronouns (2)
反身代名詞（2）

---

1 有些詞彙不能跟反身代名詞連用。

- feel
- relax
- concentrate

✗ Hannah feels herself young and energetic.

✓ Hannah feels young and energetic.

漢娜感到年輕有活力。

✗ When Jess wants to relax herself, she listens to Celtic music.

✓ When Jess wants to relax, she listens to Celtic music.

潔思想要放鬆的時候，就會聽凱爾特音樂。

✗ Patrick can't concentrate himself when the TV is on.

✓ Patrick can't concentrate when the TV is on.

只要電視開著，派屈克就沒辦法專心。

---

2 片語 each other 的意義經常和反身代名詞混淆。each other 意指「**兩個人彼此、互相**」。

We are videotaping ourselves.
↳ 大家都在影片裡。
我們自己幫自己錄影。

> **We are photographing** each other.
> 兩個人各自幫彼此拍照。↵
> 我們正在幫彼此拍照。

---

3 另一個與 each other 意義相近的片語 one another，也不能和反身代名詞的用法混淆。

one another 也是「**彼此、互相**」的意思，但 one another 只能用於「**三個人以上**」。

When playing doubles, you and your partner must always keep an eye on each other.
↳ 兩個人；這裡不能用 watch yourselves。

進行雙打的時候，
你和你的夥伴應該
要不斷彼此注意。

Everybody on the team must help one another **if we are to win the game.**
↳ 人數超過兩名

如果我們想贏得比賽，每一名隊員都應該彼此幫助。

Practice

1

請從框內選出正確的詞彙或片語填空，完成句子。不需要填任何詞彙的地方，請劃上「/」。

me

myself

himself

by herself

ourselves

each other

one another

themselves

1. I am going to take my camera with ＿＿＿＿＿＿＿.

2. Nobody taught Isabelle how to swim. She learned ＿＿＿＿＿＿＿.

3. Kent is relaxing ＿＿＿＿＿＿＿ on the back porch.

4. We didn't hire anybody. We painted our house ＿＿＿＿＿＿＿.

5. When my sister and I go swimming, we look out for ＿＿＿＿＿＿＿.

6. With the economy being so bad, we need to help ＿＿＿＿＿＿＿.

7. I feel ＿＿＿＿＿＿＿ strong and healthy.

8. You must concentrate ＿＿＿＿＿＿＿ on the book.

9. Craig didn't shave ＿＿＿＿＿＿＿ this morning.

10. My dog Lou always dries ＿＿＿＿＿＿＿ in front of the fan.

11. Brenda was dressed ＿＿＿＿＿＿＿ quickly and left her apartment.

12. They are still in love with ＿＿＿＿＿＿＿.

2

請依圖示，從框內選出適當的用語填空，完成句子。

herself

themselves

each other

one another

Lily and Nana are chasing ＿＿＿＿＿＿＿.

To win the race, everyone on the yacht must help ＿＿＿＿＿＿＿.

They are photographing ＿＿＿＿＿＿＿.

Cathy is putting together the puzzle by ＿＿＿＿＿＿＿.

Unit 26

Expressions for Quantity
表示「數量」的用語

1 a number of 意指「一些」,常用來修飾**複數可數名詞**,動詞也要用**複數動詞**。

A **large** <u>number of</u> **customers** have gathered in the shoe department for their refunds.

很多消費者聚集到鞋子部門要求退費。

比較

the number of 則表示「某物的數量」,須用**單數動詞**。

• <u>The number of</u> **unemployed teachers** in this city <u>keeps</u> rising.

這個城市的失業教師人數持續增加。

2 a group of 意指「一群」,用來修飾**複數可數名詞**,動詞也要用**複數動詞**。

<u>A group of</u> **unemployed teachers** are marching on New York City Hall, demanding teaching jobs. 一群失業教師在紐約市政府前遊行,要求教職。

3 plenty of 意指「大量的」、「比剛好還要多一點」。可修飾**複數可數名詞**,也可修飾**不可數名詞**。

We still have <u>plenty of</u> **time**. Why don't we drop by Mary's before we return to Phoenix? 我們的時間還很多,何不在返回鳳凰城之前,繞去瑪莉家一下?

plenty of **lamb**
很多羊肉

plenty of **lamb chops**
很多羊排

4 a great deal of 意指「**大量的**」,可修飾**複數可數名詞**,也可修飾**不可數名詞**。搭配的動詞視其修飾何種名詞而定。

<u>A great deal of</u> **work** needs to be done by tomorrow.

有許多工作要在明天之前完成。

Jenny has <u>a great deal of</u> **toys**. Please do not buy her any more toys.

珍妮的玩具已經很多了,請不要再買給她了。

5 a lot of 或 lots of 意指「很多」、「比剛好多很多」。可修飾**複數可數名詞**,也可修飾**不可數名詞**。

a lot of **pork**
大量豬肉

a lot of **sausages**
大量香腸

lots of **beef**
大量牛肉

lots of **steaks**
很多牛排

Practice

1 請勾選正確的答案。

1. We've got □ a plenty of □ plenty of fruit in our refrigerator.

2. □ A plenty of □ Plenty of juice □ was □ were made for the party.

3. Plenty of shops □ is □ are open if we need more supplies for the party.

4. We have plenty of □ people □ person with cars to pick up the guests at the train station and drive them to the clubhouse.

5. The company is prepared to spend □ a great deal of □ great deals of money on the new production facility in China.

6. A great deal of □ planning □ a planning has gone into this new facility.

7. A great deal of money □ was □ were required to get the land for the factory.

8. As we enter the construction phase for this project, a great deal of □ time □ the time will be required for management to complete this expansion.

9. □ A number of □ The number of the pictures we took □ is □ are astonishing.

10. □ A number of □ The number of pictures □ has □ have been ruined.

11. A number of □ problem □ problems reduced the number of usable photos.

12. Therefore, □ a number of □ numbers of pictures have to be deleted.

13. There is □ lot of □ lots of sand on this beach.

14. A lot of □ sand □ sands went into my sneakers.

15. Are you going to build a lot of □ a sand castle □ sand castles today?

16. A lot of beaches □ is □ are so rocky.

Unit 27

Indefinite Pronouns for Quantity
表示「數量」的不定代名詞

不定代名詞的個別用法，請見 Units 29-38 說明。

1 不定代名詞用來指「**不特定的人、事、物**」，經常帶有**數量**的含意。

- **a few** 一些
- **all** 全部
- **a little** 一些
- **some** 一些
- **any** 任何
- **both** 兩者
- **either** 兩者之一
- **neither** 兩者皆非
- **another** 另一個
- **each** 每個
- **half** 一半
- **many** 很多
- **much** 很多
- **more** 更多
- **most** 大多數
- **none** 完全沒有

2 不定代名詞當語意清楚時，它們**可以單獨存在**，後面不需要加名詞。

If you want some donuts, I will go buy some.
如果你想吃甜甜圈，我就去買一點回來。
I didn't count the number of no-shows, but there weren't many.
我沒算缺席的人數，但是不太多就是了。

3 上述這些詞彙，有許多都常作「限定詞」使用，可以直接放在**名詞前面**修飾名詞。

The fruit stand has some watermelons.
水果攤上有一些西瓜。
They have many types of grapes.
他們有很多不同品種的葡萄。
All the fruit is fresh. 所有的水果都很新鮮。
The fruit stand has more bananas than the grocery store. 水果攤的香蕉比雜貨店的多。

這些詞彙如果**單獨使用**，或者**先接 of** 再接名詞，它們就是**代名詞**；如果**後面直接加名詞**，就是**限定詞**。

4 不定代名詞後面接的名詞，如果已經是加了所有格或 **the/these** 的名詞（the room、her key 等），則不定代名詞後面要先接 of，再接這些帶有修飾語的名詞。

Does this store sell any of the English newspapers? 這間店裡有賣任何英文報紙嗎？
The mini-mart has a lot of your favorite soft drinks.
這間小型超市有很多你喜歡喝的飲料。
None of these soft drinks are caffeine-free. 這些飲料沒有一種是不含咖啡因的。

5 all、half 和 both 後面如果接加了**所有格代名詞或 the/these 的名詞**（the room、her key 等），則**可加 of 也可以不加**。
如果接**受格代名詞**（them、us 等），就一定要加 of。

I bought all (of) the groceries on the shopping list.
我把購物單上所有的物品都買齊了。
Half (of) the gifts have been wrapped.
一半的禮物都包裝好了。
✗ It would be helpful if you could move some of the boxes, but it is not necessary to move all them.
✓ It would be helpful if you could move some of the boxes, but it is not necessary to move all of them.
要是你能幫我搬一些箱子，就算是幫了我的忙了，不過不用搬全部的箱子。
✗ I told Sue I couldn't attend the party unless she invited both us.
✓ I told Sue I couldn't attend the party unless she invited both of us.
我告訴蘇除非我們兩個都受邀，不然我就不能去派對。

Practice

1

請勾選正確的答案，有些句子可能兩個答案皆適用。

1. There are □ some □ some of markers in the drawer.

2. □ Both □ Both of tissue bags are empty.

3. □ A few of □ A few your friends sent you birthday cards.

4. There were two phone calls, but □ neither of □ neither was for you.

5. □ All □ All of the boxes you left here are stored in the garage.

6. I only bought □ a few □ a few of apples.

7. I bought a new type of tea. I'll make you □ some □ some of.

8. I only finished □ half □ half of the spaghetti.

9. I threw out □ some □ some of them.

10. □ Most □ Most of the tourists are Chinese.

11. □ Many □ Many of them came here for the first time.

2

請將句中可省略的名詞劃除，精簡句子；必要處可以用其他代名詞替代。

1. I need some crayons. Do you have any ~~crayons~~?

2. I bought some soy milk. Would you like to drink some soy milk?

3. I ate some cherries, but not all of the cherries.

4. I borrowed some books from the library, but not very many books.

5. I've read a few articles in the newspaper, but not all of the articles.

6. I've run out of printing paper. I need more printing paper.

7. I dropped the spoon. Please give me another spoon.

8. There're five singers in the band. Each singer has his or her own fans.

9. I can't decide which shirt to buy. I think I'll take both shirts.

10. I took the whole box of grapes out of the fridge and found out half of the grapes had gone bad.

11. I can't lend you much money. I have only a little money.

12. Over two hundred students have joined our dance club. Most of the students are college students.

Unit 28

Indefinite Pronouns With Singular or Plural Verbs
不定代名詞搭配單數動詞或複數動詞

1 應該搭配**單數動詞**的不定代名詞：

- each
- either
- neither
- another
- much
- every (one)
- everyone
- everybody
- everything
- anyone
- anybody
- anything
- someone
- somebody
- something
- no one
- nobody
- nothing

No one believes his story.

沒人相信他說的事情。

Someone is knocking on the door.

有人在敲門。

Neither of the dogs has a skin problem.

兩隻狗都沒有皮膚病。

Each of the rooms is decorated in a different theme.

每個房間各自以不同的主題做裝潢。

單數意義的不定代名詞，除了動詞要使用**單數**之外，如有需要使用相對應的其他代名詞，也要使用**單數**，例如**人稱代名詞**要用 he/she/it，所有格代名詞要用 his/her/its。

- Everyone is writing his or her research paper carefully.

  每個人都全神貫注在寫自己的研究論文。

- If anything has to be done, it has to be done quickly.

  如果還有任何待辦事項，都得盡快完成。

2 應該搭配**複數動詞**的不定代名詞：

- both
- many
- (a) few
- several

Both of the clerks wear black hats. 兩名店員都戴著黑帽子。

A few vases were broken when they were transported.

有些花瓶在運送途中破損了。

Several days have passed.

已經過了好幾天。

Many of them have been to Tokyo two or three times.

他們之中，許多人已經去過東京兩、三次。

3 同時可修飾**複數可數名詞**和**不可數名詞**的不定代名詞，則要視其搭配的名詞而定。

當後面接**複數可數名詞**的時候，就要用**複數動詞**；當後面接**不可數名詞**的時候，就要用**單數動詞**。

- all
- most
- some

Some fresh blueberries are added to the fruit tea. 水果茶裡加了一些新鮮藍莓。

Most of the work is going to be done today. 大部分工作會在今天完成。

All the furniture in the store is handmade.

這家店裡賣的家具全都是手工製作的。

All the fruit tarts were sold in two hours.

所有水果塔在兩個小時內銷售一空。

Practice

1　請將括弧內的動詞以正確的形式填空,完成句子。

Most of the pieces left on the board _____ (be) white.

Some of the peppers _____ (be) red.

All of the fish _____ (be swimming) in the same direction.

Each dog _____ (have) its own personality.

Both racing cars _____ (be) fast.

Everyone _____ (work) hard in the office.

2　請勾選正確的答案。

1. ☐ Does ☐ Do anybody know when the bus will arrive?

2. Nothing ☐ was ☐ were achieved today.

3. Everybody ☐ was ☐ were yelling her name.

4. Neither of the children has ☐ their ☐ his or her cell phone.

5. Several students lost ☐ their ☐ his or her coats.

6. There ☐ isn't ☐ aren't much time left.

7. I left my cell phone on the kitchen table. I'll go and get ☐ it ☐ them.

8. Only a few of the rings ☐ cost ☐ costs a lot.

Unit 29

"Some" and "Any"
Some 與 Any

1 some 和 any 可用來修飾**複數可數名詞和不可數名詞**，表達「**不確定的數量**」。

some **messages** 一些訊息
any **messages** 任何訊息
some **food** 一些食物
any **food** 任何食物

2 一般來說，some 用於**肯定句**；
any 用於**否定句**和**疑問句**。

Christy has some **job offers.**
克莉絲蒂有一些職缺機會。
Christy doesn't have any **job offers.**
克莉絲蒂沒有獲得任何的職缺機會。
Do **you** have any **milk?**
你有牛奶嗎？
Do **you** have any **small plastic tubing?**
你有小的塑膠管線嗎？
There were some **phone calls for you.**
有幾通電話打來找你。
There weren't any **phone calls for you.**
沒有打給你的電話。

3 如果一個問句「**希望得到肯定的回答**」，也就是期待對方回答 yes，那麼就可以在**疑問句**中使用 some。

Do **you** have some **black electrical tape?**
↳ 提問的人認為對方有黑色的絕緣膠帶。
你有黑色的絕緣膠帶可以借我用嗎？
Jason, can **I** have some **of the cookies on the table?**
傑森，我可以拿一些桌上的餅乾嗎？

4 如果 any 表示「**無論哪一個都可以**」、「**隨意選擇一個**」的時候，就可以用於肯定句。

Take any **of those PVC pipes if you need one.** ↳ 你要拿哪一個都可以。
如果需要的話，你可以從那些塑膠管中拿一個去用。

5 any 可以和 never、seldom、rarely、hardly 和 without 等單字連用，強調這些單字的**否定意義**。

Fran never **helps** any **of her colleagues in her office.**
法蘭從來不幫助辦公室裡的任何同事。
Nelson seldom **calls** any **of his relatives.**
奈爾森很少打電話給親戚。

6 some 經常用於「**比較**」的句子裡，以強調「**差異性**」。

Some **of these new water heaters use a lot less electricity than the older models.**
這些新型熱水器裡，有些比舊型的省電很多。

Practice

1

請用 some 或 any 填空，完成句子。有些句子可以同時使用 some 和 any。

1. I received _____ interesting emails from an old friend.

2. I haven't received _____ messages from Mom.

3. Louis found Mary's phone number without _____ trouble.

4. If you need _____ letters of reference, I will write one for you.

5. Do you have _____ books to help me get ready for civil service examinations?

6. I don't have _____ paperclips in my drawer.

7. You can get staples from _____ business supply stores.

8. _____ people like plastic folders, but I like the paper ones.

9. Could you make me _____ coffee?

2

請用 any 將右列句子改寫為「否定句」和「疑問句」。

1. We can take some plums from the box.
   → _____
   → _____

2. I have some lip balm.
   → _____
   → _____

3. She made some strawberry milkshake in the morning.
   → _____
   → _____

3

請用括弧裡提供的詞彙改寫句子。

1. Sue doesn't buy any diamonds. (never)
   → _____

2. Tanya doesn't play any online games. (rarely)
   → _____

3. Sunny doesn't cook any fish. (hardly)
   → _____

4. We don't watch any horror movies. (seldom)
   → _____

Part 4 Quantity 數量

Unit 30

"Many" and "Much"
Many 與 Much

1 many 和 much 是**代名詞**，也是**形容詞**，意指「大量的」。

We don't have many free tickets for the circus performance. 我們沒有很多馬戲團表演的免費入場券。

Is there any orange juice left?
還有柳橙汁嗎？

Yes, but not much.
有，但是所剩不多。

2 many 用來修飾**複數可數名詞**；much 用來修飾**不可數名詞**。

many **bricks**
許多磚塊

much **concrete**
大量的混凝土

I didn't take many photos in Spain because I didn't have much free time.

我在西班牙的時候沒拍很多照片，因為我沒多少空閒時間。

3 many 和 much 多用於**疑問句**和**否定句**，少用於**肯定句**。

How much gas is in the car?

車子還有多少油？

We don't have much gas in the car.

我們車裡的油不多了。

Is there much time left?

還剩下很多時間嗎？

There isn't much time left.

剩下的時間不多了。

4 如果要在**肯定句**表示「**大量的**」，通常會用 a lot of、lots of 或 plenty of 這類的量詞，而不用 **many** 或 **much**。

✗ Cathy always has many questions.
✓ Cathy always has a lot of questions.
凱西總是有很多問題。

✗ There is much space to add another desk.
✓ There is plenty of space to add another desk.
還有足夠的空間可以增加一張書桌。

✗ The room has much light.
✓ The room has lots of light.
房間裡的光線充足。

5 many 和 much 如果搭配 too、so、as、very，就可以用於**肯定句**。

The department has too much boxes of copier paper. 部門裡的影印紙太多箱啦。

Put as much copier paper as you can in the storage room.

盡可能把影印紙放到儲藏室裡。

The secretary has so many things to do that we need to help her move the boxes. 祕書要做的事實在太多了，所以我們得幫她搬那些紙箱。

Your help is very much appreciated.

非常感謝您的幫忙。

Practice

1

請勾選正確的答案。

1. There are ☐ many ☐ much cars on the road.
2. There is ☐ a lot of ☐ many sand in my shoes.
3. How ☐ much ☐ many oatmeal is in the pot?
4. He has ☐ plenty of ☐ many clothing.
5. Do you have ☐ so many ☐ many handbags?
6. The agency doesn't have ☐ much ☐ many work this week.
7. There isn't ☐ much ☐ many time before the bus leaves.
8. There is still ☐ much ☐ a lot of room in the trunk.
9. I drank ☐ much ☐ too much tea tonight.
10. I've found ☐ many ☐ much mistakes in this proposal.

2 請從框內選用適當的用語填空，完成句子。

plenty of

many

too many

as many

much

too much

There isn't _____
wine in the decanter.

She poured _____
wine into the glass.

She is eating _____
sandwiches as she can.

We've made _____
sandwiches.

They collected _____
grapes this year.

I don't have _____
grapes to eat.

Part 4 Quantity 數量

Unit 31

"Few" and "Little"
Few 與 Little

1 few 和 little 是**代名詞**，也是**形容詞**，兩者都指「**幾乎沒有**」，帶有**否定的**口氣。
few 用於**可數名詞**，little 用於**不可數名詞**。

There is little relevant information on this topic in the briefing book.
重點手冊裡幾乎沒有和這個主題相關的資訊。

Few customers have purchased the deluxe spa services since they were introduced.
在聽過介紹後，還是沒什麼人購買豪華 SPA 服務。

2 a few 和 a little 也是**代名詞**兼**形容詞**，表示「**一些**」，通常用於**肯定句**中。
a few 用於**可數名詞**，a little 用於**不可數名詞**。

The application takes a little work so plan your time accordingly.
申請要花一點功夫，所以你要好好安排時間。

There were a few applicants for the position. 這個職位有一些應徵者。

3 few、little、a few、a little 都可不接名詞，單獨存在，作為**代名詞**使用。

Everybody complained, but few of us failed the exam.
雖然大家都在抱怨，但我們之中只有少數幾個考試沒過。

Little of my homework has been finished. 我的作業都還沒做完。

Is there any apple juice left?
還有蘋果汁嗎？

There is a little left. 剩下一些。

Just a few will do. Thanks.
只要幾個就好，謝謝。

How many bags do you need?
妳需要幾個袋子？

4 few 和 little（不加 a）屬於較正式的用語，口語中，多用 not much、not many、only a little、only a few 和 hardly any 來表達「**不多**」、「**只有一點點**」。
如果要表示「**極少**」，較常用 very little 或 very few。

There is not much tea in the pot.
茶壺裡沒有多少茶了。

Not many people have shown up.
出席的人不怎麼多。

The typhoon knocked over very few trees. 颱風只吹倒了少數幾棵樹。

The refrigerator has very little food in it.
冰箱裡的食物少得可憐。

Practice

1

請勾選正確的答案。

1. It's raining heavily. There are ☐ **few** ☐ **little** people on the streets.

2. The chicken soup was so delicious. There is ☐ **few** ☐ **little** left.

3. Could you pull the curtain? We need ☐ **little** ☐ **a little** light in the room.

4. ☐ **A few** ☐ **A little** of us have come to the conference.

5. ☐ **Few of** ☐ **Few of the** runners could finish the marathon.

6. Jack put ☐ **a few** ☐ **a little** sugar in his coffee.

7. He also poured some cream into the coffee, but just ☐ **little** ☐ **a little**.

8. We still have ☐ **little** ☐ **a little** time. Let's get some souvenirs at the duty-free shop.

9. ☐ **A few** ☐ **A few of** the passengers are sitting in the transit lounge.

2

請將括弧內的動詞以正確的形式填空，完成句子。

Very little vinegar .... (be poured) on the salad.

Very few students .... (have solved) this math question.

Not many chickens .... (be) able to fly.

There .... (be) not much preservative in this hot sauce.

Only a little light .... (penetrate) through the leaves.

Only a few plants .... (survive) in a desert.

Unit 32

Both

Both

1 both 是**形容詞**，也是**代名詞**，意指「**兩者皆是**」，是一個具有複數意義的詞彙。both 作為**形容詞**時，會接**複數可數名詞**。

Both employees won awards for their performance.

兩名員工都因為工作表現良好獲得獎賞。

The boss had a picture taken with both winners of the contest.

老闆和比賽的兩名獲獎者都合拍了照片。

2 both 可以單獨使用，作為**代名詞**。此時，動詞要用**複數動詞**。

Peter and Clive were fighting in the hallway. Both were punished by the teacher.

彼德和克里夫因為在走廊打架，雙雙被老師處罰。

The orchestra is going to play the works of Beethoven and Bach. Both are my favorite musicians.

這個管弦樂團將演奏貝多芬和巴哈的作品，兩位都是我最喜愛的音樂家。

3 both 經常放在**主詞或受詞的後面**。

The two Australian players both entered the semifinals.

兩名澳洲選手雙雙挺進四強賽。

The human resources department required them both to take an aptitude test.

人事部要求他們兩位都要做性向測驗。

4 如果句中有助動詞或 be 動詞，則 both 會放在**助動詞或 be 動詞後面**。

They will both graduate this year.

他們兩個都將於今年畢業。

Rondo and Nick are both workaholics.

朗道和尼克都是工作狂。

5 both of 後面常接帶有 **the/these/my/your** 等修飾詞的複數名詞，這種情況下，**of** 也可以省略。

Both (of) the applicants have arrived.

兩位應徵者都已經到了。

Both (of) the vice presidents are being considered for the presidency of the company.

兩位副總裁都被列入考慮擔任公司的總裁。

6 both of 後面如果接的是 **you**、**us**、**them** 等複數代名詞，則 **of** 不可省略。

✗ The company invited both them for interviews.

✓ The company invited both of them for interviews.

公司請他們兩位都來面試。

7 「both . . . and . . .」這個用法，常用來**連結兩個詞彙或詞組**。

Grace contacted both the general manager and the executive director of the agency.

機關裡的總經理和執行長兩位，葛麗絲都聯絡了。

Practice

1

請勾選正確的答案，
有些句子可能兩個答
案皆適用。

1. My cousin has two boys, and ☐ both ☐ both of them love basketball.

2. I already asked ☐ both ☐ both of your aunt and uncle to come.

3. My parents ☐ both are ☐ are both teaching in secondary schools.

4. Both Jenny and Keith ☐ is athlete ☐ are athletes.

5. ☐ Both you ☐ Both of you should respect your parents.

6. ☐ Both ☐ Both of the ideas are wonderful.

7. ☐ Both concerts ☐ Concerts both will attract many people.

8. Both volleyball ☐ and ☐ or swimming are my favorite sports.

9. ☐ Both ☐ Both of my cousins are studying at law school.

10. Sandra and Chris are best friends. You should invite ☐ both them ☐ them both.

2

請依圖示，從框內選
出適當的動詞，搭配
both，以正確的形式
和語序填空，完成句
子。

be violinists

have passed
the exam

love fishing

be Russian Blue
cats

be the best
friends of
human beings

can do the
freestyle

Mike and James ....
....

Wendy and Rita ....
....

Mumu and Lulu ....
....

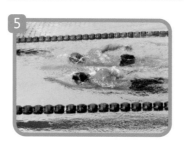

Roger and Janet ....
....

Ken and Tom ....
....

Dogs and cats ....
....

Unit 33

"Either" and "Neither"
Either 與 Neither

1 either 意指「**兩者之一**」，neither 意指「**兩者皆不**」，都是**形容詞**，也是**代名詞**。當形容詞時，後面都接**單數可數名詞**。

Either size will work. 兩種尺寸都可以用。
If neither scanner can make five mega-pixel images, then find a different one.
如果兩台掃描器都沒辦法掃出五百萬畫素的圖，那就再選別的。

2 either 和 neither 作為**代名詞**時，經常用 either of 和 neither of。它們後面都會接帶有 **the/these/my/your** 等修飾詞的**複數可數名詞**。

Will either of your children be willing to help me plant flowers?
你的兩個小孩有誰要幫我種花嗎？
Neither of the chairs was comfortable.
這兩張椅子都不好坐。

3 either of 和 neither of 後面也常接 **you、us、them** 等複數代名詞。

Can either of you fix the washing machine?
你們兩個人有誰可以把洗衣機修好嗎？
Neither of us are repairmen.
我們兩個都不是維修人員。

neither 的發音有兩種：['niðɚ]〔美式〕和 ['naɪðɚ]〔英式〕，但是並沒有規定何時要發哪一個音。選定一種發音後可以大膽說出來，不要將兩種發音混合使用，便可避免引起誤解。

4 either 不管是單獨使用，或者接**單數名詞**，或者「**either of + 複數名詞**」，動詞都用**單數動詞**。

Either was possible in the beginning, but not now.
兩種可能性一開始都有，但現在沒了。
Either of the writers has the skill to do the job. Call one of them.
兩位作者都能勝任這份工作，打電話給他們其中一個。

5 neither 如果單獨使用，或者接**單數名詞**，也是使用**單數動詞**。
但 neither of 接**複數可數名詞**時，可以用**單數動詞**，也可以用**複數動詞**，**單數動詞**多用於正式用語。

Neither is strong enough to beat the boxing champion.
兩位選手都不夠強壯，難以挑戰拳擊冠軍。
Neither machine works.
那兩台機器沒有一台是好的。
Neither of us know/knows the answer.
我們兩個都不知道答案。

6 常用句型：
either . . . or . . .（不是……就是……）
neither . . . nor . . .（不是……也不是……）

Herman indicated that either the order should be filled or the payment should be refunded. 赫曼指示，要不把訂單完成，要不就必須退費。
Neither getting a refund nor receiving the product will address the underlying issues.
不管是獲得退費或是收到產品，都不能解決潛在的問題。

1 請用 either、either of、neither 或 neither of 填空，完成句子。

1. My husband and I want to join you, but _____ us have the time.

2. We can leave on _____ Monday or Tuesday.

3. Can _____ your parents chaperone the school dance?

4. _____ withdraw the money from the ATM machine or write a check.

5. _____ us is hungry because we already ate.

6. _____ you pay now or you lose the chance.

7. _____ outbound nor inbound flights are going anywhere because of the typhoon.

2 請將括弧內的動詞以正確的形式填空，完成句子。

1. Neither of the fire lanterns _____ (be flying) high enough.

2. Neither book _____ (be) easy to read.

3. Most of the time the ducks _____ (be) either swimming or walking.

4. Neither of the tennis players _____ (have made) six double faults in this match.

5. Neither the Petronas Twin Towers nor the Taipei 101 _____ (be) taller than the Burj Khalifa.

6. Either espresso machine _____ (can make) good coffee.

7. You can choose between these two tables. Either of them _____ (be) fine with me.

Unit **34**

All
All

None   All

3   all 經常放在**主詞或受詞的後面**。

Those sports cars **all belong to Derek.**
那些跑車都是德瑞克的。
I asked them **all to go home.**
我要他們全部都回家。

1   all 指「**所有的**」，也可作為**形容詞**，也可當**代名詞**。all 可修飾**複數可數名詞**和**不可數名詞**。

　　❶ 當 all 修飾**複數可數名詞**的時候，要用**複數動詞**；
　　❷ 當 all 修飾**不可數名詞**的時候，要用**單數動詞**。

All coins are **stamped with a mint date.**
所有的錢幣上面都刻有鑄幣日期。
All old money has **some value to collectors.**
對收藏家來說，所有的舊錢都有價值。

4   如果句中有助動詞或 be 動詞，則 all 會放在**助動詞**或 **be** 動詞的後面。

We must **all finish our homework before we go to the party.**
我們去參加派對之前，得都先寫完作業。
The tableware they sell is **all silver.**
他們賣的餐具全都是銀製品。

2   all 作為**代名詞**時，常搭配**關係子句**，意義等於 **everything** 或 **the only thing**。此時 all 如果作為**主詞**，要使用**單數動詞**。

The company has all (that) it needs to make money.
= **The company has** everything (that) it needs to make money.
公司要用來生財的東西都有了。
All I need is **the address, not the phone number.**
= The only thing I need is **the address, not the phone number.**
我需要的就只有地址，不要電話號碼。

5   all of 後面常接帶有 **the/these/my/your** 等修飾詞的**複數名詞**，這種情況下，**of** 也可以省略。all (of) 後面也可接**不可數名詞**。

All (of) the people got on the bus.
所有人都上了公車。
Do you have all (of) the books I need?
你有我要的那些書嗎？

all of the books

6   all of 後面如果接的是 **you**、**us**、**them**、**it** 等代名詞，則 **of** 不可以省略。

Where is the chocolate milk? Did you drink all of it?
巧克力牛奶在哪裡？你全部喝光了嗎？
Janet told all of us about the procedures at the customs office. 珍娜把海關的所有程序都告訴我們每一個人了。

Practice

1

請勾選正確的答案，
有些句子可能兩個答
案皆適用。

1. Almost all kids □ love □ loves to visit the zoo.

2. □ Do □ Does women all love diamonds?

3. I put some cherries on the table. Have you eaten □ all them □ them all?

4. □ All □ All of pigeons can tell directions by instinct.

5. All I have □ is □ are three hundred dollars.

6. You □ should all □ all should arrive at the station by five.

7. □ All □ All of the developed countries have begun to make an effort to explore sustainable energy.

8. All wealth □ is □ are temporary.

9. Sammi bought all □ that was □ that were on the shelf.

10. Our effort □ all was □ was all in vain.

11. All □ is □ are good that ends well.

12. I gave you one hundred dollars. Did you spend □ it all □ all it?

2

請用 all 改寫句子。

1. I've sold everything I had.
   → ....

2. This lamb chop is the only one left.
   → ....

3. Do you have every book I requested?
   → ....

4. The only thing you've done right is marrying that woman.
   → ....

5. You will find everything you need in this outlet.
   → ....

6. Did you eat everything in the refrigerator?
   → ....

7. I looked up every word I didn't know in the dictionary.
   → ....

8. The only thing I read last week was *The Stolen Bicycle*.
   → ....

Part 4 Quantity 數量

Unit 35

"All," "Every," and "Whole"
All、Every、Whole

1 all 和 every 都用來指「**一整個群體**」，同時意指「**全體裡的每一個成員**」。all 可以當**形容詞**，也可以當**代名詞**。every 則是只能當**形容詞**。

Mr. Smith bought all the roses in the flower shop.
史密斯先生買下花店裡所有的玫瑰花。
Derek bought every rose in the flower shop. 德瑞克買下花店裡的每一朵玫瑰花。

2 every 只用來修飾**單數可數名詞**，並且使用**單數動詞**。

I checked the date on every coin.
我查看了每一枚錢幣上面的日期。
Every citizen has his or her responsibility.
每位市民都有責任。

3 如果要指「**所有的人**」或「**所有的東西**」，會用 everybody 或 everything，而不常用單獨的 **all**。

✗ All got on the bus.
✓ All the people got on the bus. /
They all got on the bus.
所有的人都上了公車。／他們全都上了公車。
✗ All got off the train.
✓ Everybody got off the train. /
They all got off the train.
每一個人都下火車了。／他們全都下火車了。
✗ Did you get all on the list?
✓ Did you get everything on the list?
單子上列的所有東西你都準備好了嗎？

4 whole 表示「**事物的整體**」、「**事物的每一個部分**」，可以修飾**單數可數名詞**或**不可數名詞**。

The distributor shipped the whole order to the customer.
經銷商將所有的訂貨都運送給客戶。
Jill had to stay at the trade show the whole time. 吉兒得從頭到尾一直待在貿易展。

5 whole 的前面要加上 **the/this/my** 等修飾語，後面再接**名詞**。

Did you buy the whole set, or just part of it? 你買了一整套，還是只單買一部分？
I spent my whole vacation babysitting my sister's kids.
我整個假期都花在幫我姐姐帶孩子。

6 a whole 後面只能接**單數可數名詞**。

This is my first time to write a whole novel by myself.
這是我第一次獨力寫一整本小說。

7 all、every 和 whole 的意義比較：

all 表示「**整體**」	all day 整天
	all morning 整個早上
every 表示「**頻率**」	every day 每天
	every morning 每個早上
whole 強調「**完整**」，比 all 更具強調語氣。	the whole day 一整天
	the whole morning 一整個早上

I like to listen to the radio all day.
我喜歡整天聽廣播。　　↳ 聽一整天
I like to listen to music every day.
我喜歡每天聽音樂。　　↳ 每天至少聽一次
I keep the TV on the whole day.
我讓電視一整天開著。　↳ 比 all day 強調

Practice

請勾選正確的答案。

1. ☐ All ☐ Every student likes vacation.

2. Matt loves ☐ all ☐ every classical music.

3. ☐ Everybody ☐ All enjoyed the concert tonight.

4. After ☐ everything ☐ all the help I gave you, you still didn't finish it.

5. Did you complete ☐ the whole ☐ all job?

6. I sent ☐ all the ☐ the whole thank-you letters.

7. Yesterday I spent ☐ all ☐ every day working on a book review.

8. My bowling league plays ☐ every ☐ all Wednesday night at 7:00.

9. ☐ Every one of ☐ Every your old friends has moved away.

2

請從框內選用適當的用語填空，完成句子。

all

every

whole

1. Have you changed the sheets and towels in ＿＿＿＿＿＿ guest room?

2. The police searched the ＿＿＿＿＿＿ building but found nothing.

3. ＿＿＿＿＿＿ the strawberry milk on the rack has been sold out. Let's go to another supermarket.

4. I checked the expiration date on ＿＿＿＿＿＿ bottle of milk and then picked the freshest one.

5. Did you write down ＿＿＿＿＿＿ word I said?

6. Janice spent her ＿＿＿＿＿＿ winter vacation taking driving lessons.

7. Dawn checked the ＿＿＿＿＿＿ house, but she couldn't find her passport.

8. After I read ＿＿＿＿＿＿ message on my cell phone, I deleted ＿＿＿＿＿＿ of them.

9. Can you eat a ＿＿＿＿＿＿ pizza by yourself?

10. I've bought ＿＿＿＿＿＿ the items I need. Let's go home.

Unit 36

"No" and "None"
No 與 None

1 no 是**形容詞**，可以修飾**名詞**，表示「**沒有**」，等同於 not a 或 not any，但語氣更強烈。

There is no room in the trunk of the car.
= There is not any room in the trunk of the car.
後車廂已經沒有空間了。
There are no seats available on the 11:00 flight.
= There are not any seats available on the 11:00 flight.
11 點起飛的班機已經沒有座位了。
No appointments are available until July 5.
= There aren't any appointments available until July 5.
7 月 5 日之前的預約都滿了。

2 no 可以修飾**單數可數名詞**、**複數可數名詞**和**不可數名詞**。

Today Brian has no handkerchief in his pocket. 今天布萊恩口袋裡沒有放手帕。
Betty has no shoes under her bed.
貝蒂的床鋪底下沒有鞋子。
Anna has no space in her closet.
安娜的衣櫥裡已經沒有空間了。

3 none 是**代名詞**，意指「**沒有**」。none 不能當作**形容詞**，所以後面不能接名詞。

I checked to see if we had basil, but we had none.
我檢查了一下看我們還有沒有羅勒，不過一點都不剩了。

4 none 後面如果需要接**名詞**，要使用 none of，同時後面的名詞要有**修飾語 the/this** 或 **my/your/his/her** 等所有格。

None of these cold medicines have helped. 這些感冒藥沒有一種有用。
None of my friends caught my cold.
我沒有朋友被我傳染感冒。

5 none of 後面如果接**不可數名詞**，那麼動詞就要用**單數動詞**。

None of the bread tastes good.
這些麵包都不好吃。
None of the sauce is spicy enough to go with the chicken.
這些醬料對這道雞肉來說都不夠辣。

6 none of 後面如果接**複數名詞**，那麼動詞可以用**單數**，也可以用**複數**。

None of my grandmother's home remedies have/has worked. 我外婆的那些家傳療法，沒有一種是有效的。

7 none 單獨使用時，如果是代替**複數名詞**（not any people or things），可以用**單數**或**複數動詞**。

Most of my classmates can speak good English, but none speaks/speak Spanish.
我班上大部分同學英語都講得很好，但是沒有人會說西班牙文。

I will go buy some cumin if there is none in the spice rack.
如果放調味罐的架上沒有孜然了，我會去買一點回來。

cumin

Practice

1

請用 no 或 none 填空，完成句子。

1. We have _____ carry-on luggage.

2. _____ of my friends are on the trip.

3. There are _____ connecting flights.

4. I checked for taxies and _____ were available.

5. If there are _____ taxies, then we will have to rent a car.

2

請勾選正確的答案，有些句子可能有兩個適用的答案。

1. We have ☐ no ☐ none soy sauce left.

2. I was looking for coffee beans to make an espresso, but there were ☐ none ☐ none coffee beans.

3. ☐ None of plates ☐ None of the plates ☐ None plates are clean.

4. None of today's news ☐ is ☐ are exciting.

5. None of the books ☐ is ☐ are informative.

6. She gave me lots of excuses, but none ☐ was ☐ were acceptable.

7. No one ☐ want ☐ wants to go into the water first.

8. The sign says ☐ None Smoking ☐ No Smoking.

9. None of his ideas ☐ was ☐ were accepted.

3

請用 no 的句型改寫句子。

1. There isn't any milk in the refrigerator.
   → _____

2. She doesn't trust anyone but her sister.
   → _____

3. I don't have any money with me.
   → _____

4. There aren't any rooms available today in this hotel.
   → _____

5. There isn't any room for negotiation.
   → _____

Unit 37

"One" and "Ones"
One 與 Ones

1 為了避免重複使用兩次相同的名詞，可以在語意清楚的情況下，用 one/ones 取代**第二次出現的名詞**。one 用來取代**單數可數名詞**，ones 用來取代**複數可數名詞**。

The new boss is much nicer than the old one.
新老闆比以前的老闆和善多了。
= boss ↵

Which office is yours? Is it the one by the window?
↳ = office
你的辦公室是哪一間？窗戶旁邊的那一間嗎？

Bonnie likes her new coworkers more than the last ones. 邦妮喜歡她的新同事勝於之前的同事。
↳ = coworkers

one/ones 不能代替**不可數名詞**。不可數名詞只能**重複出現**或省略不用。

• We have classical music, but we don't have any Baroque.
↳ = Baroque music
我們有古典音樂，但是沒有任何巴洛克時代的音樂。

2 one 的前面除非有**形容詞**修飾，否則不能與 **a/an** 連用。

✗ I'm looking for a job, but not just any job. I'm looking for a one.

✓ I'm looking for a job, but not just any job. I'm looking for a good one.
我在找工作，但不是什麼工作都行，我要一份好工作。

✗ Are you going to take that job? I'm waiting for a one with a high salary.

✓ Are you going to take that job? I'm waiting for one with a higher salary.
你要接受那份工作嗎？
我在等薪水好一點的工作。

3 one 的前面常加 this、that，形成 this one 或 that one。但是 ones 的前面卻不能加 **these** 或 **those**，除非 ones 的前面還有**形容詞**。

You can have this one here or that one over there. 你可以拿這邊的這一個，或是那邊的那一個。

✗ I like these red apples more than those ones.

✓ I like these red apples more than those green ones.
我喜歡這些紅蘋果勝過那些青蘋果。

✗ I like those ties more than these ones.

✓ I like those ties more than these.
我比較喜歡那些領帶，比較不喜歡這些領帶。

4 which one 或 which ones 可以構成**疑問句**，用來詢問「哪一個」、「哪一些」。

There are two trails in the botanical garden. Which one do you want to take?
植物園裡有兩條路，你想走哪一條？

There are lots of books on this shelf. Which ones are yours?
這個架子上有很多書，哪些是你的？

5 each one of 用來強調「**個別性**」。

There are ten cacti on sale. Let's look at each one of them.
有十棵仙人掌在特價拍賣，我們每一棵都來看看吧。

Practice

1 請用 one 或 ones 填空，完成句子。

1

We have some extra sandwiches.
Would you like _____?

2

I like the hat with the chin strap more
than the other _____.

3

Get the green grapes. They look better
than the purple _____.

4

I don't want a large fish. Can you give
me a small _____?

5

My apartment is the largest _____
on the third floor.

6

I like those white plates more than the
colorful _____.

7

Which shoes are yours?
Are yours the yellow _____?

8

Which puppy do you prefer? How about
the second _____ from the left?

Unit 38

Indefinite Pronouns With Some-, Any-, Every-, No-

以 Some-、Any-、Every-、No-
開頭的不定代名詞

1 以 some-、any-、every-、no- 開頭
的複合代名詞，是不定代名詞的大宗。

	some-	any-	every-	no-
-thing	something	anything	everything	nothing
-body	somebody	anybody	everybody	nobody
-one	someone	anyone	everyone	no one
-where	somewhere	anywhere	everywhere	nowhere

2 以 some- 和 any- 開頭的不定代名詞，
在用法上的差別，和 **some**、**any** 完全
一樣。

　1 something/somebody/someone/
　somewhere 用於**肯定句**；
　2 anything/anybody/anyone/
　anywhere 用於**否定句**和**疑問句**。

I want you to do something for me.
我想要你為我做一件事。
I do not want you to do anything for me.
我不要你為我做任何事。
Is there anywhere you want to go?
你想去什麼地方嗎？

3 如果一個**問句**「希望得到肯定的回
答」，也就是期待對方回答 yes，
就可以在**疑問句**中使用 something/
somebody/someone/somewhere。

Are you looking for someone?
你在找什麼人嗎？
Would you like something to drink?
你要不要喝點什麼？

4 如果表「**無論何事**」、「**無論何地**」、
「**無論何人**」都無所謂的時候，
anything/anybody/anyone/anywhere
也可以用於**肯定句**。

With that monetary prize, you can travel
anywhere you want.
有了這筆獎金，你想去哪裡旅遊都可以。
If you see anybody, please let me know.
如果你看到任何人，請通知我。

5 以 some-、any-、every-、no- 開頭
的不定代名詞，都要使用**單數動詞**。

Somebody is looking for you.
有人在找你。
Everything was at the English
department office.
所有的東西都在英語系辦公室。

6 這類不定代名詞的後面經常接「**加 to**
的不定詞」。

I have something to say.
我有話要說。

They've got nobody to rely on.
他們無依無靠。

7 everyone 和 every one 不同。
everyone 一定指「人」，只能單獨
使用，後面不接 of 片語。
every one 可以指「人」或「物」，
常**搭配 of** 使用。

Everyone had a good time in Shanghai.
每個人在上海都玩得很盡興。
Every one of the leather bags is
handmade.
所有的皮包都是手工製的。

Practice

1

請從框內選出適當的「不定代名詞」填空，完成句子。部分提供詞彙可重複使用。

something
anybody
nobody
everybody
everything
anything
nothing
somewhere
anywhere

1. I don't want to go _____ this weekend.

2. I want to go _____ hot and exciting.

3. Didn't _____ read the note I left on the table?

4. I called several times but _____ was home.

5. I would like you to get me _____ to drink.

6. I'm so hungry that I can eat _____.

7. The gangster asked _____ to put their hands on their head.

8. It was just an empty box with _____ in it.

9. I'm sorry. There is _____ I can reveal right now.

10. I've tried _____ I can do to help him.

2

請依圖示，從框內選出適當的用語，以「to + V」的形式填空，完成句子。

play with
read
eat
talk to
drink
go

I'm thirsty. I'll have something _____.

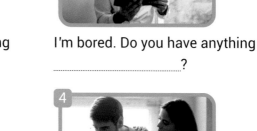

I'm bored. Do you have anything _____?

I'm hungry. I need something _____.

I feel sad. I need someone _____.

I don't want to be alone. I want someone _____.

I shouldn't have trusted this map. Now I have nowhere _____.

Unit 39

Introduction of Verb Tenses
動詞的時態介紹

時間軸

●事件

過去 ——————|——————→ 未來
現在

1 動詞依照動作進行的時間，可分為現在式、過去式和未來式；依照動作進行的狀態，又可分為簡單式、進行式和完成式。

簡單　　　　　　　　　　　　　　　進行

現在

1 現在簡單式

主詞 + 動詞現在式

Peter drives to work every weekday.
彼德每天開車去上班。

2 現在進行式

主詞 + am/is/are + 現在分詞（V-ing）

Andrew is writing a proposal to produce a series of household robots. 安德魯正在寫一份生產系列家用機器人的企畫。

過去

3 過去簡單式

主詞 + 動詞過去式

Ann passed the exam.
安通過考試了。

4 過去進行式

主詞 + was/were + 現在分詞（V-ing）

Vicky was cooking in the kitchen.
維琪那時正在廚房煮飯。

未來

5 未來簡單式

主詞 + will + 動詞原形

I will buy the tickets tomorrow.
我明天會去買票。

6 未來進行式

主詞 + will be + 現在分詞（V-ing）

Kevin will be watching a football game tomorrow night.
明天晚上凱文會看美式足球賽。

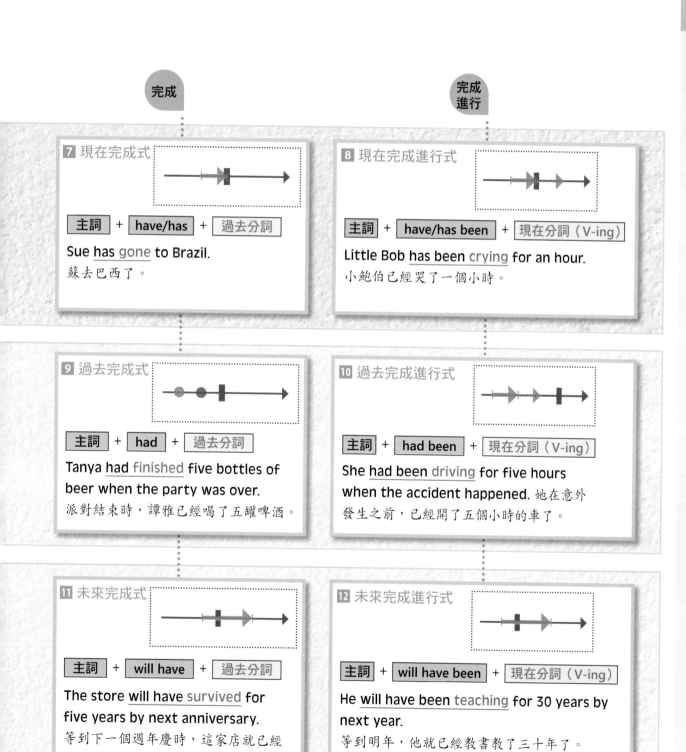

完成

7 現在完成式

主詞 + have/has + 過去分詞

Sue has gone to Brazil.
蘇去巴西了。

完成進行

8 現在完成進行式

主詞 + have/has been + 現在分詞（V-ing）

Little Bob has been crying for an hour.
小鮑伯已經哭了一個小時。

9 過去完成式

主詞 + had + 過去分詞

Tanya had finished five bottles of beer when the party was over.
派對結束時，譚雅已經喝了五罐啤酒。

10 過去完成進行式

主詞 + had been + 現在分詞（V-ing）

She had been driving for five hours when the accident happened. 她在意外發生之前，已經開了五個小時的車了。

11 未來完成式

主詞 + will have + 過去分詞

The store will have survived for five years by next anniversary.
等到下一個週年慶時，這家店就已經營業五年了。

12 未來完成進行式

主詞 + will have been + 現在分詞（V-ing）

He will have been teaching for 30 years by next year.
等到明年，他就已經教書教了三十年了。

Unit 40

Present Simple Tense
現在簡單式

● 事件

過去 ————————→ 未來
現在

Form 構句

| 肯定句的句型 | I/you/we/they listen |
| | he/she/it listens |

| 否定句的句型 | I/you/we/they do not listen |
| | he/she/it does not listen |

| 否定句的縮寫 | I/you/we/they don't listen |
| | he/she/it doesn't listen |

| 疑問句的句型 | Do I/you/we/they listen? |
| | Does he/she/it listen? |

Use 用法

1 現在簡單式可用來表示「**習慣**」和「**重複發生的行為**」。

We recycle cans and bottles once a month.
我們每月回收一次瓶罐。

He commutes downtown every weekday.
他每個工作日都要通勤往來市中心。

The news always finishes at 11:30 p.m.
新聞都在晚上 11 點 30 分播報完畢。

Do you visit relatives in the South every Chinese New Year?
你每年農曆春節都會到南部探望親戚嗎？

2 現在簡單式可以用來說明「**長期持續不變的情況**」，也就是說，過去如此、現在如此，未來也如此。

Typhoons come every year.
每年都會颳颱風。

Grandmother comes every winter.
外婆每年冬天都會來。

3 現在簡單式可以用來說明「**一件事實**」或「**正確無誤的事**」。

Julie graduates this year. 茱莉今年畢業。

Politicians fear the truth. 政客畏懼真相。

4 現在簡單式經常和一些頻率副詞搭配，形容「**規律發生的事件**」，同時指出到底「**多常發生**」。

頻率副詞
- always
- usually
- often
- sometimes
- never
- every day
- every year

My mother always cooks me breakfast.
我媽媽都會幫我準備早餐。

Jack gets up early every morning, and he is never late for school.
傑克每天早上都很早起，而且上學從不遲到。

5 現在簡單式也可以用來表示「**未來將會發生的事**」，並且是按照時刻表和計劃表「**安排好的事**」。

The client arrives at 2:00 tomorrow afternoon. 客戶將於明天下午 2 點抵達。

The train to Kyoto departs at 6 p.m.
往京都的火車於晚上 6 點發車。

What time does the earliest flight to Hong Kong leave?
飛往香港的班機最早的是幾點？

Practice

1

請將括弧內的動詞以
「現在簡單式」填空，
完成對話。

1. Q _____ you _____ (shave) every morning?
   A Yes, I _____ (shave) every morning after taking a shower.

2. Q _____ the café _____ (open) at 8 a.m.?
   A No, it _____ (open) at 9 a.m.

3. Q _____ whales _____ (migrate) to warm waters every winter?
   A Yes, whales _____ (migrate) to warm waters every winter.

4. Q _____ Brandon _____ (come) from England?
   A Yes, he _____ (come) from England.

5. Q How often _____ Brandon _____ (return) to England?
   A He _____ (return) once every couple of years.

6. Q _____ Jessie _____ (eat) pinto beans?
   A No, she _____ (not eat) pinto beans.

7. Q How many kilometers _____ you _____ (drive) to work?
   A I _____ (drive) 10 kilometers to my office every day.

8. Q Why _____ John _____ (feel) bad?
   A He _____ (feel) bad about yesterday's car accident.

9. Q When _____ the earliest MRT train _____ (depart)?
   A The earliest train _____ (depart) at 6 a.m.

10. Q How often _____ you _____ (check out) books from a library?
    A I _____ (check out) books from a library once a week.

2

請將括弧內的動詞以
「現在簡單式」填空，
完成句子。

1. Fran _____ (like) peanut butter and banana sandwiches.

2. Alice and Larry _____ (prepare) their food at home every night.

3. Aunt Sue _____ (live) in a cabin in the woods.

4. We _____ (not raise) pigs anymore.

5. _____ Emma _____ (study) hard?

6. It _____ (take) hours on high heat to roast a turkey.

7. Bernie always _____ (finish) eating before anybody else.

8. Fay always _____ (pay) her cell phone bill at the FamilyMart around the corner.

9. The sea level _____ (rise) gradually.

Unit **41**

Present Continuous Tense
現在進行式

Form 構句

● 事件

過去 ━━━━▶ 未來

現在

肯定句的句型	I am studying
	you/we/they are studying
	he/she/it is studying
肯定句的縮寫	I'm studying
	you/we/they 're studying
	he/she/it 's studying
否定句的句型	I am not studying
	you/we/they are not studying
	he/she/it is not studying
否定句的縮寫	I'm not studying
	you/we/they aren't studying
	he/she/it isn't studying
疑問句的句型	Am I studying?
	Are you/we/they studying?
	Is he/she/it studying?

Use 用法

1 現在進行式用來說明「**說話當時正在進行的動作**」。

Mavis: What are you doing?
Steve: I am peeling potatoes.
Mavis: Are you cooking dinner?
Steve: Of course, I am cooking dinner.
Why else would I be cooking potatoes?

梅菲絲：你在做什麼？
史帝夫：我在削馬鈴薯皮。
梅菲絲：你在準備晚餐嗎？
史帝夫：沒錯！我正在做晚餐。不然我何必煮馬鈴薯呢？

2 現在進行式可以用來說明「**目前這段期間在發生的事**」或「**某人目前的狀態**」，不必然是說話當下正在進行的動作。

Sam is looking for an apartment in Tokyo at this moment.
山姆現在正在找一間東京的公寓。
You're working very hard these days.
這些日子你很努力工作。

3 現在進行式可以用來說明「**正在改變或進展的事物**」。

It's getting cold at night. 晚上天氣變冷了。
Cell phones are rapidly adding new features. 手機正迅速發展出新的功能。

4 現在進行式有時用來表示「**已經安排好、未來將會發生的事**」。

I am visiting Bert and Ernie on Saturday.
我星期六將會去拜訪柏特和爾尼。
He's flying to Los Angeles on a business trip next Monday.
他下星期一要搭機前往洛杉磯出差。

5 現在進行式經常和頻率副詞 always 連用，表示「**總是、經常在做的事**」。

She's always vacationing in some exotic spots.
她總是到一些充滿異國風情的地方度假。
He's always making promises that cannot be fulfilled. 他老是在做一些無法實現的承諾。

6 有些動詞不能使用**現在進行式**（詳見 Unit 43 說明）。

✗ I am liking strawberry jam.
✓ I like strawberry jam.
　我喜歡草莓果醬。
✗ I am knowing Jane Robinson.
✓ I know Jane Robinson.
　我認識珍‧羅賓森。

Practice

1

請將括弧中的動詞以「現在進行式」填空，完成句子。

1. The global climate _____ (get) warmer every year.
2. I _____ (send) you the contract via email.
3. _____ you _____ (practice) your golf swing?
4. Tony _____ (apply for) a management job.
5. The government _____ (carry out) an environmental policy.
6. Pam _____ (sell) bubble milk tea at the night market.
7. Joe _____ (go) to a movie with his girlfriend on Saturday.
8. The crowd _____ (wait) for the President in the square.
9. Who _____ (bring) the pizza and soft drinks tonight?
10. Denise _____ (have) a birthday party on Sunday night.
11. I _____ (fly) to Osaka next Tuesday.
12. The kids _____ (enjoy) the sun on the beach.
13. Meg _____ (rock) the baby to sleep.
14. I _____ (write) a book about imaginary creatures.
15. My hair _____ (grow) white, but I _____ (not work) harder.

2

請依圖示，從框內選出適當的動詞，用「be + always + V-ing」的句型填空，完成句子。

mess

work

lose

jump

He _____ up and down on the bed.

He _____ at the computer.

He _____ up the bathroom.

He _____ his cell phone.

Unit 42

Comparison Between the Present Simple and the Present Continuous

「現在簡單式」與「現在進行式」的比較

比較

now

Are **you** drinking **your soy milk now?** ↳ 現在進行式

你正在喝豆漿嗎？

now

Do **you** drink **soy milk for breakfast every morning?** ↳ 現在簡單式

你每天早餐都喝豆漿嗎？

---

1 現在進行式用來表示「**說話當時正在進行的事**」。

It is snowing **outside now.**

現在外面正下著雪。

Are **you** eating **your dumplings?**

你正在吃水餃嗎？

現在簡單式用來表達「**習慣、重複發生的行為**」。

Do **you** cook **at home every night?**

你每晚都在家煮飯嗎？

He swears **too much.**

他滿口粗話。

---

2 現在進行式用來表示「**目前暫時發生的情況**」。

I'm wearing **a tie because I have a job interview.** 我現在打著領帶，是因為我要去面試應徵工作。

現在簡單式用來表達「**長期維持不變的狀況**」。

She always has **breakfast at the same café.**

她每天都在同一家咖啡店吃早餐。

---

3 現在進行式和現在簡單式，都可以用來表示「**未來將會發生的事**」。

Are **we** planning **to visit your mother this weekend?**

我們這個週末要去拜訪你媽媽嗎？

Do **we** plan **to visit your aunt next week?**

我們下星期要去拜訪你阿姨嗎？

Practice

1

請勾選正確的答案。

1. The sausages ☐ burn ☐ are burning.

2. Flowers ☐ are blooming ☐ bloom in the spring.

3. I ☐ eat ☐ am eating now because I missed breakfast.

4. I ☐ am hiding ☐ hides because the boss is looking for me.

5. ☐ Is Lonny reading ☐ Does Lonny read a newspaper now?

6. I ☐ often watch ☐ am often watching movies late at night.

7. ☐ Do you play ☐ Are you playing football every Saturday morning?

8. People ☐ are traveling ☐ travel overseas every year.

2

請將括弧內的動詞以「現在進行式」或「現在簡單式」填空，完成句子。

1. Julia _____ (weed) the garden now.
   She _____ (weed) the garden twice a week.

2. Do not go out because it _____ (rain) heavily outside.
   It _____ (rain) a lot this time of year.

3. Susan _____ (check) her emails right now.
   She _____ (receive) a lot of emails every day.

4. We _____ (take) the bus home now.
   We _____ (take) the bus home after work every day.

3

請將括弧內的動詞以「現在簡單式」或「現在進行式」填空，完成句子。並且從框內選出該用法的依據，填入句子後面的空格內。

> Ⓐ 事實或正確無誤的事　Ⓒ 說話當時正在進行的事　Ⓔ 已經安排好、未來將會發生的事
> Ⓑ 習慣或重複發生的行為　Ⓓ 目前這段時間在發生的事　Ⓕ 正在改變或進展的事物

1. The atmosphere of Mars _____consists_____ (consist) of 95% carbon dioxide. → __A__

2. I _____ (take) a yoga class this month. → _____

3. I _____ (not eat) meat. I'm a vegetarian. → _____

4. Africa's climate _____ (change) dramatically due to global warming. → _____

5. I can't answer the phone right now because I _____ (play) video games. → _____

6. I _____ (attend) Professor Whelan's speech tomorrow. → _____

7. The Moon _____ (orbit) the Earth. → _____

8. My English _____ (get) better and better. → _____

9. Jessie _____ (sit) in the yard with her dog and _____ (enjoy) the sunshine every morning. → _____

10. I _____ (teach) two elementary courses and one advanced course this semester. → _____

Unit 43

Verbs Not Used in the Continuous Forms
不能用於進行式的動詞

1 有些動詞不能用於**進行式**，只能用於**簡單式**。描述「思想」的動詞，通常不能用於**進行式**。

• doubt	• see	• imagine
• believe	• recognize	• forget
• understand	• suppose	• mean
• know	• remember	• realize

✗ I am knowing the answer to the question.

✓ I know the answer to the question.

我知道這個問題的答案。

✗ Are you knowing Janet's phone number?

✓ Do you know Janet's phone number?

你知道珍娜的電話號碼嗎？

2 see 和 hear 屬於「非刻意進行的動作」，也不用於**進行式**。

When I was at Gail's apartment, I saw her new painting.

我去蓋兒的公寓時，看到了她的新畫作。

When I lay in bed at night, I heard my parents talk.

深夜我躺在床上時，聽到父母親的談話。

listen、look 和 watch 則屬於「刻意進行的動作」，可以用於**進行式**。

I am listening to the song. Wait until it's finished. 我正在聽這首歌，先等我聽完。

Are you looking at that photo album? I'd like to look at it when you're finished.

你在看那本相簿嗎？等你看完，我也想要看。

3 描述「感受」的動詞，通常不能用於**進行式**。

• like
• dislike
• love
• hate
• prefer
• want
• wish

✗ Jean is loving this song.

✓ Jean loves this song.

琴很愛這首歌。

✗ Beth is not wanting a pet.

✓ Beth does not want a pet.

貝絲不想養寵物。

感官動詞和說明「思想」的動詞，如 see、hear 和 understand，常常搭配 can 或 could 使用。

Scott can see the whole office from his desk.
史考特從他的書桌，能看到整間辦公室。

Meredith could hear her grandmother snoring.
梅麗狄絲可以聽到祖母在打呼。

Louis can remember everybody's name.
路易斯能記住每個人的名字。

4 以下動詞，通常也不使用**進行式**。

• exist	• need	• consist of
• own	• include	• sound
• belong	• cost	• seem
• owe	• constrain	• deserve

✗ Are you owning a 3-in-1 printer, scanner, fax machine?

✓ Do you own a 3-in-1 printer, scanner, fax machine?

你有影印、掃描、傳真三合一的事務機嗎？

✗ Dan is not needing any more new clothes.

✓ Dan does not need any more new clothes.

丹不需要更多新衣服了。

Practice

1

請勾選正確的答案。

1. I ☐ am recognizing ☐ recognize your face.
2. He ☐ is not liking ☐ does not like durian ice cream.
3. I ☐ am having ☐ have my own bicycle.
4. Give me a minute. I ☐ think ☐ am thinking about it.
5. ☐ Are you believing ☐ Do you believe his guarantee?
6. Emma ☐ heard ☐ was hearing her neighbors arguing.
7. Be quiet. I ☐ am listening ☐ listen to an important news report.
8. Sarah ☐ deserves ☐ is deserving a holiday after such hard work.

2

哪些動詞通常用於簡單式而不用於進行式？請從框內選出適當的動詞，用「現在簡單式」填空，完成下列描述各個圖片的句子。

| cost | prefer | belong | exist | know | weigh | own | include | forget |

1
Life _____ (not) on Saturn.

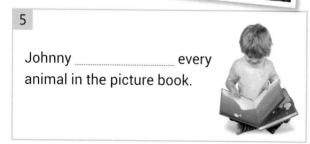

2
The jeans _____ $80.

3
Tammy always _____ her credit card password.

4
The spa set _____ essential oil, bath salt, and handmade lavender soap.

5
Johnny _____ every animal in the picture book.

6

The family _____ a black SUV.

7 Which _____ you _____, fruit or cake?

8
The peppers _____ 500 grams.

Unit **44**

Verbs Used in the Present Simple and the Present Continuous With Different Meanings
用於「現在簡單式」與「現在進行式」意義不同的動詞

---

see | see 指「明白」的時候，只能用於**簡單式**；指「會見」的時候，則可以用於**進行式**。

現在簡單式	現在進行式
Do you see my point of view? 你明白我的觀點嗎？	Are you seeing your doctor tomorrow? 你明天要去看醫生嗎？

look | look 指「看起來」時，只能用於**簡單式**；指「尋找」或「看」時，則可以用於**進行式**。

現在簡單式	現在進行式
It looks like a good job. 這似乎是個很好的工作。	Eric is looking for a job. 艾瑞克在找工作。

smell | smell 指「聞起來」或「聞到」時，只能用於**簡單式**；指「嗅聞」時，則可以用於**進行式**。

現在簡單式	現在進行式
Do you smell the bread in the oven? 你聞到烤箱裡的麵包香味了嗎？	The chef is smelling the beef stew on the plate. 廚師在聞盤內的燉牛肉。

taste | taste 指「嚐起來」時，只能用於**簡單式**；指「品嚐」時，則可以用於**進行式**。

現在簡單式	現在進行式
The soup tastes better with some rosemary. 這湯加了迷迭香之後，喝起來更美味。	The sommelier is tasting the 1944 wine. 這名品酒師正在品嚐 1944 年分的葡萄酒。

feel | feel 指「摸起來給人某種感覺」或「認為、覺得」時，只能用於**簡單式**；指「觸摸」或「感覺」時，則可以用於**進行式**。

現在簡單式	現在進行式
This silk shirt feels so soft. 這件絲質襯衫摸起來好柔軟。	I'm feeling woozy. (= I feel woozy.) 我覺得頭暈不舒服。

be | 動詞 be 通常用於**簡單式**；當動詞 be 指「（刻意）表現」時，則可用於**進行式**。

現在簡單式	現在進行式
He is cool. 他很酷。	He is being cool. 他表現得很酷。

have | have 指「擁有」時，只能用於**簡單式**；指「進行某動作」時，則可用於**進行式**。

現在簡單式	現在進行式
She has many antiques. 她有很多古董。	She is having a sandwich. 她正在吃三明治。

weigh | weigh 指「秤起來多重」時，只能用於**簡單式**；指「秤某物的重量」時，則可用於**進行式**。

現在簡單式	現在進行式
These oranges weigh 2 kilograms. 這些柳橙秤起來有兩公斤重。	The clerk is weighing the Chinese herbs. 店員正在秤這些中藥的重量。

Practice

1

請勾選正確的答案。

1. Your idea ☐ **sounds** ☐ **is sounding** very good.

2. He ☐ **cannot see** ☐ **is not seeing** the words in the book without his glasses.

3. This apartment ☐ **looks** ☐ **is looking** old.

4. Sandpaper ☐ **is feeling** ☐ **feels** rough.

5. He ☐ **is** ☐ **is being** late for his lunch meeting.

6. He ☐ **has** ☐ **is having** a shower.

7. Raymond ☐ **is looking after** ☐ **looks after** his sick dad in the hospital now.

8. I have a stuffed nose. I ☐ **can't smell** ☐ **am not smelling** anything.

2

請依據題意，將括弧內的動詞以「現在簡單式」或「現在進行式」填空，完成句子。

1

Johnny _____ (look) at a butterfly. The butterfly _____ (look) beautiful.

2

Mom and Ginny _____ (taste) the soup. The soup _____ (taste) delicious.

3

Kelly _____ (smell) the flowers. The flowers in her hands _____ (smell) good.

4

Sandy _____ (feel) the cotton towels. The cotton towels _____ (feel) soft.

5

Tina _____ (weigh) herself. David is eager to know how much she _____ (weigh).

6

Jessica _____ (have) some chocolate. She _____ (have) lots of chocolate in her refrigerator.

Part 6 Past Tenses 過去式

Unit 45

Past Simple Tense
過去簡單式

Form 構句

● 事件

過去 ——●——|——→ 未來
　　　　現在

肯定句的句型	I/you/he/she/it/we/they walked
否定句的句型	I/you/he/she/it/we/they did not walk
否定句的縮寫	I/you/he/she/it/we/they didn't walk
疑問句的句型	Did I/you/he/she/it/we/they walk?

1 規則動詞的過去式和過去分詞拼法一樣，構成也有規則可循：

1 大多數規則動詞，直接在字尾加上 ed。
- talk → talked 說話
- enjoy → enjoyed 享受

2 字尾是 e 的規則動詞，只要加 d。
- like → liked 喜歡
- phone → phoned 打電話

3 字尾是「子音 + y」的動詞，先刪除 y，再加 ied。
- study → studied 學習；研讀
- empty → emptied 清空

4 字尾是「單母音 + 單子音」的動詞，要重覆字尾，再加 ed。
- dim → dimmed 使模糊
- stop → stopped 停止

2 不規則動詞的過去式和過去分詞則要逐一牢記。詳見《Unit 46 不規則動詞表》。

- come → came → come 來
- drive → drove → driven 駕駛
- hit → hit → hit 打

Use 用法

3 過去簡單式用來形容「**過去的行為和情況**」，經常和一些表示「**過去意義**」的副詞或副詞片語連用。

- yesterday
- last month
- last night
- last year
- last week
- a year ago

He visited his aunt last weekend.
上週末他去拜訪阿姨。
They bought a house last year.
去年他們買了一棟房子。
I did not go to work last week.
我上星期沒上班。
The team did not lose the game last night.
這個隊伍昨晚並沒有輸掉比賽。
Did you drive here by yourself yesterday?
你昨天自己開車來的嗎？
Did Tina graduate from high school last month? 蒂娜上個月高中畢業了嗎？

4 過去簡單式常用來「**講故事**」。

A hundred years ago, our ancestors immigrated to this land and built up our farmstead. They started growing coffee soon after that and made their living by selling high quality coffee beans.

一百年前，我們的祖先來到這片土地，建立了我們這個莊園。不久後，他們開始種植咖啡，靠販售高品質咖啡豆維生。

Practice

1

請將括弧內的動詞以「過去簡單式」填空，完成右列段落。

Ludwig van Beethoven ❶_____ (be) born in Germany on December 17th, 1770. His father ❷_____ (give) him piano lessons at the age of five. His father ❸_____ (hope) his son was a child genius like Mozart. As a teenager, Beethoven ❹_____ (work) as a court musician. He also ❺_____ (play) in theaters and churches. Beethoven ❻_____ (compose) his first music in his late teens. By the age of 25, he ❼_____ (earn) a living from performing, composing, and teaching music. Beethoven ❽_____ (lose) his hearing in 1801. He ❾_____ (write) his most important symphonies after he became deaf. Beethoven ❿_____ (die) on March 26th, 1827.

2

請將括弧內的動詞以正確的時態填空，完成對話。

Bob: I ❶_____ (call) you yesterday, but you were not home.

Sue: I ❷_____ (go) to the fashion district.

Bob: ❸_____ you _____ (spend) a lot of money?

Sue: Well, I ❹_____ (see) some great shoes.

Bob: ❺_____ you _____ (get) a pair?

Sue: No, I ❻_____ not _____ (buy) any shoes.

Bob: ❼_____ you _____ (pick up) any nylons?

Sue: No, but I ❽_____ (buy) four pairs of socks.

Bob: ❾_____ you _____ (need) socks?

Sue: Yes, I ❿_____ (need) some socks.

Bob: How much ⓫_____ you _____ (pay)?

Sue: I ⓬_____ (get) four pairs for $100.

Bob: ⓭_____ you _____ (buy) them on sale?

Sue: No, I ⓮_____ (bargain) with the saleswoman.

Bob: You don't usually bargain with salespeople. You usually avoid arguing about prices.

Sue: But this time I did. I ⓯_____ (get) her to lower the price from $200.

Bob: Good job! Let's go see that saleswoman. I need some socks, too.

Unit 46

List of Irregular Verbs 不規則動詞表

🔖 三態同形
🔖 不同的意義下，有不同的過去
式與過去分詞。

arise	arose	arisen	升起
awake	awoke	awoken	喚醒
be	was/were	been	be 動詞
🔖 bear	bore	borne	承受；生孩子
	bore	born	誕生
beat	beat	beaten	打
become	became	become	變成
begin	began	begun	開始
behold	beheld	beheld	看見
bend	bent	bent	彎曲
🔖 bet	bet	bet	打賭
🔖 bid	bid	bid	出價
bind	bound	bound	綑綁
bite	bit	bitten	咬
bleed	bled	bled	流血
blow	blew	blown	吹
break	broke	broken	打破
breed	bred	bred	使繁殖
bring	brought	brought	帶來
🔖 broadcast	broadcast	broadcast	廣播
build	built	built	建造
burn	burned/burnt	burned/burnt	燃燒
🔖 burst	burst	burst	爆炸
🔖 bust	bust/busted	bust/busted	使失敗
buy	bought	bought	買
🔖 cast	cast	cast	投擲
catch	caught	caught	抓住
choose	chose	chosen	選擇
cling	clung	clung	黏著
come	came	come	來
🔖 cost	cost	cost	花費
creep	crept	crept	躡手躡腳地走
🔖 cut	cut	cut	切
deal	dealt	dealt	處理
dig	dug	dug	挖掘
dive	美 dived/dove	dived/dove	潛水
	英 dived	dived	
do	did	done	做
draw	drew	drawn	畫
dream	dreamed/dreamt	dreamed/dreamt	做夢
drink	drank	drunk	喝
drive	drove	driven	駕駛
dwell	dwelled/dwelt	dwelled/dwelt	居住
eat	ate	eaten	吃
fall	fell	fallen	落下
feed	fed	fed	餵養

feel	felt	felt	摸；感覺
fight	fought	fought	打架
find	found	found	找到
🔖 fit	美 fitted/fit	fitted/fit*	合身
	英 fitted	fitted	
flee	fled	fled	逃
fling	flung	flung	用力丟
🔖 fly	flew	flown	飛
	flied	flied	擊出高飛球
forbid	forbade	forbidden	禁止
🔖 forecast	forecast/ forecasted	forecast/ forecasted	預測
foresee	foresaw	foreseen	預見
forget	forgot	forgotten	忘記
forgive	forgave	forgiven	原諒
forsake	forsook	forsaken	拋棄
freeze	froze	frozen	結冰
get	美 got	gotten	得到
	英 got	got	
give	gave	given	給
go	went	gone	去
grind	ground	ground	磨碎
grow	grew	grown	成長
🔖 hang	hanged	hanged	絞死
	hung	hung	懸掛
have/has	had	had	擁有
hear	heard	heard	聽見
hide	hid	hidden	躲藏
🔖 hit	hit	hit	打
hold	held	held	握著
🔖 hurt	hurt	hurt	傷害
🔖 input	input	input	輸入
keep	kept	kept	持有
kneel	美 kneeled/knelt	kneeled/knelt	跪下
	英 knelt	knelt	
🔖 knit	knitted	knitted	編織
	knit	knit	接合
know	knew	known	知道
lay	laid	laid	放置
lead	led	led	引導
lean	美 leaned	leaned	傾身
	英 leaned/leant	leaned/leant	
leap	美 leaped	leaped	跳躍
	英 leapt	leapt	
learn	美 learned	learned	學習
	英 learned/learnt	learned/learnt	
leave	left	left	離開；遺留
lend	lent	lent	借給
🔖 let	let	let	讓

lie	lay	lain	躺
light	lighted/lit	lighted/lit	點燃;照亮
lose	lost	lost	遺失
make	made	made	製造
mean	meant	meant	意指
meet	met	met	遇到
mislead	misled	misled	誤導
mistake	mistook	mistaken	弄錯
mow	mowed	mowed/mown	割草
outdo	outdid	outdone	勝過
output	output	output	輸出
overcome	overcame	overcome	克服
overeat	overate	overeaten	吃太飽
overhear	overheard	overheard	無意中聽到
oversleep	overslept	overslept	睡過頭
overthrow	overthrew	overthrown	推翻
pay	paid	paid	支付
plead	美 pleaded/pled	pleaded/pled	懇請;辯護
	英 pleaded	pleaded	
proofread [`prufrid]	proofread [`prufrɛd]	proofread [`prufrɛd]	校對
prove	美 proved	proved/proven	證明
	英 proved	proved	
put	put	put	放
quit	美 quit	quit	放棄;辭職
	英 quit/quitted	quit/quitted	
read [rid]	read [rɛd]	read [rɛd]	閱讀
relay	relaid	relaid	轉達
repay	repaid	repaid	償還
reset	reset	reset	重置
rid	rid	rid	使免除
ride	rode	ridden	乘坐
ring	rang	rung	使成環形
rise	rose	risen	上升
run	ran	run	跑
saw	美 sawed	sawn/sawed	鋸開
	英 sawed	sawn	
say	said	said	說
see	saw	seen	看見
seek	sought	sought	尋找
sell	sold	sold	賣
send	sent	sent	寄;送
set	set	set	放;豎立
sew	sewed	sewed/sewn	縫補
shake	shook	shaken	搖
shed	shed	shed	流出
shine	shone	shone	發光
	shined	shined	擦亮
shoot	shot	shot	發射
show	showed	shown/showed	顯示;陳列
shrink	shrank/shrunk	shrunk	收縮
shut	shut	shut	關閉
sing	sang	sung	唱
sink	sank	sunk	下沉
sit	sat	sat	坐

sleep	slept	slept	睡覺
slide	slid	slid	滑動
smell	美 smelled	smelled	嗅聞;聞到
	英 smelt	smelt	
sow	sowed	sowed/sown	播種
speak	spoke	spoken	說話
speed	speeded/sped	speeded/sped	迅速前進
spell	spelled/spelt	spelled/spelt	拼字
spend	spent	spent	花費
spill	美 spilled	spilled	濺出;溢出
	英 spilt	spilt	
spin	spun	spun	旋轉
spit	美 spit	spit	吐;吐痰
	英 spat	spat	
split	split	spilt	劈開
spoil	美 spoiled	spoiled	搞砸;寵壞
	英 spoilt	spoilt	
spread	spread	spread	散布
spring	美 sprang/sprung	sprung	跳
	英 sprang	sprung	
stand	stood	stood	站立
steal	stole	stolen	偷
stick	stuck	stuck	黏貼;釘住
sting	stung	stung	刺;螫;叮
stink	stank/stunk	stank/stunk	發臭
stride	strode	stridden	邁大步走
strike	struck	struck/stricken	攻擊
string	strung	strung	(用線繩)紮
swear	swore	sworn	發誓;咒罵
sweat	sweat/sweated	sweat/sweated	流汗
sweep	swept	swept	清掃
swim	swam	swum	游泳
swing	swung	swung	搖擺
take	took	taken	拿
teach	taught	taught	教
tear	tore	torn	撕裂
tell	told	told	告訴
think	thought	thought	想
throw	threw	thrown	丟
thrust	thrust	thrust	刺
tread	trod	trodden/trod	踩
understand	understood	understood	理解
undertake	undertook	undertaken	著手做
undo	undid	undone	解開;取消
upset	upset	upset	使心煩
wake	woke/waked	woken/waked	醒來
wear	wore	worn	穿著
weave	wove	woven	編織
weep	wept	wept	哭泣
win	won	won	贏
wind	wound	wound	纏繞
withdraw	withdrew	withdrawn	收回
write	wrote	written	寫

* 在被動語態中,會用 fitted。

Unit **47**

Past Continuous Tense
過去進行式

Form 構句

```
過去 ──────▶ │ ──────▶ 未來
            現在
                        ● 事件
```

肯定句的句型 | I/he/she/it was thinking
you/we/they were thinking

否定句的句型 | I/he/she/it was not thinking
you/we/they were not thinking

否定句的縮寫 | I/he/she/it wasn't thinking
you/we/they weren't thinking

疑問句的句型 | Was I/he/she/it thinking?
Were you/we/they thinking?

1 過去進行式的構句方式是：
was/were + V-ing

I was celebrating my 26th birthday with my friends when you called.
你打電話來的時候，我正在和朋友慶祝我的 26 歲生日。

Were you driving on the highway at that time?
當時你正行駛在高速公路上嗎？

Use 用法

2 過去進行式用來形容「**過去某一時間內正在進行的行為或狀態**」。

At 9:00 last night I was doing my homework. 昨天晚上 9 點我正在做功課。

The wind was blowing this morning when I woke up.
今天早上我起床的時候，風還蠻大的。

3 過去進行式也常用來「**說故事**」，和過去簡單式搭配使用。

此時，須用**過去進行式**來說明「**故事背景**」，用**過去簡單式**來描述「**行為或動作**」。

I was dreaming about eating vanilla ice cream with chocolate chips when I heard a knock on my door. I opened the door, and my friend Jeff handed me a vanilla ice cream cone.

當我聽到有人在敲門時，我正在幻想可以吃到灑了巧克力碎片的香草冰淇淋。我把門打開，我的朋友傑夫就拿了一個香草冰淇淋甜筒給我。

4 過去進行式經常搭配 always 使用，說明「**過去時常發生的事**」。

My girlfriend was always telling me to shave my beard and get a haircut.
我女朋友老是叫我要刮鬍子和剪頭髮。

5 不能用於**進行式**的動詞，也沒有**過去進行式**。

✗ I was believing the story.
✓ I believed the story.
　 我那時相信這件事是真的。

Practice

請依圖示，用「過去進行式」回答右列各問題。

install the tiles
hang the drape
fix the pipe
put up wallpaper
inspect the bike
wash the car

Ⓐ What was she doing in the living room?

Ⓑ *She was hanging the drape.*

Ⓐ What were they doing?

Ⓑ

Ⓐ What was he doing in the kitchen?

Ⓑ

Ⓐ What was he doing in the bathroom?

Ⓑ

Ⓐ What was he doing in the garage?

Ⓑ

Ⓐ What were they doing in their new house?

Ⓑ

2 請將括弧內的動詞以正確的時態填空，完成對話。

1. Ⓐ Why didn't you open the door?
   Ⓑ I didn't hear the doorbell ring, because I _____ (take) a shower.

2. Ⓐ Why did Keith go downstairs?
   Ⓑ Keith went downstairs to pick up the parcel for me, because I _____ (change) the baby's diaper.

3. Ⓐ Did you see him go into that room?
   Ⓑ I didn't. I _____ (study) at my desk at that time.

4. Ⓐ How did he stain the shirt?
   Ⓑ He _____ (eat) some chicken nuggets and _____ (squeeze) the ketchup. He squeezed it so hard that it splattered on his shirt.

Part 6 Past Tenses 過去式

Unit 48

Comparison Between the Past Simple and the Past Continuous
「過去簡單式」與「過去進行式」的比較

1 過去簡單式通常描述的是「**過去已經結束的動作**」；過去進行式描述的是「**過去持續、尚未完成的動作**」。

I was eating **dessert.** 我當時正在吃甜點。
↳ 當時還在吃

I ate **dessert before dinner.**
↳ 已經吃完了
我在晚飯前吃了甜點。

I heard **you snoring last night.**
昨晚我有聽到你的打呼聲。

You were blasting **rock music.**
你那時在大聲播放搖滾樂。

2 過去簡單式描述的是「**過去長期的動作或情況**」；過去進行式描述的則是「**過去暫時的情況**」。

I worked **for IBM for two years.**
我曾在 IBM 任職兩年。

I was looking **for a job in a bank.**
當時我在找銀行的工作。

3 描述「**過去某段時間內的短暫動作或事件**」要用過去簡單式。若這段時間內發生了兩個短暫動作或事件，則兩者會依照發生順序，用過去簡單式分別描述。

We caught **the fish. Then we** ate **the fish.**
我們捕到魚，後來把魚吃了。

I drank **some orange juice, and I** felt **better.** 我喝了一些柳橙汁，覺得舒服多了。

4 如果是「**過去的習慣**」或「**過去反覆發生的事**」，要用過去簡單式。

I jogged **every day last year.**
去年的時候，我每天都慢跑。

I called **him four times, but he** didn't **answer.** 我打了四通電話給他，他都沒接。

5 while 經常搭配過去進行式使用，來描述一個「**持續較長時間的動作或背景**」。這時候，主要的子句會用過去簡單式。

I finished **watching my favorite TV program** while **my wife** was reading **a financial magazine.** 我太太在看財經雜誌的時候，我看完了我最愛的電視節目。

6 when 可搭配**過去進行式**使用，也可搭配**過去簡單式**使用。如果 when 後面描述的是「**短暫的動作**」，就用過去簡單式；如果描述的是「**持續較長時間的動作**」，就用過去進行式。

I was walking **down the street** when I found **some money.** 我走在街上時，發現了一些錢。

When **Yvonne** was driving **home, she** saw **a car accident.** 伊芳開車回家時，目睹了一場車禍。

My brother and I were singing when **somebody** knocked **at the door.**
我和哥哥在唱歌時，有人敲門。

We ran **into the convenience store** when it began **to rain.**
↳ 也有可能兩個動作都屬於短暫動作，都用簡單式。
開始下雨的時候，我們跑進了便利商店。

比較

- I was making **a beef pot pie when Teddy** walked in **with a lunch box. He** sat down **and** began **to eat his lunch.**
  ↳ 在一個較長動作（was making）之中，發生了三個短暫動作（walked in、sat down、began）。
  我正在做牛肉派時，泰迪拿著午餐便當走了進來，並且坐下來開始吃午餐。

- While I was eating **the beef pot pie, Teddy** went out **to buy some orange juice.**
  ↳ 在一個較長動作（was eating）之中，發生了一個短暫動作（went out）。
  我在吃牛肉派時，泰迪走出去買一些柳橙汁。

Practice

1

請將括弧內的動詞以「過去進行式」或「過去簡單式」填空，完成段落。

I ❶_____ (walk) down the street. I ❷_____ (mind) my own business. I had just left the café and ❸_____ (go) to my car. I ❹_____ (pass) a strange-looking guy. He ❺_____ (lean) against a street light. Suddenly, I ❻_____ (feel) nervous.

I ❼_____ (look) over my shoulder. The guy ❽_____ (stare) right at me.

He ❾_____ (raise) his hand and ❿_____ (say) something. I ⓫_____ (walk) faster. He ⓬_____ (run) after me. I ⓭_____ (sprint) toward my car. I ⓮_____ (stop) in front of my car. I ⓯_____ (look) for my keys. The guy ⓰_____ (slow) down and called after me, "You dropped your keys."

2

請從 A 欄和 B 欄選出適當的片語，用 when 連結，寫出完整的句子，並將括弧裡的動詞改為正確的時態。

A

I (play) football
I (fight) with my sister
I (buy) a wedding present
I (lose) my passport
I (sleep) soundly
I (crank) the volume

I (hear) you were getting married
I (blow) out the speakers
I (sprain) my ankle
the alarm clock (ring)
I (vacation) in Italy
Mom (come) home

B

1. *I was playing football when I sprained my ankle.*

2.

3.

4.

5.

6.

Unit 49

Continuous Forms With "Always" for Expressing Complaints
進行式搭配 Always 表示抱怨的用法

1 always 常和現在進行式或過去進行式搭配使用,表示「某事發生得過於頻繁,造成困擾」。

He is always tapping his fingers.
他老是在敲手指。

He was always hurrying from one place to another.
他總是來去匆匆。

簡單式	進行式
always 搭配簡單式的時候,只是表達「某事不斷發生」。	always 搭配進行式的時候,則帶有抱怨的意味。
現在式 Steven always drives at the speed limit. 史蒂芬開車總是開在速限邊緣。	Steven is always driving too fast. 史蒂芬老是愛開快車。
過去式 Tim always called when he was in town. 提姆每次進城都會打電話來。	Tim was always calling late at night. 提姆老是在深夜打電話來。

2 除了 always 以外,forever、continually 和 constantly 也常和現在進行式或過去進行式連用,表示「抱怨」。

You are forever gambling away your salary. 你永遠只會把薪水拿去輸光。
Herbert is constantly missing family holidays.
賀柏特不斷錯過和家人相聚的假期。
Francis is constantly dreaming about being rich. 法蘭西斯只想做著富貴夢。

My brothers were constantly talking about going to Antarctica on vacation.
我哥哥以前總說要去南極洲度假。

Sandy was continuously buying shoes.
珊蒂以前很愛買鞋子。

3 always 在**進行式**中,不與 **not** 連用。

✗ She is always not going to school.

✓ She is always skipping school.
她老是蹺課。

Practice

1 請將括弧內的動詞，以正確的「進行式」型態，搭配 always 填空，完成句子。

1. The faucet __was always dripping__ (drip). Fortunately, Dad repaired it.

2. My brother _____ (jump) on my teddy bear. He also kicked my purple dinosaur.

3. That computer _____ (crash) when I was doing my homework. That's why I bought a new computer.

4. Patty is grounded for a week, and she is not allowed to watch TV. However, she _____ (watch) TV when her mom is out.

5. His parents treated him better than they treated his sister. His little sister _____ (complain) about the unfair treatment.

6. Tommy _____ (play) online computer games with his friends. He plays every day after school and late into the evening every night.

7. You _____ (tell) me that your house is like a zoo, but your family is nice. You should speak more respectfully about your family.

2 請依圖示，從框內選出適當的動詞或動詞片語，搭配 always 填空，完成句子。

| pile up | drink | leave | store up | cry | scatter |

1

He _is always piling up_ his desk with books and papers.

2

My son _____ his toys all over the floor.

3

Mom _____ things where nobody can find them.

4

She _____ Coke for breakfast.

5

Little Susie _____ loudly when she is hungry.

6

I wrote a note for him because he _____ things behind.

Part 7 Perfect Tenses 完成式

Unit 50

Present Perfect Simple Tense (1)
現在完成式（I）

● 事件

過去 ——————▶ 未來
現在

Form 構句

肯定句的句型	I/you/we/they have eaten
	he/she/it has eaten
肯定句的縮寫	I/you/we/they 've eaten
	he/she/it 's eaten
否定句的句型	I/you/we/they have not eaten
	he/she/it has not eaten
否定句的縮寫	I/you/we/they haven't eaten
	he/she/it hasn't eaten
疑問句的句型	Have I/you/we/they eaten?
	Has he/she/it eaten?

Use 用法

1 現在完成式用來描述一個「從過去某個時刻開始，一直持續到現在的動作或狀態」。

How long have you driven?
↳ 從某個時刻一直開車到現在
你已經開了多久的車？

Danny has been a student for years.
↳ 從他生命的某段時間一直到現在
丹尼當學生已經好多年了。

Have you ever held a job?
↳ 從你生命的某段時間一直到現在
你有做過什麼工作嗎？

---

2 當某件事已經結束，但強調「**對現在產生影響**」，也可以使用現在完成式。

The pizza has arrived.
↳ 對現在產生的影響是：披薩已經在這裡，隨時可以吃。
披薩已經送到了。

Our meeting has been canceled.
↳ 對現在產生的影響是：會議取消，無法討論。
我們的會議取消了。

I have tried bungee jumping many times. I don't want to do it anymore.
↳ 從以前到現在發生過好幾次，對現在產生的影響是：已經不想再玩了。
我已經玩過高空彈跳好幾次，都玩到不想玩了。

past

使用現在完成式的時候，事情發生的確切時間並不重要。

Practice

1

請將括弧內的動詞，以「現在完成式」填空，完成對話。

I have been waiting for Dr. Smith since eight this morning.
I ❶_____ (read) every magazine in the waiting room.

Two hours ago, I asked a woman, "Have you been waiting long?"
She said, "I ❷_____ (not be) here very long." I sat and
waited some more. I chatted on my cell phone with everybody I
knew. Then I called the doctor's office to ask if Dr. Smith was in. The
receptionist asked, "❸_____ you _____
(see) Dr. Smith before?"

I replied, "No, I ❹_____ (never see) Dr. Smith before."
The receptionist asked me to hold on for a second. Now I
❺_____ (be) on hold on the phone for fifteen minutes!

2

請將括弧內的動詞，以「現在完成式」填空，完成對話。

Ⓐ ❶_____ you ever _____ (use) Happy Hair Shampoo?

Ⓑ No, I ❷_____ not _____ (try) it.

Ⓐ ❸_____ you _____ (see) the Happy Hair Shampoo
TV commercial?

Ⓑ Yes, I ❹_____ (see) it many times.

Ⓐ What do you think of it?

Ⓑ I don't believe it. She has too much dirt in her hair.

Ⓐ Yeah, that commercial always catches my attention.

Ⓑ I ❺_____ (hear) my friends talk about it.

Ⓐ I ❻_____ never _____ (see) such dirty hair before.

Ⓑ And after she uses Happy Hair Shampoo, her hair is beautiful.

Ⓐ Yes, and she seems really happy.

Unit 51

Present Perfect Simple Tense (2)
現在完成式（2）

Use 用法

1 　現在完成式常表示「**事情發生了多久**」，此時不能用其他現在式。

✗ He is thinking **about going to the beach** for a long time.

✓ He has been thinking **about going to the beach** for a long time.

他想著要去海灘想了好久。

✗ I expect **to see you again** since last year.

✓ I have expected **to see you again** since last year.

我從去年就期待再和你見面。

2 　現在完成式常用來表示「**事情發生的次數**」。

I have tried **fresh carrot juice** twice.

我嘗試喝過兩次鮮榨紅蘿蔔汁。

I have been **to Prague** many times.

我去過布拉格很多次。

3 　現在完成式也常用來「**發布消息**」。

The ball game has started.

球賽已經開始了。

The team has lost **the game**.

這隊輸了比賽。

4 　現在完成式不能和「**已經結束的過去時間**」連用，但是可以和與「現在」、「今天」等「尚未結束的時間」連用。

today 今天	yesterday 昨天
this afternoon 今天下午	last week 上星期
this evening 今天晚上	in 1999 在 1999 年時

✗ They've gone **to Peru** yesterday.

✓ They went **to Peru** yesterday.
↳ 事件和說話發生在不同一天，不能用現在完成式。

他們昨天去秘魯了。

I have taken **my medicine** today.
↳ 發生在同一天，可以用現在完成式。

我今天吃過藥了。

5 　been 是 be 動詞的過去分詞，have been 用來說明「**去過某處，現在已經回來了**」。

I have been **out twice today**.

我今天已經外出兩次了。

He has been **to Singapore only once**.
↳ 去過新加坡，但現在不在新加坡。

他只去過新加坡一次。

6 　gone 是 go 的過去分詞，have gone 用來說明「**去了某處，現在還在那裡**」。

She has gone **to Nova Scotia**.
↳ 人離開去了某處，還沒回來。

她去了新斯科細亞。

He has gone **to the movie theater** **without cleaning his room**.
↳ 工作尚未完成就離開，人不在房間裡了。

他沒打掃房間就去電影院了。

Practice

1

請將括弧內的動詞以「現在完成式」填空，完成段落。

I ❶＿＿＿＿＿＿＿＿＿＿ (plan) this party for a long time. We
❷＿＿＿＿＿＿＿＿＿ (invite) many guests. We now have almost
everything ready. The party ❸＿＿＿＿ not ＿＿＿＿＿ (start).
The food ❹＿＿＿＿＿＿＿ (arrive). The cleaning service
❺＿＿＿＿＿＿＿ (leave). The floor ❻＿＿＿＿＿＿＿ (dry). Let me
think. ❼＿＿＿＿ I ＿＿＿＿＿＿＿ (miss) anything? Yes, I ❽＿＿＿＿＿
not ＿＿＿＿＿＿ (throw) the garbage out. Good. Now we are ready.

2

請將右列錯誤的句子改寫為正確的句子。

1. Lawrence is working at the Flying Tomato Pizzeria for six months.
   → ＿＿＿＿＿＿＿＿＿＿＿＿＿＿＿＿＿＿＿＿＿
   ＿＿＿＿＿＿＿＿＿＿＿＿＿＿＿＿＿＿＿＿＿

2. Iris stars in a soap opera since last year.
   → ＿＿＿＿＿＿＿＿＿＿＿＿＿＿＿＿＿＿＿＿＿

3. Tom is owning this car since several months.
   → ＿＿＿＿＿＿＿＿＿＿＿＿＿＿＿＿＿＿＿＿＿

4. How long are you working on this proposal?
   → ＿＿＿＿＿＿＿＿＿＿＿＿＿＿＿＿＿＿＿＿＿

3

請依據題意，用 have/has been 或 have/has gone 填空，完成對話。

1. Ⓐ I looked for Grandpa in the house, but he's not home. Where is
   Grandpa?
   Ⓑ He ＿＿＿＿＿＿＿＿＿ to work in the garden.

2. Ⓐ Grandma looks so different. What happened to her?
   Ⓑ She ＿＿＿＿＿＿＿＿＿ to the hair salon.

3. Ⓐ The restaurant is closed. I wonder why it's closed.
   Ⓑ They ＿＿＿＿＿＿＿＿＿ on a trip to Guam.

4. Ⓐ I have always wanted to go to Brazil. Have you ever traveled to
   South America?
   Ⓑ Yes, I ＿＿＿＿＿＿＿＿＿ to Chile and Argentina.

Part 7 Perfect Tenses 完成式

Unit 52

Present Perfect Simple With Some Adverbs and Prepositions
常與「現在完成式」連用的一些副詞和介系詞

1 現在完成式常和一些表示「從某個不特定的時間一直到現在」的副詞連用，最常見的是 ever 和 never，通常放在 **have** 和主要動詞的中間。

What is the most interesting book you have ever read?
↳ 過去任何時間至今
你看過最有趣的書是哪一本？

I have never met such a big guy.
　↳ 過去任何時間至今都未發生
我從沒碰過塊頭這麼大的男生。

2 already 是「已經」的意思，常和現在完成式連用，描述「事情比預期早發生」。already 通常放在 **have** 和主要動詞的中間。

He has already left for work.
他已經出門上班了。

The cake has already cooled off.
蛋糕已經涼了。

3 just 常和現在完成式連用，表示「才剛發生的事」。just 要放在 **have** 和主要動詞的中間。

The movie has just finished.
電影剛演完。

The food has just arrived at the table.
食物才剛端上桌。

4 yet 常和現在完成式連用，並且只能用於否定句和疑問句。

■1 yet 在**疑問句**裡用來詢問「某件事發生了沒」，並且具有「期待某事發生」的意味；

■2 在否定句裡表示「某件事還沒發生」。yet 在兩種句型裡都要放在**句尾**。

Has Thomas married Mary yet?
湯瑪士和瑪麗結婚了沒？

Hasn't Anna called yet?
安娜還沒打電話來嗎？

I haven't found my keys yet.
我還沒找到鑰匙。

5 before 也可以和現在完成式連用，表示「在之前」。before 會放在**句尾**。

She hasn't been married before.
她過去從未結過婚。

I haven't eaten caviar before.
我以前沒有吃過魚子醬。

6 現在完成式常和 for 連用，說明「某件事持續進行了多久的時間」。for 的後面要接「時間單位／一段時間」。

Isabel has been pregnant for six months.
依莎貝兒已經懷孕六個月了。

I have been an editor for two years.
我做編輯已經兩年了。

7 現在完成式常和 since 連用，說明「某件事從何時開始」。since 的後面要接「一個時間點」。

They have lived in California since 2012.
他們從 2012 年開始，就在加州定居。

I have known Jim since he was four years old. 從吉姆四歲時我就認識他了。

Practice

1

請將括弧裡的動詞改寫為「現在完成式」，並將題目提示的副詞插入句中的正確位置。

1. We (eat) dinner. [already]
   → We have already eaten dinner.

2. We (not finish) our coffee. [yet]
   → _____

3. We (receive) her phone call. [just]
   → _____

4. The singer (get) her first single on the top ten chart. [just]
   → _____

5. Have you (throw away) your old books? [already]
   → _____

6. I (not discuss) the problem with my doctor. [yet]
   → _____

7. I (buy) anything online. [never]
   → _____

8. Have you (run) in a marathon? [ever]
   → _____

9. I (not be) to Russia. [before]
   → _____

10. This is the most splendid view I (see). [ever]
    → _____

2

請用 for 或 since 填空，完成句子。

1. Patti has studied at Marymount University _____ three years.

2. Tony has owned his current house _____ 2017.

3. Vivian has collected Warhol's soup cans _____ six months.

4. Duane has worked as a sales rep _____ he graduated from college.

5. Neal has been a city councilor _____ two terms.

6. I have been telling you to start studying harder for your final exams _____ last month, but you never listen.

Unit 53

Comparison Between the Present Perfect Simple and the Past Simple (1)

「現在完成式」與「過去簡單式」的比較（I）

比較

- I've been a member of the Wilderness Society for five years.
  ↳ 使用現在完成式：我現在還是會員。

  我擔任「荒野保護協會」的會員已經五年了。

- I was a member of the Wilderness Society for five years.
  ↳ 使用過去簡單式：我已經不是會員了。

  我過去有五年曾是「荒野保護協會」的會員。

	現在完成式		過去簡單式
說明「從過去發生到現在的事」，就時間上來說，是將「過去與現在連結」。	I've grown vegetables in my garden for six years. ↳ 現在我仍然在花園裡種蔬菜。 我在花園裡種蔬菜已經有六年了。	說明「過去開始並已於過去結束的事」，沒有持續到現在，與現在無關，「純粹描述一個過去事件」。	Eve collected butterflies for one summer. ↳ 她現在已經不再採集蝴蝶了。 有一年夏天伊芙曾採集蝴蝶。
	He has planted flowers in his yard for two years. ↳ 他現在還在院子裡種花。 他在院子裡種花兩年了。		Larry tried chocolate-covered ants only once. ↳ 從那次起他就沒再吃過了。 賴瑞只吃過一次巧克力螞蟻。
	How long have you been a gardener? ↳ 你現在還是園丁。 你做園丁做了多久？		How long were you a snake owner? ↳ 你現在沒有養蛇。 你以前養蛇養了多久？
強調「發生於過去的行為或事件，對現在仍產生影響」。	I have invested some money in a biotechnology company. ↳ 使用現在完成式，表示投資仍在進行，現在錢還在股票市場裡。 我投資了一些錢在一家生技公司。	描述「已經結束的事件，對現在沒有影響」。	I invested my money in a biotechnology company, but I sold the stock. ↳ 使用過去簡單式，表示投資已成為過去，錢已經不在股票市場裡，已換成現金。 我投資了一些錢在一家生技公司，不過我把股票賣了。
用來「發布消息」，或在對話時「提供初步資訊」。	My investment has doubled. 我的投資增值了兩倍。	提供更多關於此事件的「細節」。	I bought the stock at $25 per share. The stock jumped to $55 per share. I sold it at $50. I cleaned up on that stock deal. 我在每股 25 元的時候買下股票，後來升到 55 元，我在 50 元時把股票賣掉，這回股票出手我大賺了一筆。

Have you ever seen a real whale?
你有沒有看過真正的鯨魚？

No, I haven't seen a real whale, but I saw some white dolphins for the first time last year.
我沒看過真正的鯨魚，但是去年我第一次看到白海豚。

Practice

1

請將括弧內的動詞以正確的時態填空，完成句子。

1. The police _____ (search) the mountain for the suspect for three days. Now they claim that the suspect _____ (leave) the area.

2. I _____ (find) your watch under the bed.

3. The global climate _____ (change) dramatically in the last ten years.

4. A huge tornado _____ (hit) the village yesterday and _____ (cause) a great damage.

2

請用「現在完成式」搭配「過去簡單式」，來描述事件及其細節。

I ❶ _____ (adopt) a golden retriever from an animal shelter. He ❷ _____ (be abandoned) by the previous family and ❸ _____ (wander) the streets looking for food. One day, he ❹ _____ (be brought) into the shelter. He had stayed in the shelter for two weeks before we took him home. He ❺ _____ (be) so slim and dirty at that time. Now, he ❻ _____ (become) a happy, healthy, and smiley dog.

3

請依照範例，利用圖片的資訊，分別用三種句型造句。

1

went to bed

wake up now

→ Gilbert _went to bed at 1:00._

(go to bed / at)

→ Gilbert _has slept since 1:00._

(sleep / since)

→ Gilbert _has slept for four hours._

(sleep / for)

2

JULY

S	M	T	W	T	F	S
		1	2	③	4	5	6
7	8	⑨	10	11	12	13
14	15	16	17	18	19	20
21	22	23	24	25	26	27
28	29	30	31			

moved in here

still here today

→ We _____

(move in here / on)

→ We _____

(live here / since)

→ We _____

(live here / for)

115

Unit **54**

Comparison Between the Present Perfect Simple and the Past Simple (2)

「現在完成式」與「過去簡單式」的比較（2）

現在完成式 Present Perfect Simple

現在

未來

2010　過去簡單式 Past Simple　2030

現在完成式		過去簡單式	
句中出現了意味著「從過去某時一直延續到現在」之副詞或副詞片語時使用。 · recently · ever · never	**Sheena** has begun **coloring her hair** recently. ↳ 句中出現 recently，是一個不確切的時間副詞，常用現在完成式。 席娜最近開始染髮。 I've started **writing a book about economic recessions** recently. 我最近著手寫一本關於經濟衰退的書。 Have **you** ever bought **any books on the Internet?** 你在網路上買過書嗎？	句中出現了指明「過去確切時間」之副詞或副詞片語時使用。	**Shirley** began **highlighting her hair** last month. ↳ 句中出現 last month，是一個確切的過去時間，須用過去簡單式。 雪莉上個月開始挑染頭髮。 ✗ I have read **about a hot mutual fund** yesterday. ✓ I read **about a hot mutual fund** yesterday. 昨天我讀到一支熱門的共同基金的消息。 Did **you** buy **camping gear on the Internet** last week? 你上星期在網路上買了露營用具嗎？ I swallowed **a mosquito while bicycling** yesterday. 我昨天騎腳踏車時吞下了一隻蚊子。

I have never eaten a kiwi.

· yesterday
· last week
· two months ago
· in the 20th Century

現在完成式		過去簡單式	
句中出現與「今天」有關的副詞或副詞片語，但這個動作「尚未結束」。 · today · this morning · this afternoon · this evening · tonight	**Ginny** has driven **halfway to Detroit** this afternoon. ↳ 現在時間依然是今天下午，她還得繼續開車。 吉妮今天下午前往底特律的路程只開到了一半。	句中出現與「今天」有關的副詞或副詞片語，但這個動作「已經結束」。	**Ginny** drove **all the way to Detroit** this afternoon. ↳ 現在時間可能還是今天下午，或者已晚上，她已經開完整段路程。 吉妮今天下午一路開車到達底特律。
		詢問某件事「發生的時間」只能用過去簡單式。	**When** did **you** finish **painting the house** this week? 你這星期是何時完成房子的粉刷的？

Practice

1

請將括弧內的動詞以正確時態填空，完成對話。

Dialog 1

Ⓐ When ❶_____ you _____ (arrive) in Taiwan?

Ⓑ I ❷_____ (arrive) today.

Ⓐ ❸_____ you _____ (be) here before?

Ⓑ Yes, I ❹_____ (be) here twice before.

Dialog 2

Ⓐ When ❺_____ you _____ (buy) this bicycle?

Ⓑ Someone ❻_____ (give) me the bicycle last week.

Ⓐ ❼_____ you _____ (start) riding your bicycle?

Ⓑ Yes, I ❽_____ (start) riding my bicycle to work.

2

請勾選正確的答案。

Ⓐ How long have you played baseball?

Ⓑ I ❶ ☐ have played ☐ played baseball for two decades.

Ⓐ ❷ ☐ Have you ever been injured ☐ Did you injure on the field?

Ⓑ I ❸ ☐ had ☐ have had several injuries during the past fifteen years, but I'm OK now.

Ⓐ What was the longest period of time ❹ ☐ you have played ☐ you played with an injury?

Ⓑ The longest period of time I ❺ ☐ played ☐ have played with an injury was about four months.

Ⓐ When ❻ ☐ have you hurt ☐ did you hurt your arm this year?

Ⓑ I ❼ ☐ hurt ☐ have hurt my arm in April right before the season opener, but now I have full use of my arm.

Ⓐ ❽ ☐ Have you ever played ☐ Did you ever play other sports?

Ⓑ Yeah, I ❾ ☐ played ☐ have played soccer in college.

Ⓐ ❿ ☐ Have you liked ☐ Did you like to play soccer in college?

Ⓑ I ⓫ ☐ loved ☐ have loved to play soccer when I was in college.

Ⓐ ⓬ ☐ Have you ever been recruited ☐ Were you ever recruited by other teams?

Ⓑ My agent ⓭ ☐ received ☐ has received a few calls.

Ⓐ People ⓮ ☐ said ☐ have said you are a natural-born athlete. I'll see you on the baseball diamond next week. Keep on hitting those homers.

Unit **55**

Present Perfect Continuous Tense
現在完成進行式

●事件

過去 ————▶▶▶▶ 未來
現在

I have been writing a novel about secret agent dogs.

我一直在寫一本關於特務狗的小說。

Form 構句

肯定句的句型	I/you/we/they	have been listening
	he/she/it	has been listening
肯定句的縮寫	I/you/we/they	've been listening
	he/she/it	's been listening
否定句的句型	I/you/we/they	have not been listening
	he/she/it	has not been listening
否定句的縮寫	I/you/we/they	haven't been listening
	he/she/it	hasn't been listening
疑問句的句型	Have I/you/we/they	been listening?
	Has he/she/it	been listening?

Use 用法

1 現在完成進行式也是用來「**連接過去與現在**」的時態，描述「從過去一直持續到現在仍然在進行的動作」，或者「從過去一直持續到現在，才剛結束，並對現在產生影響的動作」。

He has been waiting an hour for the pizza. ↳ 到現在還一直在等

他等披薩送來已經等了一個小時。

It has been raining. 雨一直下個不停。
↳ 說明街上為何是濕的

She has been swimming in the pool at the gym. ↳ 說明某人身上為何濕答答的

她一直都在健身房的游泳池游泳。

Have you been exercising?
↳ 詢問他人為何覺得熱且流汗

你一直在運動嗎？

2 現在完成進行式可用來說明「**近期不斷重複的行為或狀態**」、「**度過時間的方式**」。

I has been jogging every weekend over the last month.
↳ 一段時間內重複的活動

上個月我每週末都在慢跑。

How long have you been using the tennis courts at the park?
↳ 詢問近期內的狀況

你在公園的網球場打球多久了？

Have you been lifting weights?
↳ 詢問近期內的狀況

你一直都有在練舉重嗎？

Practice

1 請以「現在完成進行式」改寫句子。

1. It is raining.
   → ___It has been raining.___

2. We are drinking.
   → ....

3. Those people are chatting.
   → ....

4. Camille is wearing high heels.
   → ....

5. People are boarding the plane.
   → ....

6. Have you practiced your Spanish?
   → ....

7. Did you redecorate your house?
   → ....

2 請從框內選出適當的動詞，以「現在完成進行式」填空，完成句子。

argue

rain

wash

reel

1. They're still mad. They ....
   .... for two hours.

2. It's damp in here. It ....
   .... for two days.

3. There are so many dishes.
   I .... for more than an
   hour.

4. The test is so hard. My head
   .... for hours.

Unit 56

Comparison Between the Present Perfect Continuous and the Present Perfect Simple (1)

「現在完成進行式」與「現在完成式」的比較（1）

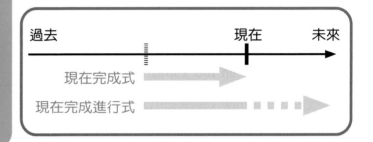

	現在完成式		現在完成進行式
動作已經結束。	**Tom** has eaten **his dinner.** 湯姆吃完晚餐了。 **Sheila** has celebrated **her promotion to Director.** ↳ 已經慶祝完，現在要回去工作 席拉慶祝了自己升上董事。	動作可能已經結束，也可能仍在進行中。	**Tom** has been eating **his dinner.** 湯姆一直在吃晚餐。 **Sheila** has been celebrating **her promotion to Director.** ↳ 還在慶祝或已經慶祝完 席拉一直在慶祝她升上董事。
強調事件在某一段時間已被完成。	**Mary** has practiced **her violin for eight hours today.** 瑪麗今天花了八小時練習小提琴。 **How many pieces of music** have **you** composed? 你已經寫完多少曲子了？	強調事件持續了多久。	**Mary** has been practicing **her violin all day.** 瑪麗一整天都在練習拉小提琴。 **How long** have **you** been composing **music?** 你寫曲子寫了多久？
說明「固定的情況」（持續較長時間）。	**Mick** has played **that song in concert for many years.** 米克在音樂會上演奏那首歌好多年了。 **Sara** has cooked **healthy food all her life.** 莎拉這輩子煮的都是健康食物。	說明「暫時的情況」（持續較短時間）。	**Mick** has been playing **that song in concert for a couple of weeks.** 米克已經好幾個星期都在音樂會上演奏那首歌。 **Sara** has been cooking **healthy food recently.** 最近莎拉煮的都是健康食物。
詢問事件發生的頻率要用**現在完成式**。	**I** have tried **fried mushrooms five times.** 我吃過五次炸蘑菇。		
		說明「度日、打發時間」的方式要用**現在完成進行式**。	**He** has been working **on the project since last night.** 他從昨天晚上就一直在處理這個案子。
不能用於進行式的動詞，即使動作還沒結束，也要用**現在完成式**。	**How long** has **Trisha** known **Tom?** 翠莎認識湯姆多久了？		

Practice

1

請用「現在完成式」或「現在完成進行式」填空，完成句子。並從框內找出作答的依據，填入題後的空格內。

Ⓐ 完成的動作或情況

Ⓑ 尚未完成的動作或情況

Ⓒ 強調事件或情況持續了多久

Ⓓ 強調事件或情況在某一段時間已被完成

Ⓔ 暫時的情況

Ⓕ 固定的情況

Ⓖ 不能用於進行式的動詞

1. How many cherries _have you eaten_ (you / eat) today? → __D__

2. Anton _____ (sit) in the café for the whole afternoon. → _____

3. Bernie _____ (clean) the staircase voluntarily for many years. → _____

4. Since when _____ (you / realize) that fact? → _____

5. You _____ (chat) with your friends all night. Turn off the computer and go to bed now. → _____

6. Ron _____ (send) strange messages since yesterday. Does his computer have a virus? → _____

7. I _____ (work) day and night recently. I need a vacation. → _____

8. I _____ (finish) five cases in the past four months. → _____

9. I _____ (imagine) life on Mars since I was little. → _____

10. Pete _____ (travel) around Europe for two months. Now he will go back to work. → _____

Unit 57

Comparison Between the Present Perfect Continuous and the Present Perfect Simple (2)

「現在完成進行式」與「現在完成式」的比較（2）

1 現在完成式和現在完成進行式都不能與**表示已經結束的時間副詞或片語**連用，這時要使用過去簡單式。

- yesterday
- at six
- until 10 p.m.

yesterday I ate six slices of cherry pie yesterday. 我昨天吃了六片櫻桃派。

today I have eaten six slices of cherry pie today.

我今天已經吃了六片櫻桃派。

I have been eating cherry pie today.

我今天一直在吃櫻桃派。

✗ Cynthia has called at 5 p.m.

✗ Cynthia has been calling at 5 p.m.

✓ Cynthia called at 5 p.m.

辛西亞傍晚 5 點的時候來過電話。

✗ Sunny hasn't gone to bed until 11:30.

✗ Sunny hasn't been going to bed until 11:30.

✓ Sunny didn't go to bed until 11:30.

桑尼 11 點半才睡。

2 有時候，使用現在完成式或現在完成進行式的差別並不大。

Paul has been dating Virginia for a year.
= Paul has dated Virginia for a year.

保羅和維吉妮亞已經交往一年了。

How long has Virginia been dreaming of marriage?

= How long has Virginia dreamed of marriage?

維吉妮亞想結婚想了多久？

3 現在完成式和現在完成進行式都常與 for 連用，說明該動作的「**持續時間**」。

Lonny has painted the room for three hours.

朗尼已經粉刷房間三個小時了。

Hans has been repairing the roof for four hours.

漢斯修屋頂已經修四個小時了。

4 現在完成式和現在完成進行式都常與 since 連用，說明該動作的「**起始時間**」。

Daniel has studied chemistry since high school. 丹尼爾從高中就開始唸化學。

Stan has been playing hockey since he was twelve.

史丹從 12 歲就開始打曲棍球。

Practice

1

請將右列錯誤的句子改寫為正確的句子。

1. I have been out for dinner last night.

   → _____

2. Roy has held a party yesterday afternoon.

   → _____

3. Sandra wrote her essay since this morning.

   → _____

4. Larry hasn't gone home until his boss left the office.

   → _____

2

請依圖示，從框內選出適當的用語，以「現在完成式」填空，再以「現在完成進行式」改寫句子。

make trips with a hot air balloon

stand by the window

take photos

decorate the Christmas tree

1

Jessica and her kids _____ for three hours.

= _____

_____

2

Emma _____ for *National Geographic*.

= _____

_____

3

Daniel _____ across America since 2019.

= _____

_____

4

Nicky _____ since 2 p.m.

= _____

_____

Unit **58**

Past Perfect Simple Tense
過去完成式

Form 構句

● 事件

過去 ●————●———■————→ 未來
　　　　　　　現在

肯定句的句型	I/you/we/they/he/she/it	had moved
肯定句的縮寫	I/you/we/they/he/she/it	'd moved
否定句的句型	I/you/we/they/he/she/it	had not moved
否定句的縮寫	I/you/we/they/he/she/it	hadn't moved
疑問句的句型	Had I/you/we/they/he/she/it	moved?

Use 用法

1 過去完成式用來描述「**兩個過去事件中，較早發生的那一個**」，強調事件的先後。

過去　　9:00　　10:00　　現在　　未來

We arrived at the airport at 10:00, but our plane had left at 9:00.

我們 10 點抵達機場，不過我們要搭的班機 9 點就起飛了。

2 過去完成式表達的是「**過去的過去**」，當說話的當下已經是過去式，要描述在那之前所發生的事，就要用過去完成式。

While I was canoeing **in the Amazon, I realized I** had forgotten **my mosquito repellant.**

在亞馬遜河划獨木舟時，我才發現自己忘了塗防蚊液了。

I said I hadn't seen **anyone in that cabin, but nobody** believed **me.**

↳ 說話（said）的當下已經是過去式，說的內容是更早發生的事，要使用過去完成式。而 believe 的動作和 said 同時發生，因此也用過去式。

我說我在那棟小屋裡沒看到任何人，卻沒人相信我。

過去簡單式		過去完成式	
只提及一個過去事件。	I smoked **my last cigarette two weeks ago.** 兩星期前我抽了最後一根菸。	提及兩個過去事件或動作，並且強調其先後順序。	**When a stranger handed me a carton of cigarettes, I** realized **I** had quit **smoking and wasn't even tempted.** ↳ 兩個過去動作：realized 和 had quit。 當一位陌生人遞了一包菸給我，我才發現自己真的戒菸成功了，我甚至連一點抽菸的欲望都沒有。
純粹描述兩個接續的過去事件，並不強調其先後順序。	I smoked **my last cigarette two weeks ago, so I** didn't smoke **any cigarette yesterday.** 兩星期前我抽了最後一根菸，所以昨天我一根菸也沒抽。		

現在完成式		過去完成式	
說明「**當下**」，描述的一個動作用**現在式**，在這之前一直持續到說話當下的動作要用**現在完成式**。	I haven't smoked **a cigarette for two weeks, so I am dying for a smoke.** 我兩星期沒抽菸了，現在我真想哈一根。	用於「**回想**」，描述的一個動作用**過去式**，在這之前發生的動作要用**過去完成式**。	I hadn't smoked **a cigarette for two weeks, so I was having a nicotine fit when I** smelled **tobacco smoke.** ↳ 提及兩件事：「戒菸兩星期」和「聞到菸味」。 我兩星期沒抽菸了，所以當我聞到菸味時，我的菸癮又來了。

Practice

1

請勾選正確的答案。

1. At about 9 p.m. we □ **called** □ **had called** to get directions to the party at Kenny Wheeler's house, but the party □ **ended** □ **had ended** at 8:30 p.m.

2. Before the guest of honor □ **had arrived** □ **arrived**, the bachelor party □ **started** □ **had already started**.

3. Terry, the guest of honor, □ **had proposed** □ **proposed** to his girlfriend over a year ago, and finally the bachelor party □ **was** □ **had been** here.

4. We □ **had wanted** □ **wanted** to go to a bar, but Terry □ **had told** □ **told** his fiancée he would go home early.

5. We □ **accepted** □ **had accepted** his request and □ **took** □ **had taken** him home around 1:00 in the morning.

2

請將括弧內的動詞以「過去完成式」或「過去簡單式」填空，完成句子。

1. When I _____ (talk) to the musician, I realized I _____ (see) his picture in the newspaper.

2. I _____ (not practice) my juggling enough, and so I often _____ (drop) balls and pins.

3. I _____ (look at) the milk container and noticed that the milk _____ (already pass) its expiration date.

4. We _____ (leave) the club after the last act _____ (be finished).

5. I knew that Philip _____ (give) many speeches about the global pandemic.

6. It _____ (not dawn) on me that I _____ (need) a full-time job until after my high school graduation.

7. After I _____ (open) the envelope from the graduate school, the rejection letter _____ (dash) my hope about staying in school.

8. I told Grandma that Frank _____ (take) all her jewelry, but she wouldn't believe.

9. They said that the ancient Egyptians _____ (build) the great pyramids by the help of aliens.

125

Unit **59**

Past Perfect Continuous Tense
過去完成進行式

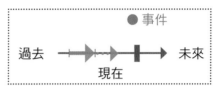

● 事件
過去 ━━━━▶▶▶ ┃ ━━▶ 未來
現在

Form 構句

肯定句的句型	I/you/we/they/he/she/it had been sleeping
肯定句的縮寫	I/you/we/they/he/she/it 'd been sleeping
否定句的句型	I/you/we/they/he/she/it had not been sleeping
否定句的縮寫	I/you/we/they/he/she/it hadn't been sleeping
疑問句的句型	Had I/you/we/they/he/she/it been sleeping?

Use 用法

1 過去完成進行式表示「**發生於過去某個動作之前的另一個動作，且該動作一直持續到某過去動作發生之時**」。

I'd been avoiding the stage at the karaoke bar for 30 minutes when Tom pushed me toward the front.

在湯姆把我推到台前時，我已經逃避了 30 分鐘不想站上卡拉 OK 的舞台。

Julia had been sitting in the restaurant for 10 minutes when she saw her ex-boyfriend arrive.

茱麗亞見到前男友到來之前，已經在餐廳裡坐了 10 分鐘。

He had been hiding in the woods when the police finally caught him.

他一直在藏匿在樹林裡，終究還是落網。

2 過去完成進行式可用來說明「**過去某個動作發生時，另一個動作正在持續進行**」。

I had been ironing my shirt when the doorbell rang.

我在燙襯衫的時候，門鈴響了。

I had been cooking lamb stew when Pete came home with two lunch boxes.

我一直在燉羊肉，結果彼特買了兩個午餐便當回來。

比較

比較現在完成進行式與過去完成進行式：

- I've been practicing my song all week, so I'm ready now.
  ↳ 從過去一直到說話的當下，持續進行的事。

  我已經練唱了一整個星期，所以現在我已經準備好了。

- I'd been practicing my song all week, so I was ready last night.
  ↳ 從更早的過去一直到回憶的過去時間，持續進行的事。

  我之前練唱了一整個星期，所以昨晚我是準備好的。

Practice

1

請將括弧內的動詞以
「過去完成進行式」
填空，完成句子。

1. Fran _____ (play) the lottery for two months when she won $1,000.

2. Irene _____ (not try) out for parts too long when she was cast in a small role.

3. How many years _____ (Charlie / crack) online games when he was busted by the police?

4. I _____ (eat) lunch at that restaurant for months before the waitress caught my eye.

5. Bobby _____ (smile) and nodding so long that everybody was shocked when they found out he was deaf.

6. Carla _____ (trade) so long in the stock market without collateral. She was surprised when she finally got a margin call.

7. Sally _____ (not live) on the 22nd floor too long before she decided she was afraid of heights.

8. I wanted to know how long _____ (Louise / plan) to become an airline pilot.

2

請從框內選出適當的動詞，以「過去完成進行式」填空，完成句子。

prepare
talk
wash
eat

Tom _____ fried chicken when Dad came home.

Jack _____ the car before it rained.

Susan _____ on the phone when the water boiled over.

Gary _____ the document for the meeting before he realized the next day was a holiday.

Part 8 Future Tenses 未來式

Unit 60

Simple Future "Will"
未來簡單式 Will

● 事件

過去 ————|——●——→ 未來
　　　　　現在

Form 構句

肯定句的句型	I/you/we/they/he/she/it	will sing
肯定句的縮寫	I/you/we/they/he/she/it	'll + sing
否定句的句型	I/you/we/they/he/she/it	will not sing
否定句的縮寫	I/you/we/they/he/she/it	won't + sing
疑問句的句型	Will I/you/we/they/he/she/it	sing?

1 平常對話時，通常會以縮寫「'll」取代正式的 will。

I'll drop by if I have a little extra time.
如果我有一點多的時間，我就會去找你。

2 當主詞是 I 或 we 時，助動詞也常用 shall，**否定句型**為 shall not，但這種用法現在已經很少見了。

We shall overcome poverty.
我們會戰勝貧窮的。
I shall veto the legislation.
我會反對那項法律。
We shall appeal the verdict.
我們將對判決提出上訴。

Use 用法

3 當我們純粹要說明一個「**未來事件**」時，就可以用未來簡單式 will。

I will be in my office next week.
下星期我會在辦公室。
Ernie will pitch the new program in June.
爾尼 6 月會開始進行新專案。
We won't leave the country until August.
我們一直要到 8 月才會出國。

4 will 可以用來「**預測未來事件**」，此時經常和某些動詞連用。

I will think about the new design.
我會考慮新的設計。
The boss will expect us to decide on the packaging by Friday.
老闆會期待我們在星期五前決定好包裝方式。
He will believe the projected costs if we show him the estimates.
如果我們告訴他評估的結果，他就會相信預估的成本了。
I will hope for the best, but you never know with our boss.
我會往最好的方面想，不過老闆會怎麼想就不得而知了。

- think
- expect
- believe
- hope

5 will 可用來表達「**說話當時所做的決定**」。

I think I will take a cup of lobster bisque, a Caesar salad, and the roast chicken, and I'll have a glass of chardonnay with that.
我要點一份龍蝦濃湯、一份凱薩沙拉、一份烤雞，還要搭配一杯夏多內紅酒。
I will go with this one.
Yeah, I will go for it.
No, I changed my mind.
That one will go better.
我要選這一個，沒錯，我選這個；等一下，我改變主意了，那個看起來好像更好。

6 will 經常用來詢問「**意願**」或「**可能性**」；won't 除了表示「**未來不會做某事**」，還常用來表示「**拒絕**」。

Will you be able to come over tomorrow?
你明天能夠過來一趟嗎？
She said, "I won't see you again."
她說：「我不想再看到你了。」

Practice

1

請將括弧內的動詞以「未來簡單式」填空，完成句子。

1. Someday people _____ (recognize) his genius.
2. My wife _____ (not be) at the gallery opening until after 4 p.m.
3. The gallery owner says she _____ (sell) one or two pieces.
4. A drunk customer wants to know if we _____ (serve) her some more wine.
5. Your kids _____ (have) to play in my backyard, not in the house.
6. The reporter from *The Times* _____ (arrive) soon.
7. The museum director _____ (not be) able to attend the meeting because she is leaving early for her trip.
8. What _____ you _____ (do) while we are getting ready for the opening?
9. I _____ (be) in the bathroom throwing up since I am so nervous about directing my first show.

2

請從框內選出適當的動詞，搭配 will 或 won't 填空，完成句子。

finish

buy

go

eat

hear

find

1. I bet I _____ a parking space around here.

2. He _____ the phone if it rings.

3. _____ you _____ the magazine so I can look at it?

4. Daddy _____ to the office because he is going out of town.

5. Mommy _____ me some new clothes later today.

6. We _____ three pieces of pizza and drink one soda.

129

Unit 61

"Be Going To" for the Future
Be Going To 表示未來意義的用法

Form 構句

肯定句的句型	am/are/is going to work
肯定句的縮寫	I'm going to work
	you/we/they 're going to work
	he/she/it 's going to work
否定句的句型	am/are/is not going to work
否定句的縮寫	I'm not going to work
	you/we/they aren't going to work
	he/she/it isn't going to work
疑問句的句型	Am I going to work?
	Are you/we/they going to work?
	Is he/she/it going to work?

Use 用法

1 be going to 常用來描述「未來事件」，具有「連結現在與未來」的意味。

I have decided that I am not going to buy a house. I am going to rent an apartment. I am going to call your aunt about her available apartment sometime next week.

我決定不要買房子，而是租間公寓。我下星期會找個時間打電話給你阿姨，問問她有沒有多的公寓。

2 be going to 常用來表示「由當前的一些跡象判斷，預測未來會發生的事」。

The snow and ice on the runway has delayed our departure. We are going to take off late. We may miss our connecting flight.

機場跑道上的冰雪導致我們無法準時起飛，飛機稍晚才會起飛，我們可能會錯過轉機。

3 be going to 常用來描述「事先做好的決定」或「意圖」。

I am going to buy a big work bench and put it in the garage.

我要去買個大型工作台放在車庫裡。

I am going to build a deck on the side of the house, but first I am going to buy a book about carpentry.

我要在房子旁邊蓋個平台，不過首先我要去買本木工的書。

I am all hot and sweaty from mowing the grass. I am going to take a shower before lunch. After lunch, I am going to watch TV for a while.

除完草後我熱得要命，全身都是汗。我要在吃午飯前先沖個澡，吃過午飯後再看一下電視。

4 如果在過去時間，要描述「過去的未來」，則使用「was/were + going to」的句型。使用這種句型通常表示「該事件並未發生」。

I was going to buy a $10,000,000 house, but I realized I couldn't afford it.

我本來打算買一間一千萬的房子，不過後來發現我根本買不起。

We were going to take a month off, but the plan was canceled.

我們本來要休假一個月，但後來取消計畫了。

He was going to sell his house, but he changed his mind.

他本來要把房子賣掉，不過後來他改變主意。

Practice

1

請從框內選出適當的動詞，以「be going to」的句型填空，完成句子。其中一字會出現兩次。

smash

work

lend

win

quit

rewrite

have

buy

get

1

This résumé doesn't look good. I _____ it.

2

I've got hired! I _____ _____ hard from now on.

3

You're a crazy driver. One of these days, you _____ _____ a bad accident.

4

Now that you have smashed up your car, how _____ you _____ to your office?

5

_____ the bank _____ you money for a new car?

6

I _____ a fast little car.

7

You are driving recklessly. You _____ your new car.

8

OK. I _____ driving my car on the sidewalk.

9

What type of bicycle _____ you _____?

10

You _____ the race and get to work on time.

Unit 62

Comparison Between the Simple Future "Will" and "Be Going To"
未來簡單式 Will 與 Be Going To 的比較

	will		be going to
「認為」未來可能會發生的事	I love my girlfriend. I will marry her someday. 我很愛我女朋友，將來有一天我會娶她。	由當前狀況可以「預見」的未來事件	Slow down! You're going to bump into that tree. 快減速！你要撞上那棵樹了。 
說話當下突然決定的事	I caught some squid in the bay this morning. I will cook them for lunch. 我今天早上在海灣抓到一些烏賊，我要把牠們煮了當午餐。		He bought a diamond ring. He is going to ask his girlfriend to marry him tonight. 他買了一顆鑽戒，打算今晚向女友求婚。
		事先就做好的決定	This afternoon I went to the fish market to get some squid for our dinner party. I am going to cook your favorite squid dish, calamari spaghetti. 我到魚市場去買晚宴派對要用的烏賊，我打算做你最喜歡的一道烏賊料理：花枝義大利麵。

比較 •••••••••••••

- I'll grill a chicken leg.
  ↳ 臨時起意
  我來烤隻雞腿吧。
- I'm going to grill a chicken leg.
  ↳ 原本就打算好
  我要烤雞腿。

Practice

1

請勾選正確的答案，有些句子可能兩個答案皆適用。

1. I think I ☐ will leave ☐ am going to leave now instead of later as I planned yesterday.

2. I ☐ am going to take ☐ will take the GEPT test tomorrow.

3. I ☐ will start ☐ am going to start my annual vacation next week.

4. ☐ I'll have ☐ I'll going to have a ham on rye bread with a sour dill pickle.

5. I ☐ will do ☐ am going to do it anytime you ask me to do it.

6. I forgot about the party. I ☐ will come ☐ am going to come immediately.

7. Jimmy ☐ will begin ☐ is going to begin his new job on Monday.

8. Kelly has just decided to drive, and I ☐ will grab ☐ am going to grab a ride with her.

2

請參考題目提示的情境，將括弧裡的動詞改寫為「未來簡單式 will」或「be going to」，完成句子。

1. Edmond _____ (apply) for a new job. (Simple future)
   → *Edmond will apply for a new job.*

2. He _____ (apply) for a job at a cookie factory. (Previous decision)
   → ....

3. He said, "I _____ (be) the best cookie tester in the world!" (Simple future)
   → ....

4. He said, "I _____ (pass) the exam with flying colors." (Intention; previous decision)
   → ....

5. He said, "First, I _____ (practice) testing some cookies." (Simple future)
   → ....

6. Lou asked, "_____ you _____ (bake) cookies as well?" (Previous decision)
   → ....

7. Lou claimed, "You _____ (burn) those cookies." (Probable future)
   → ....

8. Edmond retorted, "I _____ (bake) some cookies right away!" (Sudden decision)
   → ....

Part 8 Future Tenses 未來式

Unit 63

Present Continuous for the Future and the Comparison With "Be Going To"
「現在進行式」表示未來意義的用法，以及與 Be Going To 的比較

---

1 現在進行式也常用來表示**未來事件**，此時指的是「**計畫好的未來事件**」。

Where are you meeting the buyers from Japan?
你和日本的採購員約在哪裡見面？
I'm meeting them in the Yokosuka sales office. 我會和他們在橫須賀的業務辦公室見面。
Joanna is moving to the international sales office.

喬安娜要轉到國際業務辦公室。

---

2 現在進行式表示「**未來事件**」時，經常會在句中指出「**確切的時間**」。

- Friday afternoon
- Saturday
- this morning
- next month

What are you doing for your grandmother's birthday?
你祖母生日的那天你會有什麼表示？
We are taking her to dinner and the opera next Saturday night.
下星期六晚上，我們要帶她去吃晚餐、看歌劇。
Ruth is starting her new job on May 1st.
露絲 5 月 1 日起開始新工作。

---

be going to		現在進行式	
強調「**意圖**」	I am going to work extremely hard and buy my first house before the age of thirty. 我要非常努力，在三十歲之前買到我人生中的第一間房子。	強調「事先做好的安排」	I am signing the contract with Union Studio next Monday. Is there anything else I should know? 我將於下星期一和聯合工作室簽約，有什麼其他我該知道的事項嗎？

不過，使用 be going to 或現在進行式來描述未來事件時，兩者的差別並不大，上面所述其實只是極細微的差別，實際使用上，尤其是美式英語，兩者的意義相當。

- I am leaving for my trip tomorrow at 6 a.m.
- = I am going to leave for my trip tomorrow at 6 a.m.

我明天早上 6 點出發旅行。

---

be going to 和現在進行式都不能用來說明「**預測的未來事件**」，此時只能用未來簡單式 will。

✗ Cynthia is crying for joy when she sees this present.
✗ Cynthia is going to cry for joy when she sees this present.
✓ Cynthia will cry for joy when she sees this present.
辛西亞看到這份禮物的時候，一定會喜極而泣。

Practice

1 請從框內選出適當的動詞，以「現在進行式」填空，完成句子。

plan

cut

perform

close

transfer

inspect

1. Bella Conchita, the famous soprano, _____ at the Lyric Opera next weekend.

2. The mayor _____ the ribbon at the groundbreaking ceremony on Monday, August 15th.

3. Ellen _____ to the European sales office next month.

4. The textiles division _____ its Vietnamese factory in the next couple of months.

5. Director Van Stolten _____ the city's fire department sub-stations for compliance with the new EMT regulations all next week.

6. The IMF _____ a major review of all loan portfolios for undeveloped nations in the coming six months.

2 請將括弧內的動詞以「現在進行式」或「be going to」的句型填空，完成句子。有些句子可能兩種句型皆適用。

1. Ron *is going to leave / is leaving* (leave) on his trip to Geneva tomorrow.

2. The stock market _____ (tank) tomorrow.

3. The plumber _____ (fix) the pipes next week.

4. The gas tank _____ (run out) on Monday.

5. Bobby _____ (pay) the electricity bill on Tuesday afternoon.

6. Mary _____ (graduate) this June.

7. After the earthquake, Japan _____ (have) many economic problems.

8. The owner's son _____ (bankrupt) the company.

Part 8 Future Tenses 未來式

Unit 64

Present Simple for the Future
「現在簡單式」表示未來意義的用法

1 現在簡單式有時也會用來表示「固定、安排好的未來事件」，經常用於「時刻表」等。

What time does the family swimming time start on Sunday?

星期日家庭游泳池開放的時間是幾點？

On Sunday afternoons, the family swimming time begins at 2 p.m. and finishes at 5 p.m.

星期日下午，開放給家庭成員游泳的時間是從下午 2 點到 5 點。

The swimming pool also opens from 6 p.m. to 8 p.m. on Sunday evenings.

游泳池星期日晚上也從 6 點開放至 8 點。

OPEN
Sunday
2 p.m. – 5 p.m.
family members only
6 p.m. – 8 p.m.
all members

2 現在簡單式常用來「請求指示」，此時也具有「未來」含意。

How do I get to the National Palace Museum?

故宮博物院要怎麼去？

Where do I buy the tickets?

票要在哪裡買？

3 在「時間或條件子句」裡，當主要子句使用了 will 的未來式時，時間或條件子句要以現在簡單式來代替未來式。

- when 當……
- while 當……時
- as soon as 一……就
- after 在……之後
- before 在……之前
- until 直到
- if 如果
- unless 除非
- as long as 只要
- so long as 只要
- provided that 假若
- providing that 假若

I will get you a hot Americano when I go to buy lunch.

我去買午餐時，會幫你買一杯熱美式。

I will also choose a piece of cake for myself while I am in the café.

我在咖啡廳時，也會幫我自己選一片蛋糕。

I will rent the movie you want as soon as it arrives.

等你想看的那部電影一上架，我就去租。

We won't watch the video before we eat lunch.

我們吃完午餐才會開始看影片。

比較

若「時間和條件子句」後接的是現在完成式，則等到該子句中的行為完成後，主要子句所描述的情況才會發生。

- I will vacuum the carpet after you have picked up your clothes.

等你把地上的衣服都撿起來後，我要吸地毯。

Practice

1

請將括弧內的動詞以「現在簡單式」填空。

1. Jackson _____ (make) breakfast at home every morning at 6:15 a.m.

2. Jackson's wife _____ (wash) the dishes every morning after Jackson _____ (leave) home to catch the 7:20 train.

3. Every night Jackson's wife _____ (pick up) Jackson at the train station at 6:30.

4. When _____ (do) the aquarium _____ (open) on Sunday?

5. The aquarium _____ (open) after the fish have breakfast.

6. The cafeteria _____ (serve) fried chicken every Friday.

7. The city libraries _____ (be closed) on Mondays.

8. The band at the pub _____ (start) at 9:00 in the evening.

2

請將括弧內的動詞以「簡單未來式 will」或「現在簡單式」填空，完成句子。

1. I _____ (go) to the movies when my mom _____ (go) out.

2. I _____ (sneak out) while my family _____ (be) asleep.

3. My brother _____ (enlist) in the military as soon as he _____ (graduate) from high school.

4. I _____ (tour) the South Pole before I _____ (visit) the North Pole.

5. I _____ (stay up) late every night before I _____ (turn in) my assignment.

6. I _____ (stay) right here in this tree until you _____ (bring) a ladder.

7. The crocodile _____ (appear) in the circus act if it _____ (perform) well.

8. It _____ (be) difficult to travel to Mars unless the space shuttle's computer _____ (accept) my VISA credit card.

9. Tammy _____ (sing) as long as the music _____ (play).

10. I _____ (eat) my peas provided that you _____ (put) honey on them.

Part 8 Future Tenses 未來式

Unit 65

Future Continuous Tense
未來進行式

Form 構句

```
過去 ——————[——▶——]——▶ 未來
              現在        ● 事件
```

肯定句的句型	I/you/we/they/he/she/it	will be giving
肯定句的縮寫	I/you/we/they/he/she/it	'll be giving
否定句的句型	I/you/we/they/he/she/it	will not be giving
否定句的縮寫	I/you/we/they/he/she/it	won't be giving
疑問句的句型	Will I/you/we/they/he/she/it	be giving?

Use 用法

1 未來進行式用來描述「**未來某特定時刻正在進行的事件**」。

We will be watching TV when Mom arrives home.

當媽媽到家時,我們將會在看電視。

I will be driving at 7:30 tomorrow. It usually takes me an hour to drive to work. I often leave my house at 7 a.m. and get to my office at 8 a.m.

Tomorrow at 10 a.m., I will be drinking coffee. I won't be working at that time. I will be sitting in the coffee shop next door to my office. Will you join me for a cup of coffee tomorrow morning?

明天早上 7 點半我會在開車,開車上班通常要花一小時,所以我常常早上 7 點出門,8 點抵達辦公室。
明天早上 10 點我會喝咖啡,這時候我沒有在工作,我會坐在辦公室旁邊的咖啡店。明天早上你要和我一起喝杯咖啡嗎?

2 未來進行式可指「**確定的未來計畫**」,此時並沒有「**進行**」的意味。

Dad will be going to the library at 7:00 tonight. Do you want him to return the library books?

爸爸今天晚上 7 點要去圖書館,你要請他幫你還書嗎?

Mom will be taking a yoga class every Wednesday night from 7:00 to 9:00.

媽媽以後每個星期三晚上 7 點到 9 點要上瑜伽課。

3 未來進行式可以表示「**依照正常的發展,應該會發生的事**」,此時該事件並非人為安排或意圖,而是「**自然而然會發生的**」。

Dad won't be coming back home soon. He is still working in his office.

↳ 因為爸爸現在仍然在辦公室,照理無法馬上回家。

爸爸不會馬上回家,他現在人還在他的辦公室裡工作。

4 **請別人幫忙做事時**,可以先用「Will you be + V-ing」詢問對方的計畫、行程,再提出要求。
使用這種句型表示你並不希望因為自己的要求,而改變對方原本的計畫。

Will you be walking home past the mini-mart? Could you please pick up some soy milk on your way home?

你走路回家時會經過便利商店嗎?那你回家時可以順便幫我買點豆漿嗎?

Will you be attending the opening of the Monet show at the art museum? I was wondering if my son could have your stamped admission ticket if you are not planning to save it.

你會去參加美術館舉辦的莫內展覽開幕式嗎?如果你不想保留入場券的話,可以送給我兒子嗎?

Practice

1

右表是 **Dr. Edwards** 明天的行程，請用「未來進行式」寫出他在各時間正在進行的事。

8:00-10:00	Meet the committee members
10:00-12:00	Watch the demonstration of sterilization equipment
12:00-14:00	Eat lunch
14:00-16:00	Listen to a panel discussion about childhood disease
16:00-18:00	Present a paper about disease treatment plans
18:00-24:00	Tour the city

1. → _Dr. Edwards will be meeting the committee members at 9:00._

2. → ....

3. → ....

4. → ....

5. → ....

6. → ....

2

請將括弧內的動詞以「未來進行式」填空，完成句子，再從框內選出適當的問句接在句子後面。

Are you planning to watch it again?

Can I come to listen to you play?

Can I walk with you on the Nature Trail?

Can you buy us a pizza?

Could I get a ride from you?

Would you like to use my computer this afternoon?

1. My mom _____won't be cooking_____ (not cook) tonight.
   Can you buy us a pizza?

2. Dad .... (not drive) tomorrow.
   ....

3. I .... (leave) the office around noon.
   ....

4. I .... (return) the video later tonight.
   ....

5. When .... you .... (walk) the Nature Trail?
   ....

6. .... you .... (play) the cello at the music school?
   ....

139

Unit 66

Future Perfect Tense and Future Perfect Continuous Tense
「未來完成式」與「未來完成進行式」

未來完成式的形式

肯定句的句型	will have watched
否定句的句型	will not have watched
否定句的縮寫	won't have watched
疑問句的句型	Will . . . have watched?

未來完成進行式的形式

肯定句的句型	will have been drinking
否定句的句型	will not have been drinking
否定句的縮寫	won't have been drinking
疑問句的句型	Will . . . have been drinking?

未來完成式的用法

1 未來完成式表示「現在尚未完成，但在未來某特定時刻將會完成的動作」。這裡的 have 代表事情的完成，不可省略。

He will have finished his novel by the end of July. 他會在 7 月底前寫完小說。
He will have written the editorial by 2:00 this afternoon.
今天下午 2 點以前他會把社論寫好。

2 未來完成式可以表示「期待在未來某特定時刻完成的動作」，此時句中通常會有一個表示「直到未來某時刻」的時間副詞或片語。

I will have reinstalled my operating system before bedtime tonight.
↳ 此句表示期待能完成安裝
我會在今晚睡覺前把作業系統重新灌好。

- before next Monday
- by tomorrow
- by next Christmas
- by noon

By tomorrow, I will have debugged my operating system.
↳ 表示期待到時能解決作業系統問題
到明天時，我會把作業系統的問題都解決。

未來完成進行式的用法

3 未來完成進行式表示「在未來某特定時刻之前持續進行的動作」。

I will have been riding my bicycle for four hours when I arrive at the top of the mountain.
我抵達山頂時，將已經騎了四個小時的自行車。

4 未來完成式和未來完成進行式所描述的動作，都可能開始於「過去」。

Sue will have worked for the FBI for 35 years by the time she retires.
= Sue will have been working for the FBI for 35 years by the time she retires.
等到蘇退休時，她就已經在聯邦調查局工作 35 年了。

Practice

1　請將括弧內的動詞以「未來完成式」填空，完成句子。

1. I ＿＿＿＿＿＿＿＿＿＿＿＿ (move) into my new apartment by next week.

2. By next month, I ＿＿＿＿＿＿＿＿＿＿＿ (settle) in my new house.

3. I ＿＿＿＿＿＿＿＿＿＿ (climb) to the top of the mountain via the north trail by lunch.

4. I ＿＿＿＿＿＿＿＿＿＿ (start) down the mountain via the east trail by 2 p.m.

5. Jerry ＿＿＿＿＿＿＿＿＿ (finish) his research project by early July.

6. Jerry ＿＿＿＿＿＿＿＿＿ (begin) his new job by early August.

2　請將各題提供的用語，以 How long 搭配「未來完成進行式」的句型，寫出問句；再依圖示回答問題。

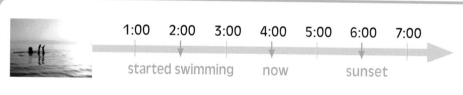

1. How long / he / swim in the ocean / by sunset?

Q　*How long will he have been swimming in the ocean by sunset?*

A　*He will have been swimming in the ocean for four hours by sunset.*

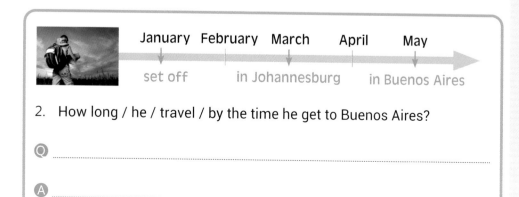

2. How long / he / travel / by the time he get to Buenos Aires?

Q　＿＿＿＿＿＿＿＿＿＿＿＿＿＿＿＿＿＿＿＿＿＿

A　＿＿＿＿＿＿＿＿＿＿＿＿＿＿＿＿＿＿＿＿＿＿

Unit 67

"Have" and "Have Got"
Have 與 Have Got 的用法

Form 構句

在英式英語裡，經常將 have 當作助動詞一般地變化，此時否定句會用 have not 或 has not，疑問句會用「Have/Has . . .?」。

have

肯定句的句型	have/has money
否定句的句型	do not / does not have money
否定句的縮寫	don't/doesn't have money
疑問句的句型	Do/Does . . . have money?

have got

肯定句的句型	have got / has got money
肯定句的縮寫	've got / 's got money
否定句的句型	have not got / has not got money
否定句的縮寫	haven't got / hasn't got money
疑問句的句型	Have/Has . . . got money?

1 have 和 have got 都可以指「**擁有**」，此時兩者的意義完全相同。

I have got a new cell phone. = I have a new cell phone. 我有一支新手機。
He hasn't got a scooter. = He doesn't have a scooter. 他沒有摩托車。
Have you got a date? = Do you have a date?
你有約會嗎？

對於何時該使用 have 和 have got 有很多不同的說法，其中一種是認為美式英語多用 **have**，英式英語則多用 **have got**。另一種說法是認為 **have got** 是用在非正式的對話裡，**have** 則多用於正式場合或寫作中。

2 have 常用來說明「**重複發生的事件**」；have got 則多用於說明「**單一事件**」。

That clothing store often has sales.
那家服飾店常打折。
That clothing store has got a sale right now. 那間服飾店現在有折扣。

3 have 和 have got 當作「**擁有**」解釋時，沒有**進行式**，也不能用於**被動語態**。

✗ Shelly is having got a new suit.
 ↳ 不能用進行式
✗ The new suit is had by Shelly.
 ↳ 不能用被動語態
✓ Shelly has a new suit.
✓ Shelly has got a new suit.
 ↳ 要使用簡單式及主動語態
雪莉有一件新衣服。

4 have got 只能用於**現在式**，沒有過去式。如果要表示「**過去擁有**」，要使用 have 的過去式 had；否定句和疑問句也要用過去式助動詞 did 來構成。

Sally had a cute collie for about 13 years, but he died of old age last week.
莎莉有一隻養了 13 年的牧羊犬，不過狗狗上星期過世了。

"Did you have a big house while working in Detroit two years ago?"
「你兩年前在底特律工作時，就有了大房子了嗎？」

"No, I had a small apartment."
「沒有，我那時只有一間小公寓。」

5 have got 也不能用於**未來式**，如果要表示「**未來擁有**」，要使用 will have。

✗ I will have got a new sports car.
✓ I will have a new sports car.
 我將會擁有一輛新的跑車。

6 have got 的問句，簡答要使用 have 來回答，不能加 got。

A: Have **you got a toothpick**? 請問你有牙籤嗎？

B: **Yes,** I have. 是的，我有。

B: **No,** I haven't. 不，我沒有。

Practice

1

請勾選正確的答案。

1. ☐ **Have you got** ☐ **Have you** your bowling ball?

2. I ☐ **have got** ☐ **have not** three children.

3. She ☐ **has not** ☐ **does not have** any time to take a break.

4. It ☐ **does not have got** ☐ **does not have** a battery.

5. ☐ **Does she have** ☐ **Does she have got** any idea about this blog?

2

請以 have、have got 或「助動詞」填空，完成句子。如果 have、have got 兩個用語都可以，請兩個都填。

I _____ a happy family.

Everyone will _____ a pay raise next month.

Have you got a pencil sharpener?
Yes, I _____.

Do you have any hand cream?
No, I _____.

143

"Have" for Action
Have 當作行為動詞的用法

---

1 have 經常用來描述「**動作**」，此時不可用 **have got** 代替。

表示「喝飲料」

have a soft drink 喝飲料
have a cup of tea 喝杯茶
have a cup of coffee 喝杯咖啡
have a Coke 喝可樂

表示「吃東西」

have a bite 吃一口
have breakfast 吃早餐
have lunch 吃午餐
have dinner 吃晚餐

表示「休假、遊樂」

have a day off 放一天假
have a holiday 放假
have a party 舉辦派對
have a good time 玩得開心

表示「說話」

have a conversation 對話
have a talk 交談
have a chat 聊天
have a meeting 開會

表示「疾病」

have a headache 頭痛
have a sore throat 喉嚨痛
have diarrhea 拉肚子
have a runny nose 流鼻水

表示「爭論」

have a disagreement
意見不合
have a fight 吵架
have a quarrel 爭吵
have an argument 爭論

表示「沐浴梳洗」

have a shower 淋浴
have a bath 洗澡
have a shave 刮鬍子

其他用語

have a try 試試看
have a baby 生小孩
have a look 看看

---

2 have 作「**行為動詞**」時，可以使用進行式。

Alfred is having dinner at this time.
阿爾發此刻正在吃晚餐。
Are you still having dinner?
你們還在吃晚餐嗎？
We're not having dinner.
We're having dessert.
我們沒有在吃晚餐，我們在吃甜點。

---

3 have 作「**行為動詞**」時，不能用 **have got** 代替。

✗ I always have got a cup of coffee during my break.
✓ I always have a cup of coffee during my break.
休息時我都會來上一杯咖啡。

---

4 have 作「**行為動詞**」時，**否定句**和**疑問句**要使用助動詞 do/does 或 did 來構成。

I don't usually have lunch before 1 p.m.
我通常下午一點之後才吃午餐。
Where do you have lunch?
你都在哪裡吃午餐？
Did you have lunch at the new restaurant?
你去那家新開的餐廳吃午餐了嗎？

---

5 have 作「**行為動詞**」時，不能縮寫為「**'ve**」，has 不能縮寫為「**'s**」，had 不能縮寫為「**'d**」。

✗ I've a meeting in a few minutes.
✓ I have a meeting in a few minutes.
幾分鐘後我有個會要開。

Practice

1 請從圖中選出適當的片語並以正確的形式填空，完成句子。

have a look

have a glass of orange juice

have a fight

have a baby

have a bubble bath

have a bowl of soup

1. I _____ with my neighbor last night.

2. Laura is pregnant. She is _____ in June.

3. Let's buy some orange juice. I want to _____ while I'm watching TV.

4. Irma usually _____ for dinner.

5. I love to _____ in our bathtub on winter nights.

6. Did you _____ at the newspaper this morning?

2 請選出正確的答案。

_____ 1. Dad and Mom usually _____ after dinner every night.
Ⓐ have a nice day　Ⓑ have a nightmare　Ⓒ have a walk

_____ 2. Have you _____ already? There is so much left.
Ⓐ had a piece of apple pie　　Ⓑ have your shoes washed
Ⓒ have a nap

_____ 3. We _____ in Taitung. We will definitely visit it again.
Ⓐ had everything ready　　Ⓑ had a good time
Ⓒ had nothing to do

_____ 4. I _____ yesterday afternoon, so I went home, leaving all the work undone.
Ⓐ had a headache　Ⓑ had a picnic　　Ⓒ had a dream

_____ 5. I am _____ tomorrow. Shall we go to a movie?
Ⓐ having a day off　Ⓑ having a feeling　Ⓒ having some wine

Unit 69

Be Being
Be Being 的用法

---

1 「be + 形容詞」可表達一種「狀態」。

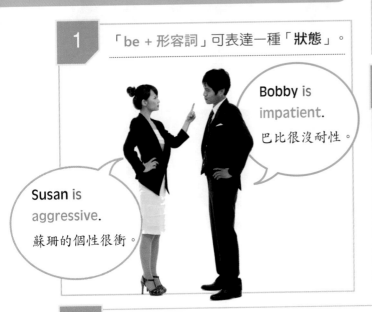

Bobby is impatient.
巴比很沒耐性。

Susan is aggressive.
蘇珊的個性很衝。

---

2 be being 可以視為 be 動詞的進行式，being 就是 be 的現在分詞。此時後面雖然也接形容詞，但其實描述的是一種「動作」而非「狀態」，而且是「暫時的動作」。

What's wrong with you? You are being very rude today.
↳ 其實是 You are acting rude today.
怎麼了你？今天怎麼會這麼失禮。

---

3 be being 表示：個性並非如此，但今天卻表現的不一樣。

She is being naughty today.
↳ 她個性並不調皮，但今天表現得比較調皮
她今天表現得比較調皮。

Yesterday Mrs. Wang was being very hospitable.
↳ 暗示她平時並不是一個好客的人
王太太昨天表現得很好客。

---

4 並非所有形容詞都適合接在 be being 的後面。

可以用於 be being 句型的形容詞			不適用於 be being 句型的形容詞	
bad	impolite	pleasant	beautiful	old
careful	kind	polite	handsome	short
careless	lazy	quiet	happy	sick
foolish	naughty	reasonable	healthy	tall
funny	nice	rude	hungry	thirsty
generous	noisy	serious	lucky	well
impatient	patient	unreasonable	nervous	young

比較

✗ Sam is being tall.
✓ Sam is tall.
↳ tall 並不是一個暫時的動作，不適用 be being 的句型。
山姆很高。

比較

✗ Larry was being happy to help.
✓ Larry was happy to help.
↳ happy 只適合用於描述狀態，不適合描述動作。
賴瑞很樂意幫忙。

Practice

1 請勾選出正確的答案。如果在語意和文法上兩個答案都可以，可都勾選。

1. Judy ☐ is ☐ is being healthy.

2. I don't think he was sincere. He ☐ was just ☐ was just being polite.

3. Today Lily ☐ was ☐ was being naughty in scattering the dog cookies all over the floor.

4. Joe ☐ was ☐ was being very rude to talk like that.

5. Nancy ☐ was ☐ was being lucky to win the lottery.

6. Sam ☐ is ☐ is being sick. He has been lying in bed for several days.

7. Normally Stanley is a careful person, but yesterday he ☐ was ☐ was being careless when looking after his brother in the hospital.

8. Heather's little girl ☐ is ☐ is being very cute.

9. I ☐ was ☐ was being foolish to give him with all my savings.

10. Selina ☐ was ☐ was being generous to help me when I was unemployed.

11. I ☐ was ☐ was being very nervous on my first day of work.

12. Alice ☐ was ☐ was being quiet in the meeting.

13. I ☐ am ☐ am being hungry. When will lunch be ready?

Unit 70

Linking Verbs 連綴動詞

1 連綴動詞是用來「**描述主詞狀態**」的動詞，與一般描述動作的動詞不同。
連綴動詞後面要接**主詞補語**，也就是**名詞**、**代名詞**或**形容詞**，通常不能接副詞。
最常見的連綴動詞就是 be 動詞。

Wade is the product manager of our firm.

↳ be 動詞後面接名詞 product manager，補充說明主詞 Wade 的身分狀態。

韋德是我們公司的產品經理。

It was he who opened the jewel box.

↳ be 動詞後面接代名詞 he。這是一個強調句型：It is/was . . . who/that . . .

就是他打開珠寶盒的。

Danny is smart but lazy.

↳ be 動詞後面接形容詞 smart 和 lazy，補充說明主詞 Danny 的狀態。

丹尼很聰明，但是很懶惰。

2 感官動詞也屬於連綴動詞，後面可以直接加形容詞或「**like + 名詞**」。

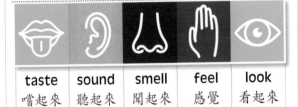

taste	sound	smell	feel	look
嚐起來	聽起來	聞起來	感覺	看起來

The stinky tofu smells like some used socks that haven't been washed for a week, but it tastes wonderful.

臭豆腐聞起來像是一星期沒洗的臭襪子，但是好吃極了。

The Milan Cathedral looks solemn.

米蘭大教堂的外觀莊嚴肅穆。

A caterpillar feels soft and hairy.

毛毛蟲摸起來軟綿綿、毛茸茸的。

He sounds depressed. What happened?

他的口氣聽起來很沮喪，發生什麼事了？

3 連綴動詞還包含一些表示「**狀態**」或「**狀態的改變情況**」的動詞。

- appear 似乎
- go 變得
- remain 維持
- become 變成
- grow 變得
- seem 似乎
- get 變得
- prove 證明是
- turn 變得

The man seems lost. Shall we go over and give him a hand?

那個人看起來迷路了，我們要不要過去幫他一下？

Everything went wrong.

每件事都不順利。

When I grow old, I'll move to a nursing home and chat with other elderly people all day.

等我年紀大了，我要搬去老人院，整天和其他老人聊天。

4 上述連綴動詞，同時也是**一般動詞**。

Taste the soup before you serve it.

把湯端上桌之前，記得嚐一下味道。

What are you looking at?

你在看什麼？

Can you get a jar of marmalade for me?

幫我買一罐橘子果醬好嗎？

I think I can feel the rain. Let's move fast.

好像有雨滴在我身上，我們走快一點。

Gary turned his head and saw a man in black following him.

蓋瑞回過頭，發現他遭到一名黑衣男子尾隨。

You don't want to smell my shoes.

你不會想聞我的鞋子的。

Practice

1

請勾選正確的答案。

smell

1. The coffee beans smell □ fruit □ fruity.

2. The coffee beans smell □ raspberry □ like raspberry.

3. We can smell □ the aroma □ aromatic of their home-made coffee from outside the house.

look

4. Do I look □ a graceful woman □ graceful in this silk dress?

5. In that dress, you look like □ the most beautiful lady □ the most beautiful in the world.

6. How did you know? You didn't even look □ me □ at me.

taste

7. Would you like to taste □ my Mapo tofu □ like my Mapo tofu?

8. Hmm, it tastes □ like spicy □ spicy.

9. It tastes □ like a dish □ a dish Dad would love.

feel

10. Yesterday, I saw an unusual plant on the path to our wooden hut in the valley. I reached out my hand to touch it. It felt □ cool and hairy □ like cool and hairy.

11. Soon after I touched it, I realized that it was poisonous, because I couldn't feel □ like my finger □ my finger.

others

12. My finger began to swell and turned □ like red □ red.

13. I put on some ointment, but my finger didn't seem to get □ better □ well.

14. The swelling grew □ a bigger one □ bigger.

15. At last I had to see a doctor. He said my finger had gotten □ more badly □ worse.

16. I could have lost my finger if I had turned □ him □ to him any later.

17. He gave me a prescription and told me to get □ the medicine □ medicinal at the pharmacy next to the clinic.

18. My finger appears □ normal □ normality today.

Causative Verbs: Make, Have, Get
使役動詞 Make、Have、Get 的用法

1 使役動詞是用來「**使另一個動作發生**」的動詞。

- make it happen 使之發生
- have her call back 請她回電
- get it done 把它做完

2 make 可以當作使役動詞，句型為：

| make | + | 人／物 | + | 原形動詞 |

表示「**讓某人或某物去做某個動作**」。

No one can make him change his mind.
沒人可以改變他的心意。

He tried using magic to make that glass move, but it stayed on the table.
他試著施展魔法移動那個杯子，但杯子還是停在桌子上。

3 have 可以當作使役動詞，句型為：

❶ | have | + | 人／物 | + | 原形動詞 |
❷ | have | + | 物 | + | 過去分詞 |

表示「叫某人或某物去做某個動作」或「讓某物接受某個動作」。

I'll have Jason rewrite the proposal.
我會請傑森重寫企畫案。

Please have the proposal rewritten. It's awful.
這份企畫書寫得不好，請重寫一份。

4 get 可以當作使役動詞，句型為：

❶ | get | + | 人 | + | 加 to 的不定詞 |
表示「叫某人去做某個動作」。
❷ | get | + | 物 | + | 過去分詞 |
表示「讓某物接受某個動作」。

No one can get me to do the things that I don't want to do.
沒人能叫我做我不願意做的事。

Did you get the air conditioner fixed?
你找人修好冷氣了沒？

5 這三個字當中，make 的語氣最強烈，get 次之，have 的語氣最和緩。

Norman can't make his son eat vegetables.
諾曼無法逼他兒子吃青菜。

He can't get his son to do dishes either.
他也叫不動他兒子去洗碗。

At least, he had his son take ping-pong lessons.
至少，他讓兒子上桌球課了。

6 這三個字除了作為使役動詞之外，都可以當作**一般動詞**使用，分別有它們的意義在。

Jeffery is making a wooden chair at his yard.　↳ 製造
傑弗瑞正在院子裡做木頭椅子。

Jennifer had lunch with her teammates at
↳ 吃
a Chinese restaurant yesterday.
昨天，珍妮佛和她的隊友在一家中式餐館吃了午餐。

Patti got a new cell phone from her
↳ 獲得
boyfriend last week.
上星期，佩蒂的男友送了她一支新手機。

1

請選出正確的答案。

.... 1. Kelly saw a giant spider in her room, but she couldn't get it _____ out of the window.

 Ⓐ move   Ⓑ to move   Ⓒ moving   Ⓓ moved

.... 2. If I don't have Isabella _____ for her bad manner, how do I teach other kids to behave?

 Ⓐ punish   Ⓑ to punish   Ⓒ punishing   Ⓓ punished

.... 3. What makes you _____ he'll win the race? He is falling behind other runners now.

 Ⓐ to believe   Ⓑ believed   Ⓒ believing   Ⓓ believe

.... 4. Jimmy is not in now. I'll have him _____ you back when he returns.

 Ⓐ call   Ⓑ to call   Ⓒ calling   Ⓓ called

.... 5. The air conditioner is not working! I must get it _____ as soon as possible. I can't stand the heat this summer.

 Ⓐ repair   Ⓑ to repair   Ⓒ repairing   Ⓓ repaired

.... 6. You can't get things _____. I suggest you let it go.

 Ⓐ undo   Ⓑ to undo   Ⓒ undoing   Ⓓ undone

2

請勾選屬於「使役動詞」的用法。

☐ make a fire   ☐ make her go away

☐ make the baby cry   ☐ make a birthday card for Lisa

☐ get him a glass of water   ☐ get him to move over a little

☐ get the coffee cup washed   ☐ get me a coffee cup

☐ have her write an article   ☐ have a writer's block

☐ have a terrible dream   ☐ have the pillowcase changed

Unit **72**

Causative Verb: Let
Let 當作使役動詞的用法

1 let 是使役動詞，句型為：

| let | + | 人／物 | + | 原形動詞 |

表示「讓某人或某物去做某個動作」。

Joe let me drive his car to school.
喬讓我開他的車上學。

Susan let the dog rest before the next race started.

下一場比賽開始前，蘇珊讓狗狗休息了一下。

2 let's 常用來「提議」，會接「不加 to 的不定詞」，形成祈使句。let's 句型被視為「第一人稱複數」的祈使句。

Let's get away from it all.
我們全都離它遠一點吧！

Let's go now before they realize we're not busy.

趁他們還不知道我們很閒的時候快走吧！

3 let me、let us 和 let's 有所區別。

Let me explain in detail.
↳ 說話者一個人解釋

讓我詳細解釋給你聽。

Let's get / Let us get started right now.
↳ 建議聽者和說話者一起行動

我們立刻行動吧。

We can't be of any help here. Why don't you let us go?
↳ 要走的人不包含聽者

我們在這裡也沒用，你何不讓我們走？

4 | let's | + | not | + | 不加 to 的不定詞 |

可以形成否定祈使句。

Let's not stay at this boring meeting.
我們別待在這麼無趣的會議吧。

Let's not get caught leaving early.
別被人家抓到我們提早離開。

let's 和 **don't** 放在一起的用法很少見，有些人認為這是老式的用法，不過大多數人都認為這是錯誤的文法。

✗ Don't let's finish this food.
✓ Let's not finish this food.
我們別把這些食物吃光。
✗ Let's don't take the 295 bus.
✓ Let's not take the 295 bus.
我們不要搭 295 號公車。

5 在 let's 句子的句尾加上附加問句「shall we?」，也可以加強語氣。

Let's order another round of soft drinks, shall we? 我們再點一次飲料，好嗎？
Let's go on the roller coaster one more time, shall we?
我們再玩一次雲霄飛車，好不好？

let me 只包含「說話者」。

let us 包含「包括說話者的群體」，但不包括「聽者」，這種情況不用 **let's**。

let's 包含「說話者一方和聽者」，這種情況也可以用 let us（= let's）。

1 請將句中錯誤的用語劃上底線，並寫出正確的用語（不須寫出完整的句子）。

1. One of the employees said to the boss, "Please don't fire us. <u>Let's</u> stay and keep working here. We promise not to make such a serious mistake again."
   → *Let us* ....

2. Let's not to have dinner in the same restaurant every day. I want to try something different.
   → ....

3. Sarah lets her daughter to go to a bilingual school. However, I doubt if it's a good idea.
   → ....

4. Let's build another sand castle, don't we?
   → ....

5. Let's don't cry. We'll have another chance someday.
   → ....

6. Let's hang up your coat on the rack over there.
   → ....

7. Father won't let's come near the stove in the kitchen, but I want to help Mom with the cooking.
   → ....

8. Let's do make a cake for Trent. It's his birthday.
   → ....

9. Let us race to the bridge, do we?
   → ....

10. Let's not entering that house. It looks spooky.
    → ....

11. Let me to have a talk with him. Maybe he'll listen to me.
    → ....

12. Don't let's go to that beach. The undertow is dangerous this time of year.
    → ....

Part 10 Infinitives and -ing Forms
不定詞與動名詞

Unit 73

Infinitives and -ing Forms
不定詞與動名詞

1 動詞可分為**不定詞**與**動名詞**。動名詞就是 V-ing 的形式，具有**動詞**的性質，也有**名詞**的性質。

Picking strawberries at a local farm is fun.↳ picking 是動名詞，而非進行式中的動詞。

到地方農場採草莓很有趣。

2 不定詞主要指「加 to 的不定詞」。大部分動詞後面，都可以接「加 to 的不定詞」。

We want to join the June Mediterranean tour group.

我們想參加 6 月的地中海旅行團。

3 「不加 to 的不定詞」則用於 make、let、have 等使役動詞後面，或是助動詞後面。

That movie made my sister cry. Let's go to a movie tonight.

那部電影我妹看得都哭了，我們今晚也去看吧。

Mary must go to the hospital to get a copy of her birth certificate.

瑪麗得去醫院拿一份出生證明。

4 動名詞和「加 to 的不定詞」都可以當作**主詞**，但是「加 to 的不定詞」當作主詞是比較老式的用法。

Painting is the easiest of the building trades. 粉刷是建築工程業最簡單的一種。
Moving a house is not easy.

移動房子不是一件容易的事。

Selling houses is a tough job with long hours. 賣房子是得花長時間的難差事。

5 以 it 為虛主詞的句子，後面會以「加 to 的不定詞」作為真正的**主詞**。

It is a good idea to keep your job skills current.
↳ 真正的主詞是 to keep your job skills current。

讓工作技巧不斷符合現狀的需求是最好的。

Is it practical to cross train for all the jobs in your department?
↳ 真正的主詞是 to cross train for all the jobs in your department。

在你的部門內就所有工作做交叉訓練，可行嗎？

6 動名詞和「加 to 的不定詞」都可當作**受詞**，但何時該用何種形式，請見後面單元說明。

I can't stand playing volleyball in the hot
↳ 動名詞片語，是動詞 stand 的受詞。
sun. Why don't we find an indoor court?

我受不了在豔陽下打排球，能不能找一個室內球場？

I love to jog for an hour at night.
↳ 不定詞片語，是動詞 love 的受詞。

我喜歡晚上慢跑一小時。

Practice

1

請選出正確的答案。

.... 1. Lawrence can _____ 100 words per minute on his computer.
Ⓐ type   Ⓑ to type   Ⓒ typing

.... 2. I ran _____ the bus.
Ⓐ catch   Ⓑ to catch   Ⓒ catching

.... 3. My mom let me _____ at my friend's home last night.
Ⓐ sleep over   Ⓑ to sleep over   Ⓒ sleeping over

.... 4. _____ the right decision may not be easy.
Ⓐ Make   Ⓑ To make   Ⓒ Making

.... 5. The kids enjoy _____ in the puddle.
Ⓐ play   Ⓑ to play   Ⓒ playing

2

請從框內選出適當的動詞，以「動名詞」或「加 to 的不定詞」填空，完成句子。

stretch

drive

enjoy

roast

compete

1 _____ go-carts is fun for teenagers.

2 It is a tricky business _____ almonds at home.

3 It is not easy _____ in a triathlon race.

4 _____ before exercise is important.

5 _____ the cool water at the beach sounds like a good idea on a hot day.

Unit **74**

Verbs Followed by Infinitives
要接不定詞的動詞

1 大多數的動詞後面如果要接另一個動詞，都要接「加 to 的不定詞」。

- afford
- agree
- appear
- arrange
- ask
- attempt
- care
- decide
- expect
- fail
- hope
- learn (how)
- manage
- mean
- offer
- plan
- prepare
- pretend
- promise
- refuse
- seem
- threaten
- want
- wish

We can't afford to buy new living room furniture. 客廳要買新家具，我們負擔不起。
We agreed to save 25% of our combined income every month. 我們同意要把每個月合計薪資的 25% 存起來。
Buying new furniture for our house appears to cost too much for our meager budget. 要為我們房子購買新家具，顯然超出我們微薄的預算太多。
Don't attempt to persuade me to get rid of my favorite armchair. 別試圖說服我丟掉我最愛的那張扶手椅。
We already decided to save more money, not spend it on new furniture.
我們已經決定要多存一點錢，不花錢買新家具了。

2 上述動詞後面如果要接**否定意義的不定詞**，句型是「動詞 + not to . . .」。

You promised not to hit your little brother again. 你答應過不會再打你弟弟的。
You can pretend not to be guilty of hitting him, but I saw you punch him twice. 你可以裝作沒有打過他，不過我親眼看到你揍他兩次了。

3 口語中，「加 to 的不定詞」可以**省略動詞部分**，來避免重複。

Mom, I want to go with you. I want to.
I want to.
↳ = I want to go with you.
媽咪，我要跟妳一起去。我要去！我要去！

4 有些動詞要先接疑問詞，再接「加 to 的不定詞」。

- explain
- know
- teach
- show
- tell

Do you know how to make a cup of cappuccino?
你知道如何泡出一杯卡布奇諾嗎？

Alison can explain what to do with an espresso machine.
愛莉森會說明濃縮咖啡機要怎麼用。
Edna doesn't know how to explain the method for making a cheesecake.
艾德娜不知怎麼解釋要如何做起司蛋糕。
Nick had taught me how to play backgammon, but I forgot the rules.
↳ teach 要先接受詞，再接疑問詞和「加 to 的不定詞」。
尼克教過我怎麼玩西洋雙陸棋，不過我忘記規則了。
Can you show my son where to put his shoes and change into his swimming suit?
↳ show 要先接受詞，再接疑問詞和「加 to 的不定詞」。
你可以告訴我兒子要把鞋子放在哪裡，還有要去哪裡換泳衣嗎？

Practice

1

attend
use
tell
find
be able
play

請從框內選出適當的動詞，以「加 to 的不定詞」形式填空，完成句子。

I hoped ＿＿＿＿＿＿＿＿＿ my cousin's wedding in Hawaii.

I need ＿＿＿＿＿＿＿＿＿ a smaller size to try on.

I promise not ＿＿＿＿＿＿＿＿＿ anybody until you announce your engagement.

Totomi pretended not ＿＿＿＿＿＿＿＿＿ to speak English while traveling in France.

I offered ＿＿＿＿＿＿＿＿＿ his camera and take a picture of him and his son.

Randy learned how ＿＿＿＿＿＿＿＿＿ the piano when he was very young.

2

請從框內選出適當的「疑問詞 + 動詞」組合，以正確的形式填空，完成句子。

how / contact
what / watch
what / wear
when / arrive
where / find

1. Can you please tell me ＿＿_how to contact_＿＿ Mr. Greenwood?

2. Can you tell me ＿＿＿＿＿＿＿＿＿ the X-ray department?

3. Could you advise me ＿＿＿＿＿＿＿＿＿ for my TV appearance?

4. Could you inform me ＿＿＿＿＿＿＿＿＿ at the ceremony?

5. Could you describe ＿＿＿＿＿＿＿＿＿ for at the airport security gate?

Unit 75

Verbs Followed by Objects and Infinitives
要接受詞再接不定詞的動詞

1 有些動詞在接「加 to 的不定詞」之前，要先接一個受詞，其句型為：

| 動詞 | + | 受詞 | + | 加 to 的不定詞 |

- advise
- allow
- cause
- compel
- convince
- encourage
- forbid
- force
- instruct
- invite
- order
- permit
- persuade
- recommend
- remind
- request
- require
- teach
- tell
- train
- urge
- warn
- would like

The boss forced Allan to work during the weekend. 老闆強迫艾倫週末也要上班。
The salesman persuaded Virginia to apply for the credit card.

這位業務員說服維吉妮亞申辦了信用卡。
My uncle Ian invited us to visit him in the summer.

我叔叔伊恩邀請我們這個夏天去拜訪他。

2 這種句型可以改寫為被動式，此時不定詞前面就不需要受詞。

The soldier was ordered to holster his weapon. 這名軍人奉命把槍收進皮套裡。
I was persuaded to buy this set of books.

我被說服買了這套書。

- advise
- allow
- encourage
- permit
- recommend

3 有些動詞可以接受詞再接「加 to 的不定詞」，也可以不用受詞。

- ask
- beg
- choose
- expect
- get
- mean
- help
- want
- promise

Cathy wants Roland to help with the recycling project on Sunday.

凱西要羅蘭幫忙做星期日的資源回收。
Isaac wants to put woofers in the trunk of his car to improve the sound quality.

艾薩克想在後車廂放重低音喇叭，改進音響的聲音品質。
Gladys expected Rupert to call, but he never did. 葛蕾蒂絲很期待魯伯特打電話給她，但是他卻一直沒打。
Sarah expected to leave by noon.

莎拉希望中午前能出發。
Margie helped Sidney (to) wash his new car. 瑪琪幫席尼洗他的新車。
Ted helped (to) install a new navigation system in his dad's car.

泰德幫老爸在車上裝了新的導航系統。

> help 後面可接「加 to 的不定詞」，也可接「不加 to 的不定詞」，意義相同。

4 上述有些動詞除了接「受詞 + 加 to 的不定詞」之外，也可以接動名詞。

① I wouldn't advise traveling in some parts of Africa.

我不建議去非洲某些地區旅遊。
I wouldn't advise you to travel to some parts of Africa.

我不建議你去非洲某些地區旅遊。

② This bank doesn't allow depositing or withdrawing money on Saturday and Sunday. 這家銀行在星期六、日不能存提款。
This bank doesn't allow you to deposit or withdraw money on Saturday and Sunday. 這家銀行在星期六、日不能讓你存提款。

Practice

1

請勾選正確的用語。

1. Bobby invited Traci □ to have □ have dinner with him.

2. Sam asked Nancy □ to help □ helping with the dinner dishes.

3. Barbara wouldn't recommend □ going □ to go to that restaurant.

4. Jane was invited □ joining □ to join the beach party.

5. Amy's dad doesn't want her □ go □ to go to the cast party.

6. The boss □ ordered Melvin to attend □ ordered to attend the meeting at the client's office.

7. Kirk doesn't want you □ to calibrate □ calibrating the weighing scales for him.

2

請將括弧內提供的詞語以「to V」或「受詞 + to V」的形式填空，完成句子。

1. Grandma taught _____ (Colleen / knit) on the weekends.

2. Clarissa persuaded _____ (Dolly / accept) the job offer.

3. Daniel warned _____ (me / not exceed) the speed limit.

4. Trent promised _____ (drop by) this afternoon.

5. The storm caused _____ (the airport / close) for six hours.

6. The manager reminded _____ (us / finish) the work before 6 p.m.

3

請將下列各「主動句」改寫為「被動句」。

1. They instructed us how to key in the code to open the gate.
   → _____
   _____

2. Mr. White encouraged Simon to take part in the speech contest.
   → _____
   _____

3. They advised Hal to wear a suit for the press conference.
   → _____
   _____

Part 10 Infinitives and -ing Forms
不定詞與動名詞

Unit 76

Verbs Followed by -ing Forms
要接動名詞的動詞

1 許多動詞要接動名詞。

• admit	• feel like	• miss
• avoid	• finish	• postpone
• consider	• give up	• practice
• delay	• can't help	• put off
• deny	• imagine	• risk
• dislike	• involve	• stand
• enjoy	• keep on	• suggest
• fancy	• mind	• understand

Amy **admitted** being in love with Tom.
愛咪承認自己愛上了湯姆。
Faith **avoided** doing exercise whenever possible. 菲絲盡可能逃避做運動。
Beryl **considered** getting to her office on time a top priority.
貝瑞兒將準時上班視為最重要的事。

2 這些動詞後面如果要接**否定意義的動名詞**，句型是：

動詞 + not + 動名詞

Mike **imagined** not having children.
麥可幻想自己沒有孩子。

Hanna **enjoyed** not following the traditional path.
漢娜樂於不遵循傳統行事。

3 前述有些動詞在接動名詞之前，可先接受詞，句型為：

動詞 + 受詞 + 動名詞

Daniel **heard** me asking where to find the department office.
丹尼爾聽到我問系辦公室在哪裡。
Can you **imagine** Tina jogging with a Labrador? 你能想像蒂娜和一隻拉不拉多一起慢跑的畫面嗎？
I **dislike** you wearing tights and flip-flops.
我不喜歡你穿緊身褲配夾腳拖。

4 do 經常搭配動名詞，來表示「**工作**」。句型是：

do + the/some + 動名詞

I **do** the driving when we go on a long trip. 我們出門長途旅行時都是我開車。
Rosie **does** the ordering for the department.
部門採購的工作都是蘿西在做。

5 go 經常搭配動名詞，來表示「**運動**」或「**休閒活動**」。句型是：

go + 動名詞

Roger likes to **go** roller-skating on campus. 羅傑喜歡在校園裡溜冰。
Ray **goes** bicycling in the evenings.
雷都在傍晚騎腳踏車。

6 mind 後面如果接「**受格代名詞 + 動名詞**」，是較為不正式的用法；正式用法應該接「所有格 + 動名詞」。

Would you **mind** me sending you a sample of our new product?
= Would you **mind** my sending you a sample of our new product?
你介意我寄我們新產品的樣品給你嗎？

Practice

1

請從框內選出適當的動詞，以「動名詞」的格式填空，完成句子。

eat

smoke

shop

vacuum

offend

invite

read

cook

1. Fran admitted _____ a box of candy before dinner.

2. Howard finished _____ dinner for his girlfriend.

3. Let's go _____ in the morning so we can have an early lunch.

4. Rosemary risked _____ her guests when she cut loose with a loud burp.

5. Melanie postponed _____ her mother-in-law for afternoon tea.

6. I will do the _____ when we clean the house next week.

7. Sam missed _____ the newspaper during lunch.

8. Would you mind not _____ your cigar inside the house?

2

請從框內選出適當的動詞，以「not + 動名詞」的句型填空，完成句子。

use

have

watch

deliver

listen

1. Florence admitted _____ the package to Mrs. Poe yesterday.

2. I suggest _____ the talk show tonight.

3. I can't imagine _____ a cell phone for three days of my life.

4. Would you mind _____ to that loud music for half an hour?

5. Belinda enjoys _____ to rush to the office every day.

3

請將括弧內的動名詞搭配 do 或 go 填空，完成句子。

1. Arthur loves to _____ (fishing) when he is on vacation.

2. Conrad always _____ (some reading) before he sleeps.

3. Would you like to _____ (the painting) of the outer wall?

4. Sandra always _____ (swimming) on Friday nights.

5. Who's _____ (the washing) today?

Unit 77

Verbs Followed by -ing Forms or Infinitives With the Same Meaning
接動名詞或不定詞意義相同的動詞

1 有些動詞後面可以接動名詞，也可以接「加 to 的不定詞」，並且意義相同。

- begin
- love
- hate
- continue
- start
- like
- prefer
- can't bear

Lauren began to juggle when she was sixteen years old.
= Lauren began juggling when she was sixteen years old.

蘿倫從十六歲起開始練習雜耍。

Margaret continued to practice magic during senior high school.
= Margaret continued practicing magic during senior high school.

瑪格莉特高中的時候繼續練習變魔術。

Lynn loved to perform on the stage.
= Lynn loved performing on the stage.

琳恩喜愛在舞台上表演。

2 但有時，這些動詞接動名詞或不定詞仍有極細微的差異。

1「like + 動名詞」表某人很愛做某事。

2「like + 加 to 的不定詞」強調「習慣」。

Carl likes volunteering at the history museum. ↳ 某人很愛當義工。

卡爾喜歡在歷史博物館當義工。

Joy likes to put lots of sugar in her tea.
↳ 強調習慣。

喬伊喝茶喜歡加很多糖。

3 begin、start 和 continue 若已使用進行式，後面就不要用動名詞，避免重複。

Frank is beginning to grow herbs.
法蘭克正開始種植藥草。

4 begin、start 和 continue 後面，如果接的是 **know**、**realize** 或 **understand** 這類的動詞，要用不定詞的格式。

✗ Sally began realizing her limitations as a gardener.

✓ Sally began to realize her limitations as a gardener.

莎莉開始明白她身為園藝家的限制。

5 這四種句型都是用來「泛指」，指「比較喜歡；寧可」：

❶ prefer to do *something*
❷ prefer doing *something*
❸ prefer to do *something* rather than do *something* else〔美式〕
❹ prefer doing *something* to doing *something* else〔英式〕

但是 would prefer 用來特指一個決定，則會用：

would prefer	+	加 to 的不定詞	+	rather than	+	不加 to 的不定詞

Ginny prefers to grow vegetables rather than raise chickens. 吉妮喜歡種菜更勝養雞。

It's cold today. I would prefer to stay at home rather than go to the park.

今天天氣冷，我不去公園，寧願待在家裡。

6 上述動詞如果搭配 would，變成 would like、would love、would hate、would prefer，那麼通常會接「加 to 的不定詞」。

Willa would like to teach a class in house restoration techniques.

薇拉想要開一堂建築修復技巧的課。

Janet would hate to see the restoration plan being postponed.

珍妮不希望見到重建計畫被拖延。

比較

would like 是「**想要**」，like 是「**喜歡**」兩者意義不同。

- Would you like to rebuild this old temple?

你想要重建這間老寺廟嗎？

- Do you like restoring old buildings?

你喜歡整修老舊建築嗎？

Practice

1

請將括號裡的單字以正確的「動名詞」或「不定詞」格式填空，某些題目中可以同時使用兩種格式。

1. Bill loves _barbequing / to barbeque_ (barbeque) on the deck.

2. Phil started _____ (heat) the grill.

3. Calvin likes _____ (fast) for a couple of days each month.

4. Would you like _____ (join) me for a workout at the gym?

5. Do you like _____ (exercise)?

6. I prefer to watch sports rather than _____ (participate) in them.

7. I would prefer _____ (read) a book today rather than _____ (play) basketball.

8. Sandy is beginning _____ (feel) faint.

9. I began _____ (realize) that there was something wrong with the medication.

10. I started _____ (feel) bad for Quentin.

2

請從框內選出適當的動詞，以「不定詞」的形式填空，完成句子。

reduce　　spend　　buy　　help

1. Whitney would love _____ you with this report.

2. Verna would like _____ the new Coach perfume.

3. Luther would hate _____ money on interior decoration.

4. The editor would prefer _____ the budget for the illustrations in the book.

3

請從圖片中選出適當的用語，以「動名詞」或「不定詞（加 to 或不加 to）」的形式填空，完成句子。

1. Would you prefer to go snorkeling rather than _____?

2. Do you prefer swimming in the ocean or _____?

3. I prefer _____ rather than climb a mountain on my vacation.

relax on a tropical island

ride a banana boat

climb a mountain

Unit **78**

Verbs Followed by -ing Forms or
Infinitives With Different Meanings (1)
接動名詞與不定詞意義不同的動詞（ I ）

有些動詞後面可以接動名詞，
也可以接「加 to 的不定詞」，
但是意義不同。

- remember   · stop   · regret
- forget   · go on
- try   · mean

1 remember 和 forget 如果接動名詞
（V-ing），表示這事是「已經做過的」。

Joanne remembered writing her resignation letter.

瓊安記得她已經寫好辭呈了。

Tiffany forgot mailing a gift to her grandmother.

蒂芬妮忘記她已經把禮物寄給祖母了。

2 remember 和 forget 如果接「加 to 的
不定詞」，表示這件事是「還沒做的」。

Joanne remembered to write her resignation letter.

瓊安記得要寫辭呈。

Tiffany forgot to mail a gift to her grandmother.

蒂芬妮忘記要把禮物寄給祖母了。

3 try 後面接動名詞（V-ing），表示「實驗性
地做某事」、「試試看結果會如何」。

Did you try smiling at the security guard to see if you could get into the building? 你有試著對警衛微笑，看看他願不願意讓你進大樓嗎？

Have you tried negotiating with your mom to keep the cat?

你有嘗試和媽媽溝通要把貓留下來養的事嗎？

4 try 如果接「加 to 的不定詞」，
表示「非常盡力做某事」。

Yesterday I tried to climb to the top of the mountain, but I failed.

我昨天想攻頂，但是沒有成功。

I tried to negotiate with my mom to keep the cat. 我有試著和媽媽溝通把貓留下來養的事。

5 stop 如果接動名詞（V-ing），
表示「停止做某件事」。

Timmy stopped smoking cigarettes three years ago after his daughter was born.

提米三年前女兒出生後，就不再抽菸了。

The weather had been sweltering, so I stopped buying hot coffee.

天氣熱得不得了，
所以我不再買熱咖啡了。

6 stop 如果接「加 to 的不定詞」，表示
「停止手邊的事，去做另一件事」，
常用來說明「停止做某事的原因」。

Timmy stopped to smoke a cigarette outside because his wife doesn't let him smoke in the house.

提米停了下來，要到屋外抽菸，因為他太太不讓他在屋裡抽菸。

The weather was sweltering, so I stopped to buy an ice cream cone.

天氣熱得不得了，所以我停下來買個冰淇淋甜筒。

Practice

1

請勾選正確的答案。

1. I forgot ☐ to bring ☐ bring my lunch box to school. Now I'm so hungry.

2. Here are your books. Have you forgotten ☐ to lend ☐ lending them to me?

3. The jar won't open. Have you tried ☐ running ☐ to run the cap under hot water?

4. I tried ☐ sending ☐ to send my résumé to as many companies as possible, but none of them has ever contacted me.

5. I lost my running shoes, so I stopped ☐ to jog ☐ jogging.

6. Since my shoe came untied, I stopped ☐ to rest ☐ resting.

2

請將括弧內的動詞以正確的「動名詞」或「不定詞」填空，完成句子。

1. Brian forgot _____ (put) the leftovers into the refrigerator, and now the food has gone bad.

2. Chuck forgot _____ (finish) the last piece of apple pie. He had rummaged in his refrigerator for five minutes, but he couldn't find any sweets.

3. I remember _____ (take) this garbage bag outside. Who brought it back in?

4. I'll remember _____ (pay) the telephone bill on time, so they won't have the service cut next month.

5. I tried _____ (talk) to him, but he wouldn't listen.

6. I tried _____ (stay) calm, but what he said was really infuriating.

7. I stopped _____ (hang) out with my friends every day after I got married.

8. Momo had been barking near the door for ten minutes. He stopped _____ (drink) some water and then went back to the door and bark some more.

Unit 79

Verbs Followed by -ing Forms or Infinitives With Different Meanings (2)
接動名詞或不定詞意義不同的動詞（2）

1 go on 接動名詞，表「**繼續做某事**」。

She goes on swimming lap after lap without stopping.

她持續游泳，游了一趟又一趟不停止。

John went on eating all afternoon at the free buffet. 約翰整個下午都在免費的自助餐廳吃個不停。

2 go on 接「**加 to 的不定詞**」，表示「**繼續做事，但改做不同的事**」。

She went on to run on the track after swimming in the lap pool.

她在直線泳區游完後，接著又去跑道跑步。

John ate his jumbo burger, and then he went on to finish my French fries.

約翰吃完他的超大漢堡後，接著又把我的薯條吃完了。

3 mean 接動名詞，表示「**意味著**」。

If Tony signs the contract, it will mean playing baseball in this city for three years.

如果湯尼簽了約，就表示他將在此城市打棒球打三年。

4 mean 接「**加 to 的不定詞**」，表示「**打算、意圖**」。

I'm sorry. I didn't mean to tell her the sad truth. 很抱歉，我不是故意要告訴她這個令人傷心的真相的。

Did you mean to break into the house of a police officer? 你的意思是說，要闖入警察的家？

5 regret 接動名詞，表示「**對已發生的事感到悔恨**」。

Miranda regrets accepting Jonathan's marriage proposal.

米蘭達懊悔接受強納森的求婚。

I regret giving up chocolate.

我很後悔沒吃巧克力。

6 regret 接「**加 to 的不定詞**」，表示「**對於不得不做的決定表達遺憾**」。

Miranda regrets to say that she is unable to accept Jonathan's marriage proposal. 米蘭達很遺憾的說，她無法接受強納森的求婚。

I regret to say that I gave up chocolate.

我很遺憾地說我不吃巧克力了。

regret to say 是一種正式的用語。

Please inform the Minister of the Interior that the Deputy Secretary regrets to say he is unable to attend the council meeting this afternoon in Senate Conference Room 10. 請轉告內政部長，祕書長很抱歉無法參加今天下午在參議院 10 號議事廳舉辦的議會。

Practice

1

請勾選正確的答案。

1. Kevin went on □ playing □ to play □ play the same song over and over.

2. She has been doing very well in college. She may go on □ becoming □ to become a lawyer.

3. Ted regrets □ withdrawing □ to withdraw his name from the speech contest.

4. I regret □ to cancel □ cancel □ canceling the trip to India.

2

請將括弧內的動詞以正確的「動名詞」或「不定詞」填空，完成句子。

1. Now that we've come to a conclusion on this issue, shall we go on _____ (discuss) the next one?

2. The HR manager got a phone call in the middle of the meeting. Now that he has hung up the phone, we can go on _____ (discuss) a new topic.

3. When you bring a stray dog home, it will mean _____ (take) care of him for the rest of his life. You should think it through.

4. I understand. You mean _____ (feed) him, _____ (play) with him, _____ (love) him, and never _____ (abandon) him.

5. When you say going mountain climbing, do you mean _____ (walk) up hundreds of steps to the small park on the top?

6. I didn't mean _____ (lie) to you. We just wanted to give you a surprise.

7. Do you regret _____ (move) to the city and living on your own?

8. I regret _____ (tell) you that your proposal has been rejected.

9. I regret _____ (not join) their picnic at the beach as they had so much fun.

10. Jenny regrets _____ (recommend) the dinner in this restaurant.

Infinitives Used as Complements and
Infinitives of Purpose
不定詞當作補語與表示「目的」的用法

1 「加 to 的不定詞」經常放在**名詞**或**代名詞**的
後面當作**補語**。

Holly bought a newspaper to look in the
classified ads for a used car.
荷莉買了一份報紙，要看分類廣告的二手車資訊。
Would you like something to drink?
你想要喝點東西嗎？
Do you want him to meet you at the café?
你想要他到咖啡廳跟你碰面嗎？
The decision to quit my current job and
to enter a new field is very hard to make.
要我離開目前的工作，投入另一個新的領域，是
個困難的決定。

2 「加 to 的不定詞」也可以放在**形容詞後面**，
當作**補充說明**。

The university is honored to announce
a hundred million dollar gift from the family
of Dr. Chambers. 大學很榮幸地宣布獲得來自錢
伯斯博士一家人捐贈的一億元。
I am pleased to explain that the terms of the
gift from Dr. Hogan include an endowed chair
and a new science center.
我很開心能說明霍根博士捐贈的項目，包括一個
基金教授職位，和一座新的科學中心。

3 「It is/was + 形容詞 + of somebody」的**後
面**，會用「加 to 的不定詞」當作**補充說明**。

It is very kind of *Dr. Lampert* to contribute to
the endowment funds of our university.
藍伯特博士真是非常的好心，他對這次的大學捐
獻基金也做了捐贈。
It was so generous of *the Winthrop family*
to donate a new building.
溫索柏家族非常慷慨地捐贈了一棟新大樓。

4 「It is/was + 形容詞 + for
somebody」後面，也會用「加 to
的不定詞」當作**補充說明**。

It's not easy for *Barbara* to get
airline tickets over the holiday.
芭芭拉很難在假期間買到機票。
It is important for *Michelle* to visit
her family members in her hometown.
對蜜雪兒來說，回家鄉去探望家人是很
重要的。

5 「加 to 的不定詞」，也常用於說
明「**某人從事某活動的目的**」。

Mary is planning to save money for
a house. 瑪莉計畫要存錢買房子。
Eddie went to the store to buy
some milk. 艾迪去商店買了些牛奶。

6 表示「**目的**」時，用 in order to
或 so as to，是比**單用 to** 更正式
的方法。
否定句型是 in order not to 和
so as not to。

Kathryn proposed the reform in
order to help those orphans.
為了幫助那些孤兒，凱瑟琳提出改革方
案。
Joseph retired early so as to spend
more time with his family.
喬瑟夫為了有多點時間與家人相處，所
以提早退休。
Pam takes the bus in order not to
pay for parking.
為了不要付停車費，潘選擇搭公車。
Randy picks up his children at school
every day so as not to miss their
formative years.
藍迪每天放學都去學校接孩子，就是為
了不要錯過他們的人格發展期。

Practice

1

請勾選正確的答案。

1. Would you like something ☐ to drink ☐ drinking?

2. I need somebody ☐ to help ☐ helping me paint the house.

3. ☐ We are happy to hear ☐ It is happy for us to hear from you.

4. It is considered ill-mannered ☐ to ask ☐ for asking a woman her age.

5. It is ☐ you clever to open ☐ clever of you to open the car door without a key.

6. It is ☐ polite of you to knock on ☐ polite for you to knock on the door before entering a room.

7. It won't be necessary ☐ to mail ☐ for mailing the certificate.

8. It is a mistake for children in an unsafe neighborhood ☐ to play ☐ playing in the park after dark.

2

請從框內選出適當的動詞，以正確的「不定詞」形式填空，完成句子。

| buy | see | celebrate | help | update | check |

1. Sarah went to the phone store __to buy__ a new battery.

2. June bought some aspirin _____ reduce the pain in her back.

3. Emma made a cake _____ her son's birthday.

4. Felix called the kindergarten _____ on his daughter.

5. Avery went to the zoo _____ the baby koala.

6. Barry sent an email to his boss _____ her on the project.

3

請從圖中選出適當的用語填空，完成句子。

1. Lisa left the office early so as to _____ in the hospital.

2. Brenda goes to the gym every weekend to _____.

3. Amanda brought her own coffee cup to the office in order to _____ and help save the planet.

4. Ethan took his dog to a vet to _____.

visit her daughter

reduce paper waste

keep fit

cure his eye disease

Part 10 Infinitives and -ing Forms
不定詞與動名詞

Unit 81

Prepositions With -ing Forms
介系詞接動名詞

1 介系詞at、of等,可用來說明「**關係**」或「**連結**」,介系詞後要接名詞,因此如果要接動詞,就要使用動名詞。

Are you interested in sending this letter by certified mail? └ 用動名詞

你想以掛號郵件寄出這封信嗎?

I am thinking of sending it by express mail. 我在考慮用快遞寄送。

Richard is looking forward to getting the product samples.

李察很期待收到貨物樣品。

Jack is planning on placing an order in the next day or two.

傑克計畫一兩天後下單訂購。

2 不要混淆不定詞中的to和介系詞to。以**to開頭的介系詞片語**,並不是動詞的一部分。

不定詞的 to If you want to send this parcel overnight, └ to 是代表不定詞,不是介系詞。
then you need to use a package delivery service.

如果你想要今晚連夜送達包裹,那你得選包裹快遞服務。

不定詞的 to Do you want to insure your package? └ 不定詞

你的包裹要加保險嗎?

介系詞 to Take your attempted delivery notice to window number 12.
└ 以 to 開頭的介系詞片語,to 是介系詞。
請你拿取件通知單到 12 號窗口辦理。

介系詞 to Couriers can't deliver parcels to post office boxes. └ to post office boxes 是介系詞片語。
快遞員不能把包裹送到郵政信箱裡。

3 be used to是慣用語,表示「**習慣於**」。這裡的to是介系詞,因此要接名詞或動名詞。

Jordan is used to wearing sandals with socks. 喬登已經習慣了穿著襪子穿涼鞋。

Sofia isn't used to long price negotiations with street vendors.

蘇菲亞不習慣在街上和小販討價還價。

get used to 意指「**逐漸習慣某事**」,也要接動名詞。

• Heather is getting used to buying vegetables in the street markets near her apartment.

海瑟漸漸習慣在公寓附近的市場買菜。

比較 但是沒有 be 動詞的 used to 後面則是接不定詞。

Jordan used to wear sandals without socks all year round.

喬登以前整年都只穿涼鞋不穿襪子。

Practice

1

請從框內選出適當的介系詞，搭配括弧中的動詞，以正確的形式填空，
完成句子。

on

at

about

before

of

in

for

to

1. Jean is planning _on paying_ (pay) her electricity bill at the convenience store.

2. Gary is thinking _____ (get) some money at the ATM machine.

3. This area with the white lines is _____ (park) motorcycles.

4. Check the map _____ (drive) to the meeting.

5. Aren't you tired _____ (listen) to talk radio?

6. Chuck is good _____ (find) lost packages in the warehouse.

7. Curtis isn't interested _____ (collect) Pokémon figures.

8. Are you looking forward _____ (travel) around China next week?

2

請將括弧內的動詞以「to + 動名詞」或「to + 不定詞」的形式填空，
完成句子。

1. I am getting used _to hopping_ (hop) on my scooter when I need to go somewhere.

2. When I was a teenager, I used _____ (ride) a dirt bike on the hills behind my parent's house.

3. My family used _____ (own) several ATVs that we rode all over the farm.

4. I am not used _____ (fight) the intense traffic in the city.

5. It won't take long to get used _____ (navigate) a scooter in the city.

6. I am getting used _____ (move) other scooters out of the way when I need a parking place.

Unit 82

"Need" and "See" With -ing Forms or Infinitives
Need 與 See 接動名詞與不定詞的用法

need 接動名詞與不定詞

1 need 當作**一般動詞**用時，後面經常接「加 to 的不定詞」。

Danielle needs to read more books and watch less TV.

丹尼爾得多讀點書，少看點電視。

Earl doesn't need to buy any more books. He needs to donate his old books to a library. 厄爾不需要再買書了，他應該把他的舊書捐給圖書館。

2 need 當作**一般動詞**用時，也可以接動名詞，此時句子具有「**被動意義**」，這是英式英語的用法，美式用「to be + 過去分詞」。

The library needs expanding because there isn't enough room for the new children's collection.

圖書館得擴建了，因為原有的空間不夠放新的兒童藏書。

Small independent bookstores need protecting or they will all disappear.

獨立的小書店需要被保留下來，否則將會完全消失不見。

3 need 當作一般動詞用時，也可以接「to be + 過去分詞」，此時句子也是「**被動意義**」，和使用動名詞是一樣的。

The bookstore needs to be renovated and redesigned. 這間書店得重新設計翻修。

In this age of multimedia, book readers need to be supported. 在這個多媒體的時代，傳統書籍的讀者應該受到鼓勵。

see 接動名詞與不定詞

4 see 和 hear 後面要先接受詞，再接動名詞或「不加 to 的不定詞」，且兩者的意義不同。

see 和 hear 接動名詞的時候，強調看到聽到的是「**連續動作的其中一部分**」。

Yesterday I saw Sue talking to her dog.
↳ 只看到動作「說話」的部分。

昨天我看到蘇在對她的狗說話。

Jessica heard Tom arguing with someone in the hallway.
↳ 只聽到動作「爭吵」的一部分。

潔西卡聽到湯姆和人在走廊上爭吵。

As I walked by the store, I saw Danny raising the shutters. 我經過商店的時候，看到丹尼正在把百葉窗拉起來。

5 see 和 hear 若接「不加 to 的不定詞」，則表看到聽到的是「**從頭到尾的動作**」。

Carol saw Dr. Shaw arrive at his office.
↳ 目睹整個抵達的經過。

卡蘿看見蕭博士抵達他的辦公室。

Jessica heard Sherman unlock the door.
↳ 聽到整個開鎖的過程。

潔西卡聽到雪曼打開門鎖。

As I sat in the park across from the store, I saw Danny raise the shutters.

當我坐在商店對面的公園，看見丹尼窗簾拉起了百葉窗。

6 要注意的是，如果 see、hear 後面本來接「不加 to 的不定詞」，則 see、hear 的**被動式**須接「加 to 的不定詞」。後面本來如果接動名詞則不影響。

Someone saw Sam leave the building at approximately 5:00.

→ Sam was seen to leave the building at approximately 5:00.

有人看到山姆約於 5 點時離開這棟大樓。

Practice

1 請從框內選出適當的動詞，搭配 need，以正確的形式填空，完成句子。

set

fix

buy

pick up

clean

wash

1. Can you move your stuff off the dining room table? I ___*need to set*___ the table for dinner.

2. The refrigerator is full. We don't _____ any more food.

3. The faucet on the sink in the bathroom is dripping. The faucet _____ or we will waste water and run up the water bill.

4. There is a mound of laundry in the twins' room. Their clothes _____ or they won't have anything to wear.

5. There is some toothpaste on the mirror in the bathroom. The mirror _____ before your parents come.

6. There are toys all over the living room floor. The toys _____ and putting away before you go to bed tonight.

2 請將括弧內的動詞，以「動名詞」、「不加 to 的不定詞」或「加 to 的不定詞」填空，完成句子。

1. As I walked into the building, I saw the security guard _____ (watch) a movie on TV.

2. While we were waiting at the airport, we heard a man _____ (announce) our names over the public address system.

3. I saw him _____ (leave) this package at the front desk.

4. As I walked to the store, I saw a man _____ (walk) his pet cat on a leash.

5. I looked up for a moment and saw a man _____ (float) down to earth in a parachute.

6. Jerry was heard _____ (rush) downstairs.

7. The man was seen _____ (run) across the street with a package in his hand.

173

Participle Phrases and Participle Clauses
分詞片語與分詞子句

1 動詞又可分為現在分詞和過去分詞，現在分詞的形式也是 V-ing。像是**進行式**就要使用現在分詞。

Mike is <u>selling</u> sausages at the lotus flower farm. 麥克正在蓮花園賣香腸。

2 現在分詞也可以當作**形容詞**使用。

Zelda thinks furniture design is interesting. 薩爾達覺得設計家具很有趣。
Lillian says furniture shopping in Milan, Italy, is exciting. 莉莉安說，在義大利米蘭買家具很讓人興奮。
Eco-tourism is a <u>thriving</u> business.
↳ 動詞 thrive 的現在分詞 thriving，用來修飾名詞 business。

生態旅遊是個熱門的生意。

3 現在分詞可以作為一個**片語的開頭**，這種片語稱為分詞片語。

Marvin is the guy <u>standing by the office doorway</u>.
馬爾文就是站在辦公室門口的那個傢伙。

4 分詞片語可以當作形容詞使用，對名詞或名詞片語「提供更多資訊」。

The tall man <u>shouting at the office workers</u> is our boss. 我們老闆就是對著辦公室員工大吼大叫的那位高大男人。
The man <u>waving at you</u> is the inspector general from the city government.
那個正在對你揮手的人是市政府的監察長。

5 現在分詞可以作為一個子句的開頭，這種子句稱為分詞子句。分詞子句可以當作**副詞**使用，提供關於「**時間**」的訊息。

當一個短暫行為發生在一個較長行為中間時，較長行為可以用分詞片語。
While <u>staying</u> at the hospital with her father, Lindsay had a premonition.
↳「產生預感」是發生於「在醫院陪爸爸的時候」。
琳賽在醫院陪爸爸的時候，有了不安的預感。

<u>Fearing</u> for the worst, Lindsay pushed the nurse call button.
↳ 先「擔心最糟的情況會發生」，再「按下呼叫鈴」。
琳賽擔心最糟的情況會發生，於是按了護士呼叫鈴。

<u>Opening</u> his eyes, Lindsay's father looked around the hospital room.
↳ 先「張開雙眼」，再「環顧四周」。
琳賽的父親張開雙眼後，四面環顧著醫院病房。

一前一後發生的動作，也可用現在分詞的完成式來說明「**第一個動作**」。

- <u>Having called</u> for a nurse, Lara stared at her father.
  呼叫護士之後，拉蘿緊盯著父親。

6 分詞子句可以用來說明「**事情發生的原因**」。

<u>Wanting</u> to know why his son Lester was sitting here, Papa asked him what he was doing. 爸爸想知道兒子萊斯特為何坐在這裡，便問他在做什麼。
<u>Trying</u> to explain that Papa had hit his head, Linda showed how he had been knocked unconscious.

為了解釋爸爸撞到頭的事，琳達演示了他是如何撞到失去意識的。

Practice

1

請將括弧內的詞語以「分詞片語」或「分詞子句」的形式填空，完成句子。

1. Angela is the woman __brushing her hair__ (brush her hair).

2. The man _____ (look at himself in the mirror) is Victor.

3. While _____ (shop at the department store), Rose bought a two-piece suit.

4. _____ (think about buying a pair of new shoes), Ann got on the elevator.

5. _____ (have purchased a three-piece suit), Greg decided to buy a matching belt.

6. _____ (have bought a new dress), Maggie looked for a matching purse.

7. _____ (know she had to look sharp for her presentation), Rachel bought a whole new outfit.

8. _____ (have an attractive new hair style), Flora began to improve her use of makeup.

2

請以「分詞片語」或「分詞子句」改寫句子。

1. Howard bit his tongue while he was eating the glazed strawberries on a stick.
   → *While eating the glazed strawberries on a stick, Howard bit his tongue.*

2. Irene lay on the bed and thought about the next day's presentation.
   → _____

3. Who is that woman? The woman is talking on a cell phone.
   → _____

4. After she took some medicine, Mary started to feel better.
   → _____

5. John had the ambition to win the championship, so he practiced extremely hard.
   → _____
   _____

6. Because Trudy wanted to have a bubble bath after work, she bought a cedar bathtub last week.
   → _____
   _____

Unit 84

Phrasal Verbs: Two Words, Transitive, and Separable

片語動詞：兩個字、及物、可分

片語動詞是一組具有特定意義的動詞片語，由動詞搭配副詞或介系詞所構成。

片語動詞的類型眾多，第一種由「**動詞 + 副詞**」搭配受詞組成，屬於「**可分的**」片語動詞，受詞可放在**副詞後**，也可放在**動詞和副詞中間**。

❶ 動詞 + 副詞 + 受詞
→ 受詞放在副詞後

❷ 動詞 + 受詞 + 副詞
→ 受詞放副詞前，但當受詞是**代名詞**時，只能放動詞和副詞中間。

Jake took off the shoes when he entered the room.
Jake took the shoes off when he entered the room.
Jake took them off when he entered the room.
傑克進入房間的時候，脫了鞋子。

bring back 帶回

Can you bring back some coffee for me?
你可以幫我買一些咖啡回來嗎？

bring in 拿進來

Lisa, please bring in those files.
莉莎，請把那些檔案拿進來。

call off 取消

The host called off the game because of the rain.
主辦單位因雨取消了賽事。

fill up 加油

Do I need to fill it up before I return the car?
還車之前需要加滿油嗎？

bring up 養育

Kenny brought up two children by himself.
肯尼獨力扶養兩個小孩。

carry out 實行；實現

She finally carried out her dream to sail around the world.
她終於實現了「帆」遊世界的夢想。

figure out 理解

I can't figure the whole thing out. It's too weird.
這整件事太奇怪了，我無法理解。

find out 發現

He couldn't believe it when he found out the truth.
當他發現真相時，他無法置信。

bring up 提出

Sophie brought up a wonderful proposal yesterday.
蘇菲昨天提出了一個絕佳方案。

fill out 填寫

Please fill out the registration form.
請填寫這張登記表。

hand in 繳交

We need to hand in the paper tomorrow.

我們明天要交報告。

hand out 分發

Santa hands out gifts on Christmas.

聖誕節時,聖誕老人都會發禮物。

hang up 懸掛

He took off his coat and hung it up. 他脫下大衣,並且把它掛起來。

look over 檢查

You should look over your test paper before handing it in.

繳交考卷之前,應該檢查一遍。

look up 查閱

Sam looked up this topic in an encyclopedia.

山姆翻閱百科全書查過這個主題。

make up 編造

He made up the whole story.

整個故事都是他捏造出來的。

pick up 接

Shall I pick you up at eight?

我 8 點去接你好嗎?

point out 指出

Mr. Sanchez pointed out the key to efficient management.

桑切斯先生指出了有效管理的關鍵。

put away 收好

Put away your pens and books after finishing your homework.

做完功課,要把筆和書本收好。

put off 拖延

The manager put off the meeting until tomorrow.

經理將會議延至明天。

put on 穿

I'll put on the new dress and go to the party.

我要穿新洋裝,然後去參加舞會。

put out 撲滅

The fire fighter arrived in five minutes and put out the fire.

消防人員在五分鐘內抵達,並且撲滅了火勢。

set off 使爆炸

People aren't allowed to set off fireworks in many countries.

許多國家禁止人民施放煙火。

shut off 關掉

Shut off the gas and electricity before you leave the house.

外出之前,記得關閉瓦斯及電源。

take out 拿出去

Luisa, please have Johnny take out the garbage.

露薏莎,麻煩叫強尼把垃圾拿出去。

talk over 討論

Jason, I think we need to talk over the merger. 傑森，我認為我們應該要就合併案進行討論。

try on 試穿

Would you like to try on the high-heels?

你要不要試穿這雙高跟鞋？

tear down 拆除

The government decided to tear down the old bazaar building.

政府決定拆除老舊的商場大樓。

turn down 將（音量）調小

Will you turn down the radio? I'm doing my research.

我在做研究，你把收音機關小聲點好嗎？

turn up 將（音量）調大

Please turn up the TV. I want to listen to the news.

電視開大聲一點，我要聽新聞。

turn off 關掉

Lily turned off the computer and left for work.

莉莉關了電腦去上班。

turn down 拒絕

You shouldn't have turned down such a good offer. 你實在不該拒絕這麼好的工作機會。

turn on 打開

It's cold in here. I'll turn on the heat.

這裡好冷，我要打開暖氣。

think over 考慮

I'll think it over and let you know.

我會考慮看看，再告知你。

write down 寫下

Write down five titles of your favorite movies.

寫下你最愛的五部電影名稱。

throw away 丟棄

Don't throw away the plastic bottles. They're recyclable.

塑膠瓶可以回收，不要丟棄。

這些片語動詞因為是「**及物**」的，因此也可以使用**被動語態**。

The party was called off last night.

昨晚，派對被宣布取消了。

The green building issue was talked over at the international conference on the environment.

綠建築的議題在這次的國際環保會議中被提出討論。

Practice

請將左欄的句子與右欄相對應的「片語動詞」連接。

1. You should _____ the TV when you are on the phone.

2. Children should always _____ their toys after playing.

3. You had better _____ the shoes before you buy them.

4. You'd better _____ the timetable before you go to the station.

5. You should _____ that offer carefully before you accept or refuse it.

6. You need to _____ if you want to reach an agreement.

- put away
- try on
- think over
- turn off
- talk it over
- look up

2

請從框內選出正確的「片語動詞」，並以「代名詞」為受詞填空，完成對話。

write down

hang up

call off

pick up

bring in

make up

turn down

figure out

1. Ⓐ How does Helen go to the office?
   Ⓑ I ____pick her up____ on my way to the office.

2. Ⓐ I thought you're having a meeting now.
   Ⓑ The manager _____, so I have some free time.

3. Ⓐ The explanation is beyond my understanding.
   Ⓑ I can't _____, either.

4. Ⓐ It is starting to rain.
   Ⓑ The laundry is still outside. We have to _____ quickly.

5. Ⓐ Let me give you my phone number so that you can reach me.
   Ⓑ I'll get a pen and paper to _____.

6. Ⓐ Where are the keys?
   Ⓑ I _____ on the nail by the front door.

7. Ⓐ Do you think I should accept the invitation?
   Ⓑ I think it's a good chance to meet some local politicians. You shouldn't _____.

8. Ⓐ Do you believe the story on the front page?
   Ⓑ No, I don't. I think the reporter _____.

Unit 85

Phrasal Verbs: Two Words, Transitive, and Nonseparable (1)
片語動詞：兩個字、及物、不可分（1）

第二種是由「**動詞 + 介系詞**」搭配受詞組成，但屬「**不可分的**」片語動詞，也就是受詞只能放在**介系詞後面**，不能放在動詞和介系詞中間。

動詞 + 介系詞 + 受詞

---

call on 拜訪
We will call on an important customer next Monday.
我們下週一將拜訪一位重要客戶。

(be) made from
由……製成（原料本質改變）
Paper is made from wood.
紙張是木漿製的。

(be) made of
由……製成（原料本質不變）
The dress is made of silk.
這件洋裝是絲做的。

apply for 申請
We'll apply for a permission to hold the demonstration.
我們會提出示威遊行的申請。

arrive in 抵達
Mr. and Mrs. Harper arrived in London yesterday morning.
哈波夫婦於昨天早上抵達倫敦。

belong to 屬於
The diamond ring belongs to Ms. Sophia.
這只鑽戒為蘇菲雅小姐所有。

---

come across 偶遇
We came across a vagrant on our way to school.
我們上學途中遇到一個流浪漢。

depend on 倚靠；端賴
Whether we can win the trip to France depends on this test. 我們有沒有機會去法國玩，就看這次考試了。

get over 克服
She cannot get over her fear of heights.
她無法克服自己的懼高症。

keep off 遠離
The sign says, "Please keep off the newly seeded grass."
牌子上寫道：「請勿踐踏新種植的草皮。」

look after 照顧
Samuel looked after his grandfather for three years.
山謬照顧他的祖父三年了。

---

look for / search for 尋找
Tony is looking for his necktie.
湯尼在找他的領帶。

look into 調查
The detective will look into the murder case personally.
警探將親自調查這件謀殺案。

pull for 為……喝采
The crowd are pulling for the host team.
群眾為地主國加油。

run into / run across 偶遇
I ran into Mr. Jefferson at the post office this afternoon.
我今天下午在郵局遇到傑佛遜先生。

take after 像
He takes after his father. They are real artists.
他和他父親很像，都是十足的藝術家。

wait on 為……送餐
We'll wait on the president.
我們將負責為總統送餐點和飲料。

Practice

1

請從下面框內選出適當的「片語動詞」，搭配圖中的受詞填空，完成句子。

take after

come across

look after

apply for

wait on

keep off

a scholarship   Table 2   Puffy   the grass   a stray dog   her twin sister

1. Susan cannot come to the English club today, because she has to _____look after Puffy_____. He has been sick for two days.

2. Let's walk on the path and _____. There might be snakes in it.

3. I'm _____, Table 4, and Table 6 today.

4. Lucy _____. I can hardly tell them apart.

5. We _____ on our way to school. It was so cute and friendly, but our teacher said we couldn't keep it as our school dog.

6. I've _____. If everything goes well, I'll be able to study abroad next year.

2

請從框內選出正確的「片語動詞」填空，完成句子。

be made of

be made from

get over

pull for

1

I've been studying in Frankfurt for three years, but I still can't _____ my homesickness.

2

The fans came all the way from their own countries to _____ their teams.

3

Caramel pudding _____ eggs, sugar, and cream milk.

4

The columns _____ marble stones.

Unit 86

Phrasal Verbs: Two Words, Transitive, and Nonseparable (2)
片語動詞：兩個字、及物、不可分（2）

believe in 相信

Martin believes in the importance of giving his children stability and a regular schedule.

馬丁相信讓孩子們生活穩定、作息規律，是很重要的。

bump into 巧遇

I bumped into Andy's tutor this morning. 我今天早上遇到安迪的家教老師。

care about 在意

Amanda cares about feeding her family healthy food. 亞曼達很在意家人要吃健康的食物。

care for 想要（某物）

Would you care for some tea or coffee?

你想要喝點茶或咖啡嗎？

concentrate on 專心於

Sidney needs to concentrate on his career a little more and spend less time hanging out with his friends.

席尼得更專注於他的事業，少花點時間和朋友混在一起才行。

crash into / drive into 撞上

Ellen nearly crashed into her ex-boyfriend's car.

愛倫差點撞上她前男友的車子。

die of 死於

Lorraine thought she was going to die of embarrassment.

羅蘭覺得自己快糗死了。

dream about / dream of 夢見

Last night I dreamed about/of my dear departed grandmother.

昨晚我夢到已逝的親愛祖母。

dream of 夢想；考慮

Richard has been dreaming of taking a break from his high-stress job. 李察一直夢想能從他壓力很大的工作中喘口氣休息一下。

Richard needs a break, but he wouldn't dream of quitting his job. 李察需要休息一下，但他不會考慮辭職。

hear about 聽說

Have you heard about the cold front that is coming in tomorrow?

你有聽說明天有冷鋒面會來嗎？

hear from 收到（某人的）來信；接到（某人的）電話

Have you heard from your friend Herman since he got married?

你朋友賀曼結婚後，你還有聽過他的消息嗎？

hear of 聽說

Have you heard of a dark chocolate that is 99 percent or more pure cocoa?

你知道有純可可含量99% 或99% 以上的黑巧克力嗎？

laugh at 嘲笑

Are you laughing at me or with me? 你是在嘲笑我，還是在和我一起笑？

shout at 對……吼叫

Stop shouting at me.

別對著我大吼大叫。

suffer from 受苦

I'm not sleeping. I am suffering from a case of extreme boredom.

我沒有在睡覺，我正為一個超無聊的案子在受苦。

think about 想著

I think about you all the time. 我一直想著你。

think of 認為

What do you think of the strategic plan written by Sue?

你對蘇撰寫的策略計畫有什麼想法？

Practice

1

請用正確的「介系詞」填空，完成句子（包含 Units 85-86 所介紹的片語動詞）。

1. Dominique applied _____ a job as an assistant manager.

2. He believes _____ her innocence.

3. That minivan belongs _____ the Sanders family.

4. Adam doesn't care _____ eating healthy food.

5. It's not easy to start a business. You will have to get _____ many difficulties.

6. Call me immediately as soon as you arrive _____ Taipei.

7. We want to sell our house, but the deal depends _____ the buyer getting a bank loan.

8. There is no use getting angry and shouting _____ me.

9. Gladys suffers _____ an inflated opinion of her self-importance.

10. Uncle Gerald died _____ old age just before his 95th birthday.

11. Byron was thinking _____ starting his own company.

12. Have you ever heard _____ an allergy turning into an infection?

13. Ed is looking _____ an excuse to invite Mary to lunch.

14. Della dreams _____ marrying Wallace, but the two have never spoken to each other.

15. We are depending _____ you to get us to the ballpark before the first inning.

16. Tom ran _____ a deer on the road, but nobody was hurt except the deer.

17. Why is that guy laughing _____ you and pointing at your hair?

18. When Jerry was a university student, he dreamed _____ traveling around the world.

Part 11 Phrasal Verbs 片語動詞

Unit 87

Phrasal Verbs: Two Words and Intransitive
片語動詞：兩個字、不及物

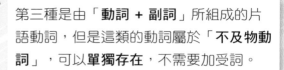

第三種是由「動詞 + 副詞」所組成的片語動詞，但是這類的動詞屬於「不及物動詞」，可以**單獨存在**，不需要加受詞。

動詞 + 副詞

My truck broke down on the highway.
我的卡車在高速公路上拋錨了。

---

break out 爆發
The Persian Gulf War broke out in 1990 and ended the next year. 波斯灣戰爭於 1990 年爆發，隔年結束。

fall down 跌倒
He tripped over a bucket and fell down.
他絆到一個水桶而跌倒。

go off 響起
The alarm went off in the morning.
鬧鐘早上響起。

speak up 大聲地說
Could you speak up, please? It's noisy here. I can't hear you. 你可以大聲一點嗎？這裡很吵，我聽不見。

start over 從頭來過
I spoiled it again. Let's start over.
我又搞砸了，再來一次吧。

come out 出來；出現
Who's there? Please come out.
誰在那裡？請快出來。

grow up 成長
Vincent grew up in the country and moved to the city when he was sixteen. 文森在鄉下長大，16 歲時才搬到城市裡。

dine out 外出吃晚餐
We're out of food. Let's dine out tonight.
家裡沒東西吃了，我們今晚去外面吃吧。

stay up 熬夜
Jane stayed up last night to finish the report.
珍昨晚熬夜趕完報告。

show up 出現
The magician showed up from behind the curtain and began the show. 魔術師從布幕後現身，表演便開始了。

take off 起飛
Our flight is going to take off in thirty minutes. 我們的班機將在三十分鐘後起飛。

dress up 裝扮
I need five more minutes to dress up. Why don't you sit down? 我還要五分鐘才能裝扮好，你先坐一下好嗎？

shut up 閉嘴
Please shut up, will you?
拜託你閉嘴好嗎？

throw up 嘔吐
I feel like throwing up. Can you bring me an airsickness bag? 我有點想吐，可以給我一個嘔吐袋嗎？

184

Practice

1

找出與劃線字同義的「片語動詞」，改寫句子。

start over

come out

dress up

stay up

break out

throw up

1. The wolf <u>showed himself</u> from behind the tree and blocked the path of Little Red Riding Hood.

   → *The wolf came out from behind the tree and blocked the path of Little Red Riding Hood.*

2. Gin is <u>burning the midnight oil</u> to watch *Emily in Paris*.

   → ....

3. I feel like <u>vomiting</u>. I'll go to the bathroom.

   → ....

4. The fire <u>started</u> in the middle of the night and spread very quickly.

   → ....
   ....

5. I've come up with an idea. Let's <u>do it again</u>.

   → ....

6. My sister is <u>putting on her clothes</u> for the masquerade.

   → ....

2

圖中發生了什麼事？請將各事件依正確的順序排列，並從下框內選出適當的「片語動詞」完成句子。

The smoke alarm ....

The police shouted, " .... of the building."

I .... while running out.

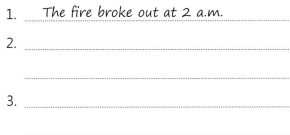

The fire .... at 2 a.m.

After I got out, I started to shake and then ....

The fire department ....

throw up	go off
break out	come out
fall down	show up

1. *The fire broke out at 2 a.m.*

2. ....
   ....

3. ....

4. ....
   ....

5. ....
   ....

6. ....

Phrasal Verbs: Three Words
片語動詞：三個字

第四種片語動詞由三個字組成，
一般來說是「**動詞 + 副詞 + 介系詞**」的組合，
通常**不可分**，而且要加**受詞**。

| 動詞 | + | 副詞 | + | 介系詞 | + | 受詞 |

I'm fed up with his temper.
我受夠了他的脾氣。

---

come up with 想出

He hasn't come up with a solution yet.

他還沒想出解決方案。

keep away from 遠離

We should keep away from the fire area.

我們應該遠離火災事故現場。

keep up with 跟上

You have to study extra hard to keep up with your classmates.

你要格外用功，才能跟得上同學。

take care of 照顧

Phyllis is taking care of her elderly parents.

菲莉絲正在照顧她年邁的雙親。

stand up for 捍衛

You must stand up for yourself.

你一定要站出來為自己說話。

look forward to 期待

We look forward to serving you again.

期待下次再為您服務。

move away from 搬離

They want to move away from the city and start a new life.

他們想要搬離都市，展開全新的生活。

put up with 忍受

I can't put up with the noise of the railway.

我受不了鐵路的噪音。

其中有些三個字的片語動詞，其實是由**兩個字**的「**不及物**」片語動詞衍生而來，為了接**受詞**，要加上一個**介系詞**，使之成為「**及物**」的片語動詞。

Elaine and George broke up last night.

↳ break up 作為「不及物」的片語動詞，可以單獨存在，不需要受詞。

Elaine broke up with George last night.

↳ 當句子需要一個受詞的時候，則使用 break up with。

伊蓮昨晚和喬治分手了。

catch up (with) 趕上

I missed two classes last week. It'll be difficult to catch up. 我上星期缺了兩堂課，進度很難趕上。

The other team has a very high score. It's not easy for us to catch up with them.

另外一隊的分數很高，我們很難追上。

move in (to) 住進（某處）

When are you moving in? 你什麼時候要搬進去？

We're planning to move in to our new apartment next week.

我們下星期要搬進新公寓去。

get through (with) 辦完

We have so much work to get through.

我們有好多工作要做。

We need to get through (with) the work by tomorrow.

我們得在明天以前把事情辦完。

come along (with) 一起來

We're going to Palm Beach next week. Do you want to come along?

我們下星期要去棕櫚灘，你要一起來嗎？

Jerry came along with Kevin to the party.

傑瑞和凱文一起來參加派對。

move out (of) 搬出（某處）

My roommate is moving out tomorrow.

我的室友明天就要搬走了。

My grandparents moved out of their old house and into a new apartment.

我的祖父母搬離他們的老家，住進一棟新的公寓。

come over (to) 順道來訪

Pan came over to my office and hand this to me.

潘順道來了我的辦公室，把這個東西交給我。

go on (with) 繼續下去

You can't go on like this. You need a job.

你不能一直這樣下去，你需要一份工作。

Grandpa took a sip of the tea and went on with the story.

爺爺小啜了一口茶，繼續講述這則故事。

I'm free this afternoon. Would you like to come over for some tea?

我今天下午沒事，你要不要過來喝杯茶？

hang on (to)
握住（某物）不放

Ken, hang on! We're coming for you.

肯，抓好啊，我們就來救你了。

Ken hung on to a branch until the rescue team arrived.

肯緊握住一根樹枝，直到救難大隊抵達現場。

set out (for)
出發（前往某處）

We'll set out at dawn.

我們預定清晨出發。

Jerry and Annie set out for Hokkaido yesterday.

傑瑞和安妮昨天出發前往北海道了。

get along (with) 相處

Jim and Lynn can't get along.

吉姆和琳恩處不來。

Jack couldn't get along with his colleagues, so he quit.

傑克和同事處不來，就辭職了。

drop in (on) 順道拜訪

Please do drop in someday.

哪天一定要來坐坐。

I dropped in on Grandma on my way to the office.

我去上班之前，先去了奶奶家一趟。

sign up (for) 登記

I want to join the cruise tour. When shall I sign up?

我想參加郵輪之旅，什麼時候應該報名？

He just signed up for the psychology experiment at Northern Michigan University.

他剛報名做北密西根大學的一項心理學實驗。

hang out (with)
（和某人）一起出去

We should hang out some time. 有空我們應該聚聚。

Janet usually hangs out with Lisa on the weekends.

週末時，珍娜通常和莉莎在一起。

drop out (of) 退出

I dropped out when I realized the offer wasn't fair.

當我得知他們給的酬勞很不公平時，我就退出了。

He dropped out of school to wait on tables for a while.

有一段時間，他輟學跑去當服務生。

run out (of)
被用完；用完某物

The tank had a hole, and the water ran out. 水槽破了一個洞，水都流光光了。

The car has run out of gas. I'm going to buy a gas can and some gas. 車子沒油了，我要去買一個汽油桶和一些汽油。

watch out (for) 小心

Watch out! There's a car coming. 小心！有車來了。

We should watch out for falling rocks around this area.

我們要小心這一區的落石。

Practice

1 請從框內選出適當的「片語動詞」填空，完成句子。

1. I am _____ her constant complaints.

2. _____ the stove. It's very hot.

3. Debby and I are both excited about the vacation.
   We're _____ our trip to New Zealand.

4. You don't have to submit to such humiliation. You should _____ yourself.

5. Our production line is not fast enough. Our production cannot _____ the market demand.

6. Have you _____ any solutions yet?

come up with

keep away from

look forward to

fed up with

stand up for

keep up with

2

請從圖中選出適當的受詞加入句子中，並加上適當的「介系詞」。

banana peel   tissue paper   buoy   the team

the bus tour

1. Watch out!
   → *Watch out for the banana peel!*

2. We will set off on Friday.
   → _____

my office

3. Why are you moving out?
   → _____

4. Have you signed up yet?
   → _____

Venice

5. The tissue paper is running out.
   → We _____

6. Hang on! I'll pull you up.
   → _____

7. Please come over to sign the contract.
   → _____
   _____

the apartment

8. I don't want you to drop out. We really need you.
   → _____
   _____

有些片語動詞，可能因為**主詞的不同**，而在用法上有所差異。這些狀況，通常在意義上也有差異，但差異不大。

blow out

使熄滅 → 及物、可分

Joe made a wish and blew out the candles.

喬許了個願之後，吹熄蠟燭。

吹離 → 不及物

A lot of dust blew out the first time I turned on the air conditioner this summer.

我今年夏天第一次開冷氣的時候，吹出來了一堆灰塵。

blow up

炸毀 → 及物、可分

They blew up a bridge to cut off the supply line of the enemy. 他們摧毀一座橋，以截斷敵方的補給路線。

爆炸 → 不及物

The missile blew up in the air.

導彈在空中爆炸。

calm down

使鎮靜 → 及物、可分

We tried to calm the old man down.

我們試圖使這位老人家冷靜下來。

鎮靜下來 → 不及物

The old man finally calmed down.

這位老人終於冷靜下來了。

cheer up

使高興起來 → 及物、可分

Jimmy cheered me up by telling a joke.

吉米說了一個笑話逗我開心。

高興起來 → 不及物

Cheer up! Nothing is impossible.
開心一點嘛！沒有什麼不可能的事。

wake up

喚醒 → 及物、可分

Sam, please wake me up tomorrow morning at 6:00. I've got an important meeting.

山姆，明天早上6點叫我起來，我有一個重要的會議要開。

醒來；起床 → 不及物

Hey, wake up! It's eight already!

嘿，快起床，已經8點了。

work out

解決 → 及物、可分

We're trying to work out the problem.

我們正設法解決這個問題。

有好結果 → 不及物

Our plan has worked out.

我們的計畫成功了。

Practice

1

請從框內選出正確的「片語動詞」填空，完成句子。

calm down

blow out

work out

wake up

cheer up

blow up

1. Susan was outraged by the policy. However, she _____ in a few minutes.

2. The explosive device _____ the train car.

3. The lunar rocket _____ 32 seconds after the launch.

4. Last night I had a nightmare and _____ with tears on my face.

5. _____! At least, the worst is past.

6. This good news will definitely _____ her _____. Let's go and tell her.

7. A strong wind _____ our campfire.

8. Lonny was disappointed after the contest, but he _____ when he heard that he had won the award.

9. The nurse gave that woman some medicine to _____ her _____.

10. _____, will you? You'll frighten the child by screaming like that.

11. The team is _____ a proposal to improve the product.

12. However, the method didn't _____. They'll have to find another solution.

13. Make three wishes before you _____ the candles _____.

14. A loud noise _____ me _____ in the middle of the night.

15. I _____ my husband and asked him to find out what was going on.

16. He lit a match, but it _____ instantly, so he lit up another one.

Unit **90**

Modal Verbs: General Use (1)
情態動詞的一般用法（I）

1 情態動詞又稱為情態助動詞，通常與一般動詞搭配，表示「**可能性、意願、能力、義務、確定性、許可**」等意義。

- can
- could
- may
- might

- will
- would
- shall
- should

- ought to
- must
- need
- dare

可能性 The bus might be late.
公車可能會遲到。

請求 Will you lower your voice?
請你小聲一點好嗎？

能力 Can your brother draw?
你弟弟會畫畫嗎？

義務 You must get up at 6 a.m.
你得在早上 6 點起床。

建議 You have an oil leak from your car engine. You should fix the leak.
你的車引擎漏油，應該要把漏洞修好。

請求許可 May I have some chicken nuggets?
我可以吃一些雞塊嗎？

2 情態動詞的格式固定，**沒有變化形**，即使主詞為第三人稱單數也**不加 s**，沒有不定詞、分詞變化和時態變化。

✗ He mights vacation in Prague.
✓ He might vacation in Prague.
他可能去布拉格度假。

3 因為情態動詞只有一種格式，如果要描述特定情況，要用**同義詞彙或片語代替**。

✗ The sun can to produce radiation storms.
✓ The sun is able to produce radiation storms.
太陽會產生輻射風暴。

✗ Carlos may to enter the building.
✓ Carlos is allowed to enter the building.
卡洛斯獲准進入大樓。

✗ Thomas must to go on a business trip last week.
✓ Thomas had to go on a business trip last week.
湯瑪士上星期得出差。

4 所有的情態動詞後面都接「**不加 to 的不定詞**」，唯一的例外是 ought 固定用 ought to。

Nina should exercise.
= Nina ought to exercise.
妮娜應該運動。

Ducks can dive.
鴨子會潛水。

Practice

1

請勾選正確的答案。

1. Ruby would like to ☐ **be able to play** ☐ **can play** tennis.

2. Betty ☐ **had to leave** ☐ **must leave** the office early yesterday.

3. Margaret ☐ **must** ☐ **can** work late today. She doesn't have a dinner date.

4. Nicolas ☐ **will** ☐ **wills** be in San Francisco this time next year.

5. You ☐ **ought to** ☐ **should to** ride on the bikeway.

6. You ☐ **oughtn't** ☐ **shouldn't** allow your children to play on the main road.

7. ☐ **Could** ☐ **Must** you step aside please?

8. I ☐ **must to** ☐ **have to** go home to feed my dog now.

9. Adam ☐ **can do** ☐ **cans do** 25 laps around the track.

2

請以括弧內提供的「情態動詞」改寫句子。

1. He drank ten bowls of miso soup. (could)

   → *He could drink ten bowls of miso soup.*

2. Jeffery explains everything. (will)

   → ....

3. Dad quits smoking and drinking. (must)

   → ....

4. Alison files the documents. (should)

   → ....

5. We get lost without a GPS system. (might)

   → ....

6. You take off your dirty shoes and socks. (ought to)

   → ....

7. Denise speaks five languages. (can)

   → ....

Unit 91

Modal Verbs: General Use (2)
情態動詞的一般用法（2）

1 肯定句中的情態動詞，應放在主詞和動詞之間。

| 主詞 | + | 情態動詞 | + | 一般動詞 |

My mom will clean the house.

我媽媽會打掃房子。

Little Johnny should call his grandfather.

小強尼應該打電話給他爺爺。

2 否定句的構成，是在情態動詞後面加 not。

| 主詞 | + | 情態動詞 | + | not | + | 一般動詞 |

I can't find my glasses.

我找不到我的眼鏡。

Penelope could not find her ballet slippers. 潘妮洛普找不到她的芭蕾舞鞋。

3 疑問句的構成，是在句首加上情態動詞。

| 情態動詞 | + | 主詞 | + | 一般動詞 |

肯定句 I may go for a walk.

我可以去散步。

疑問句 Mom, may I go for a walk?

媽，我可以去散步嗎？

4 不管是否定句或疑問句，情態動詞都不會和助動詞 do/does/did 連用。

✗ Sheila doesn't can come to the phone.

✓ Sheila can't come to the phone.

席拉無法過來接電話。

✗ Does Sheila can call me?

✓ Can Sheila call me?

席拉會打電話給我嗎？

YOU SHOULD KNOW!

肯定句	否定句	否定縮寫	疑問句
can	cannot	can't	Can I
could	could not	couldn't	Could I
should	should not	shouldn't	Should I
may	may not	-	May I
might	might not	mightn't*	Might I
will	will not	won't	Will I
shall	shall not	shan't*	Shall I
ought to	ought not to	↳ * 不常見 -	-
must	must not	mustn't	Must I
need	need not	needn't	Need I
dare	dare not	-	Dare I

5 情態動詞可以和 be 動詞連用。

| 情態動詞 | + | be | + | 現在分詞 |

The baby must be sleeping.

小嬰兒一定是在睡覺。

Edgar might be coming here tomorrow night. 艾德加明晚可能會來這裡。

6 情態動詞可以用於「情態動詞 + have + 過去分詞」的句型，表示「過去可能發生或沒有發生的事件」。

| 情態動詞 | + | have | + | 過去分詞 |

Joe hasn't arrived. He may have gotten stuck in traffic. ↳ 他可能遇上塞車，不過無法確定。

喬還沒到，他可能被塞在車陣裡了。

The service at this restaurant is so slow. They should have hired more kitchen staff. ↳ 他們沒有僱用足夠的廚師和助手。

這間餐廳的服務太慢了，他們當初該多請一些廚房人手的。

Practice

1

請勾選正確的答案。

1. We ☐ should go ☐ go should to the hot pot restaurant now.
2. ☐ Megan can run ☐ Can Megan run in the marathon?
3. Andrew really ☐ must go ☐ must be go now or he will miss the bus.
4. Carl ☐ may have left ☐ have may left home already.
5. Doug ☐ should not ☐ not should tell lies.
6. Oscar ☐ will not win ☐ will win not the game.
7. ☐ Do I shall ☐ Shall I make you a cup of tea?
8. You ☐ should not ☐ should don't have spicy food so frequently.
9. ☐ Could you have thrown ☐ Could have you thrown the memo away by accident?

2

請依圖示，從框內選出適當的動詞片語，搭配題目提供的主詞和「情態動詞」，以正確的形式填空，完成句子。

observe the lunar eclipse   play the accordion

ride his snowboard all day   have fallen off his horse

be feeding pigeons in the park

....
.... (Karl / can)

....
.... (Audrey / will)

....
.... (Elwood / may)

....
.... (Julio / can / ?)

....
....
.... (Jasper / must)

Unit 92

Ability: Can, Be Able To

表示「能力」：Can、Be Able To

• 表能力
• 否定形：
  cannot /
  can't

can

• 可取代 can，較
  正式，較不常用
• 可代替 can，
  用於過去式

be able to

1 can 可用來說明「**能力**」，否定形式為 cannot 或 can't。

I can do 200 sit-ups.
我能做兩百下仰臥起坐。

How many push-ups can you do?
你能做多少下伏地挺身？

Can you do any bench presses?
你會做臥舉嗎？

I can't do any running today because my knee hurts.
我膝蓋有傷，今天不能跑步。

3 由於 **can** 沒有不定詞、V-ing 和過去分詞等形態，因此遇到這些情況時，要以 be able to 等同義用語取代，來表示「**能力**」。

Marcy would like to be able to enroll her daughter at Bunny Bear Kindergarten.
↳ 不能說 Marcy would like to can enroll . . .
瑪西希望她女兒能進入小熊幼稚園就讀。

Marcy's daughter, Elizabeth, enjoys being able to play with blocks.
↳ 不能說 . . . enjoys canning to play . . .
瑪西的女兒伊莉莎白，很開心能夠玩積木。

Elizabeth has been able to play well with other children since she was three years old.
↳ 不能說 Elizabeth has could play . . .
伊莉莎白從三歲起，就能和其他小朋友一起玩得很開心。

2 is/are able to 可以取代 can，表示「**能力**」，但是較為正式，也比較不常用。

Are you able to handle your job stress?
= Can you handle your job stress?
你能夠排解自己的工作壓力嗎？

Practice

1

請用 can 或 be able to 填空，完成句子。

1. ＿＿＿＿＿＿＿＿ you meet me at the hotel?

2. Will I ＿＿＿＿＿＿＿＿ surf the Internet in my hotel room?

3. I would like to ＿＿＿＿＿＿＿＿ run in a marathon.

4. If Anna ＿＿＿＿＿＿＿＿ juggle flaming torches, she can have her own circus act.

5. I want to ＿＿＿＿＿＿＿＿ pilot a plane one day.

6. Will you ＿＿＿＿＿＿＿＿ to get there on time?

7. Neal ＿＿＿＿＿＿＿＿ sing well.

8. Anita must ＿＿＿＿＿＿＿＿ read people's minds.

2

請依圖示，從框內選出適當的動詞或動詞片語，搭配 can 或 can't 填空，完成句子。

skate

do bike tricks

swim

maintain her balance

paint with watercolors

Donny ＿＿＿＿＿＿＿＿＿＿＿＿＿＿＿＿＿＿＿＿＿.

Howard ＿＿＿＿＿＿＿＿＿＿＿＿＿＿＿＿＿＿＿.

Karla ＿＿＿＿＿＿＿＿＿＿＿＿＿＿＿＿＿＿＿.

Paul ＿＿＿＿＿＿＿＿＿＿＿＿＿＿＿＿＿＿＿＿.

Ian ＿＿＿＿＿＿＿＿＿＿＿＿＿＿＿＿＿＿＿＿＿.

Part 12 Modal Verbs (1) 情態動詞 (1)

Unit 93

Ability: Could, Be Able To
表示「能力」：Could、Be Able To

1 could 可以用來說明「**過去具備的能力**」，這種意義之下，可以視為 **can** 的過去式。否定形式為 could not 或 couldn't。

Mozart could read music at the age of 4.

莫札特四歲時就會看譜。

Beethoven could hear his symphonies in his head.

貝多芬能在腦海裡聽見自己創作的交響樂。

2 was/were able to 可以取代 **could**，表示「**過去具備的能力**」，或「**在某種條件下可能做到的事**」。

Bach was able to compose one cantata a week for years. 有好幾年的時間，巴哈能一星期作出一首聖樂。

3 could not 和 couldn't 常用來描述「**過去不具備的能力**」，或者「**在某種條件下所不具備的能力**」。

My uncle couldn't drive, but he owned a car.

以前，我叔叔不會開車，卻擁有一輛汽車。

My uncle could not even see a car on the street in front of his house without wearing his glasses. 叔叔要是沒戴眼鏡，連住家前面馬路上的車子都看不到。

4 上述 2 的情況，若「**該行為較為困難**」，也常用 managed to 或 succeeded in，而不用 **was/were able to**。

The coach told me to stay at home, but I managed to hobble over to the field and watch the game.

教練叫我待在家裡，但是我跛著腳走到球場去看比賽。

Despite the fact that the team lost two crucial games during the regular season, they succeeded in getting into the playoffs.

雖然球隊在賽季輸了兩場重要的比賽，他們還是成功擠進了季後賽。

5 威官動詞和表達「思想」的動詞經常與 could 連用，說明「**過去的情況**」。

I could smell the muffins baking.

我聞到烤瑪芬的味道。

I could hear the bacon sizzling. 我能聽到煎培根滋滋作響的聲音。

I could feel Nancy pull my arm as we walked past the restaurant. 我們路過餐廳時，我能感覺到南西拉了一下我的手。

- see
- smell
- taste
- feel
- understand
- remember

6 「could have + 過去分詞」的句型用來說明某人「**在過去具備做某事的能力，但卻沒有去做**」。

Sam could have played professional baseball, but he preferred a career in business. 山姆本來可以去打職業棒球，不過他比較喜歡做生意。

The contender could have beaten the champion, but he took a nasty fall and never recovered.

那名挑戰者本來可以擊敗拳王的，不過後來一個擊倒，他就出局了。

198

Practice

1

請從框內選出適當的用語填空，完成句子。

could

could have

was able to

were able to

being able to

1. I _____ hear someone speaking German.

2. Even though the train was delayed, I _____ arrive on time.

3. The company _____ gone bankrupt, but it was saved by the government.

4. The boat _____ capsized, but it managed to stay afloat.

5. I love _____ backpack in New Zealand.

6. I _____ understand why he had turned down so many good offers at that time.

7. When I embraced my wife, I _____ feel her shivering from the cold weather.

2

請用括弧內提供的詞語改寫句子。

1. I saw the sunrise over the ocean from my hotel window. (could)

   → _____

   _____

2. I didn't read English newspapers before I was twelve. (couldn't)

   → _____

   _____

3. I didn't get out of the bed by myself. My mom helped me. (be able to)

   → _____

   _____

4. I walked to the bathroom while holding the IV bottle above my head. (manage to)

   → _____

   _____

5. I remember those crazy summers when we were hanging out together at the beach all the time. (could)

   → _____

   _____

Unit 94

Permission: Can, Could, May
表示「許可」：Can、Could、May

1 can、could 和 may 都可用於「**請求許可**」。

can 是簡便的非正式用法，could 較 can 有禮貌，may 又比 can 和 could 更正式有禮。

正式與禮貌性	高		低
	may	could	can

Can I use your bathroom?
我可以用你的廁所嗎？
Could I take an hour off?
我可以請假一小時嗎？
May I leave early today?
請問我今天可以早點離開嗎？

> might 也可以用來「**請求許可**」，但 might 是非常正式的用法，非常少用。
>
> Might I be excused from the ceremony?
> 可以容許我離開典禮嗎？

2 若要表示「**許可**」對方做某事，只能用 can 或 may，不能用 **could** 或 **might**。

You can use this pass anywhere in the building.
你可以持這張許可證在大樓裡通行無阻。
You may call me at home if you like.
如果你願意，可以打電話到家裡給我。

3 法律或規定上表明「**不許可**」的事，要用 can/cannot 或 be (not) allowed to。

You can't stay in the room after 11 a.m.
上午 11 點之後，您就不能再待在房間。
You are not allowed to leave your suitcases unattended at any time.
不論什麼時候，你都不能把行李放在這裡沒人看管。

4 如果是「**過去事件**」，則使用 could 和 was/were allowed to 在意義上有所差異。

1 could 用於「**過去一般事件**」的許可；
2 was/were allowed to 用於「**過去特殊事件**」下的許可。

Before they put up the fence, we could take a shortcut across their property.
在他們築起圍籬之前，我們還可以抄小路穿過他們的土地。
This morning we were allowed to look for our lost baseball in Mr. Hudson's backyard.
今天早上，我們獲准到哈德森先生家的後院，去找我們不見的棒球。

Police officer: Could I please see your ID?
Ted: Here it is, sir. ↳ 用疑問句「請求許可」則可用 could。
警員：我可以看一下你的身分證嗎？
泰德：可以。

Customs officer: May/Might I see your travel documents?
Betty: Here they are, sir. ↳ 用疑問句「請求許可」，可用 may 也可用 might。
海關官員：請出示您的旅遊文件好嗎？
貝蒂：好的。

Practice

1

請勾選正確的答案。

1. □ Can □ Be allowed to I join your club?

2. When I was in senior high school, I □ was allowed to □ may stay out late on the weekends.

3. □ May □ Can I offer you my arm for this stroll in the park?

4. She □ can □ was allowed to go camping when she was 14.

5. You □ can't □ couldn't hang your clothes outside on the clothes line because there isn't any room left.

6. You □ may □ might eat one dessert at the end of your dinner.

2

請從框內選出適當的用語填空，完成對話。

can
can't
could
couldn't
may
may not
might
are (not) allowed
was (not) able

1. Ⓐ Can I borrow some of these periodicals from the library?

   Ⓑ No, you _____ take these periodicals out of the library. You _____ read them in the library.

2. Ⓐ Can I write notes in the library books?

   Ⓑ No, you _____. You must not deface library property.

3. Ⓐ Could I please have another cup of chocolate milk?

   Ⓑ No, you _____. We have to save some for Peggy.

4. Ⓐ May I take your plate, sir?

   Ⓑ Yes, you _____. I'm finished.

5. Ⓐ Could I use your cell phone to call my mom?

   Ⓑ Of course you _____. Here you are.

6. Ⓐ Might I announce his resignation at the press conference?

   Ⓑ No, you _____. The terms of his dismissal remain to be worked out.

7. Ⓐ Can I carry this suitcase on board?

   Ⓑ No, you _____. This one is too big to put in the overhead compartment. You _____ to carry a smaller one.

8. Ⓐ Did you go to the book fair yesterday?

   Ⓑ No, I didn't. I _____ to attend the fair because it was only open to publishers on the first day.

Obligation and Necessity: Must, Have To
表示「義務與必要」：Must、Have To

have to 並不是情態動詞，它只是與 **must** 的意義相同。

1 must 與 have to 都用來說明「**個人的義務和必須做的事**」。

義務 I must call my mom before 10 p.m. because I said I would.
↳ 說話者說明自己的義務。

我晚上 10 點以前得打電話給我媽，因為我跟她說了我會打給她。

必要 I have to call before 10 p.m. because the pizza shop closes then.
↳ 特定事實所形成之必要性。

我得在晚上 10 點以前打電話，因為披薩店 10 點就會打烊了。

必要 You must put down money before you can make an offer.
↳ 地產專員對買家說明購屋的程序。

你在正式出價前，必須先支付訂金。

必要 We have to put down money before we can make an offer.
↳ 說明購屋的程序。

我們在正式出價前，必須先支付訂金。

2 must 只能用來說明「**現在或未來的義務**」，它本身沒有過去式。

如果要表達「**過去的義務或必要**」，則要用 had to。

現在的義務 To get there on time, I must leave right now.

我現在就得出發，才能準時到達。

未來的義務 I must leave in about twenty minutes or I will be late.

我 20 分鐘內得出發，不然會遲到。

過去的義務 Last night I felt sick and had to leave the party before it was over.

昨晚我覺得不舒服，不得不在派對結束前就離開。

3 由於 must 沒有不定詞、V-ing 和分詞形式，因此在要使用這類動詞形式時，要以**其他同義用語**取代，例如 have to。

✗ Did you must leave the party and go to the after-hours club?

✓ Did you have to leave the party and go to the after-hours club?

你一定要提早離開派對趕去通宵俱樂部嗎？

✗ She hates musting go home early.

✓ She hates having to go home early.

她討厭得早點回家。

✗ She hates musting go home early.

✓ She hates having to go home early.

她討厭得早點回家。

✗ She musted check out every club in town.

✓ She had to check out every club in town.

她得到城裡的每一間俱樂部都看看。

4 have to 不是情態動詞，是一般動詞，因此它的**疑問句**和**否定句**是用 do/does/did 來構成。

When do you have to finish the report?

你得在哪一天完成報告？

Roger doesn't have to work so hard on that report.

羅傑不需要太努力做那份報告。

Did you have to give your boss a draft of the report yesterday?

昨天你得先交一份報告的初稿給老闆嗎？

Practice

1

請用 must 或 have to 的正確形式填空，完成句子。

1. You _____ use a pencil when filling in the answers on a machine-readable answer sheet.

2. You _____ deliver the samples now as per the contract.

3. Did you _____ stay in the office because of your meeting with your clients?

4. She's mad at _____ do the same thing every day.

5. I _____ read two hundred pages last night for today's class discussion.

6. _____ I drink this cough syrup?

7. Do I _____ wash the dishes right now?

2

請從框內選出適當的動詞，搭配 must 填空，完成對話。

have

take

show

Two friends, Charlotte and Jane, are visiting the consulate to prepare for their trip. Charlotte talks to an immigration officer.

Officer: You ❶ _____ a visa to enter the country.

Charlotte: I'm just staying for five days.

Officer: Even a tourist needs a visa. You ❷ _____ your passport and go to window 12.

Charlotte: What else do I need to do?

Officer: You ❸ _____ proof that you have had the appropriate vaccinations and paid the visa application fee.

3

請從框內選出適當的動詞，搭配 have to 填空，完成對話。

apply

take

process

Charlotte explains to Jane what she just learned from the visa officer.

Jane: What did the immigration officer say?

Charlotte: He said we ❶ _____ for tourist visas.

Jane: How does that work?

Charlotte: He said we ❷ _____ our documents to window 12.

Jane: Can we do that now?

Charlotte: He said we ❸ _____ our paperwork at least ten days before the trip.

Part 13　Modal Verbs (1) 情態動詞 (1)

Unit 96

Obligation and Necessity: Have To, Have Got To

表示「義務與必要」：Have To、Have Got To

1　have to 和 have got to 都可以用來說明「義務或必要」，其中 have got to 是非正式英式英語的用法。

非正式美式　Do you have to call tonight?

你今晚得打電話嗎？

非正式英式　Have you got to call tonight?

你今晚得打電話嗎？

非正式美式　I have to talk to Tommy now.

我現在得和湯米談一談。

非正式英式　I have got to talk to Tommy now.

我現在得和湯米談一談。

2　have got to 只能用於「單一事件」。如果這種義務或必要是「重複在發生的事件」，就要用 have to，不能用 **have got to**。

這種情況下經常搭配頻率副詞如 always 或 often 來強調次數。

Does Cathy often have to rush to get to her office?

凱西經常得趕著去上班嗎？

Cathy always has to hurry to get to work on time.

凱西總是得趕著準時上班。

英式　Has Cathy got to rush to get to her office today?

凱西今天要趕到辦公室嗎？

英式　Cathy has got to hurry to get to work on time today.

凱西今天得趕著準時上班。

3　have got to 只用於**現在式**，沒有過去式。如果要說明「**過去的義務或事件**」，要用 had to，不能用 had got to。

✗ Calvin had got to work in his office last Saturday afternoon.

✓ Calvin had to work in his office last Saturday afternoon.

上個星期六下午，凱文得進辦公室上班。

✗ Jack had got to pay a $100 ticket for parking illegally.

✓ Jack had to pay a $100 ticket for parking illegally.

傑克必須繳交一百元違規停車的罰款。

4　have to 有未來式 will have to，用來表示「**未來的義務或必要**」。

muffins

I will have to make twenty muffins for the party on Saturday.

我得為星期六的派對做二十個瑪芬。

You will have to find a job after you graduate. 你畢業之後，得找一份工作。

He will have to drive fifty minutes to his girlfriend's house.

他得開五十分鐘的車，才能到女友的住處。

Practice

1

請從框內選出適當的動詞，搭配 have got to 填空，完成對話。

hurry

eat

give

Charlotte and Jane rush to the immigration window.

Charlotte:　The office closes soon. We ❶.. .

Jane:　　　 I'm hungry. I ❷... something.
　　　　　　We missed lunch.

Charlotte:　We don't have time. We ❸... our
　　　　　　documents to the clerk at window 12 now.

Jane:　　　 OK. Let's go. We can eat later.

2

請勾選正確的答案。

1. You always ☐ have to ☐ have got to sort your recyclable garbage.

2. I ☐ had to ☐ have got to pack these gift boxes right now. The courier will be here in any minute.

3. Sonia ☐ had to ☐ had got to cook dinner for her parents, so she didn't join us for the dinner party.

4. ☐ Do you always have to ☐ Have you always got to say such negative things about my parents?

5. I ☐ had to ☐ will have to fly to New York for a seminar on international finance next month.

6. ☐ Does Nancy have to ☐ Has Nancy often got to wash her dog in the bathroom instead of outside in the backyard?

7. I ☐ will have to ☐ have got to see the manager now. It's an emergency.

8. ☐ Would you have to ☐ Will you have to edit her book after she finishes writing it?

9. I ☐ had got to ☐ had to call a locksmith because I locked myself out when I took the garbage out.

Part 12 Modal Verbs (1) 情態動詞 (1)

Unit 97

Obligation and Choices: Mustn't, Don't Have To, Haven't Got To, Don't Need To, Needn't, Didn't Need To

表示「**義務與選擇**」：**Mustn't、Don't Have To、Haven't Got To、Don't Need To、Needn't、Didn't Need To**

1 mustn't 和 don't have to 的意義不同，差別在於一是**義務**、一是**選擇**。
mustn't 表示「**有義務不做某事**」；
don't have to 表示「**選擇不做某事**」。

You mustn't touch the freshly painted walls. 你不可以去碰剛漆好的牆壁。

You don't have to help me paint the house if you don't want to.
如果你不想，你可以不必幫我油漆房子。

2 除了 don't have to，haven't got to、don't need to 和 needn't 都是表示「**可以選擇不做某事**」。
haven't got to 是**英式非正式用語**。

You don't need to be here next weekend.
你下週末不用過來。
You don't have to come with us.
你不必和我們一起來。
You needn't skip your meeting to join us.
你不必為了陪我們而不去參加會議。

3 「**允許別人可以不用做某事**」時，用 needn't 是最禮貌的說法，不過目前已經少有人用 needn't，也被視為過時的說法。

You needn't trouble yourself over this trifle. 你不必為這件芝麻小事操心。

4 didn't need to 也是表示「**沒有必要做某事**」，但這種用法並沒有明確指出「事情是否已經做了」，除非句子裡有另外說明。

I didn't need to clean the guest room.
↳ 沒有必要打掃，但卻沒說到底做了沒有。
我那時其實不必打掃客房的。

I didn't need to change the towels and sheets, but I did.
↳ 沒必要換，但後面的句子說明了「事情已經做了」。
我那時沒必要換毛巾和床單，可是我換了。

如果 didn't need to 的句子裡，沒有明確指出事情到底做了沒，那麼「**沒有做**」的可能性是比較高的。

I didn't need to cook extra food because we weren't sure if my husband's parents were coming for dinner.
↳ 我們不確定他們會不會來，所以我沒多準備食物。
我應該不用多準備食物，因為那時我們不確定我公婆會不會來吃晚餐。

5 美式英語 didn't need to 可以與 **needn't have done something** 意思一樣，表示某人已經做了一件沒必要做的事；口語中，可以藉由加重 need 的音調來表示這個意思。

You didn't need to prepare all that extra food. I said my parents would call if they were coming to dinner.
你實在沒有必要多準備那些食物，我已經說過如果我爸媽要來，他們會先打電話。

6 但如果用「needn't have + 過去分詞」，則表示「**雖然某件事沒必要，但卻已經做了**」，這個用語稍微過時，但仍有人在用。

I needn't have avoided the office since my co-workers did not have any work for me.
↳ 我那時沒必要刻意遠離辦公室，但是我卻做了。
我根本沒必要刻意躲開辦公室，同事又不會派給我任務。

Practice

1

請勾選正確的答案。

1. You ☐ **mustn't** ☐ **don't have to** cross the yellow line on the train platform.

2. I ☐ **mustn't** ☐ **don't have to** pick up my daughter after her archery class.

3. The nurse says they ☐ **mustn't** ☐ **haven't** got any physical therapy appointments this afternoon.

4. You ☐ **mustn't** ☐ **needn't** work this weekend if your project is already done.

5. Janet ☐ **mustn't** ☐ **don't have to** drink any alcohol because of her medication.

6. The committee finished selecting textbooks so they ☐ **mustn't** ☐ **didn't have to** schedule another meeting.

7. The sign says, "No Littering," so we ☐ **have to** ☐ **don't have to** throw our trash in the garbage can.

8. Today is Monday. The sign says, "Visitors Free on Mondays," so we ☐ **have to** ☐ **don't have to** pay.

9. I'm the teacher, and if I say you ☐ **mustn't** ☐ **don't have to** turn in the assignment this week, then you can give it to me next week.

10. The boss says you ☐ **must** ☐ **have to** stop surfing the internet and get to work.

11. The boss's wife says you ☐ **mustn't** ☐ **don't have to** listen to the boss.

2

請以「didn't need to」或「needn't have + 過去分詞」的句型填空，完成句子。

1. I _____ (bring) my passport with me when I went to exchange some money so I kept it locked up.

2. Rudy _____ (go back) to get his keys because his mom was at home the whole time.

3. We _____ (buy) extra water and food. The typhoon turned and went far to the south of us.

4. You _____ (call) the landlady about the power. She left a message on my cell phone that said the whole block had lost electricity.

5. You _____ (get up) so early. Today is a holiday. Go back to bed.

6. Last night Sheila _____ (work) late on her part of the project. She's almost done with it and will finish it in the morning.

Unit **98**

Obligation and Advice:
Should, Ought To, Shall

表示「**義務與建議**」：
Should、Ought To、Shall

1 should 和 ought to 都用來「**說明義務**」或「**提供意見**」。但 should 後面接「**不加 to 的不定詞**」，ought 後面則一定要加 to。

Fred should pick up the crayons on the carpet.
= Fred ought to pick up the crayons on the carpet.

佛瑞德應該把地毯上的蠟筆撿起來。

✗ You should to do your homework now.

✓ You should do your homework now.

你現在應該做家庭作業了。

✗ You ought do your homework now.

✓ You ought to do your homework now.

你現在應該做家庭作業了。

You should stop jumping on the couch.

你不應該在沙發上跳來跳去。

Mom says you ought to stop jumping on the couch now or you'll get into trouble.

媽媽說你應該馬上停下來在沙發上跳來跳去，不然你就要倒大楣了。

2 「should have + 過去分詞」用來表示「**過去該做而未做的事**」。這種情況下也可用「ought to have + 過去分詞」。

I should have called her. Now she's even madder at me. ↳ 我沒打電話，這是個錯誤。

我應該打電話給她的，現在她氣我氣得更厲害了。

I ought to have gone to see her. Now she won't even speak to me.
↳ 我沒去找她，這實在是個天大的錯誤。

我應該去找她的，現在她甚至連話都不跟我說了。

3 「shouldn't have + 過去分詞」則用來表示「**過去不該做卻做了的事**」。

You shouldn't have hit your sister on the head. She has been crying for twenty minutes because of you.
↳ 你不該打，但你打了。

你不該打妹妹的頭，她被你一打已經哭了二十分鐘了。

You shouldn't have embellished your résumé. Now your application has been rejected.
↳ 你不該過度美化，但你美化了。

你不該過度美化你的履歷的，現在你的應徵被駁回了。

4 shall 通常只搭配**第一人稱代名詞**來「**徵求對方的建議**」，一般對話比較少用。

What shall I do? 我該怎麼做？

Shall we go? 我們要去嗎？

Practice

1 請依括弧提示，用 should、shall 或 ought to 回應問句，來給予建議、說明義務或詢問意見。

1. Do you think it is a good idea for me to go to the auction? (should)

   → *I think you should go to the auction.*

2. Do you think it is a good idea for me to bid on the small statue? (ought to)

   → ....

3. Do you think it is a good idea for me to offer $2,000 for the statue? (should)

   → ....

4. Do you think it is a good idea for me to use an online auction company? (ought to)

   → ....

5. You can give the statue to your mother. (shall / ?)

   → ....

2 請用 should have 或 shouldn't have 搭配過去分詞的句型，回應句子。

1. I didn't bring in the laundry before it started to rain. Now it's all wet.

   → *You should have brought in the laundry before it started to rain.*

2. I didn't simmer the sauce for five more minutes. Now it doesn't taste right.

   → ....

   ....

3. Angus poured too much soy sauce on the fried noodles. Now they are too salty.

   → ....

   ....

4. I've thrown away the receipt. Now I want to return the electric steamer.

   → ....

   ....

3 請將括弧內的動詞以「ought to have + 過去分詞」的句型填空，完成句子。

1. I .... (tell) the truth. Now the wrong man has been punished by mistake.

2. You .... (know) that she was depressed. Now she has left home and we don't know where to find her.

Part 13 Modal Verbs (1) 情態動詞 (1)

Unit 99

Obligation and Advice: Had Better, Be Supposed To
表示「義務與建議」：Had Better、Be Supposed To

1 「had better + 不加 to 的不定詞」這個句型，常用來表達「**強烈的建議**」，口氣比 should 或 ought to 還重。had better 經常縮寫為'd better。

Connie <u>had better</u> tell her mother she got divorced.
康妮最好跟她媽媽說她已經離婚了。

You <u>had better</u> be careful what you tell the boss about me. 你跟老闆談到我的時候，說話最好小心一點。

You'<u>d better</u> put your wet umbrella in a plastic bag before you go into the store.
你最好把濕答答的雨傘放進塑膠套裡，再進到店裡。

2 had better 不是**過去式**的用法，它說明的是「**現在或未來的情況**」。沒有 have better 這種用法。

I hear your phone ringing. You had better answer it.
我聽到你的電話在響，你應該去接電話。

Tax time is almost over. You had better finish your tax return soon.
報稅時間快要截止了，你最好趕緊完成報稅。

3 had better 的否定形式為 had better not，表示「**強烈建議不要做某事**」。

You had better not borrow Mom's scooter. 你最好別跟媽媽借摩托車。
You had better not arrive late.
你最好別遲到。

4 「**預期他人應該要做某事**」時，常用 be supposed to 這個句型。小至每個月理髮，大如當兵等重要事項，都可以用這個說法，是說明「**義務**」很基本的用語。

According to the terms of the contract, our company is supposed to provide engineering support for two years.
根據合約內容，我們公司應該要提供兩年的工程支援。

Mark is supposed to pick you up from work today.
馬克今天應該要去接你下班。

5 說明「**限制或禁止做某事**」時，可用 be not supposed to。

You're not supposed to be in your sister's room. 你不應該進你姐姐房間。
We're not supposed to go out without telling Mom. 我們不應該沒告訴媽媽就出門。

6 如果使用 was/were supposed to，則表示「**該發生卻沒有發生的事**」。

The vendor was supposed to deliver the prototype today, but it's not finished.
賣家今天原本要把樣本送來給我，但是到現在還沒完成。

We were supposed to change planes in Tokyo, but our flight has been rerouted because of bad weather, and now we are in Seoul. 我們本來應該在東京轉機，可是班機因為天候不佳改變航線，結果現在我們來到了首爾。

7 be supposed to 也可以用來表達「**對某件事的看法**」。

It's supposed to be a good art exhibit. My friend at work said so.
這應該會是不錯的藝術展，我在工作上認識的朋友說的。

Practice

1

請勾選正確的答案。

1. You □ **had better** □ **have better** not open the lid. The pot is extremely hot now.

2. I □ **hadn't better** □ **had better not** wake him. He worked late last night.

3. You'd better □ **leave** □ **to leave** now, or I'll call the police.

4. □ **Are you supposed to** □ **Had you better** work on weekends?

5. We □ **are supposed not to** □ **are not supposed to** spend too much time on social media.

6. The soup □ **wasn't supposed to** □ **had better not** taste sweet. Did she add any sugar to it?

7. It □ **is supposed to** □ **was supposed to** be a good hot spring hotel, but the owners haven't maintained it very well.

2

請依括弧提示，用 had better 或 be supposed to 回答問句，來給予建議或說明義務。

1. Do you think I should clean the house before the guests arrive? (had better)

   → *I think you had better clean the house before the guests arrive.*

2. Should I take a number and wait for my turn? (be supposed to)

   → ....

3. Should I invite my motorcycle club to the party? (had better not)

   → ....

4. Should I cut in the line? (be not supposed to)

   → ....

5. Do you think I should vacuum the rug? (had better)

   → ....

6. Should I fill out my deposit ticket while I am waiting? (be supposed to)

   → ....

7. Should I let the dog into the house? (had better not)

   → ....

8. Should I just hand the passbook and the cash to the clerk? (be supposed to)

   → ....

Part 13 Modal Verbs (2) 情態動詞 (2)

Unit 100

Possibility: May, Might, Could
表示「可能性」：May、Might、Could

1 may、might 和 could 都是用來說明「**現在與未來可能發生的事**」，may 的可能性高於 might，而 could 的可能性最低。

可能性	高		低
	may	**might**	**could**

Roger may get us tickets.
↳ 羅傑去買票，有這個可能性。
羅傑可能會幫我們買票。

Jane might come with us.
↳ 珍或許會和我們一起去。
珍可能會跟我們一起去。

Roger could have one last extra ticket for your sister.
↳ 雖然不太可能，不過羅傑或許有多出一張票。
羅傑說不定會多出一張票可以給你妹妹。

2 may 的**否定形式**是 may not，沒有縮寫；might 的**否定形式**為 might not，縮寫是 mightn't，不過很少用；而 **could** 的**否定形式**無法用來表達「可能性」。

There may not be any seats left.
↳ 很可能已經沒有空餘的位子了。
座位可能都沒有剩了。

There might not be any parking spaces in the lot.
↳ 很可能已經沒有空的車位了。
停車場或許沒有任何車位了。

✗ There could not be a place to sit in the balcony.

✓ There could be a place to sit in the balcony.
↳ 只能使用 could 的肯定形式來表達「可能性」
露台或許會有位子可以坐。

3 說明可能性時，也可以使用**現在進行式**，表示「現在可能正在發生的事」。

may/might/could	+	be	+	V-ing

Bobby may be looking for a parking space right now.
巴比現在可能正在找停車位。

William might be circling the block and looking for a place to park his car as we speak. 在我們說話的同時，威廉或許正繞著街道在尋找停車位。

Ron could be hunting for a place to park his car by the university.
榮恩此刻說不定正在大學旁邊找停車位。

4 如果要說明「**過去可能發生的事**」，則要用：

may/might/could	+	have	+	過去分詞

Victoria may have bent the rules a little bit. 薇多莉亞可能已經有點違反了規定。
Patti might have driven her car through the garden.
派蒂或許已經開車穿過花園了。
Wendy could have chipped your aunt's teapot.
溫蒂可能把你阿姨的茶壺敲破了一個缺口。

5 但是某件事如果是「**過去可能發生，實際上卻沒發生的事**」，則會使用：

could/might	+	have	+	過去分詞

may 不會用在這種用法裡。

That bee might have stung you but I whacked it.
那隻蜜蜂本來可能會螫你，不過我已經把牠揮走了。

Your new scarf could have shrunk if you had used hot water to wash it.
如果你當時用熱水清洗，你的新圍巾可能已經縮水了。

Practice

1 請用括弧裡提示的「情態動詞」改寫句子。

1. It is possible that Bonnie will go out with us tomorrow night. (may)

   → *Bonnie may go out with us tomorrow night.*

2. Perhaps the plane will be delayed because of the fog. (might)

   → ....

3. It is possible that the movie star has arrived by now. (could)

   → ....

4. The police think perhaps Carl has stolen a Ming dynasty vase. (may)

   → ....

   ....

5. It is possible that the chocolate-flavored pastry has sold out. (might)

   → ....

   ....

6. It is possible you have sprained your ankle. (could)

   → ....

2 請依圖示，用括弧內提供的詞語，搭配 could have 或 may have 填空，
完成句子。

Bob .... (get up) in time, but he smashed the alarm and went on sleeping.

He .... (present) the report well at the meeting, but he stayed up late last night writing the report and didn't sleep well.

He .... (spend) too much time driving to our party, because he isn't a good driver.

Part 13 Modal Verbs (2) 情態動詞(2)

Unit 101

Possibility: Can, Should, Ought To
表示「可能性」：
Can、Should、Ought To

1 can 用來說明「理論上的可能性」，在此用法下，can 的意義和 **sometimes** 相似。

Any one of you can win the race.
↳ 你們當中的每一個人都可能是勝利者。
你們任何一個人都有可能贏得比賽。
The habit of sitting for too long can be dangerous. 久坐的習慣可能傷害身體。
↳ 久坐的習慣有時候就是有害的。

2 can 不能說明「現在或未來可能發生的事」，這種情況要用 may、might 或 could。

✕ The winner can be announced tonight.
✓ The winner may be announced tonight.
今晚可能就會宣布優勝者。
✕ The water is deep. You can drown.
✓ The water is deep. You could drown.
水很深，你可能會溺水。

3 may 也可用來說明「理論上的可能性」，此時，和 can 有程度上的差異。

You may win. 你可能會贏。 ↳ 說不定你會贏。
You can win. 你可能會贏。 ↳ 有時候你會贏。

4 can 不能說明「過去可能發生的事」，這種情況要用「could + have + 過去分詞」。

We could have lost the game, but we pulled through in the last five minutes.
我們本來可能會輸掉比賽的，但是我們撐過了最後五分鐘。

5 should 和 ought to 可以用來說明「現在或未來可能發生的事」。

I'd better get ready to leave. Jimmy should be picking me up soon.
↳ 吉米可能很快就會抵達。
我最好趕緊準備離開，吉米應該很快會過來接我。
My cousin Jessica ought to be graduating soon. I need to call and congratulate her.
↳ 潔西卡可能不久後就要畢業了。
我表妹潔西卡應該就快畢業了，我得打個電話恭喜她。

6 「should + have + 過去分詞」和「ought to + have + 過去分詞」常用來說明「預期可能會發生，但不確定是否已經發生的事」。

Bruce should have received word from the school about his son's registration.
↳ 學校應該已經通知布魯斯了，不過還不確定。
布魯斯應該已經收到兒子學校的註冊通知才對。
Mary ought to have filed the Power of Attorney form by now.
↳ 她可能已經提出申請，不過還不確定。
瑪麗現在應該已經提出授權書的申請了。

7 「should + have + 過去分詞」和「ought to + have + 過去分詞」也可以說明「預期可能會發生，實際上卻沒有發生的事」。

We should have gone home an hour ago, but we wanted to stay for dessert.
我們一個小時前就應該回家了，但是我們想留下來吃甜點。
You ought to have read the instructions before trying to assemble the gas grill.
你應該在組合瓦斯烤架之前先看說明書的。

Practice

1

請從框內選出適當的動詞，搭配 can 填空，完成句子。

sell

connect

make

scan

locate

1. Many printers ___can scan___ documents.

2. Many notebook computers _____ to wireless networks.

3. Many cars with GPS systems _____ street addresses.

4. Many vending machines _____ both beverages and snacks.

5. Many smartphones _____ digital video recordings.

2

請勾選正確的答案。

1. The package ☐ should be ☐ should have been here now.

2. You ☐ can ☐ could have missed the exam if you hadn't found your examination permit in time.

3. The letter ☐ ought to arrive ☐ ought to have arrived there by now.

4. She ☐ should have received ☐ should receive my email about that job opportunity by now.

5. Don't eat too many salty crackers. You ☐ can ☐ may get thirsty.

6. He ☐ ought to contact ☐ ought to have contacted them as soon as he can.

7. She ☐ ought to have heard ☐ ought to hear from them soon.

8. They ☐ should know ☐ should have known the results in an hour or two.

9. You ☐ can ☐ could succeed if you work hard.

Unit **102**

Deduction: Must, Can't
表示「推論」：Must、Can't

1 must 用來表示「**肯定的推測**」，有想必、一定是、八成的意思。

You are holding roofing shingles, a hammer, and nails. It must be time for me to help you fix the leak in your roof.
↳ 我確定現在該幫你了。

你手上拿著修屋頂用的瓦片、槌子和釘子，我該幫你修屋頂的裂縫了吧。

She must be very tired after her long trip to Tibet.

在去西藏的長途旅行之後，她應該會很累。

2 can't 用來表示「**某件事應該不可能發生**」，**mustn't** 不能用來表示推斷。

Oh, no! That can't be true.
喔，天哪！那不可能是真的。

I saw him this morning. He can't be in New York.

我今天早上才看到他，他不可能在紐約呀。

3 表示推斷的句型也有**現在進行式**。

| must | + | be | + | V-ing |
| can't | + | be | + | V-ing |

可以表示「**想必正在發生的事**」或「**想必沒有在發生的事**」。

She must be eating right now. You'd better call her later.

她想必正在吃飯，你最好晚點再打給她。

She can't be out dancing at some party because she has a big test tomorrow.

她現在不可能在派對上跳舞，因為她明天有一個大考。

4 當我們要「**對過去的事件做推論**」，要使用：

| must | + | have | + | 過去分詞 |
| couldn't | + | have | + | 過去分詞 |

I can't believe you cooked us such a nice dinner. You must have spent all day cooking.

我不敢相信你為我們做了一頓這麼豐盛的晚餐，你一定花了一整天準備吧。

This is such a unique and beautiful sweater. You couldn't have bought it from a store. You must have knitted it yourself.

這件毛衣很特別也很好看，不可能是在店裡買的，這一定是你自己織的。

5 表示「**對過去的事件做推論**」時：

| 美式 | must | + | have | + | 過去分詞 |
| 英式 | couldn't | + | have | + | 過去分詞 |

美式 The remodeling of your house is wonderful. You couldn't have done it all by yourselves.

英式 The remodeling of your house is wonderful. You can't have done it all by yourselves.

你的房子整修得太棒了，不可能全都是你自己做的。

6 表示推論的句子也有**疑問句**，如果要詢問「**過去某件事情發生的必然性**」，可以用：

| could | + | have | + | 過去分詞 |

Could they have finished fixing the roof already? 他們有可能已經完成屋頂的修繕了嗎？
Could they have left work without telling me they were going? 他們有沒有可能已經結束工作離開，卻沒告訴我？

7 如果是「**一般推論的疑問句**」，則用 can。

We put a whole new roof on your house. Where can that water be coming from?

我們幫你的房子換了全新的屋頂，那麼水究竟是從哪裡來的？

Practice

1

請勾選正確的答案。

1. The squirrel has disappeared. It ☐ must ☐ can't have crawled into a hole.

2. I hear a beautiful voice coming from Joey's room, but he doesn't know how to sing. It ☐ can't ☐ must be him.

3. The barbershop is closed today, so you ☐ must ☐ can't get a haircut.

4. You slept late this morning. You ☐ can't ☐ must have been tired.

5. I saw some migratory birds going south. They ☐ must ☐ can't have come from a colder climate.

6. That weird-looking guy is wearing a seal skin coat and is carrying a harpoon. He ☐ mustn't ☐ couldn't have bought that harpoon around here.

7. Somebody said Mary ate your lobster. She ☐ couldn't ☐ must have eaten the lobster because she is allergic to seafood.

8. How ☐ can ☐ can't it be possible to cross the river at this time of year?

9. ☐ Could ☐ Must they have found the document and given it to the police?

2

請從框內選出適當的詞語，以正確的形式填空，完成句子。

talk with

make a fortune

drink in the bar

buy this villa

1 You couldn't have _____ with your salary. It's too expensive.

2 Susan can't be _____ Matt. He's on the plane to London now.

3 Sandra must have _____. How else is she able to buy such jewelry?

4 Murray must be _____ right now. He goes there every time when he loses a job.

Unit 103

Requests: Can, Could, May, Will, Would

表示「要求」：
Can、Could、May、Will、Would

1 can、could 和 may 都可以用於「請求許可」。can 是最不正式的用法，could 比 can 正式，may 是三者中最正式的用語。

正式與禮貌性 高 ──────────── 低
may could can

Can I change the channel on the TV?

我可以轉台嗎？

Can I eat the last piece of fruit?

我可以吃最後一塊水果嗎？

Could we watch a variety show instead of this movie? 我們可不可以看綜藝節目，不要看這部電影？

Could I finish the cake?

我可以把蛋糕吃完嗎？

May I please sit in this armchair?

請問我可以坐這張扶手椅嗎？

May I make myself a cup of your special tea? 請問我可以泡一杯你那種很特別的茶嗎？

2 如果要「要求得到某物」，可以用：

can/could/may	+	I/we	+	have

Can I have another piece of cake?

我可以再吃一塊蛋糕嗎？

Could I have your cell phone number, please? 可以給我你的手機號碼嗎？

May I have your attention, please?

請注意一下這裡好嗎？

3 can you 和 could you 可用來「請求對方做某事」。could 的語氣比 can 禮貌而婉轉。

Can you help me to move this box? It's pretty heavy.

你可不可以幫忙搬這個箱子？它實在很重。

4 will you 和 would you 也可以用來「請求對方做某事」。would 的語氣比 will 禮貌而婉轉。

Will you help us move this sofa?

你要幫我們搬這張沙發嗎？

Will you walk the dog and feed the cat?

你會幫忙遛狗和餵貓嗎？

Would you be so kind as to help us for a few minutes? 可以麻煩你好心幫忙我們幾分鐘嗎？

5 「would you mind + 過去式」可以用來「詢問對方是否介意某事」。此時要注意回答如果是肯定句，表示「介意、反對某事」，如果是否定句，才是「不介意、同意某事」。

Would you mind if I turned down the music?

我把音樂關小聲一點你不介意吧？

No, I would not.
(= No, that would be fine.)
↳ would not 表示「不介意」、「可以關小一點」。

好啊。

Would you mind if I drove?

我開車你介意嗎？

No, I would not.
(= No, that would be nice.)
↳ would not 表示「你可以開車」。

不介意啊。

6 「I would like you to + 過去式」是一種禮貌性「請求對方做某事」的用法，可以縮寫為「I'd like you to . . .」。

Things have not worked out well for you at this company. I'd like you to consider a career change. 你在這間公司的表現並不是太好，我希望你考慮一下轉換職業跑道。

Could you give me a hand with this box?

可以麻煩你幫我搬這個箱子嗎？

Practice

1

請用括號內的「情態動詞」將句子改寫成問句，但不能改變語意。

1. I want to have a cup of coffee. (can)

    → *Can I have a cup of coffee?*

2. I want you to answer the phone for me. (would / please)

    → ⟶

3. I want you to turn off the air conditioner. (will)

    → ⟶

4. I want to use the bench press when you are finished. (may)

    → ⟶

5. I want to take a nap on the sofa if you are not going to watch TV. (could)

    → ⟶

6. I want you to go jogging with me tomorrow morning at 5:30. (can)

    → ⟶

2

請從圖示中選出適當的用語，以正確的形式填空，完成句子。

open the gift

borrow this book

pass me a tissue

get off the phone

turn the light on

a copy of the application form

fix the fence

1. Can I ⟶ on your bookshelf? I've always wanted to read it.

2. Would you ⟶ , please? I'm expecting an important call.

3. Can I have ⟶ ? I'd like to apply for the job.

4. May I ⟶ now? I really want to know what's in it.

5. Will you ⟶ ? I feel like blowing my nose.

6. Would you mind if I ⟶ ? I'm afraid of the dark.

7. I'd like you ⟶ today. The kids next door keep sneaking into our garden and picking flowers.

Unit **104**

Offers: Will, Shall, Can, Could, Would
表示「提供幫助或物品」：
Will、**Shall**、**Can**、**Could**、**Would**

1 I will 可以用來表示「**願意或提議幫對方做某事**」。

I will cook dinner for you.
我會幫你做晚餐。
Don't worry. I'll take care of it.
別擔心，我會處理的。

I will help you set the table for afternoon tea. 我會幫你把下午茶的餐具擺好。

2 will you 可用於「**提供物品**」或「**邀請對方做某事**」。

Will you join us for our outing to the beach? 你要和我們一起去海灘玩嗎？
Will you please take the last piece of French toast?
請你把最後一片法式土司吃了吧？

3 shall I 可用來表示「**提議**」，多半是對方已經預期由你來做某事，相當於「**Do you want me to . . . ?**」。

Shall I give the kids their baths tonight?
今天晚上由我幫孩子們洗澡嗎？
Shall I wash the dishes since you cooked such a lovely dinner? 既然你做了這麼一頓豐盛的晚餐，應該讓我來洗碗吧？

4 can/could 表示「**有做某事的能力**」，也常用於「**提議幫忙做某事**」。

I can take care of your baby for an hour if you have a doctor's appointment.
如果你已經預約了看醫生的話，我可以幫你照顧你的小寶寶一個鐘頭。
I could keep your kids overnight if you are going to be out of town. 如果你要出城，我可以幫你照顧孩子們一晚。

5 can/could 表示「**請求許可**」，有時也有「**提議幫忙**」的意味。這種用法是禮貌性提議幫忙做事，而不是要等別人許可。

Can I read the kids a book while you cook dinner? 你煮晚餐的時候，我可以唸書給孩子們聽嗎？
You look a bit unhappy. Could I give you a glass of orange juice? 你看起來心情不是很好，要我幫你倒杯柳橙汁嗎？

6 要有禮貌地「**提供對方某物**」，可用 would like、would prefer 和 would rather。

Would you prefer some hard rock?
你要聽一些重搖滾樂嗎？
Would you rather I played some R&B?
要我為你放一些節奏藍調的音樂嗎？

Would you like to listen to some heavy metal music?
你想聽一些重金屬樂嗎？

No, thanks.
不了，謝謝。

Practice

1 請用括號內的「情態動詞」將句子改寫成問句，但不能改變語意。

1. I want you to sew this button back on my pajamas. (will)

   → *Will you sew this button back on my pajamas?*

2. I want to carry that big heavy suitcase for you. (shall)

   → ....

3. I want to help you change that light bulb. (can)

   → ....

4. I want to have your daughter's hand in marriage. (may)

   → ....

5. I want to know if you would like to go out to a French restaurant for dinner this evening. (would)

   → ....

   ....

6. I want you to try a glass of white wine with the meal. (will)

   → ....

   ....

2 比較各組用語，請勾選屬於「提供幫助或物品」或「邀請」的用法。

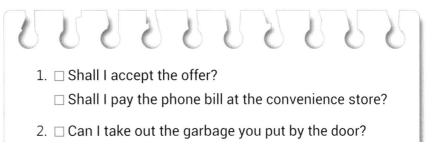

1. ☐ Shall I accept the offer?
   ☐ Shall I pay the phone bill at the convenience store?

2. ☐ Can I take out the garbage you put by the door?
   ☐ Can I have another cup of green tea?

3. ☐ Will you please have another cookie?
   ☐ Will you clean the screens on our windows?

4. ☐ I could fry an egg for your breakfast.
   ☐ I could eat two tea eggs and some rice soup.

5. ☐ I would like to hear your excuse.
   ☐ Would you like to hear my explanation?

6. ☐ I can walk the dog for you tonight.
   ☐ I can run faster than your dog.

Unit **105**

Suggestions: Shall, Let's, Why Don't We, How About, What About, Can, Could

表示「建議」：
Shall、Let's、Why Don't We、How About、What About、Can、Could

1 shall we 可以用於「尋求建議」和「提出建議」。

What **shall** we do about our phone bill?

我們的電話帳單該怎麼辦？

Shall we try a new long distance phone service?

我們要試試新的長途電話服務嗎？

Shall we look into one of these data plans? 我們要從這些資費方案中選一個嗎？

2 let's 可用來「提出建議」，後面要接「不加 to 的不定詞」。

Let's call in sick and take the day off.

我們打電話請一天病假吧。

3 why don't we 可用來「提出建議」，後面要接「不加 to 的不定詞」。

Why don't we quit our jobs and backpack around Australia?

我們何不辭了工作，背著包包環遊澳洲？
Why don't we fry some shrimp cakes tonight? 我們今晚炸一些蝦餅來吃怎麼樣？

4 how about 和 what about 可用來「提出建議」，後面要加名詞或動名詞。

How about a swim in the lake?

去湖邊游泳如何？

What about finding a quiet island with white sand beaches?

何不找一個海邊布滿白沙灘的平靜島嶼？
How about quitting this crazy rat race and living in the mountains?

我們何不拋開這種瘋狂競爭的生活，到山中居住？

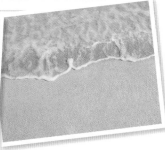

5 can/could 用來「提出建議」的時候，主要是在提出一些「可能的行為或想法」。

We can pick berries and make our own jam. 我們可以撿一些莓果自己做果醬。
We could open a bed and breakfast near the top of the mountain.

我們可以在靠近山頂的地方開一間民宿。

Practice

1

請勾選正確的答案。

1. Where □ shall we □ let's go shopping for some second-hand clothes?

2. I don't have any money. □ Can □ Let's spend the afternoon in the library.

3. □ Why don't we □ How about go to the wholesale fashion market?

4. □ Shall we □ Let's buy some cute T-shirts and try to sell them?

5. □ How about □ Shall we selling them at the night market near the MRT station?

6. □ We can □ Why don't we double the price we paid.

7. We □ let's □ could sell them to teenagers and make some money.

8. Then □ we could □ how about go shopping.

2   請依據題意，從圖中選出適當的用語，以正確的形式填空，完成句子。

take a coffee break

visit the wine factory

go bicycling

make dumplings

join the health club

wait for five more minutes

1. How about _____ on the second day of our tour?

2. How about _____? If Jack still doesn't come home, then we'll quit waiting and go buy some dog treats.

3. We've got some ground pork in the fridge. Why don't we _____ ourselves?

4. Why don't we _____ as soon as we get our new bicycles?

5. Shall we _____ before going on to the next issue?

6. Shall we _____? They are having a special discount on six-month memberships.

Unit **106**

Habits: Used To
表示「習慣」：Used To

1 used to 用來談論「**過去的習慣**」和「**過去經常從事的活動**」，而這些習慣或活動「**已經結束且不會再發生**」。

Peggy used to walk to school when she was in junior high school, but now she is a senior high school student at another school and has to take a bus.
↳ 現在不走路上學了。

珮琪以前讀國中時走路上學，不過不過她現在在另一所學校上高中，得搭公車上學。

Dean used to collect seashells on vacation, but now he takes motorcycle trips when he has time off.
↳ 現在不蒐集貝殼了。

過去迪恩度假時會蒐集貝殼，但是現在他休假時會騎著摩托車旅遊。

2 used to 也可以用來說明「**過去的狀態和情況**」。

Chuck used to be a student, but he graduated last spring and got a job.

查克以前是學生，不過他去年春天畢業了，也找到了工作。

Barbara used to have a boyfriend, but she dumped him last month.

芭芭拉以前有一位男朋友，不過她上個月把他給甩了。

3 used to 只能用於**過去式**。如要說明**現在的習慣和情況**，要使用**現在簡單式**。

Rosemary is a vice president now.
蘿絲瑪麗現在是副總裁。

Pam likes to drive to work now that she has a car. 潘喜歡開車上班，因為她現在有車子。

4 used to 的**否定式**為 didn't use to（注意不是 didn't used to）。

Norman didn't use to commute to the city. 諾曼以前不常通勤到市中心。

5 used to 的**疑問句型**是：「did . . . use to . . . ?」，用來「**詢問過去的習慣**」。

Did you use to go ice skating with Tom?
你以前常和湯姆一起去溜冰嗎？

Where did you use to go ice-skating?
你以前常去哪裡溜冰？

6 used to 和 be used to 的意義完全不同。

1 used to 是「**過去的習慣**」，後面接「**不加 to 的不定詞**」；

2 be used to 則是「**逐漸習慣於做某事**」，後面要接**動名詞**。

Andrew used to ride his unicycle all the time. 安德魯過去經常騎著他的單輪腳踏車。

Helen is used to riding a unicycle.
海倫已經習慣騎單輪腳踏車。

a unicycle

Practice

1

請勾選正確的答案。

1. Linda ☐ used ☐ used to knit, but now she crochets.

2. Naomi used to ☐ spend ☐ spending a lot of money on clothes.

3. Carol used to ☐ work ☐ worked in a clothing store.

4. Amy ☐ use to ☐ used to play computer games in the morning, but now she has to go to work at a mall.

5. Neal ☐ used to go ☐ used to going to bed early.

6. Irene ☐ loves to ☐ used to jog these days.

2

請用括弧內的詞語改寫句子。

1. She drank a cup of black tea when reading a book. (used to)

   → *She used to drink a cup of black tea when reading a book.*

2. He sips a glass of wine before going to bed. (be used to)

   →

3. Kristine watched horror movies. (used to)

   →

4. Did Karl stay in his office overnight to work? (use to)

   →

5. Sam was naive, but now he is a mature young man. (used to)

   →

6. Where did you go bowling? (use to)

   →

7. I write a journal every day. (be used to)

   →

8. Do you read a newspaper before going to work? (be used to)

   →

Habits: Will, Would
表示「習慣」：Will、Would

1 will 也可以用來說明「**目前經常從事的行為**」。

He prefers to drive. He will drive for ten hours to visit his parents instead of flying.

他比較喜歡開車，他會開十小時的車去探望父母，卻不搭飛機去。

2 would 可以用來說明「**過去經常從事的行為**」。

在以上這兩種用法中，will 和 would 都不必以重音強調。

He would always drive down to visit his parents.

他以前總是開車南下去探望父母。

He would often stand in a line for three hours to get a concert ticket.

他以前會排隊三個小時，只為了買一張演唱會門票。

3 以**重音**強調 will 和 would 時，原句便轉而帶有「**批評**」的意味。

You know she will lose it. She is so disorganized.

你明知道她會弄丟的，
她就是這麼一個做事沒有條理的人。

He would always have some lame excuse. He was so lazy.

他老是會有一些爛藉口，他就是這麼懶散。

4 would 和 used to 都用來說明「**過去的習慣**」。

Terry used to give up his seat on the bus to the elderly.

泰瑞過去總是會在公車上讓位給老人家。

Terry would always offer his seat to pregnant women and little kids.

過去泰瑞都會讓位給孕婦和小孩。

5 但是 **would** 不能說明「**過去的狀態**」，這種情況只能用 used to。

✗ My father would like to take the bus to work.

✓ My father used to like to take the bus to work.

以前我爸爸喜歡搭公車上班。

Practice

1

請勾選正確的答案。

1. She ☐ will ☐ would jog every day if she can.

2. When David was a boy, he ☐ would ☐ will read comic books for hours.

3. Jack ☐ would ☐ used to shave his head, but now he has started to let his hair grow long.

4. Don't tell her our plan. She ☐ will ☐ would let everybody know.

2

請從框內選出適當的詞語，用 will 的句型來描述圖中人物「目前」的習慣。

often sneak onto the bed

always go to the beach

always spread a lot of peanut butter

always sing loudly

Polly _____ _____ and sleep by her owner.

They _____ on Saturdays.

Lisa _____ _____ when taking a shower.

He _____ _____ on his bread.

3

請從框內選出適當的詞語，用 would 的句型來描述圖中人物「過去」的習慣。

often sit by Grandpa

often chat with friends

always doze off

always eat her breakfast

She _____ on Facebook Messenger all day.

Little Sam _____ in the park for the whole afternoon.

Claire _____ _____ while driving to work.

He _____ _____ in front of the TV.

227

Unit **108**

Other Uses of "Will," "Won't," and "Wouldn't"

Will、Won't、Wouldn't 的其他用法

won't、wouldn't 表示「拒絕」

1 won't 可以表達「拒絕」，並且是「目前拒絕做某事」。

Mommy, Julie won't let me play with her doll house.

媽咪，茱莉不讓我玩她的娃娃屋。

Daddy, Lydia won't come out of the bathroom and she is crying.

爹地，莉蒂雅關在廁所哭，不肯出來。

The door on the toy sports car won't open. 玩具賽車的車門打不開。

2 wouldn't 也可以表達「拒絕」，並且是「過去拒絕做某事」。

Katrina wouldn't let me wear her pink jumper. 凱翠娜不讓我穿她的粉紅色連身裙。

My car door wouldn't open this morning.

我的車門今天早上打不開。

Joy wouldn't talk to me for a whole week.

整整一個星期，喬伊都不肯跟我說話。

will 表示「強調承諾」

3 will 可以用於「強調承諾」。

I will remember our anniversary this year. I promise.

我這次一定會記得我們的週年紀念，我保證。

I won't forget your mother's birthday. I promise.

我不會忘記你媽媽的生日，我保證。

will 表示「威脅」

4 will 可以用於「威脅」。

You'll be in big trouble if you forget my dad's birthday.

要是你忘了我爸爸的生日，那你可就麻煩大了。

You'll fail the exam if you don't study hard. 你不用功，考試就會不及格。

You'll have dark circles around your eyes if you don't go to bed early.

你不早點睡，就會有黑眼圈。

Practice

1 請用 won't 或 wouldn't 改寫句子。

1. Kathy refuses to change her opinion.

   → Kathy won't change her opinion.

2. Kenny refuses to come out of his room.

   →

3. Yesterday I invited Lionel to the party, but he refused to go.

   →

4. I suggested Yvonne get a new suit for the interview, but she refused to buy one.

   →

5. The washing machine refuses to work properly.

   →

2 請用 will 或 won't 改寫句子。

1. If you don't stay out of my room, I am going to tell Mom.

   → If you don't stay out of my room, I will tell Mom.

2. If you let me use your computer, I am going to be careful with it.

   →

3. If you tell Dad what I did, I am not going to forget and you'll regret it.

   →

4. I took your favorite doll. Unless you stop kicking my sheep, I am not going to tell you where your doll is.

   →

5. If you tell me where Mom hid the cookies, I am going to buy you snacks next time.

   →

Unit **109**

"Would Rather" and "May/Might As Well"
Would Rather 與 May/Might As Well
的用法

would rather

1 would rather 用來表示某人的「偏好」，後面要接「不加 **to** 的不定詞」。

Albert would rather cut the grass.
艾伯特寧願去除草。
Would you rather give the baby a bath or take out the garbage?
你是要幫孩子洗澡，還是要倒垃圾？

2 would rather 的否定句型是 would rather not。

Martha would rather not compost fresh food waste. 瑪莎寧願不用廚餘做堆肥。
I would rather not watch this stupid movie. 我寧可不要看這齣爛電影。

3 如果要比較兩件事，可以用「would rather . . . than . . .」，動詞都要用「不加 **to** 的不定詞」。

Rita would rather clean the kitchen than read the kids a goodnight story.
麗塔寧願清理廚房，也不想唸故事哄孩子們睡覺。
I would rather walk to school than take a bus with no air conditioning. 我寧可走路去上學，也不要搭沒有冷氣的公車。

4 「would rather + somebody + did something」用來表示「寧願由某人做某事」，did something 要用過去式動詞。

Richie doesn't want to do it. He would rather Valerie did it.
瑞奇不想做這件事，他寧願讓薇拉莉去做。
I would rather you didn't turn off the air conditioner.
我寧可你不要把冷氣機關掉。
Pam would rather Jessica called earlier in the evening.
潘希望潔西卡晚上早點打電話。

may/might as well

5 may/might as well 表示「沒有強烈理由不做某事」，後面會接「不加 **to** 的不定詞」。

Louis is going to be late. We may as well grab a bite to eat while we are waiting for him. 路易斯會遲到，我們等他的同時可以先吃點東西。
Rob won't be here for another 30 minutes. We may as well get a cup of coffee while we are waiting for him.
羅伯再過三十分鐘才會到，我們等他的時候可以順便喝杯咖啡。

Practice

1

請從框內選出適當的動詞，搭配 would rather 或 would rather not 填空，完成對話。

drink

hunt

continue

jump

1. Ⓐ Do you want to drink some tea?
   Ⓑ I _____would rather drink_____ coffee.

2. Ⓐ Let's try base jumping off a tall building. What do you say?
   Ⓑ I _____ off a tall building.

3. Ⓐ I want to try bear hunting. Do you want to try it?
   Ⓑ I _____ bears.

4. Ⓐ Ivan wants to meet with you before continuing to work on the project. Do you want him to continue without you?
   Ⓑ I _____ he _____ without me.

2

請用「would rather + somebody + did something」的句型續寫句子。

1. Liz doesn't want to do the dishes. She would like Lisa to do the dishes.
   → _She would rather Lisa did the dishes._

2. Joe doesn't want Mary to revise too much of his paper.
   → _____

3. I want you to go to the play with me. I don't want to go alone.
   → _____

4. I don't want you to cook chicken for dinner every day.
   → _____

3

請從框內選出適當的動詞，依括弧提示，搭配 may as well 或 might as well 填空，完成句子。

ride

wash

order

go

read

have

1. Since there's nothing interesting on TV tonight, I ___may as well go___ to bed early. (may as well)

2. Since the refrigerator is empty, we _____ pizza. (may as well)

3. If nobody wants to do anything tonight, I _____ my book. (may as well)

4. If Tommy is driving to school, we _____ with him. (might as well)

5. When we finish swimming, we _____ a snack at the concession stand. (might as well)

6. If you're not using the washing machine, I _____ my clothes. (might as well)

Important Uses of "Should"
Should 的重要用法

1 should 經常出現在表示「**建議**」或「**要求**」的句子中。

當主要子句裡使用了下列動詞，那麼**附屬子句**就使用 should（英式）或原形動詞（美式）。

- suggest
- ask
- insist
- propose
- request
- recommend

Jasmine suggests (that) I take / I should take the car to the repair shop.
↳ that 可以省略。

潔絲敏建議我把車送去修車廠。

Ray requests (that) you call / you should call him when you finish playing chess.

雷要你下完棋之後打電話給他。

The National Theater requires (that) we pay / we should pay in advance for the season tickets.

國家戲劇院要我們先購買季票。

2 important、essential、vital 這類的形容詞，也很常用這種搭配 should（英式）或原形動詞（美式）的句型。

Marjorie says it is important (that) you emphasize / you should emphasize your circuit design experience during the interview.

瑪喬莉說，在面試時強調你有電路設計的經驗是很重要的。

Donald said it was essential (that) I bring / I should bring my graphics and photography portfolio to the presentation.

唐納德說，把我的繪圖和攝影集帶去發表會是很必要的。

此時不管**主要子句**是現在式或過去式，**附屬子句**都用 should 或原形動詞。

現在時態 **Buddy suggests (that) we visit / we should visit the National Concert Hall on Sunday.**

巴迪建議我們星期天去看看國家音樂廳。

過去時態 **Cornelia insisted (that) I pick up / I should pick up her father before going to get her.**

康妮莉亞堅持要我去找她之前，一定要先去接她父親。

Practice

1

請用「that . . . should」的句型，改寫句子。

1. The nurse asked me to consult the doctor about the bump on my leg.
   → The nurse suggested *that I (should) consult the doctor about the*
   bump on my leg   .

2. The butcher said it would be better to fry the meat quickly with high heat.
   → The butcher recommended ....
   ....

3. The flight attendant told me to walk around by the lavatory.
   → The flight attendant suggested ....
   ....

4. The teacher told the child, "You must finish your homework every night."
   → The teacher told the child, "It is important ....
   ...."

5. While packing for vacation, the wife told the husband because of his sensitive skin, he should pack the sunscreen.
   → While packing for vacation, the wife told the husband because of his sensitive skin, it was vital ....

6. The man behind the two teenagers in the movie theater said, "Would you please watch the movie and not talk?"
   → The man behind the two teenagers in the movie theater said, "It is important ...."

2

請將下列使用 should 的句型，改寫為「不使用 should 的句型」。

1. They say it is important that you should drive without talking on your phone.
   → ....
   ....

2. The mayor ordered that free food should be distributed to the poor.
   → ....
   ....

Part 14 Adjectives 形容詞

Unit 111

Form, Position, and Order of Adjectives
形容詞的形式、位置與順序

1 形容詞的形式只有一種，不會隨任何情況改變。不管修飾單數或複數名詞，格式都一樣。

a healthy boy 一位健康的男孩

two healthy boys 兩位健康的男孩

an anxious child 一位焦慮的孩子

anxious children 焦慮的孩子們

2 名詞也常用來修飾名詞，當作形容詞用，此時當形容詞用的名詞多用「單數形」。

✗ a fifteen-minutes run

✓ a fifteen-minute run 十五分鐘的跑步

✗ two summers breaks

✓ two summer breaks 兩個暑假

3 形容詞通常位於名詞的前面。

a busy schedule 忙碌的行程

a heavy burden 沉重的負擔

4 形容詞也可以放在 be 動詞和連綴動詞、感官動詞的後面。

Craig is busy. 克雷格很忙。

The job looks hard.
這件工作看起來很難。

The assignments are difficult.
這些任務都很困難。

* be
* look
* appear
* seem
* feel
* taste
* smell
* sound

5 有些形容詞「只能」放在 be 動詞或連綴動詞後面，不能放在名詞前面。遇到這種情況，如果要修飾名詞，則會採用同義的其他形容詞形式。

✗ The baby is an asleep baby.

✓ The baby is asleep.
小寶寶熟睡著。

Let a sleeping dog sleep.
〔喻〕別惹麻煩。

位於 be 動詞或連綴動詞後	位於名詞前
asleep	sleeping
alive	living
afraid	frightened
ill/sick	sick
well	healthy

6 有一種情況下，形容詞可以放在名詞的後面，就是談論「度量」的時候。

The boy is ten years old. 這位男孩十歲。

The girl is 130 cm tall.
這位女孩身高一百三十公分。

7 多個形容詞連用時，「詮釋意見的形容詞」通常會放在「描述事實的形容詞」之前。

a controversial new book
一本極具爭議的新書

an attractive red blouse
一件迷人的紅色上衣

8 多個形容詞連用時，請依照下列原則排列順序。

尺寸 → 形狀 → 年齡 → 顏色 → 來源 → 材料 → 目的

the Egyptian cotton dress 埃及製的棉洋裝
↳ 來源 + 材料

a plastic watering can 一個塑膠的澆水壺
↳ 材料 + 目的

my old green running shoes
↳ 年齡 + 顏色 + 目的
我那老舊的綠色跑步鞋

1

請將括弧內的形容詞，搭配各組詞語，重組出一個有意義的句子。

1. (old) / the / sat / man / on the bench

   → _The old man sat on the bench._

2. (delicious) / tea / this / tasted

   → ....

3. (tall) / is / woman / 160 cm / the

   → ....

4. (blue) / coat / is / the / mine / large

   → ....

5. (hot) / we / weather / have had / three weeks of

   → ....

6. (sleeping) / shelter / on the second floor / the / has / quarters

   → ....

2

請將右列錯誤的句子改寫為正確的句子。

1. The rope is long 45 cm.

   → ....

2. We had a two-hours walk after dinner.

   → ....

3. It was a crystal lovely lamp.

   → ....

4. Did you see my blue silk Japanese dress?

   → ....

5. I'm going to visit my ill Grandpa tomorrow.

   → ....

6. Is your bird still living?

   → ....

7. I fell sleeping.

   → ....

8. We have a schedule tight.

   → ....

Unit 112

Comparative and Superlative Adjectives: Forms
形容詞比較級與最高級的形式

Form 形式

單音節形容詞 + er/est

thick → thicker → thickest
short → shorter → shortest

字尾「單母音 + 單子音」的單音節形容詞 → 重複字尾 + er/est

thin → thinner → thinnest
big → bigger → biggest

字尾 e 的單音節形容詞 + r/st

close → closer → closest
wide → wider → widest

字尾 y 的雙音節形容詞 → 去 y + ier/iest

funny → funnier → funniest
naughty → naughtier → naughtiest

字尾非 y 的雙音節形容詞 → more/most

modern → more modern → most modern
serious → more serious → most serious

三音節以上的形容詞 → more/most

expensive	comfortable
→ more expensive	→ more comfortable
→ most expensive	→ most comfortable

more/most 是具有「**正面意義**」的比較級和最高級，如果要表示**負面意義「較不」**、「**最不**」，則改用 less/least。

- less expensive
- least expensive

1 左表構成形容詞比較級與最高級的原則，也有例外。有些**字尾非 y 的雙音節形容詞**，卻是加 (e)r/(e)st 構成比較級和最高級。

narrow → narrower → narrowest
cruel → crueler/crueller → cruelest/cruellest
gentle → gentler → gentlest
remote → remoter → remotest
subtle → subtler → subtlest

2 有些**雙音節的形容詞**，有兩種比較級和最高級形式。

· common	· handsome	· simple
· obscure	· clever	· stupid
· mature	· quiet	

common → commoner → commonest
common → more common → most common
obscure → obscurer → obscurest
obscure → more obscure → most obscure

3 有些形容詞的比較級和最高級是**不規則變化**，請逐一牢記。

good → better → best
bad → worse → worst
little → less → least
many → more → most
much → more → most

4 有些**形容詞**有兩種不同的比較級和最高級，且**意義上有差異**。

far → farther → farthest ↳ 距離上的遠
far → further → furthest ↳ 程度上的進一步
old → older → oldest ↳ 可形容人或物
old → elder → eldest ↳ 英式：只能形容人／只能用在名詞前

Practice

1 請將括弧內的形容詞以「比較級」或「最高級」填空，完成句子。

1. These shoes are too small. Do you have a pair in a _____ (big) size?

2. Who is the _____ (young) child in our school?

3. I think bubble milk tea is the _____ (delicious) drink.

4. The weather is OK. It is cloudy. It could be _____ (sunny), but at least it's not raining.

5. How many kilometers do we have to drive? How much _____ (far) do we have to go to get there?

6. The flight from Taipei to Tokyo is _____ (long) than the flight from Taipei to Hong Kong.

2 將左欄圖片中的名詞，與右欄相對應的描述結合，並將括弧內的形容詞改為「最高級」，寫出完整的敘述句。

1 **Mount Everest**

2 **The Louvre**

3 **The Mariana Trench**

4 **Shakespeare**

5 **Solar energy**

6 **Cirque du Soleil**

is the (high) mountain in the world.

is one of the (famous) museums in the world.

is the (innovative) contemporary circus.

is considered to be one of the (great) poets and dramatists.

is the (deep) place in the ocean.

is one of the (important) sources of energy.

1. *Mount Everest is the highest mountain in the world.*

2. _____

3. _____

4. _____

5. _____

6. _____

Part 14 Adjectives 形容詞

Unit 113

Comparative and Superlative Adjectives: Use
形容詞比較級與最高級的用法

1 形容詞比較級用於**比較兩件事物**，通常會用「比較級 + than」的句型。

Sandy is smarter than **Judy.**
珊蒂比茱蒂聰明。

Sharon is more energetic than **Harriet.** 雪倫比哈里特更有活力。

2 形容詞比較級也常用「比較級 + and + 比較級」的句型，來表示「**逐漸增加或減少**」、「**愈來愈⋯⋯**」。

Computers are getting faster and faster. 電腦的速度變得愈來愈快。
Hard drives are getting more and more compact. 硬碟的體積變得愈來愈小。

3 可以結合兩個「the + 比較級」的子句，來表達「**兩件事物互相影響、改變的關係**」。

The more cheese on the pizza, the better it will be.
披薩上的起司愈多愈好吃。
The better Internet phones become, the more money traditional phone companies will lose.
網路電話發展的愈好，傳統電話公司損失的金錢就愈多。

4 比較級的前面，可以用 (very) much、a lot、a bit、a little bit 等來描述其程度。

very much brighter 明亮非常多
a lot paler 蒼白很多
a little bit shallower 比較淺一點

5 比較三個以上的人或事物，則要使用形容詞的最高級。最高級前面要加 the。

- the happiest 最開心的
- the most pragmatic 最實際的

This is the ripest **one of the five mangoes on the table.** 桌子上的五個芒果，就這一個最熟了。

Kirk is the quietest **child in the family.**
科克是家裡最安靜的孩子。

The office on the right is the most spacious.
右邊那間辦公室最寬敞。

6 形容詞最高級的前面，可以用 by far（顯然）或 easily（顯然）來強調其「**獨特性**」。

by far the most realistic 顯然最實際的
easily the cleverest 顯然最聰明的

7 若要表示「**兩個事物一樣（或不一樣）**」，會用「(not) as + 形容詞原級 + as」的句型。

The appetizer was as good as **the main meal.**
開胃菜就和主菜一樣美味。

The tea is as strong as **the coffee at this café.**
這間咖啡廳的茶就和咖啡一樣濃。

The park didn't have as many **visitors today as it did yesterday.**
今天公園裡不像昨天人那麼多。

It isn't as hot **now as it was this morning.**
今天早上不像平常那麼熱。

8 在「as . . . as」的句型中，口語常用 me 或 him 等受詞代名詞，在正式用法中通常會使用「主詞代名詞 + 動詞」，如 I 或 he。

You aren't as cool as me. 你沒有我酷。
↳ 口語

You couldn't represent the citizens of our district as well as I **could.**
↳ 正式
你無法像我一樣代表本區的全體市民。

Practice

1

請勾選正確的答案。

1. Tonya is ☐ short ☐ shorter than Lesley.
2. Helen is the ☐ happy ☐ happiest child I've ever seen.
3. Adam is ☐ honester ☐ more honest than Max.
4. Alvin is the ☐ more careful ☐ most careful child in his class.
5. This is the ☐ worse ☐ worst milk tea I've ever had.
6. Too bad this dress isn't ☐ cheaper ☐ more cheap.
7. The summer is getting ☐ hotter and hotter ☐ hottest.
8. The colder the air conditioning is, the ☐ more ☐ most I like it.
9. I am not as emotional as ☐ she ☐ she is.

2

請將括弧內的形容詞，以正確的「原級」、「比較級」或「最高級」填空，並視需要加上 than、the 或「as . . . as」，完成句子。

1. I'll let you use the phone first. Your call is a lot _____ (important) mine.
2. In general, the larger a diamond is, _____ (expensive) it is.
3. Lemons may be _____ (sour) of all fruit.
4. Today is not _____ (hot) as yesterday.
5. We're getting _____ (close) to sending people to Mars.
6. This is by far _____ (boring) movie I've ever seen.
7. This corporate profile is too general. Can you make it a little _____ (specific)?

3

請從框內選出適當的形容詞，以「as . . . as」的句型填空，完成句子。

hip
neat
smart
high
frugal
fast

1. If you get new sunglasses, then you can be _____ me.
2. I got a higher test score, so you're not _____ me.
3. I can't afford these prices, so if you want to be _____ me, then we can go shopping at the night market.
4. You were not _____ me. I ran two laps in the time it took you to run one.
5. If you cleaned up your room as often as I clean my room, then your room would be _____ mine.
6. The mountain called K2 in Pakistan is almost _____ Mount Everest.

Adverbs of Manner
狀態副詞／方式副詞

1 狀態副詞／方式副詞用於描述「某事發生的方式」。

The press conference was run professionally. 那場記者會進行得很專業。

Jeff remembers the accident distinctly.

傑夫清楚記得那次的意外。

Pan is doing the research passionately.

潘積極投入這次的研究。

2 狀態副詞通常由形容詞加 ly 衍生而來。

- high → high**ly**
- sincere → sincere**ly**
- mischievous → mischievous**ly**

professional + ly = professionally

Walter is a professional manager.

華特是一名專業的經理。

Walter manages the department professionally.

華特十分專業地管理部門。

confident + ly = confidently

Anthony is a confident guy.

安東尼是個有自信的人。

Anthony talks about the future confidently.

安東尼信心滿滿地高談未來。

confidential + ly = confidentially

It was a confidential letter.

這是一封機密信函。

Please treat this letter confidentially.

請將這封信的內容保密。

3 狀態副詞／方式副詞可以放在**動詞的前面或後面**，也可以放在**句首**。

Natalie whispered into the phone angrily.
= Natalie angrily whispered into the phone.
= Angrily, Natalie whispered into the phone.

娜塔莉憤怒地對著電話低語。

4 有些**以 ly 結尾的詞彙**，實際上是**形容詞**，不是**副詞**。這類的形容詞沒有對應的副詞，因此如果要修飾動詞，會用「in a . . . way」的句型。

- friendly
- lovely
- lonely
- silly
- ugly

Sally smiled in a friendly way as we drove off.

我們駕車離開時，莎莉友好地微笑著。

5 **副詞**也有**比較級**和**最高級**，構成方式和形容詞一樣。

Daryl runs faster than Chad.

德瑞跑得比查德快。

As Maria talked longer, I began to know the whole story. 瑪麗亞說得滔滔不絕，我開始瞭解事件的始末。

The later Valerie arrives, the longer we will have to wait.

薇拉莉愈晚抵達，我們就得等愈久。

Of the girls in our class, Cornelia runs the fastest.

我們班上的女生，就屬可娜麗雅跑得最快。

I am hammering as hard as I can on these two pipes, but they are still stuck together.

我盡量用力敲打兩支管子，不過它們還是黏在一起了。

例外

good 是一個例外，它的副詞是 well。

- He is a good supervisor.

  他是一位很好的管理者。

- He supervises the department well.

  他把部門管理得很好。

Practice

1

請勾選正確的答案。

1. Margery is a ☐ graceful ☐ gracefully dancer.

2. Gabriel manages the lab ☐ efficient ☐ efficiently.

3. That is an ☐ absurd ☐ absurdly story.

4. Clara is an ☐ inspiring ☐ inspiringly speaker.

5. You're acting ☐ silly ☐ in a silly way.

6. Wendell handled the press conference ☐ impressive ☐ impressively.

7. Florence answered the question ☐ tentative ☐ tentatively.

8. She talked to her mother ☐ ugly ☐ in an ugly way.

9. Sarah finished her work ☐ quickly ☐ in a quickly way.

2

請將括弧內的副詞以正確的形式填空，可視需要加上 more、most、than、the 和 as 等字。

1. Penelope jumps _____ (high) as Lisa.

2. The house was _____ (beautifully) decorated.

3. Our team played _____ (well) the other team.

4. Don arrived _____ (late) of all the people.

5. I want to move _____ (far) possible away from this city.

6. Vivian needs to _____ (carefully) prepare her reports.

7. No one can solve this problem _____ (intelligently) than he can.

8. Buffy called me back _____ (soon) I expected.

9. The rain was pouring _____ (heavy) all night.

10. Larry dealt with the murder case _____ (emotionlessly).

3

請將括弧內的形容詞以「in a . . . way」的句型填空，完成句子。

1

Huck licked the boy _____
_____ (friendly).

2

The little girl is smiling _____
_____ (lovely).

Part 15 Adverbs 副詞

Unit 115

Adverbs of Time and Place
時間副詞與地方副詞

1 地方副詞用來描述「**事件發生的地點**」，通常位於**動詞或受詞的後面**。

- here
- there
- upstairs
- downstairs
- behind the shed

Linus rode his bike to the laboratory.
↳ to the laboratory 是地方副詞片語，放在「動詞 + 受詞」後面。
李納斯騎腳踏車到實驗室。

Bonnie signed here. 邦妮在這裡簽了名。

2 時間副詞用來描述「**事件發生的時間**」，通常位於**動詞後面**或「**動詞 + 受詞**」後面。

- now
- today
- immediately
- next month

Larry rode his bike home after the concert.
↳ after the concert 是時間副詞片語。
音樂會結束後，勞瑞騎著他的腳踏車回家。

Stella withdrew from the competition yesterday. 史黛拉昨天退出了比賽。

3 有些時間副詞通常放在**動詞或助動詞的前面**。

Natasha just laughed **at her boyfriend.**
娜塔莎剛才嘲笑她男友。

Jerome still couldn't **believe what he had seen.** 傑洛姆還是不敢相信他所看到的。

4 當句中同時出現了**狀態動詞**、**地方副詞**、**頻率副詞片語**和**時間副詞**時，語序為：
狀態動詞 → 地方副詞 → 頻率副詞 → 時間副詞。

Max calculates effortlessly in his head.
　　　　　　　↳ 狀態副詞 + 地方副詞
麥克斯心算起來毫不費力。

Donald stops at the diner every morning.
　　　　　　　↳ 地方副詞 + 頻率副詞
唐諾每天早上都會光顧那個餐車。

Della sneaks quietly up the back stairs at night.　　↳ 狀態副詞 + 地方副詞 + 時間副詞
黛拉夜裡會悄悄地從後面的樓梯溜上去。

5 狀態副詞、地方副詞、頻率副詞片語和時間副詞都不會放在**動詞和受詞的中間**。

✗ **Archie watched** silently **the football game.**
✓ **Archie watched the football game** silently.
亞契靜靜地觀看美式足球賽。

✗ **Frances cheered** loudly **Jimmy.**
✓ **Frances cheered Jimmy** loudly.
法蘭西絲大聲地為吉米加油。

✗ **Joyce played** yesterday **video games.**
✓ **Joyce** played **video games** yesterday.
喬伊絲昨天在玩電視遊樂器。

6 狀態副詞、地方副詞、頻率副詞片語和時間副詞都可放在**句首**，產生「**強調**」的效果。

Longingly, **Martina stared at the map of New Zealand.**
瑪蒂娜充滿渴望，直盯著紐西蘭的地圖。

At the Sydney airport, **Holly finally felt a twinge of excitement.**
在雪梨的機場，荷莉總算感到一陣興奮。

In just a couple of hours, **Billie would finally arrive in her ancestral home.**
就在幾小時後，比莉終將抵達祖先的故鄉。

Practice

1　請將括弧內的詞語以正確的語序填空，完成句子。

1. Ariel devoured _____ (hungrily / the food).

2. The Executive Vice President _____ (works / in this office).

3. The attorney entered our office _____ _____ (at 2:30 in the afternoon / casually).

4. The tech support team reacted _____ _____ (quickly / last week / in the office).

5. The contender punched _____ _____ (last night / hard / at the champion).

6. We _____ (the fight / excitedly / watched), forgetting that we should call the police.

7. An earthquake occurred _____ (this afternoon / in the south).

8. He threw a book _____ (angrily / at his brother).

2　請將下列錯誤的句子改寫為正確的句子。

1. Trent put here the box.

   → _____

2. Sally poured some milk into her coffee just.

   → _____

3. Sonia left at 10 a.m. the library.

   → _____

4. I will buy some books tomorrow at the bookstore.

   → _____

5. Mom won't still let me go to the party.

   → _____

6. Jacky jumped off quickly the tree.

   → _____

Unit **116**

Adverbs of Frequency
頻率副詞

頻率副詞
Adverbs of Frequency

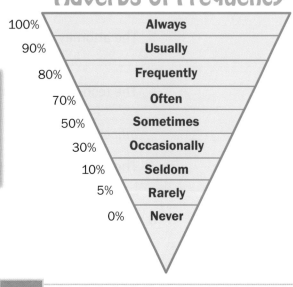

100%	Always
90%	Usually
80%	Frequently
70%	Often
50%	Sometimes
30%	Occasionally
10%	Seldom
5%	Rarely
0%	Never

1 頻率副詞用來表示「**事件發生的頻率**」，通常放在**主要動詞的前面**，或者 **be** 動詞和助動詞的後面。

- always
- normally
- usually
- frequently
- often
- sometimes
- occasionally
- rarely
- seldom
- hardly ever
- never
- ever

Clifford always puts **condensed milk in his tea**. 克里佛總是在茶裡加奶精。

Winnie is normally **a kind and gentle soul**.
溫妮平常是個善良溫柔的人。

Frank can usually work **all day without stopping.**
法蘭克通常可以工作一整天不休息。

These socks have never **been worn.**
↳ 即使較長的助動詞組 have been worn，頻率副詞 never 還是放在第一個助動詞的後面。
這些襪子還沒穿過。

2 部分的**頻率副詞**可以放在**句首**或**句尾**。

- sometimes
- usually
- normally
- frequently
- often
- occasionally

Do you eat hot and spicy curry often?
你常吃口味又重又辣的咖哩嗎？

Sometimes **I buy foreign products in that luxurious supermarket.**
有時候我會在那家高級超市購買外國的產品。

3 頻率副詞片語如 every morning、once a day 等，通常會放在**句尾**，不過有時候也會放在**句首**。

Cecilia practices tai chi in the park every morning.
西西莉雅每天早上在公園裡練習太極拳。

Bart takes a calcium supplement tablet once a day. 巴特每天吃一個鈣片。

Every night **Joyce has to take a sleeping pill before she goes to bed.**
喬伊絲每晚睡前都要吃一顆安眠藥。

4 一些「**明確指出多久**」的頻率副詞，會放在**動詞後面**，也就是**句尾**的位置。

We do file transfers daily.
我們每天交換檔案。

The website is updated monthly.
這個網站每月都會更新。

- daily
- weekly
- monthly
- twice a week

Practice

1

請將括弧內的「頻率副詞」放入句中正確的位置，改寫句子。

1. Trisha gets up at 6:30 in the morning. (usually)

   → *Trisha usually gets up at 6:30 in the morning.*

2. Ester is late for work. (never)

   → _____

3. Vanessa will bring a box of donuts for her coworkers. (sometimes)

   → _____

4. Does Brigit take time off work? (often)

   → _____

5. Felix goes to a client's office. (once a week)

   → _____

6. Irvin writes up his sales report. (daily)

   → _____

2

請依圖示，從第一個框內選出適當的「動詞片語」，第二個框內選出適當的「頻率副詞」，以正確形式搭配填空，完成句子。

have a sandwich for breakfast

has his car maintained

go biking

go to a yoga class

have Thai food

---

every three months

every weekend

every day

once a week

monthly

1. My family _____.

2. I _____.

3. Kim _____.

4. We _____.

5. James _____.

Adverbs of Probability
可能性副詞

1 可能性副詞用來表示「事件發生的可能性」，通常放在**主要動詞的前面**，或者 **be** 動詞和助動詞的後面。

❶ 可能性副詞 + 主要動詞

❷ be 動詞／助動詞 + 可能性副詞

- certainly
- definitely
- obviously
- probably

Probability

Daniel definitely understands the textile business.

丹尼爾一定對紡織業很了解。

Conrad is obviously ready to sign the contract.

顯然康瑞德已經準備好要簽合約了。

Josh is probably talking on the cell phone in the stairwell.

喬許可能正在樓梯間講手機。

Colleen can probably arrange for the first shipment on Monday.

可琳或許能在星期一安排第一批貨運。

Byron will certainly get caught smoking in the bathroom.

拜倫在廁所抽菸一定會被抓到。

Isaac certainly knows his way around the back alleys of this town.

艾薩克想必對城裡的小巷弄熟悉得很。

perhaps		surely	definitely
possibly	maybe	probably	certainly
可能性低			可能性高

2 在「否定句」裡，可能性副詞通常會放在 won't、isn't、not 這些詞彙的**前面**。

The bread definitely won't rise if you forget to add yeast.

如果沒有加酵母，麵包就發不起來。

The price is obviously not cheap, but the quality is excellent.

價格顯然並不便宜，但是品質極佳。

The engagement cake probably won't be ready until tomorrow.

訂婚蛋糕可能要到明天才會好。

3 perhaps 和 maybe 也是可能性副詞，perhaps 比 maybe 來得正式。這兩個副詞只能放在**句首**。

Perhaps we should provide cinnamon rolls during the coffee break.

我們或許應該在休息時間提供肉桂捲。

Maybe I'll call Derek and see if he can swing by with some cookies.

說不定我可以打電話給德瑞克，看他能不能帶點餅乾過來。

Practice

1

請勾選正確的答案。

1. Kristy ☐ knows definitely ☐ definitely knows the subway system in Tokyo since she's been there over ten times.

2. Johnny ☐ certainly won't ☐ won't certainly believe you because he has learned his lesson.

3. The stone is ☐ not obviously ☐ obviously not naturally shaped.

4. ☐ Stanley will perhaps ☐ Perhaps Stanley will visit Busan next month.

5. Sonia ☐ probably is ☐ is probably watching a Wimbledon match in the Center Court.

6. ☐ Maybe Jill ☐ Jill maybe has gone to the Villa Breeze Spa.

2

請將括弧內的「頻率副詞」放入句中正確的位置，改寫句子。

1. Beryl will run in the 100 meter race. (probably)

   → *Beryl will probably run in the 100 meter race.*

2. Amy swims faster than anybody I know. (certainly)

   → _____

3. Luke is in the running for a medal. (definitely)

   → _____

4. Jenna won't continue dancing after her injury. (obviously)

   → _____

5. Kathleen isn't the best teacher, but she is well loved. (certainly)

   → _____

6. Mort is not going to get promoted this year. (probably)

   → _____

7. Shirley can fill in for you while you're gone. (maybe)

   → _____

8. Rod will play his guitar in a concert for the earthquake survivors. (perhaps)

   → _____

Part 15 Adverbs 副詞

Unit 118

Adverbs of Degree
程度副詞

1 程度副詞強調「**事件到什麼程度**」，通常用來修飾**形容詞和其他副詞**，因此，**程度副詞**會放在它們修飾的形容詞或副詞**前面**。

- fairly
- pretty
- almost
- quite
- very
- simply
- rather
- really
- extremely

She was dressed fairly well.
她衣服穿得非常好看。　↳ 修飾副詞

The scent was quite good.
這個味道很好聞。　↳ 修飾形容詞

2 以「**強調的程度**」來說，very、fairly、quite、rather、pretty 這幾個字的語氣強弱如下：

強			弱
very	rather/pretty	quite	fairly

Jerry is a fairly good runner.
傑瑞是個相當不錯的跑者。

Darla is quite hungry. She says let's eat as soon as we can.
黛拉滿餓的，她說我們盡量早點吃飯。

I had a rather long visit with Aunt Edna.
我去艾德娜阿姨那裡待了很久。

Richard is pretty boring, isn't he?
↳ pretty 和 rather 的語氣差不多，但 pretty 較不正式。
李察這個人滿無趣的，是吧？

This restaurant has very large portions.
這個餐廳的食物份量很多。

3 quite 若遇到 a/an，要放在 a/an 前面，其他程度副詞都是放在 a/an 後面。

Tanya is quite a good singer.
譚雅是位很不錯的歌手。

Portia is a fairly good fiddler.
波莎是個很不錯的小提琴手。

4 有些程度副詞也可以修飾**動詞**，如 quite、rather、almost、simply 等，可以放在**主要動詞的前面**，或 **be 動詞和助動詞的後面**。

Brad rather enjoyed himself tonight.
布萊德今晚玩得很盡興。

Carrie is quite pleased with herself these days. 這些日子凱莉對自己的表現頗為滿意。

5 如果要修飾**形容詞比較級**，只能用 rather。

Today's weather is rather colder than yesterday's. 今天的天氣比昨天冷多了。

Today our street is rather noisier than usual. 今天我們街上比平常更吵了。

6 如果要修飾具有「**絕對**」意義的形容詞或副詞，可用 quite，此時 quite 表「**完全**」。

The parrot is quite dead.
這隻鸚鵡已經死了。

No, it's not. That parrot is quite alive. It's just sleeping soundly. Please don't wake it up.
不，牠沒有死，那隻鸚鵡還活著，牠只是睡得很熟，請別把牠吵醒。

Your son behaved quite well today.
你兒子今天表現得很好。

Practice

1

請勾選正確的答案。

1. Polly is ☐ quite ☐ fairly a helpful person.

2. Samuel is a ☐ fairly ☐ quite friendly neighbor.

3. Tim ☐ pretty ☐ quite enjoyed the art exhibit.

4. Warren is ☐ fairly ☐ rather enjoying the party tonight.

5. Aaron is ☐ rather ☐ quite more sincere than I expected.

6. Clive was ☐ fairly ☐ quite a perfect gentleman.

7. The top of the mountain is ☐ extremely cold ☐ cold extremely.

8. Today our class is ☐ rather ☐ very quieter than usual.

9. You are ☐ rather ☐ quite right.

10. Let's hurry. We're ☐ almost there ☐ there almost.

11. She is ☐ rather ☐ quite more professional than I expected.

12. Pam ☐ is quite ☐ quite is good at tennis.

2

請將括弧內的「程度副詞」放入句中正確的位置，改寫句子。

1. Antone is a famous chef. (quite)

   → ....

2. Meg was satisfied with the result. (rather)

   → ....

3. I feel depressed. (fairly)

   → ....

4. Louis drove faster than usual. (rather)

   → ....

5. Tim pushed the "Start" button. (simply)

   → ....

6. Larry is a smart person. (pretty)

   → ....

7. Mom's roast beef is delicious. (really)

   → ....

Unit **119**

Adverbs "Still," "Yet," and "Already"
副詞 Still、Yet、Already 的用法

1 still 是時間副詞，描述「**目前的時間**」、「**較預期晚的時間**」或「**特定的時間**」。
still 可以放在**主要動詞的前面**，或者 **be** 動詞和助動詞的後面。

目前的
情況
My sister **still drives** to work for an hour one way every day.
我姐姐還是每天開一小時的車去上班。

某特定
時間
Stephanie says it **is still** Tuesday in California, but it is Wednesday in Taipei right now.
史黛芬妮說現在加州還是星期二，不過台北已經星期三了。

較預期
晚的時間
Chris **can still get** it done before the end of the day, but he has other things he needs to do first.
克里斯還是可以當天完成工作，只不過他有別的事需要先做。

2 still 可以在**否定句**裡表達「**驚訝**」、「**不耐**」的情緒。此時 still 會放在 won't、haven't 等否定詞彙的**前面**。

The lab tests **still haven't** been completed.
實驗室的測試還有沒完成。

3 yet 是時間副詞，描述「**目前的時間**」、「**較預期晚的時間**」或「**特定的時間**」。
yet 只用於**疑問句**和**否定句**，通常放在**句尾**。

Have you left your office **yet**?
你已經離開辦公室了嗎？
When I last checked, the committee had not finished that project **yet**. 我最後一次查看時，委員會還沒有完成他們的專案。

4 yet 的**否定簡答句**經常用 not yet。

Alan popped in to see if I was ready to go to the gym, but I said, "**Not yet**."
艾倫跑進來看我是不是準備好要去健身房了，但是我說：「還沒有。」
Betsy said, "**Not yet**." I said, "OK. When will you be ready?" 貝西說：「還沒。」我說：「好吧！那什麼時候會好？」

5 already 是時間副詞，描述「**目前的時間**」、「**較預期早的時間**」或「**特定的時間**」。
already 可以放在**主要動詞的前面**，或者 **be** 動詞和助動詞的後面。

The Curry Restaurant chain **has already opened** two more locations.
這家咖哩連鎖餐廳已經多開了兩家分店。
The company **has already filed** the legal papers for its initial public stock offering.
公司已經繳交法律文件申請股票上市。
When I finished visiting all the clients, it **was already** 2:00 and I had missed lunch.
我拜訪完所有的顧客時已經 2 點了，我還沒吃午餐。

6 already 也可放在**句尾**，來「**加強語氣**」。

It's only March, and Darryl has sold his annual quota **already**. 現在才 3 月，德瑞爾就已經把他的年度配額量賣完了。
How did he finish it **already**?
他是如何現在就已經完成的？

They said they would end by noon, but when I checked they had not wrapped up their meeting **yet**.
他們說中午會結束，不過我進去看時，發現他們還沒開完會。

Practice

1

請勾選正確的答案。

1. Clive: Have you picked up little Johnny yet?
   Jenny: ☐ **Not yet** ☐ **Yet not**.

2. Lydia ☐ **knits still** ☐ **still knits** her grandmother a sweater every winter.

3. It ☐ **is still** ☐ **still is** raining outside. It has been raining for two days.

4. We ☐ **can still** ☐ **still can** catch the train if we take a cab.

5. ☐ **Already I have weeded** ☐ **I have already weeded** the garden twice this week.

6. I ☐ **have already warmed up** ☐ **have warmed up already** for twenty minutes. Now I'm going to swim for an hour.

7. I ☐ **cooked already** ☐ **already cooked** two vegetarian dishes. Now I'm going to fry some chicken.

8. Julia hasn't passed the driving test ☐ **still** ☐ **yet**.

9. Have you sold your textbooks ☐ **yet** ☐ **still**?

10. I ☐ **haven't gone to bed yet** ☐ **haven't yet gone to bed**.

2

請用 still、yet 或 already 填空，完成句子。

1. I have _____ called him.

2. He hasn't finished his science report _____.

3. I can _____ remember my trip to Japan five years ago.

4. I _____ look at the photos I took at that time.

5. I have not had an opportunity to go back to Japan _____.

6. Murray has _____ realized his dream of working in Japan.

7. Murray went to Japan two years ago and is _____ there.

8. I thought it was _____ early, but it is actually almost 12 o'clock.

9. It is _____ midnight. You'd better call tomorrow.

10. He has gone to the airport _____.

11. The shoes are _____ on sale. You're lucky.

Unit 120

Adverbs "Too" and "Enough"
副詞 Too 與 Enough 的用法

1 too 和 enough 都可修飾**形容詞和副詞**，但 too 要放在形容詞或副詞**前面**；enough 要放在形容詞或副詞**後面**。

Jacob is too pushy. 雅各實在太過積極了。

Fritz is not persistent enough.

弗里茲不夠有毅力。

2 too much、too many 和 enough 如果修飾**名詞**，則一律放在名詞的**前面**。

Toby gets too many messages.

托比收到太多訊息了。

Sebastian gets too much spam.

賽巴斯丁收到太多垃圾郵件。

Adele has enough cash for the whole trip.

愛黛兒的現金足夠走完整趟旅程。

3 too much、too many 和 enough 也可以單獨使用，當作**代名詞**。

Did you get enough? 你得到的夠嗎？

You gave me too much. 你給我太多了。

I already have too many. 我已經擁有太多了。

4 too 具有**負面意義**，若要表達**正面意義**，要用 very。

Gregory is very tall, but his feet don't stick out of the bed. 葛瑞戈里很高，不過他的腳還不會伸出床鋪外面。

Chester is too tall, and his head and feet both stick out of the bed. 切斯特太高了，他的頭和腳都已經超過床沿了。

5 too 和 enough 的片語後面，可以接 for *somebody*。

I can't take all the leftover food home because it is too much for me.

我沒辦法把剩菜都帶走，那些對我來說太多了。

My knapsack isn't big enough for me to carry all this food.

我的背包不夠大，沒辦法裝下所有這些食物。

6 too 和 enough 的片語後面，可以接「加 to 的不定詞」。

1 「too . . . to . . .」
意指「太……以致於不能……」；

2 「. . . enough to . . .」
意指「夠……而可以……」。

Wally is too young to marry Selma.

威利年紀太輕，還不能娶賽瑪。

Wayne isn't old enough to retire from his job. 偉恩還不到可以退休的年紀。

7 too 和 enough 的片語後面，可以先接 for somebody，再接「加 to 的不定詞」。

It is too early for us to plan the wedding.

現在就計畫婚禮，對我們來說還太早。

Hiram and Stephanie have not been dating long enough for her parents to start thinking about wedding plans.

希來姆和史黛芬妮交往的時間，還沒有久到讓她父母開始考慮婚禮的計畫。

8 too 前面可用 much、a lot、far、a little、a bit 或 rather 來修飾，但 **enough** 不行。

I think we improvised a bit too much when we were assembling the grill.

我想我們在組裝烤肉架的時候多做了一些步驟。

The instructions were much too complicated.

說明書實在太複雜了。

Unfortunately, there are far too many leftover nuts and bolts.

不巧的是還剩下了太多的螺帽和螺絲釘。

Practice

1

請勾選正確的答案。

1. Elizabeth is ☐ too ☐ enough late, and she will miss dinner.

2. Faye says the oven is hot ☐ too ☐ enough now to put in the roast.

3. Lorrie has ☐ too many ☐ too much shoes in her closet.

4. Jill has ☐ too many ☐ too much clothing in her dresser.

5. Martin needs more socks because he doesn't have ☐ enough ☐ too.

6. Sidney wants to move because his apartment is ☐ enough small for him ☐ too small for him.

7. Geraldine says it is ☐ too early to look ☐ enough early to look for a new job.

8. Malcolm says his salary is ☐ much enough high ☐ much too high for him to leave the company.

9. Dinah has ☐ coins enough ☐ enough coins for the tolls on the highway.

2

請依圖示，從框內選出適當的用語填空，完成對話。

too

too many

much

enough

Ⓐ I've prepared ❶ _____enough_____ fruit for your diet today.

Ⓑ Those are ❷ _____ for me. I only need one apple today.

Ⓐ Maybe you'll be interested in some blueberries. They are a little sweet and sour, but not ❸ _____ sweet and sour.

Ⓑ Thanks, but I had ❹ _____ blueberries yesterday. I think I'll have some orange juice now.

Ⓐ I know there isn't ❺ _____ orange juice left, but I'd like to have a glass, please.

Adverbs "So," "Such," "Anymore/Longer," and "No Longer"

副詞 So、Such、Anymore/Longer、No Longer 的用法

so/such

1 such 通常放在**名詞的前面**，該名詞可以帶有**形容詞**，也可以沒有。
名詞前面如果有 a/an，則 such 要位於 a/an 之前。

I've never seen such a big motorcycle.
我從沒看過這麼大的摩托車！
I felt happy to have achieved such an accomplishment.
對於達到如此的成就我覺得很開心！

2 so 則是修飾**形容詞或副詞**，不直接修飾**名詞**。

Derek is so agile. 德瑞克是如此敏捷！

Don't be so selfish. 別這麼自私！

Brian prepared for yesterday's department meeting so thoroughly that his boss was very impressed.
布萊恩為了昨天的部門會議做了十足的準備，他的老闆很滿意。

3 so 可以搭配 many 和 much 來表達**數量**，但 **such** 沒有這種用法。

There were so many customers in the meeting room that I had to stand.
會議室裡的顧客太多了，我不得不站著。

Gary has so much money that he doesn't know what to do with it.
蓋瑞有太多錢，不知道該如何用。

4 such 可以搭配 a lot (of) 來表達**數量**，**so** 則不行。

We have such a lot of cheese. Maybe we should have pizza every night for a week.
我們有這麼多的起司，也許這個星期的每天晚上我們都應該吃披薩。

Stuart has such a lot of work. I am going to help him.
史都華有這麼多工作得做，我要去幫他的忙。

5 so 和 such 都可以搭配 that 子句，來表示「**事情的結果**」，但句型不同。

❶ | so | + | 形容詞 | + | that 子句 |
❷ | such | + | 名詞 | + | that 子句 |

The meeting went so long that I missed lunch. 會議開得太久，害我錯過了午餐。
It was such a successful presentation that everybody wanted to shake the speaker's hand. 那場發表會實在太成功了，大家都想去和演講者握手致意。

anymore / any longer / no longer

6 「not . . . anymore」和「not . . . any longer」用來表示「**情況已經改變**」、「**事情已不再如此**」，通常放在**句尾**。

Candice is not single anymore.
康蒂絲已經不再是單身了。
Edna does not work for our airline any longer. 艾德娜已經不在我們航空公司上班了。

7 no longer 也表示「**情況已經改變**」、「**事情已不再如此**」。no longer 會放在**主要動詞**前面，或 **be** 動詞和助動詞後面。

Jasper no longer volunteers at the hospital.
賈士柏沒有在醫院當義工了。
Tracey is no longer delivering newspapers.
崔西現在已經沒有送報紙了。
My parents can no longer afford my tuition.
我的父母再也負擔不起我的學費了。

8 no more 的意義和「**not . . . anymore/longer**」以及
no longer 很類似，但沒有 no anymore 這樣的用法。

✗ The mother told the babysitter no anymore dessert
for the twins.

✓ The mother told the babysitter no more dessert for
the twins.

這位母親對保姆說，不要再給雙胞胎吃點心了。

Practice

1

請用 so 或 such 填空，
完成句子。

1. After the party, the house was _____ a mess.

2. Why has Sue had _____ many headaches since she became
pregnant?

3. Why are you walking _____ slowly?

4. Annabelle is _____ kind and generous.

5. It was _____ a good performance that the band gave two encores.

6. Bruce is _____ a tough kid that we never have to worry about him.

7. The scenery was _____ amazing that no one wanted to stop taking
pictures.

8. There are _____ many phone calls this morning. I could hardly
concentrate on my work.

2

請從括弧內選出適當
的「副詞片語」，插
入句子中改寫句子。

1. Victoria doesn't wear glasses. (anymore / no longer)

→ *Victoria doesn't wear glasses anymore.*

2. Matthew watches auto racing on TV. (no longer / any longer)

→

3. Laurie doesn't read comic books. (anymore / no longer)

→

4. Sandy is very tired. She can't drive today. (no more / any longer)

→

5. Andy will play in the Asian Cup. (no longer / any longer)

→

Unit **122**

Linking Words of Time: When, As, While, As Soon As, Before, After, Until

表示「時間」的連接語：

When、As、While、As Soon As、Before、After、Until

1 如果要說明「**兩件同時發生的事情**」，常用 when、as 和 while 來連接**兩個子句**。其中 when/as/while 的子句裡，會用進行式來表示「**持續時間較長的動作**」。

When I am swimming, I don't use goggles.
我游泳的時候不戴泳鏡。

As I am swimming up and down the lane, I count my laps. 我在水道來回游泳時，計算了自己游了幾趟。

As I am swimming up and down the lane, I feel something like a runner's high. 當我在水道中游泳時，感覺到一陣運動的快感。

When I start out, I swim slowly, but later I swim hard and fast.
↳ 要注意的是，while 不能用於「短暫的動作」；when 才可以。

當我開始游時，我游得很慢，不過接著我加快速度賣力地游。

2 說明「**兩件同時發生的事情**」時，可以用 just as 來描述「**持續時間較短的動作**」。

My adrenaline peaks just as I hit the water. 就在我揮手拍打水面時，我的腎上腺素急速分泌。

3 如果要說明「**直到某個時候**」，會用 until 和 till。

Susan worked in the garden until sunset.
蘇珊在花園裡工作直到日落。

Al studied at the library till midnight.
艾爾在圖書館裡唸書直到午夜。

4 如果要說明「**兩件接連發生的事情**」，可以用 when、as soon as、before 和 after 來連接**兩個子句**。

After I got my haircut, I called home to check on the kids. 當我剪完頭髮後，便打電話回家確認孩子有沒有事。

The nanny said she would serve dinner as soon as I got home. 保姆說我一到家，她就會把晚餐端上桌。

I said I might not get home before the kids had dinner.
我說孩子們吃晚餐前，我可能沒辦法回到家。

As it turned out, I was delayed and didn't get home until after the kids had a bath.
結果我耽擱了，一直到孩子們洗完澡才回到家。

5 when 的用法十分靈活，在某些情況下，when 的意義常相當於 while、as、before 或 after。

When/While/As Lena was washing the dishes, she heard a crash in the living room. 莉娜洗碗的時候，聽到客廳傳來一陣巨大的聲響。

A different real estate agent had sold the house when/before we had a chance to look at it. 我們還沒有來得及去參觀那棟房子時，房子已經被另一名房屋仲介售出了。

When/After Arthur had finished mowing the lawn and trimming the bushes, the property looked great. 在亞瑟除過草、修剪過樹叢之後，整個建築景觀看起來棒極了。

6 when、as soon as、before 所引導的子句，可以用現在簡單式來表達「未來」意義。

I have told the housekeeper we'll talk about the weekend schedule as soon as I get home. 我告訴管家等我回到家，我們再討論週末的安排。

Practice

1

請勾選正確的答案。

1. ☐ **When** ☐ **Just as** I was flying between Kaohsiung and Sydney, I read the whole book.

2. ☐ **While** ☐ **When** Jessica finished mopping the kitchen floor, she cleaned the bathroom.

3. I will call my uncle ☐ **as soon as** ☐ **while** I get home.

4. The basketball coach waited ☐ **until** ☐ **when** all the players had finished running ☐ **before** ☐ **until** beginning skill drills.

5. Mark usually takes a shower ☐ **as soon as** ☐ **before** he gets up.

6. I drank a cup of tea ☐ **while** ☐ **until** I was reading the newspaper.

2

請用括弧內的「連接詞」合併句子。

1. I counted the steps. I was walking home from the MRT station. (when)
   → *I counted the steps when I was walking home from the MRT station.*

2. You have food in your mouth. Do not speak. (when)
   →

3. I was making a cup of cappuccino. I got grains of instant coffee all over the table. (while)
   →

4. Mom was humming a lullaby. The baby fell asleep. (while)
   →

5. The light went out. We were playing cards. (as)
   →

6. I lost eight pounds. I quit eating hamburgers and French fries. (after)
   →

7. Dad checked on the electricity, gas, and windows. We set off for our vacation. (before)
   →

8. I ran to my computer and checked the email. I got home. (as soon as)
   →

Unit **123**

Linking Words of Contrast:
Although, Even Though, Though, However,
In Spite Of, Despite, While, Whereas
表示「對比」的連接語：**Although**、
Even Though、**Though**、**However**、**In**
Spite Of、**Despite**、**While**、**Whereas**

1 連接詞 although 和 even though 都用來連結「**相反的概念**」，意指「**雖然**」。兩者都要連接主句和子句。
even though 的語氣比 although 來得強烈。

Although we were on the ninth floor, we didn't have a view because of the fog.
雖然我們身在九樓，但是卻看不到什麼景觀，因為都被霧遮住了。

We went up to the rooftop garden, even though we knew it was rainy and overcast. 雖然我們知道天氣陰雨，但還是上去了屋頂花園。

Even though you are late for work, I will let it go this time.
雖然你上班遲到，不過這次我就算了。

2 連接詞 though 的意義和 **although** 一樣，但 though 多用於非正式用語中。

Though it was cold, we enjoyed our picnic in the park.
天氣雖然很冷，我們還是很享受在公園裡野餐。

Though you've explained the plan thoroughly, I still don't understand.
雖然你已經鉅細靡遺地解釋了這個計畫，我還是不懂。

3 however 是副詞，也可以用來連接兩個「**對比的概念**」。

An old car requires constant maintenance. However, keeping an old car is cheaper than buying a new car.
一輛舊車得持續保養，但是養一部舊車比買一部新車便宜多了。

比較

though 如果放在**句尾**，意義就等同於 **however**。

• The cost of the building is high, but it is quite spacious though.
這棟大樓的價格很高，不過空間卻也很寬敞。

4 in spite of 和 despite 也用於表示「**對比的概念**」，但兩者都是介系詞（片語），後面要接**名詞**，而不是接子句。

In spite of Clint's negative reaction, we went ahead with the plan.
儘管科林特反對，我們還是繼續進行計畫。

Despite Blake's connections, he couldn't get an interview. 雖然布雷克有人脈關係，卻還是沒得到面試的機會。

5 如果要連接**主句**和**子句**，要用 in spite of the fact that 或 despite the fact that，兩個句型中的 that 都**可以省略**。

In spite of the fact (that) only half the sales reps showed up, the event was a success. 儘管只有一半的業務員現身，整場活動依然非常成功。

Despite the fact (that) there was no advance preparation, somehow the whole thing worked out fine.
雖然沒有預先準備，但整件事進展順利。

6 although 的意義和用法與 **in spite of the fact** 相當（後面接名詞），但用法不同於 **in spite of**（後面接子句）。

In spite of the fact that Dina and Gordon could have walked home, they took a taxi.
= Although Dina and Gordon could have walked home, they took a taxi.
雖然蒂娜和高登可以走路回家，但他們還是搭了計程車。

7 連接詞 while 和 whereas 也可以用來連接「對比的概念」。

I like to go fishing whereas my sister Jane likes to go mountain climbing.
= I like to go fishing while my sister Jane likes to go mountain climbing.
我喜歡釣魚，而我姐姐珍喜歡爬山。

Practice

1 請用括弧內的「連接詞」，合併句子。

1. Kathy likes toy dinosaurs, but she doesn't like dinosaur movies. (although)
   → ....

2. The plot was silly, but we enjoyed the movie. (despite)
   → ....

3. The movie was a little long, but it was great. (though)
   → ....

4. We planned to have dinner in the Italian restaurant before the movie, but we didn't have time. (though)
   → ....

   ....

5. The movie received bad reviews, but we went to see it anyway. (in spite of)
   → ....

6. Hank planned to stay up for the late movie, but he fell asleep before it started. (even though)
   → ....

7. Alan looks very conservative, but his wife is totally wild and artistic. (while)
   → ....

8. Jerry likes to get up at dawn, but his wife likes to sleep until noon. (whereas)
   → ....

Unit **124**

Linking Words of Reason: Because, Because Of, As, Since, Due To

表示「原因」的連接語：Because、Because Of、As、Since、Due To

1 because 表「**原因**」，後面要接**子句**，這種子句因為修飾整個主要子句，因此屬於**副詞子句**。because 子句可以位於**句首**，也可以位於**句尾**。

Because my brother was addicted to online games, Dad refused to buy him a new computer. 我哥哥因為沉迷網路遊戲，老爸不願意幫他買新電腦。

My mother fed the children some soup because they were hungry. 我媽媽餵孩子們喝了點湯，因為他們肚子餓了。

The kids slept at my mother's house because it was late when we returned.
孩子們睡在我媽媽家，因為我們回去時已經太晚了。

2 because of 表示「**原因**」，屬於**介系詞片語**，後面要接**名詞**，不能接子句。

We like downhill skiing because of the thrill. 我們喜歡下坡滑雪，因為很刺激。
We don't go skiing often because of the cost.
我們不常去滑雪，因為很花錢。

3 as 可以表示「**原因**」，as 子句可以位於**句首**，也可以位於**句尾**，意義等同 **because**。

As I had no idea what they were talking about, I just kept my mouth shut and nodded every now and then. 因為我根本不知道他們在說些什麼，只好閉上嘴，不時點點頭。

4 since 可以表示「**原因**」，since 子句可以位於**句首**，也可以位於**句尾**，意義等同 **because**。

Since you know about the topic, why not give a short presentation on it and share your point of view?
既然你對這個議題已經完全瞭解，何不做個簡短的報告，跟大家分享你的觀點呢？

I was stunned when they asked me to stand up and say something since it seemed to them that I knew everything about the topic. 他們好像以為我對這個主題瞭如指掌，所以當他們要我站起來發言時，我整個人傻眼。

5 due to 是**介系詞片語**，可表示「**原因**」，後面要接**名詞**而不接子句。根據傳統語法，「due to + 名詞」片語只能當做**形容詞**，置於 be 動詞後面，但現在也可以用作**副詞**，意思相當於 **owing to**、**because of**、**as a result of**。

All the flights to Hong Kong were cancelled due to the nasty weather.
所有飛香港的航班，都因天候不佳而取消了。

6 due to 後面如果要接**子句**，要用 due to the fact that。

Due to the fact that vitamin C has a great effect on anti-oxidization, it has been widely applied in skin care products. 維他命 C 具有優異的抗氧化效用，已被廣泛運用於肌膚保養品之中。

Everybody assumed that I already knew all about the topic as I didn't ask any questions. 由於我沒發問，大家都假定我對這個主題已經完全瞭解。

Practice

1

請勾選正確的答案。

1. Arnold was tired ☐ because ☐ because of he stayed up late the previous night.

2. ☐ Since ☐ Due to Jim was delayed, everybody had to wait.

3. Gabriel didn't buy the house ☐ since ☐ because of the price.

4. I changed designers ☐ due to ☐ due to the fact that the first one was so irresponsible.

5. ☐ As ☐ Due to I know he has a large house mortgage, I won't invite him on our trip to New Zealand.

6. ☐ So ☐ Because you don't want my opinion, I won't say anything from now on.

2

請用括弧內提供的「連接語」取代原句的粗體連接語，改寫句子。

1. **Because** he is miserly, I won't ask him for help. (because of)
   → *Because of his miserliness, I won't ask him for help.*

2. **Because** it was raining, we had to stay home. (because of)
   → ....

3. **Because of** his generosity, we survived the hard times. (because)
   → ....

4. They decided to close the front gate after sunset **due to** security concerns. (since)
   → ....
   ....

5. **Due to the fact that** cherries are rich in vitamins, they are good for our health. (due to)
   → ....
   ....

6. He can't play tennis as well as before **because of** his ankle injury. (as)
   → ....

7. **Since** he didn't play fair in the final, he was deprived of the title two days after the match. (as)
   → ....
   ....

261

Unit 125

Linking Words of Result: So, As A Result, Therefore, So . . . That, Such . . . That

表示「結果」的連接語：So、As A Result、Therefore、So . . . That、Such . . . That

1 連接詞 so 常用來表示「**結果**」，後面會接**子句**。so 引導的表示結果的子句要放在**主句後面**，常用**逗號**跟主要子句分開。

I had already eaten, so I said that I wasn't hungry. ↳ 以逗號分開

我已經吃過了，所以我說我不餓。

Bonnie was tapping her foot in time to the music, so I asked her if she wanted to dance.

邦妮隨著音樂節奏用腳打拍子，所以我問她想不想跳舞。

2 as a result 也用來表示「**結果**」，是一個**副詞片語**，在句中可有多種位置。

I hadn't eaten any dessert for two months. As a result, I lost five pounds. ↳ 位於句首

= I hadn't eaten any dessert for two months. I lost five pounds as a result.

我已經兩個月沒吃甜食了，所以瘦了五磅。 ↳ 位於句尾

✗ There were no jobs in my hometown as a result I moved to the city.

✓ There were no jobs in my hometown and as a result I moved to the city.

↳ 因為 as a result 是副詞片語，不是連接詞，所以不能用來連接兩個子句，這裡搭配了 and 使用。

我家鄉沒有工作可做，所以就搬到城市來。

3 therefore 可以用來表示「**結果**」，屬於比較**正式**的用法。therefore 本身是**副詞**，在句子中可以有多種位置。

I didn't have any friends or relatives in the city, and therefore I had to get my own place to live.

↳ 因為 therefore 是副詞，不是連接詞，所以不能用來連接兩個子句，這裡搭配了 and 使用。

我在城市裡沒有朋友，也沒有親戚，所以得自己找地方住。

The apple pie was delicious. Therefore, I asked for a second piece. ↳ 位於句首

= The apple pie was delicious. I, therefore, asked for a second piece. ↳ 位於句中

那塊蘋果派非常美味，結果我又點了第二塊。

I didn't have enough money to buy a house, and I therefore decided to rent an apartment. ↳ therefore 可以直接接動詞，但這種用法較不普遍。

我的錢不夠買一棟房子，所以我決定租一間公寓。

4 「so . . . that」片語可以表示「**結果**」，意思是「**太……以致於**」。so 後面要接**形容詞**，也就是「so + 形容詞 + that 子句」。

The tea was so good (that) I drank several cups. ↳ that 可以省略。

茶太好喝了，所以我喝了好幾杯。

5 「such . . . that」片語也表示「**結果**」，意思是「**太……以致於**」。such 後面要接**名詞**，也就是「such + 名詞 + that 子句」。

It was such a good price (that) I bought five boxes of the tea. ↳ that 可以省略。

因為價格太划算，於是我買了五盒茶。

Practice

1

請勾選正確的答案。

1. □ As □ So Vera felt exhausted, she closed her eyes for a couple of minutes.

2. Joey was in a comfortable armchair, and □ as a result □ since he fell fast asleep.

3. There was a traffic jam on the highway, □ so □ because we took side streets.

4. The traffic on the route Monica took was slow. □ As a result □ since, she was late.

5. Linda is □ so □ such a good cook that even a simple meal at her house is a gourmet feast.

6. Yesterday was □ so □ such hot that I stayed indoors all day.

2

請依據範例，將括弧內的「副詞片語」分別以兩種位置改寫句子。

1. Grandma was sick. We had to put off our trip. (as a result)

   → *Grandma was sick. As a result, we had to put off our trip.*

   → *Grandma was sick. We had to put off our trip as a result.*

2. We didn't have vegetables at home. We went out for dinner. (therefore)

   → ....

   → ....

3. I left home late this morning. I was caught in the traffic. (as a result)

   → ....

   → ....

3

請將下列使用 so 的句子以 such 改寫；反之，使用 such 的句子以 so 改寫。

1. Those peaches were so sweet that I ate three of them.

   → ....

   ....

2. It was such splendid scenery that we took hundreds of pictures.

   → ....

   ....

3. The show was so amazing that the audience applauded the performers for three minutes.

   → ....

   ....

Unit **126**

Linking Words of Purpose: To, In order To, So As To, For, So That

表示「目的」的連接語：To、In Order To、So As To、For、So That

1 「加 to 的不定詞」常用來表示「目的」。

Let's stop at this convenience store to buy a bottle of water.

我們在這間便利商店停下來買瓶水吧。

Dave uses Skype to communicate with his son who is studying abroad.

戴夫使用 Skype 來和在國外求學的兒子聯絡。

2 in order to 和 so as to 也用來表示「目的」，兩者後面都是加不定詞。

Can I use your truck in order to move some furniture and boxes?

我可以借用你的卡車搬些家具和箱子嗎？

We vacuum pack the rice so as to prevent it from being spoiled.

我們用真空包裝白米是為了防止腐壞。

3 in order to 和 so as to 的**否定句型**是 in order not to 和 so as not to，表示「目的是不要……」。

✗ Did you call in sick not to miss your son's gymnastics meet?

✓ Did you call in sick in order not to miss your son's gymnastics meet?

你打電話請病假，是為了不想錯過兒子的體操比賽嗎？

I sneaked into the room so as not to wake you up.

我躡手躡腳溜進房間，因為不想吵醒你。

4 如果要接**子句**，可以用 in order that 的句型。

Steve leaves a light on every night in order that he won't trip over something when he uses the bathroom at night.

史帝夫每晚都留一盞燈，以便半夜上廁所時不會絆到東西。

5 for 也是常用來表「**目的**」的介系詞，後面要接**名詞**或**動名詞**。

Use these noodles for dinner.

用這些麵條來煮晚餐吧。

Eve is going to Seoul for plastic surgery.

伊芙要去首爾做整型手術。

This razor is good for shaving legs.

這把剃刀用來刮腿毛很好用。

Mick uses his room for storing samples.

米克把他的房間用來存放樣品。

6 so that 可以說明「**目的**」，後面要接**子句**，子句裡常使用 can、can't、will、won't 等助動詞。**that 可以省略**。

Conrad always breaks a big bill before taking a cab so (that) he can pay the driver the exact fare.

康瑞德會在搭計程車前先把大鈔換成零錢，這樣就可以給計程車駕駛剛好的車費。

Ellen takes the bus so (that) she won't have to spend money on cabs. 愛倫選擇搭公車，就不必把錢花在計程車費上。

7 so that 也可以搭配 could、couldn't、would、wouldn't，說明「**過去的目的**」。

Nicole called her friend Jay <u>so (that) he</u> <u>could</u> help translate a letter from Poland.

妮可打電話給她的朋友傑，請他幫忙翻譯來自波蘭的信。

Liz hired a limo to pick up Greg at the airport <u>so (that)</u> he wouldn't have to take the bus.

莉茲租了禮車去接機場接葛瑞格，他就不必搭巴士了。

Practice

1

請用括弧提示的「連接語」，將兩個句子合併。

1. William brought his own bag. He needs to carry his groceries. (to)
   → *William brought his own bag to carry his groceries.*

2. The dog wants to go for a walk. The dog needs to go to the bathroom. (so as to)
   →

3. Lauren got to the store early. She wanted to avoid the rush. (in order to)
   →

4. Kevin often eats dinner out. He wants to avoid messing up his kitchen. (so as not to)
   →

5. Paulina bought some shrimp. She will have shrimp for lunch. (for)
   →

6. Lawrence has a knife with a serrated edge. The knife is good for cutting bread. (for)
   →

7. Nadia will give you some money. You can buy a new dress. (so that)
   →

8. Tamara closed the window. That way it wouldn't get too cold. (so that)
   →

Unit **127**

Linking Words of Purpose: In Case
表示「目的」的連接語：**In Case**

1 in case（以防）可以用來表示「**目的**」，說明「**做某事的目的是什麼**」。
in case 的後面會接子句，當表示「**未來的目的**」時，會用現在簡單式。

Bring a bottle of water **in case** you get thirsty.

帶一瓶水免得你口渴。

Please give me your business card **in case** I need to contact you.

請給我一張名片，好讓我能跟你聯絡。

2 in case 和 if 不同，if 說的是「**假設**」，in case 則是「**明確要做準備**」。in case 用來談論預防措施，意思是「**以防、免得**」。

Save a seat for Randy **in case** he comes.
↳ 確定要為藍迪過來而找好位子。
幫藍迪留個位子，他要是來了就有得坐。

We will find a seat for Randy **if** he comes.
↳ 如果藍迪過來，才會幫他找位子。
如果藍迪過來，我們會幫他找個位子。

3 in case 如果用來說明「**過去做某件事的目的**」，則會用過去簡單式。

I ordered a lunch box for Rhonda **in case** she forgot to buy one.

我替蘭達點了一個便當，以防她忘了買。

I invited all the parents **in case** they wanted to come. 我邀請了所有的家長，這樣他們想來就可以來。

4 in case 後面所接的事件，如果**發生的機率不太確定**，則會在子句中使用 should。

Reserve a later connecting flight **in case** your first flight is delayed.
↳ 認為飛機延誤的可能性不小
轉接的班機訂晚一點，以免你的頭一班飛機延誤。

Reserve a later connecting flight **in case** your first flight should be delayed.
↳ 不太確定飛機會不會延誤
轉接的班機訂晚一點，以防你的頭一班飛機延誤。

比較

in case of 和 in case 不同。in case of 是指「**萬一**」、「**如果某事發生的話**」，後面會接名詞。

• **In case of** emergency, dial 119.

萬一發生緊急事件的話，就撥 119。

Practice

1

請用 if 或 in case 填空，完成句子。

1. Bring your coat _____ it gets cold.
2. Let's make more sandwiches _____ Joey comes for lunch.
3. Write down your mailing address _____ I need to forward any mail.
4. I called to reserve another table _____ your sister's family comes.
5. Go back to your office _____ you haven't finished your report.
6. I will pack our swimsuits _____ the hotel has a pool.

2

請分別自 A 欄和 B 欄選出語意搭配的子句，以 in case 連結，造出句子。

A ▶

take your purse with you	lock your cell phone keypad
give me your phone number	give Mary a call
call him later	back up your files every day

B ▶

 you accidentally make a call

 I need to reach you

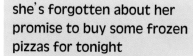 she's forgotten about her promise to buy some frozen pizzas for tonight

 your computer crashes

 you want to buy anything while walking the dog

 he hasn't arrived at the office

1. _Take your purse with you in case you want to buy anything while walking the dog._
2. _____
3. _____
4. _____
5. _____
6. _____

Unit **128**

Prepositions of Place:
Basic Meanings of "In," "At," and "On"
表示「地點」的介系詞：
In、At、On 的基本意義

in the vehicle
在裡面

on the vehicle
上方；有接觸到

at the end
在一個點上

1 in 表示「在一個三度空間裡」。

Put the book **in your backpack**.
把書放進你的背包裡。
We will be **in the garden**.
我們會在花園裡。

2 on 表示「在一個平面上」。

Please pick up your socks **on the floor**.
請把你地板上的襪子撿起來。
Sign your name **on the lease**, and give them the deposit.
請你在租約上簽名，再把保證金交給他們。

3 at 表示「在一個點上」。

Let's meet **at the train station**.
我們約在火車站見面吧。
I was standing **at the main entrance** to the museum.
我當時就站在博物館的主要入口前。

4 in 也可以表示「在一個特定的範圍內」。

Your name is mentioned **in the email message**.
電子郵件的訊息裡有提到你的名字。
I think that city is somewhere **in Brazil**.
我想那座城市位在巴西的某個地方。

5 on 也可表示「在一條線上」。

A squirrel is standing **on the fence**.
有一隻松鼠站在籬笆上。

It's risky to stand **on the edge** of a cliff.
站在懸崖邊緣是很危險的。

Practice

1

請用 in、at 或 on 填空，完成句子。

1. Tina is waiting _____ the ticket window.

2. Your keys are _____ the kitchen table.

3. Get off the highway _____ the Cedar Point exit.

4. I put your watch _____ the drawer. Did you see it?

5. Can you put this dictionary _____ the top shelf for me?

6. Jeffery left his suitcase _____ the sofa again.

2

請依圖示，用 in、at 或 on 填空，完成句子。

1 Lulu was told to sit _____ the dike and wait.

2 Migu is looking at the goldfish _____ the aquarium.

3 Sunny and Moony wait _____ the front door every evening.

4 The little boy is hanging the laundry _____ the clothesline.

5 Muddy is _____ the door ringing the bell. He wants to get inside.

Unit 129

Prepositions of Place:
"In," "At," and "On" With Different Locations
表示「地點」的介系詞：
In、At、On 說明各種地點的用法

1 in、at、on 常用來說明「**實際地點**」。

Yvonne's office is in the Hancock Building. 伊芳的辦公室就在漢考克大樓裡。

The elevator in the Guangzhou CTF Finance Center is the fastest in the world.
廣州周大福金融中心的電梯是全世界速度最快的。

We ate lunch in/at the food court in the basement of the Taipei 101 building.
我們在台北 101 樓下的美食街吃午餐。

2 如果特別強調「**在一棟建築物內進行活動**」，也就是強調「**建築物的功能**」的話，常用 at。

Henry is getting money at the bank.
亨利正在銀行領錢。

Trudy is studying at/in college.
楚蒂正在大學唸書。

Terrence is paying his overdue bill at the phone company office on Central Avenue. 泰倫斯正在位於中央大道的電話公司繳交過期的帳單。

3 說明「**在某個城市、城鎮內**」，要用 in。

The brewery is in Sapporo.
啤酒廠就位於札幌市。

Reporters from many countries gathered in New York to broadcast the World Series. 許多國家的記者進駐紐約，轉播美國職棒總冠軍賽。

4 但如果只是「**旅途中經過某個城市或城鎮**」，則要用 at。

The bus will stop at the park after we have lunch.
等我們吃完午餐，巴士會在公園停下來。

We will stop at Tokyo, Yokohama, and Kamakura on this trip. 我們這次的行程將會參觀東京、橫濱和鎌倉。

5 in、at、on 經常拿來說明「**地址**」，既定用法如下：

國家、洲名、城市 → **in**

I lived in Australia for three years.
我在澳洲住了三年。

街道 → **on**

We live on Wentworth Street, near the corner of Forest Avenue. 我們住在溫沃斯街，接近佛瑞斯特大道的轉角。

含門牌號碼的地址 → **at**

I live at 421 Judson Avenue.
我住在賈德森大道 421 號。

樓層 → **on**

Our apartment is on the third floor.
我們的公寓在三樓。

6 說明「**在某條河川、海岸**」，會用 on。

We cruised on the Yangtze River and enjoyed the scenery along its banks.
我們航行於長江之上，欣賞沿岸風光。

We stayed on the East Coast for two weeks.
我們在東岸停留了兩週。

Practice

1

請用 in、at 或 on 填空，完成句子。

1. Fred is _____ the garage.

2. There is a historic house _____ my neighborhood.

3. The house is _____ Old River Road.

4. We live _____ the town of West Milton.

5. The meeting will be held _____ our office.

6. There are two large conference rooms _____ our office building.

7. My grandmother lives _____ 201 East 74th Street.

8. I went to the bookstore _____ Angel Avenue last night.

2

請依圖示，用 in、at 或 on 填空，完成句子。

1 Three old boats are floating _____ the river.

2 Lisa studied the Patent Act _____ graduate school.

3 The train will stop _____ Union Station.

4 The 2022 FIFA World Cup will take place _____ Qatar.

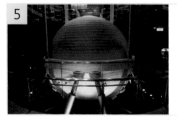

5 A tuned mass damper _____ the Taipei 101 building is a technique to control seismic vibration.

Unit 130

Prepositions of Place:
Over, Under, Above, Below, Underneath
表示「地點」的介系詞：Over、Under、Above、Below、Underneath

over the boat
正上方；未接觸到

under the boat
正下方；未接觸到

above the boat
上方（不必正上方）

below the boat
下方（不必正下方）

1 over 表示「某物的位置高於另一物」，通常是垂直的相對關係，也就是「正上方」。

Turn on the light that is over the table.
把桌子上方的燈打開。

2 under 表「某物的位置低於另一物」，通常是垂直的相對關係，也就是「正下方」。

Clean up the food on the floor under the table. 把桌子底下地板上的食物清理乾淨。
I saw a mouse under the sofa this afternoon!
我今天下午在沙發底下發現一隻老鼠！

3 over 也可以表示「覆蓋」；under 也可以表示「被覆蓋」。

Pour the sauce over the vegetables.
把醬汁倒到蔬菜上。

The rice should be under the omelet.
白飯應該被蓋在歐姆蛋下面。

4 above 表「某物的位置高於另一物」，但不在同一垂直線上，也就是「非正上方」。

The birds glided above the lake and trees.
鳥兒飛過湖泊和樹木上空。

5 below 表示「某物的位置低於另一物」，但不在同一垂直線上，也就是「非正下方」。

Bob was standing below the birds.
鮑伯就站在鳥兒下方。
From the top of the Taipei 101 building, we could see the city below.
我們可以從台北 101 的頂樓眺望整座城市。

6 underneath 的意義和用法等同於 under。

He's hiding underneath/under the blanket. 他躲在毯子下面。

272

Practice

1

請勾選正確的答案。

1. The ball rolled □ under □ below the sofa.
2. The mobile dangled □ over □ under the baby's crib.
3. Be sure to sweep the dirt □ under □ below the floor mat.
4. Aren't those snow-capped mountains □ above □ over the village beautiful?
5. You can spread out the jigsaw puzzle pieces □ above □ over the whole table.
6. Who is that guy talking and laughing □ above □ below our tree house?

2

請依圖示，從框內選出適當的「介系詞」填空，完成句子。

over　　under　　below　　above

1

Pour some tarragon sauce _____ the grilled salmon and garnish it with vegetables before you serve the dish.

2

A meerkat is an animal that lives _____ the ground.

3

The moon hangs quietly _____ our city.

4

A lionfish swam _____ the diver.

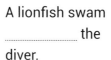

5

Jenny is snorkeling _____ the surface of the ocean.

6

Susan kept her money _____ the mattress.

Unit **131**

Prepositions of Place: In Front Of, Behind, Between, Among, Opposite
表示「地點」的介系詞：In Front Of、Behind、Between、Among、Opposite

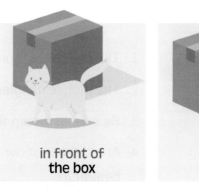

in front of **the box**

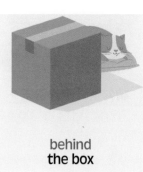

behind **the box**

1 in front of 指「在某物／人的前面」。

Ernie is standing in front of the elementary school.

爾尼正站在小學的前面。

Do not stand in front of the car when it's being started.

車子發動的時候，不要站在車子前面。

2 behind 意指「在某物／人的後面」。

The children are playing behind the bus shelter. 孩子們正在公車亭後面玩耍。

I was scared by a stray dog coming out from behind the tree. 我被樹後面跑出來的一隻流浪狗給嚇到了。

3 between 意指「在兩個物品／人物的中間」。

Sonny's motorcycle is between the tree and the fire hydrant.

桑尼的摩托車就停在樹木和消防栓之間。

Who is that girl sitting between Johnny and Annie?

坐在強尼和安妮中間的那個女生是誰？

4 among 意指「在三個以上之物品／人物的中間」。

Peter is the best singer among his classmates. 彼得是全班最會唱歌的人。

between **the boxes**

among **the boxes**

opposite

5 opposite 表示「在對面」。

The lion and the hyenas stood opposite each other, ready to fight for the dead antelope.

獅子和土狼群為了爭奪一頭死掉的羚羊而對峙，準備打鬥。

Practice

1 請依圖示，勾選正確的答案。

There is a woman ☐ opposite ☐ in front of the gate.

Lily was ☐ between ☐ among the students who raised their hands to answer the teacher's question.

The puppies are kissing their mother, who is sitting ☐ among ☐ between them.

Do you recognize the boy ☐ behind ☐ opposite the chain link fence?

2 請從框內選出適當的「介系詞」填空，完成句子。

between

among

behind

in front of

opposite

1. May I stand _____ you? You're taller than me. I can't see the singer on the stage.

2. Can we buy some sugar cane juice from the drink vendor on the _____ side of the street?

3. Who's there hiding _____ the curtain?

4. Do you have to travel _____ the clinic and your house every day?

5. Our teacher let us discuss it _____ ourselves before explaining in detail.

Part 17 Prepositions of Place and Movement
表示地點與移動方向的介系詞

Unit 132

Prepositions of Place: Near, Next To, By, Beside, Against, Inside, Outside
表示「地點」的介系詞：
Near、Next To、By、Beside、
Against、Inside、Outside

inside
the box

outside
the box

near
the box

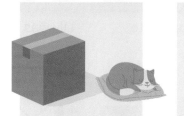
next to
the box

by/beside
the box

against
the box

---

1 near 表示「在附近」。

The university is near the town of Amherst. 這所大學離安赫斯特鎮很近。
The kids are playing near the lake.
孩子們在湖泊附近玩耍。

2 next to 表示「比鄰著」。

The dormitory is next to the Sports Center. 宿舍就在體育中心旁邊。
Would you mind if I sat next to you?
你介不介意我坐在你旁邊？

3 by 和 beside 的意義相同，都指「在旁邊」。

The Science Center is by the front gate.
= The Science Center is beside the front gate. 科學中心與前門相鄰。
The engineering building is by the Performing Arts Center.
= The engineering building is beside the Performing Arts Center.
工程大樓在表演藝術中心隔壁。

4 against 表示「靠著；倚著」。

A woman is leaning against the wall.
有名女子倚靠在牆上。

5 inside 表「在裡面」，意義與 in 相同。

The extra blankets are inside the chest.
= The extra blankets are in the chest.
多餘的毯子都放在衣櫃裡。
Are you sure the thieves are still inside the house? 你確定小偷還在屋內嗎？

6 outside 表示「在外面」。

The maid stood outside her room for 30 minutes.
女僕在自己的房間外站了30分鐘。
Can you let my dog in? I don't want to leave him outside the house.
可以讓我的狗狗進去嗎？我不想留牠在屋外。

Practice

1 請依圖示，勾選正確的答案。

1

Jason parked his scooter ☐ outside ☐ inside the house.

2

Matilda left her scooter ☐ by ☐ on the wall.

3

Those new scooters are standing ☐ outside ☐ against the rental shop.

4

There is an old bicycle ☐ along ☐ against the wall.

5

Sam parked his scooter ☐ inside ☐ near the forest.

6

The sisters are sitting ☐ against ☐ next to each other.

7

The laundry is hanging ☐ outside ☐ near the house.

8

A man is standing ☐ beside ☐ inside the car.

Unit **133**

Prepositions of Movement:
In, Into, Out Of, On, Onto, Off
表示「移動方向」的介系詞：
In、Into、Out Of、On、Onto、Off

on the box
在上面

in the box
在裡面

on/onto the box
到上面

off the box
脫離

in/into the box
進入

out of the box
出來

1 in 表示「在裡面」。

My car is in the repair shop.
我的車在修車廠。

2 in 和 into 都可表示「進入某處」。

Put the trash in the garbage can.
= Put the trash into the garbage can.
把垃圾丟到垃圾桶裡。
Larry put his hands into his pockets to avoid the cold wind.
賴瑞把手放進口袋裡，免得被冷風吹。

3 out of 表示「從某處出來」。

Take your clothes out of the washer.
把你的衣服從洗衣機拿出來。

4 on 表示「在上面」。

The bananas are on the counter.
香蕉就在櫃台上。

5 on 和 onto 都可表示「到某處上面」。

Put the tea kettle on the stove.
= Put the tea kettle onto the stove.
把茶壺放到火爐上。
Please step on the scale.
= Please step onto the scale.
請站到體重計上面。

6 off 表示「脫離某處」。

Take your feet off the coffee table.
把你的腳從咖啡桌上移開。
Gary, get off the wall right now.
蓋瑞，現在立刻從牆上下來。

Practice

1 請從框內選出適當的「介系詞」填空，完成句子。有些空格的答案不只一個。

in

on

into

out of

off

1. Tom dove _____ the swimming pool.

2. Sandy took the cake _____ the oven.

3. The villains were hiding _____ their secret cave.

4. The jewel thief put the fake ring _____ the counter.

5. Put the plates _____ the table.

6. Take your hat _____ the bust of Beethoven.

7. The sugar is _____ the cabinet.

8. Victoria was sitting _____ Bobby's motorcycle.

2 請依圖示，勾選正確的答案。

Jennifer squeezed some lotion ☐ on ☐ into the back of her hand.

Molly is taking her bicycle ☐ off ☐ out of the car.

The mother and daughter put the cookies ☐ in ☐ onto the oven.

Lily, get your paws ☐ off ☐ out me.

I poured some milk ☐ into ☐ on the coffee.

Simon sprinkled some parsley ☐ in ☐ onto the dish and served it.

A goldfish jumped ☐ onto ☐ out of the tank.

Unit **134**

Prepositions of Movement:
Up, Down, From, To, Toward
表示「移動方向」的介系詞：
Up、Down、From、To、Toward

up the stairs

down the stairs

1 up 意指「往上」。

My big cat is <u>up</u> that tree.
我的大貓上到了那棵樹上。
Father went <u>up</u> the hill for rare herbs.
父親上山去採集稀有草藥了。

MAU...

2 down 意指「往下」。

I fell <u>down</u> the stairs and broke my leg.
我跌下樓梯，摔斷了腿。
George went <u>down</u> the mine to look for his daughter.
喬治走下礦坑去找他女兒。

3 from 表示「出發點」、「從某處來」。

My family came <u>from</u> the countryside.
我的家人來自鄉村。
We drove <u>from</u> the suburbs to the mall downtown.
我們從郊區開車前往市區的購物中心。

4 to 表示「到某處」、「目的地」。

My parents moved <u>to</u> the city when I was ten years old.
我父母在我十歲的時候搬到這座城市。
I drive <u>to</u> work every day.
我每天開車去上班。

5 toward 或 towards 表「往某處移動」。

Let's walk <u>toward</u> the park so I can see something green.
我們往公園走，讓我看看綠色植物吧。
I've been thinking about moving the couch <u>toward(s)</u> the windows.
我一直想把沙發搬到靠窗一點的地方。

6 表示「到達一個城鎮、城市或國家」，可以用 get to 或 arrive in。

When will we <u>get to</u> Dubai?
= When will we <u>arrive in</u> Dubai?
我們什麼時候會抵達杜拜？
Jennifer <u>got to</u> Bangkok yesterday morning.
= Jennifer <u>arrived in</u> Bangkok yesterday morning.
珍妮佛昨天早上抵達曼谷。

7 如果是「抵達一個比較小的地方」，則會用 get to 或 arrive at。

We <u>got to</u> the Prado Museum in Madrid at 1:00.
= We <u>arrived at</u> the Prado Museum in Madrid at 1:00.
我們一點的時候抵達馬德里的普拉多美術館。
When will the directors <u>arrive at</u> the office for the board of directors?
董事們何時會抵達公司召開董事會？

Practice

1 請依圖示，勾選正確的答案。

1

The firefighter climbed □ **up** □ **down** the ladder to the rooftop.

2

Tears keep falling □ **from** □ **down** her face.

3

Larry walked □ **up** □ **down** the hill to the lake.

4

The guest wanted to make a phone call □ **toward** □ **from** the hotel room.

2 請從框內選出適當的「介系詞」填空，完成句子。

up

down

from

toward

to

at

1. We walked slowly _____ the hill and got _____ the top at around 2:30 p.m.

2. We saw a bird resting in a tree, so we moved slowly _____ the tree to get a closer look.

3. We tried not to disturb the bird. However, it flew away _____ the tree when it saw us.

4. We headed _____ the hill in the afternoon and arrived _____ a restaurant at the foot of the hill by night.

5. The head waiter walked _____ us and took us _____ our table.

6. After we had a good meal, we sipped some coffee and then drove back _____ our apartment.

Unit **135**

Prepositions of Movement: Along, Across, Over, Through, Past, Around
表示「移動方向」的介系詞：Along、Across、Over、Through、Past、Around

along the path

across the path

over the bridge

past the tree

around the tree

1 along 表示「沿著」。

Drive along the shoreline and look for a place to picnic.

沿著海岸線開，找個可以野餐的地方。

Walk along the main road, and you'll see a blue building. That is the gallery.

沿著大路走，你會看到一棟藍色的建築，那裡就是畫廊。

2 across 表示「橫越」。

She is swimming across the river.

她游泳橫越了這條河。

3 over 也有「穿越」的意思。

Let's walk over the bridge and look around on the other side of the stream.

我們走過橋到溪的對岸看看吧。

比較

但 across 和 over 有差別，over 通常是「穿越一個高起的物體」。

- I saw him walking across the street.

  我看到他穿越了馬路。

- ✗ Michelle drove across the mountains to see her cousins in the valley.

- ✓ Michelle drove over the mountains to see her cousins in the valley.

  蜜雪兒開車越過山脈，去拜訪住在山谷裡的表親。

4 through 也表示「穿越」。

Walk through the woods, and you'll see our village.

穿過樹林後，你就可以看到我們的村莊了。

5 past 表示「經過」或「超過」。

As we walked past the bakery, we could smell cinnamon rolls in the oven.

在我們走過麵包店時，可以聞到烤箱裡肉桂捲的香味。

Let's speed up and get past that slow truck ahead of us.

我們加速超越我們前面那輛開得很慢的卡車吧。

6 around 或 round 表示「環繞」。

We walked around the fountain and watched the water shoot up from different directions.

我們繞著噴泉走，看著水柱從各種角度噴出。

We sat round the table, talked, and laughed. 我們圍桌談笑。

around 和 round 還有「到處」的意思。

另外美式英語常用 around，比較少用 round。

Practice

1 請勾選正確的答案（包含 **Units 128-135** 所介紹的「介系詞」）。

1. I will meet you ☐ **in front of** ☐ **from** the main entrance to the zoo.

2. I'm going to sneak a cigarette ☐ **towards** ☐ **behind** the store.

3. Set up the chess pieces on the ☐ **opposite** ☐ **around** sides of the board.

4. Park ☐ **up** ☐ **between** the lines, or you will get a ticket.

5. The pub is so ☐ **close to** ☐ **next to** here that we should pop in for some pizzas and beer.

6. Pull up a chair ☐ **next to** ☐ **through** your brother and join us for dinner.

7. There is an umbrella rack ☐ **by** ☐ **between** the front door.

8. Let's ☐ **stroll along** ☐ **arrive at** the promenade and see the sights.

9. You can save a few steps cutting ☐ **near** ☐ **across** the parking lot.

10. Since it's raining, let's walk ☐ **through** ☐ **opposite** the mall to the car.

11. The elevated highway goes right ☐ **over** ☐ **get to** the old meat packing district.

12. This street will take us ☐ **between** ☐ **across** town.

13. Why don't we go up ☐ **to** ☐ **along** the men's department on the seventh floor?

14. I will be walking ☐ **around** ☐ **in** the second floor of the history museum.

15. We just walked ☐ **past** ☐ **at** a guy sleeping face down on the sidewalk.

16. Step ☐ **over** ☐ **between** the construction material, and don't fall into the hole.

17. Take the bus ☐ **from** ☐ **up** downtown ☐ **over** ☐ **to** the university.

18. When we get ☐ **near** ☐ **behind** San Jose, you will see Silicon Valley.

19. Tell me when we will ☐ **near** ☐ **arrive at** Harrods Department Store.

20. I will be ☐ **at** ☐ **between** home all night.

21. Can we go ☐ **around** ☐ **over** the traffic circle again?

22. Walk ☐ **across** ☐ **around** the pedestrian walkway and turn right.

Unit **136**

Transport: Get In, Get Out Of, Get On, Get Off, By, On, In

表示「交通方式」的詞彙：Get In、Get Out Of、Get On、Get Off、By、On、In

1 「位於轎車內」要用 in。

Mike left the flyers in his car.
麥克把傳單留在車上了。

2 「上車」要用 get in 或 get into；
「下車」要用 get out of。

Jerry got in(to) his car and sped off.
傑瑞上了車後加速離開。
Tommy, get out of the car now.
湯米，現在就下車。

3 搭乘大眾交通工具、飛機、船舶，都用 on。

Joan's suitcase is already on the train.
瓊的行李箱已經在火車上了。
This is a non-smoking flight. Please do not smoke on this plane.
本班機為禁菸航班，請勿在機上吸菸。
All the cargoes have been put on the ship. 所有的貨物都放到船上了。

4 「上大眾交通工具、飛機、船舶」，
都用 get on 或 get onto；
「下大眾交通工具、飛機、船舶」，
都用 get off。

I saw the man get on(to) the train with a suspicious box. 我看到那個男子提著一個可疑的箱子上了火車。

Patsy got off the plane and walked across the tarmac.
派西下了飛機後就步行穿過停機坪。

5 「上下機車或單車」也用 get on(to) 或 get off。

Nancy hesitantly got on(to) the back of Stan's motorcycle.
南西有些遲疑地坐上史丹的摩托車後座。
Nick got off the bike and went into the post office. 尼克下了腳踏車，走進郵局。

6 如果是表示「**交通方式**」，會用「by + 交通工具」，並且不能加 **the**。

In the old days, people traveled by horse and wagon. 過去人們是搭乘馬車旅行的。

When people started to travel by car, the automobile was called the horseless carriage.

人們剛開始乘坐汽車時，這種交通工具被稱為「無馬馬車」。

7 唯獨「走路」的固定片語是 on foot。

It's too close to take a cab. Let's go on foot.
太近了，不需要搭計程車，我們走路去吧。

8 如果交通工具前面有**冠詞 a、an、the**，或**所有格 my、his、her** 等，則不能用 **by**，要用「in ... car」或「on ... 其他交通工具」。

Willa offered to drive us to the pet store in her car. 薇拉說要開車載我們去寵物店。
Alice said she would never ride on a motorcycle again.
艾麗絲說她以後絕不再坐摩托車了。
Fritz wants to travel around Europe on his bicycle. 費利茲想要騎自行車漫遊歐洲。

Practice

1

請從框內選出適當的「介系詞」填空，完成句子。

in
into
on
by

1. Tell your brother to get _____ the car. We're leaving.

2. My car is being repaired, so I came _____ subway.

3. The best way to learn your way around a new place is _____ foot.

4. I don't want to go _____ train.

5. I would rather go _____ plane.

6. Don't take your car. Both of us can ride _____ Sue's van.

7. Which shipping method is cheaper, _____ train or truck?

8. I usually get to work _____ taxi, but sometimes I go _____ foot.

9. Stanley left his suitcase _____ a subway train.

2

請依圖示，勾選正確的答案。

The little boy is sleeping ☐ in ☐ on a car.

The boy is getting ☐ into ☐ on the bus.

We will be having our lunch ☐ on ☐ in the plane.

The woman asked her son to ☐ get on ☐ get off the boat. They were going for a ride.

The woman ☐ got out ☐ got off the train at the wrong station. She had no idea what to do.

Part 18 Prepositions of Time
表示時間的介系詞

Unit 137

Prepositions of Time: In, At, On (1)
表示「時間」的介系詞：In, At, On（1）

1 「較長的一段時間」多半用 in，如**年分、月分、世紀**。

in January 在 1 月

in 2021 在 2021 年

in the ten years from 2011 to 2021
在 2011 年到 2021 年間的 10 年

in the twentieth century 在二十世紀

2 說明「**季節**」要用 in。

in spring 在春天

in summer 在夏天

in autumn / in the fall 在秋天
↳ fall 前要加 the

in winter 在冬天

3 說明「**星期**」、「**週末**」，要用 on。

on Monday 在星期一

on Friday 在星期五

on Sundays 在每個星期日

on the weekend 在週末

on weekends 在每個週末

4 說明「**日期**」，要用 on。

on November 22nd 在 11 月 22 日

on the first of December 在 12 月 1 日

on December 22nd, 2023
在 2023 年 12 月 22 日

5 表示「**一天中的一個時段**」，要用 in。

in the morning 在上午

in the afternoon 在下午

in the evening 在傍晚

> 例外
>
> at night 和 at midnight
> 是例外的慣用語。

6 表示「**一天中的一個確切時間**」，要用 at。

at three o'clock 在 3 點

at noon 在正午

at 5:32 在 5 點 32 分

at dinner time 在晚餐時間

at 10 p.m. 在晚上 10 點

7 表示「**國定假日**」，通常用 at。但是如果有提到 day、eve 等表示「**假日當天**」的用語，則要用 on。

at Thanksgiving 在感恩節

at Easter 在復活節

on Memorial Day 在陣亡將士紀念日

on Halloween 在萬聖節

on Christmas Day 在聖誕節

on New Year's Eve 在除夕

at/on Christmas 在聖誕假期間
↳ Christmas 用 at 或 on 都可以。

Practice

1

請以 in、at 或 on 填空，完成句子。

1. I will call you _____ 1:00.
2. Shall we go to watch the fireworks _____ the evening?
3. We go to a tropical island on vacation _____ winters.
4. I have a lunch appointment _____ Friday.
5. Movable type printing was invented by Bi Sheng _____ approximately 1040.
6. Printing was applied extensively across the world _____ the eighteenth century.
7. Irving was born _____ August 19th.
8. A stranger called _____ midnight yesterday.
9. Do you usually go bowling _____ the weekend?
10. Rice is planted _____ spring and harvested _____ summer or autumn.
11. Meet me _____ lunch time.
12. The night is the longest _____ winter solstice.
13. Traditionally, Chinese families gather for their annual reunion dinner _____ Chinese New Year's Eve.

2 請從圖中選出與敘述相對應的節日，並搭配正確的「介系詞」填空。

Halloween

Chinese New Year

Christmas

New Year's Eve

the Mid-Autumn Festival

1. We eat moon cakes and look at the full moon _____.

2. Families and friends will get together and exchange cards _____.
   Also, doors and windows will be decorated with lights and mistletoes.

3. Children in ghost costumes will go from house to house playing "trick or treat" _____.

4. People shoot off fireworks _____ all over the world.

5. Every family thoroughly cleans the house to sweep away ill luck _____.
   People also call or visit their friends to wish them a happy and wealthy new year.

Prepositions of Time: In, At, On (2)
表示「時間」的介系詞：In, At, On（2）

1 如果 morning、evening 等字的前面還有提
到「**星期**」，則要用 on。

on Tuesday **morning** 在星期二早上

on Thursday **afternoon** 在星期四下午

on Saturday **evening** 在星期六傍晚

2 如果 morning、evening 等字的前面還有提
到「**昨天、明天**」等，則完全**不加介系詞**。

tomorrow **morning** 在明天早上

yesterday **afternoon** 在昨天下午

✗ Mona has agreed to help you on tomorrow
afternoon.

✓ Mona has agreed to help you tomorrow
afternoon.
夢娜已經答應明天下午要幫你。

3 時間的前面如果有 next、some 等
限定詞，不需要再加任何**介系詞**。

some **day** 總有一天

last **night** 在昨天晚上

next **summer** 在明年夏天

✗ Kate will arrive on next Friday.

✓ Kate will arrive next Friday.
凱特將於下星期五抵達。

✗ Gerald goes to see Sheryl at every weekend.

✓ Gerald goes to see Sheryl every weekend.
傑瑞德每週末都去看雪柔。

- next
- last
- every
- each
- some
- any
- one

4 「in + 一段時間」用來表示
「**多久之後**」。

in five minutes 過五分鐘

in two months 兩個月後

Joanna will have finished getting
her hair done in an hour.
↳ 從現在起的一小時之後
瓊安娜再過一小時就做完頭髮了。

Charlotte has to finish writing her
master's thesis in one month.
↳ 從現在起的一個月之後
夏綠蒂得在一個月內寫完她的碩士論
文。

You can have the car in two hours.
↳ 你要等兩小時。
再過兩小時你就能拿到這輛車。

You will get your score reports in
three weeks.
↳ 需要三星期才能收到成績單。
三星期後你們就會收到成績單。

5 in 也可和「所有格 + time」的用
語搭配，一樣表示「**多久以後**」。
但這種所有格結構不簡潔。in a week 比
in a week's time 簡潔且自然。

You will hear from Megan again
in a week's time.
一週內你就會再收到梅根的消息。

You will see Trisha in about two
weeks' time.
大約兩星期後，你就會見到翠莎了。

6 what time 通常不加 **at**。at
what time 雖非錯誤，但已經是
過時的用法，**when** 前面不能用 **at**。

What time are we meeting?
我們幾點碰面？

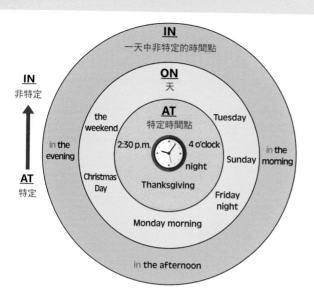

Practice

1

請以 in、at 或 on 填空，完成句子。如果不需要介系詞，
請在空格內劃上「/」。

1. Are we going to meet _____ the afternoon?

2. Let's meet _____ Monday night instead.

3. I will go on a tour to Jakarta _____ next Wednesday.

4. He will finish his homework _____ twenty minutes.

5. You will lose five pounds _____ a month if you follow this diet carefully.

6. If you are ready now, then you can get there _____ ten minutes.

7. She visits her grandma _____ every weekend.

8. Where were you _____ yesterday morning? I kept calling you, but you never answered.

9. I'm going to the bookstore _____ this afternoon. Do you want me to buy any books for you?

10. When did you hear the noise _____ last night?

11. Do you think you can finish the project _____ two weeks?

12. Since I have to find the illustrations from the picture bank, I might be able to finish this book _____ two months.

13. My parents went to the farmers' market twice _____ last week.

14. The spokesman for the Ministry of Foreign Affairs is having a press conference _____ tomorrow night.

15. Will you join the company outing _____ next weekend?

16. You can meet me _____ any time _____ tomorrow afternoon.

17. I saw him in the laundromat _____ one day.

Part 18 Prepositions of Time
表示時間的介系詞

Unit 139

Prepositions of Time: For, Since, Before (Compared With the Adverb "Ago")
表示「時間」的介系詞：For、Since、Before（與副詞 Ago 比較）

1 for 用來說明一個事件「持續了多久」。for 後面會接「一段時間」，可以用於**過去**、**現在**或**未來**時態。

We waited in line for two hours.
我們排隊等了兩小時了。
Most of the time we wait here for about two hours.
多數的時候，我們在這裡要等兩小時左右。
We will have to wait for two hours.
我們將在這裡等上兩小時。

2 說明一個事件的「**開始時間**」，會用 since。since 後面會接「一個確切的時間」。

I have lifted weights since high school.
我從高中開始練舉重。
He's lived in Atlanta since 2015.
他從 2015 年開始，就住在亞特蘭大。

3 for 和 since 都常和現在完成式搭配，說明**事情持續了一段時間**。

Norton has been going to cram school for five months.
諾頓上補習班已經五個月了。
I've waited for you for two hours. Why are you so late? 我已經等你等了兩個小時了，你怎麼這麼晚才到？
Nancy has been at the cram school since 5:00. 南西從 5 點開始就一直在補習班。
I've waited for you since 4 p.m.
我從下午 4 點就開始等你了。

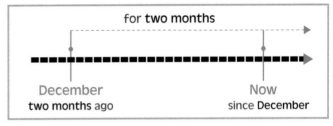

4 ago 是副詞，不是介系詞，用來說明「**在此之前**」，是從說話的當下往前推算。ago 只能用於過去簡單式，不能用於**完成式**。

The time is now 3:30 p.m., and Heidi left two hours ago. 現在時間是下午 3 點 30 分，而海蒂是兩個小時以前離開的。

✗ Franz has left three hours ago.
✓ Franz left three hours ago.
法藍茲是三小時前離開的。

5 ago 也常用於 how long ago 這樣的問句，來詢問「**多久以前**」。

How long ago did April start preparing for her wedding?
艾波多久以前開始準備她的婚禮？

How many years ago did you quit smoking? 你是幾年前開始戒菸的？

6 for 和 ago 雖然都具有「多久」的意義，但用法完全不同。

1 for 是「**持續多久**」，可以銜接「**描述過去、現在或未來的任何一段時間**」；
2 ago 是「**多久之前**」，一定是由「**說話的時間往回推算**」。

Simone was the top-ranked tennis player one year ago.
↳ 從現在往前推的一年前
一年前，席夢是排名頂尖的網球選手。

Simone was the top-ranked tennis player for one year.
↳ 過去某段時間，未必與現在銜接。
席夢曾有一年時間是排名頂尖的網球選手。

Practice

1

請以 for、since 或 ago 填空，完成句子。

1. Nat lived with his uncle _____ three years while he was a university student.
2. Ivan has been living in the faculty dorm _____ 1995.
3. Jamie graduated from the university one year _____.
4. How long _____ did Martina finish graduate school?
5. Next year Jake will be coming back for a visit _____ one month.
6. Wes has been staying in the haunted house _____ two days, and so far nothing has happened.
7. The reporter has been interviewing the actor _____ 2 p.m.
8. Sammi moved to Paris five months _____.
9. I have been thinking about the project _____ yesterday.
10. I have helped in my mom's restaurant _____ I was twelve.

2

請依據括弧提示回答問題。

1. How long have you been playing the piano? (fifteen years)
   → *I have been playing the piano for fifteen years.*
2. How long have you studied the history of art? (2005)
   →
3. How long ago did you start your YouTube channel? (three years)
   →
4. How long will you stay in Toronto? (six months)
   →
5. When did you arrive? (four hours)
   →
6. Since when have you been selling fried chicken in the night market? (last year)
   →

Part 18 Prepositions of Time
表示時間的介系詞

Unit 140

Prepositions of Time: During (Compared With "In," "For," and "While")

表示「時間」的介系詞：
During（與 In、For、While 比較）

1 說明「介於某段時間之中」，可以用 in 或 during，意思相同。

Lily wore a chicken costume <u>in/during</u> <u>the parade</u>.
莉莉在遊行時穿著小雞的道具服。

The phone rang many times <u>in/during</u> <u>the night</u>. 電話一晚上響了很多次。

2 說明「在某個活動從頭到尾的完整期間」，要用 during，此時不能用 **in**。

✗ The dog had his head out of the window <u>in the whole car ride</u>.

✓ The dog had his head out of the window <u>during the whole car ride</u>.

在搭車這段時間，狗狗一直把頭伸出車窗外。

✗ We met the principal <u>in our visit</u> to the elementary school.

✓ We met the principal <u>during our visit</u> to the elementary school.

我們去小學參觀的時候，遇到了校長。

✗ <u>In breakfast</u>, we talked about our plans for the day.

✓ <u>During breakfast</u>, we talked about our plans for the day.

吃早餐的時候，我們談了當天的計畫。

3 during 和 for 雖然都指「一段時間」，但 during 是指「事情發生在某事件的期間」，經常接的是「一個事件」，for 是指「事情發生了多久」，要接「一段時間」。

❶ It rained <u>during our vacation</u> in Hawaii.
我們去夏威夷度假期間有下雨。

It rained <u>for almost a week</u> in Hawaii.
夏威夷下了快一星期的雨。

❷ We were in Mexico <u>during the spring break</u>. 春假的時候，我們人在墨西哥。

We were in Mexico <u>for two weeks</u>.
我們在墨西哥待了兩個星期。

4 during 和 while 的意義相同，都是「在……期間」，但 during 要接名詞，while 可以接子句。

❶ Marsha arrived <u>during dinner time</u>.
瑪莎在晚餐時抵達。

Cyrus arrived <u>while we were eating dinner</u>.
賽勒斯在我們吃晚餐的時候到達。

❷ Tiffany fell asleep <u>during the opera</u>.
蒂芬妮聽歌劇時睡著了。

Frankie fell asleep <u>while he was watching the opera</u>.
法藍奇去看歌劇的時候睡著了。

Practice

1

請勾選正確的答案。

1. My parents went to Sydney □ during □ while the winter.

2. Christina was at her office □ for □ in the whole day.

3. □ During □ In dinner we watched TV.

4. Marla was sleeping □ during □ for the morning.

5. Laura has scuba dived □ for □ during two hours.

6. □ During □ While the party, Alyssa lost her remote control for the TV.

7. Mary hid in her bedroom □ while □ during my in-laws were visiting.

8. Hillary was out of town □ for □ while ten days.

2

請將 A 欄句子和 B 欄的「介系詞片語」搭配，寫出完整的句子。

 A

 B

A	B
I burned my fingers	while my wife was taking a shower and getting ready to go
I had to go to the bank	in the cooking class
I watched a basketball game	during my lunch break
I ate a lot of ramen and pork chops	for the whole week
I've been busy with the bank merger	during my vacation in Tokyo

1. ....

....

2. ....

....

3. ....

....

4. ....

....

5. ....

....

Unit **141**

Prepositions of Time:
By, Until, From . . . To, From . . . Until,
Before, After

表示「時間」的介系詞：
**By、Until、From . . . To、From . . .
Until、Before、After**

1 by 意指「**在某個時間之前**」，不能晚於該時間。

I have to leave by 7 p.m.
　　　　　↳ 最晚 7 點要離開。
我得在晚上 7 點以前離開。
I can finish proofreading the articles
by tomorrow afternoon.
我明天下午以前可以校對完這些文章。

2 until 或 till 意指「**直到某個時候**」，事件要到該時間才會結束。

I can work until/till 11 p.m.
我可以一直工作到晚上 11 點。
**The engineer is checking the power
system. We won't have the power back**
until/till 10 p.m. 工程師正在檢查電力系統，要到晚上 10 點才會恢復供電。

3 「from . . . to」和「from . . . until」的意義相同，都是「**從一個時刻直到另一個時刻**」。

I will need the car from 6:00 to 8:00 **this
evening.** 我今晚 6 點到 8 點要用車。
Can I use your truck from 3:00 until 5:00?
我 3 點到 5 點之間可以借用你的卡車嗎？

4 before 指「**在某個時間或活動之前**」。

Let's leave before 2:00.
我們 2 點之前出發吧。
We set off for the airport before dawn.
我們天亮之前就出發前往機場。

5 after 意指「**在某個時間或活動之後**」。

Do you want to come over after 3:00?
你要不要 3 點之後順道過來？

We walked along the coast after dinner.
晚飯之後，我們沿著海岸散步。

6 before 和 ago 都具有「**之前**」的意義，before 可以當作介系詞，也可以當作副詞，但 ago 只能當作副詞。

Tom arrived in Wellington two weeks
ago, **and Susan arrived in Wellington
three days** before **him.**
↳ Tom 從現在往前推的兩個星期前抵達；
　 Susan 比 Tom 早三天抵達。
湯姆兩個星期前抵達威靈頓，而蘇珊又比他早三天到達。

Practice

1

請從框內選出適當的「介系詞」填空。

- by
- until
- from
- to
- before
- after

1. _____ 1:00 _____ 3:00 we are having an open house.
2. I'll stay at the house _____ you come home.
3. I have to leave for the meeting _____ 1:00 this afternoon.
4. We are busy _____ December 1st _____ December 10th.
5. This is our second visit. We were here once _____.
6. We have to get to the airport _____ 2 p.m.
7. We usually go for some snacks _____ swimming.
8. I had a cup of coffee _____ resuming my work.
9. I won't go home _____ I finish these papers.
10. She has to get a job _____ graduation.

2

請依圖示,同樣用上一題框內的「介系詞」填空,完成句子。

Bill got up early since he had to get to the office _____ seven.

He had a quick breakfast _____ he left for work.

He had an important meeting _____ nine _____ ten.

The meeting did not end _____ twelve.

_____ the meeting, he went to the buffet next to his office for lunch.

He relaxed a little _____ a hard day's work.

Unit **142**

Individual Usage of Prepositions:
With, By, In, On
一些介系詞的個別用法：
With、By、In、On

with

1 with 常用來描述「**某人或某物擁有的東西**」。

Melvin thinks he knows that guy **with the briefcase**. ↳ 那個男人有個公事包

梅爾文覺得他認識拿著公事包的那個男人。

April works for a company **with two** ↳ 那間公司有兩個海外分支

overseas subsidiaries.

艾波在一間有兩個海外分支的公司工作。

2 with 常用來描述「**做某事所使用的工具**」，此時不能用 **by**。

Open the wine bottle with the corkscrew.
用這個開瓶器開紅酒。

What are you going to buy with this money? 你打算用這筆錢買些什麼？

by

3 by 用來表示寫作、作曲、作畫的「**作者**」，此時不能用 **of**。

Hamlet **is a famous play** by Shakespeare.
《哈姆雷特》是莎士比亞的知名劇作。

"When I Have Fears That I May Cease to Be" **is a poem** by John Keats.
《每當我害怕》是約翰·濟慈的詩作。

This is a painting by an artist named Smith.
這幅畫是一名叫做史密斯的畫家所畫的。

in

4 說明**書寫、作畫**的「**方式**」要用 in。

in oils	in chalk	in ink	in watercolors
用油墨	用粉筆	用鋼筆	用水彩

Anita drew a picture in oils.
艾妮塔用油墨作了一幅畫。

May I fill in the form in pencil?
我可以用鉛筆填表嗎？

5 in 可以用來說明「**穿著**」。

Tammy looks great in her new shawl.
譚美穿著新披肩很好看。

Margaret has decided to go to the interview in her suit.
瑪格麗特決定穿著套裝去面談。

on

6 on 常常用來說明「**行程的目的**」。

- on a **trip** 旅遊
- on a **journey** 旅遊
- on (a) **holiday** 放假
- on **business** 洽公
- on a **vacation**〔美式〕/ on **vacation**〔英式〕度假

William will be away on business **for a week**.
威廉將出差一星期。

Practice

1

請從框內選出適當的「介系詞」填空。

with
by
in

1. Do you want to go to a restaurant _____ private rooms?

2. Doris is going to the party _____ her new jeans.

3. Laurie knows the girl _____ the yellow umbrella.

4. Do you like oatmeal cookies _____ raisins?

5. The kids can go to the cram school _____ their uniforms.

6. I am reading a book _____ Charles Dickens.

7. Chop up these carrots _____ a chef's knife.

2

請依圖示，從框內選出適當的詞語，並搭配正確的「介系詞」填空。

Andrew Lloyd Webber

pen

a gray scarf

two garage doors

(a) vacation

the soap

Sign your name at the bottom
_____.

My family went to Florida
_____.

Cats is an opera _____
_____.

That house
_____ belongs to the Simpsons.

Wash your hand thoroughly
_____.

I don't recognize the woman
_____.

Unit **143**

Individual Usage of Prepositions: Like, As (Compared With "As If")
一些介系詞的個別用法：
Like、As（與連接詞 As If 比較）

like

1 like 可當作介系詞，用來說明兩種事物的**相似性**，此時後面要接**名詞**、**代名詞**或**動名詞**。

The woman looks just like you.
那個女人看起來和你很像。

She speaks like a native speaker of English.
她說話聽起來很像是英語的母語人士。

Talking to her is like talking to a diplomat.
跟她說話，就好像在跟外交官說話一樣。

2 like 經常用來「**舉例**」。

Darleen can cook gourmet food like soufflés and raspberry tortes.
達琳會烹飪精緻的食物，如舒芙蕾和覆盆子蛋糕。

as

3 as 可當作介系詞，用來說明「**某人的工作**」或「**某物品的功能**」。

When Louis was young, he worked as a draftsman. 路易斯年輕時，工作是繪圖員。

The little girl used the coffee table as a doll house. 這個小女孩把咖啡桌拿來當娃娃屋。

比較

as 和 like 都可能接「**一個職業或功用**」，但意義不同。使用 as 表示那是「**真正的職業**」，使用 like 表示「**類似該職業，但其實不是**」。

- **Amy works as an actress.** 艾美的工作是演員。
  ↳ 她真的是演員。
- **Amy looks like an actress.** 艾美看起來像演員。
  ↳ 她不是真的演員。

4 as 也可以表示「**如同；像**」，但多半屬於**連接詞**的用法，後面接子句為多。

The village was not as far away as we had expected to be.
村莊沒有我們想像中的遠。

as if

5 as if 屬於連接詞，但是它的用法常和 like 或 as 混淆。as if 後面要接子句。

Ron looks as if he is tired.
朗恩看起來很累。

The restaurant looks as if it will close soon.
這間餐廳看起來像是很快就要打烊了。

6 as if 經常用於「**假設語氣**」的句型，接**過去簡單式**來表示「**與現在事實相反**」，接**過去完成式**來表示「**與過去事實相反**」。

Barney orders us around as if he were our boss.
↳ 巴尼並不是老闆；在假設語氣中用 were 來取代 was，是更正式的用法。
巴尼不斷指揮我們，就好像他是老闆一樣。

Joan felt as if she had been transported back in time to her childhood. 瓊安覺得她彷彿被帶回過去，回到她的兒童時期。

7 **as if** 可以用 as though 取代。

The Senator says we have to address this evolving situation as though it were a matter of life and death.
參議員說，我們必須因應這個變化的情勢，彷彿這是什麼攸關生死的大事。

The house looked as though it hadn't changed in 40 years. 這房子看上去就好像四十年來從未改變過。

Practice

1

請用 like、as 或 as if 填空，完成句子。

1. Jerome's apartment is a lot _____ mine.

2. Gene has been promoted _____ I predicted.

3. This novel is so boring that it is _____ reading a phone book.

4. Sonny started his career in the hotel industry _____ a bellhop.

5. Willie looks _____ a professional athlete.

6. Jordan looks _____ he needs a strong cup of coffee.

7. Don't follow me around _____ you were a lost dog.

8. It looks _____ we will be going on the stage next.

9. James is good at many ball games _____ basketball and volleyball.

2

請勾選正確的答案。

1. Julia is working ☐ as ☐ like a secretary at our company.

2. Do you want to use this wood box ☐ like ☐ as a tea table?

3. Why is Lorelei dressed ☐ as if ☐ like an old lady?

4. He attended the conference ☐ as ☐ like the firm's representative.

5. You talk ☐ as ☐ as if you didn't know anything.

6. There was a big thunderstorm last night, but today everything is quiet and it seems as if nothing ☐ happened ☐ had happened.

7. Larry generously offered us the food and drinks ☐ as ☐ as though he were the host.

8. I can cook simple dishes ☐ as ☐ like fried rice and tomato salads.

9. He acted ☐ as ☐ like a professional performer.

10. Your ten-year-old car looks ☐ as if ☐ as it were new.

Unit **144**

Indirect Objects With or Without "To" and "For"
To 與 For 搭配間接受詞的用法

1 有些動詞如 give 和 buy，會同時有直接受詞和間接受詞。直接受詞通常是「**物**」，間接受詞通常是「**人**」，句型為「動詞 + 間接受詞 + 直接受詞」。

✗ Larry <u>gave</u> a gift Kate.

✓ Larry <u>gave</u> Kate a gift.
> 動詞要先接間接受詞（接受物品的人），再接直接動詞（物品）

賴瑞送給凱特一份禮物。

✗ Amanda <u>is buying</u> lunch Daniel.

✓ Amanda <u>is buying</u> Daniel lunch.

亞曼達在幫丹尼爾買午餐。

2 有些動詞如果先接**直接受詞**，要再加介系詞 to，才能接**間接受詞**，句型：

| 動詞 | + | 直接受詞 | + | to | + | 間接受詞 |

這類動詞有：

• bring	• pass	• read	• take
• give	• pay	• recommend	• tell
• lend	• post	• sell	• throw
• offer	• promise	• send	• write
• owe	• reach	• show	

Cliff <u>gave the ring to</u> **April.**
克里夫將戒指送給艾波。

Steven <u>lent his notebook computer to</u> **Lara.** 史蒂芬把他的筆記型電腦借給蘿拉了。

3 有些動詞若先接**直接受詞**，要再加介系詞 for，才能接**間接受詞**，句型：

| 動詞 | + | 直接受詞 | + | for | + | 間接受詞 |

這類動詞有：

• bring	• cook	• get	• prepare
• build	• do	• keep	• save
• buy	• fetch	• knit	
• change	• find	• make	
• choose	• fix	• order	

Belinda <u>bought a ticket for</u> **Diane.**
貝琳達買了一張票給黛安。

Belinda <u>bought a ticket for</u> **Diane, not Martha.**
> 在句中增加「否定子句」，可以更強調間接受詞。

貝琳達買了一張票給黛安，不是給瑪莎。

Jimmy is going to <u>order wedding cakes for</u> **Vera.** 吉米會幫薇拉訂購婚禮蛋糕。

She <u>knitted a sweater for</u> **herself.**
她為自己織了一件毛衣。

4 **直接受詞**如果是代名詞，則通常會放在**間接受詞**的前面。

✗ Eric <u>gave</u> the guy it at the door.

✓ Eric <u>gave</u> it to the guy at the door.
艾瑞克把它交給門口的那個人了。

There are many stories in this book. I used to <u>read</u> **them to my kids when they were little.** 這本書裡有很多故事，我在孩子還小時會唸給他們聽。

Practice

1 　請將下列各句子改寫為「不用 to 或 for 的句子」。

1. Bella will give the letter to Trevor.

   → *Bella will give Trevor the letter.*

2. Phil will forward the email to Dave.

   →

3. John is going to buy a coat for Mindy.

   →

4. Mark bought the teapot for Rita.

   →

5. Can you read the news to Grandpa?

   →

6. I will show the ingredients to you.

   →

7. I am going to build a house for my parents.

   →

2 　請將下列各句子改寫為「使用 to 或 for 的句子」。

1. Morris is going to bring Gabriel the paint.

   → *Morris is going to bring the paint to/for Gabriel.*

2. Gerald is going to pay Kate the money.

   →

3. Suzanne is going to read her son a book.

   →

4. Larry will recommend Gail a restaurant.

   →

5. I'll buy you lunch.

   →

Adjectives With Specific Prepositions (1)
形容詞所搭配的特定介系詞（ I ）

about

- **excited about** 對⋯⋯感到興奮
- **worried about** 對⋯⋯感到擔心
- **nervous about** 對⋯⋯感到緊張
- **angry about** 對⋯⋯感到生氣
- **annoyed about** 對⋯⋯感到惱怒
- **furious about** 對⋯⋯感到憤怒
- **mad about** 對⋯⋯感到著迷

Josephine is excited about visiting her family for a week.

要回去探望家人一星期，喬瑟芬感到很興奮。

Sophia is furious about her son's behavior at school. 蘇菲亞對她兒子的在校行為感到氣憤。

for

- **famous for** 以⋯⋯聞名
- **well-known for** 以⋯⋯聞名
- **responsible for** 對⋯⋯負責

Sue is responsible for the purchase. 蘇負責採購。

This café is famous for chicory coffee and French crullers.

這家咖啡館的菊苣咖啡和法式甜甜圈很出名。

at

- **good at** 擅於
- **bad at** 不擅於
- **clever at** 擅於
- **hopeless at** 極不擅於
- **mad at** 對⋯⋯生氣

Billy is good at ping pong.
比利很會打乒乓球。

John is hopeless at board games.
約翰對棋盤遊戲一竅不通。

- **surprised at/by**
  對⋯⋯感到驚訝
- **astonished at/by**
  對⋯⋯感到驚異
- **shocked at/by**
  對⋯⋯感到震驚
- **amazed at/by**
  對⋯⋯感到驚奇

Joan was surprised at receiving the full scholarship.
= Joan was surprised by the full scholarship she received.
瓊很驚訝能拿到全額獎學金。

We were all shocked at/by the news. 我們全都對這則新聞大為震驚。

with

- **pleased with**
  對⋯⋯感到滿意
- **bored with**
  對⋯⋯感到無聊
- **disappointed with**
  對⋯⋯感到失望
- **happy with**
  對⋯⋯感到開心
- **satisfied with**
  對⋯⋯感到滿意

The boss was pleased with your translation of the contract. 老闆對你翻譯的合約很滿意。

We were all bored with his speech. 我們都覺得他的演講很無聊。

- **angry/annoyed/ furious with** + *sb.* (+ for *sth.*)
  為了某事生某人的氣

Don't be angry with your mother for overfeeding our kids when we go over to her house.

我們去你媽媽家的時候，你可別因為她餵孩子們吃太多就生氣。

Practice

1

請從框內選出適當的「介系詞」填空。

- about
- at
- with
- by
- for

1. There is no reason to be worried _____ looking for a new job.

2. I hope you're good _____ hiding your job search effort from our boss.

3. You will be surprised _____ how many job offers you will get.

4. You are well-known _____ your research work in biology.

5. My wife would be unhappy _____ me if I took time off to relax and she still had to go to work every day.

6. Is Andy still mad _____ me?

7. Both my brother and I are mad _____ modern art.

8. My wife is hopeless _____ housework.

9. O. Henry's short stories are famous _____ clever and unexpected endings.

2

請依圖示從 A 框和 B 框中選出搭配的詞語填空完成句子。

A

- amazed by
- good at
- nervous about
- bored with
- satisfied with

B

- our teacher's long and uninformative speech
- the dolphin show
- solving a Rubik's cube
- our son's English exam score
- having dinner with my girlfriend's parents

1. We were _____ _____ at Ocean Park.

2. We were _____ _____.

3. We were _____ _____.

4. She is _____ _____.

5. I'm _____ _____.

Unit 146

Adjectives With Specific Prepositions (2)
形容詞所搭配的特定介系詞（2）

to

- **engaged to** *sb.* 與某人訂婚
- **married to** *sb.* 嫁給某人
- **similar to** 與……相似

My brother is engaged to a charming woman.

我哥哥和一位迷人的女子訂婚了。

Fiona is getting married to Andy in June. 菲歐娜和安迪將於 6 月結婚。

- **nice to** *sb.* 對某人好
- **kind to** *sb.* 對某人好
- **good to** *sb.* 對某人好
- **friendly to** *sb.* 對某人友善
- **polite to** *sb.* 對某人有禮
- **rude to** *sb.* 對某人無禮

You should be nice to your little sister. 你應該對你妹妹好一點。

You shouldn't be rude to your classmates. 你不應該對同學無禮。

of

- **afraid of** 害怕
- **frightened of** 恐懼
- **scared of** 害怕
- **proud of** 驕傲
- **ashamed of** 羞愧
- **jealous of** 嫉妒
- **envious of** 羨慕
- **suspicious of** 懷疑
- **aware of** 注意到
- **conscious of** 意識到
- **capable of** 有能力
- **fond of** 喜愛
- **tired of** 厭倦
- **short of** 缺乏
- **full of** 充滿

Chester is afraid of being seen as a mama's boy.

切斯特怕被當成「媽寶」。

Alisa is fond of water skiing.

愛莉莎熱愛滑水。

others

- **different from/to** 與……不同

The house my grandparents live in has been remodeled and looks different from the way it looked twenty years ago.

我祖父母的家改造之後，看起來和二十年前很不一樣了。

The living room in your apartment looks different to mine. 你公寓的客廳看起來和我的不一樣。〔美式不用 to，英式可以用 to〕

- **nice of** *sb.* **(to do . . .)**
  某人很好心（做了某事）
- **kind of** *sb.* **(to do . . .)**
  某人很好心（做了某事）
- **good of** *sb.* **(to do . . .)**
  某人很好心（做了某事）
- **friendly of** *sb.* **(to do . . .)**
  某人很友善（做了某事）
- **polite of** *sb.* **(to do . . .)**
  某人很有禮貌（做了某事）
- **rude of** *sb.* **(to do . . .)**
  某人很無禮（做了某事）
- **stupid of** *sb.* **(to do . . .)**
  某人很愚蠢（做了某事）

It was nice of Ted to offer to pick you up at your house.

泰德提議到你家去接你，他人真好。

It was rude of you to push your little brother.

你那樣推你弟弟很粗魯。

- **interested in**
  對……有興趣

Are you interested in learning how to dance?
你有興趣學跳舞嗎？

- **keen on** 熱衷於

Archie is keen on Korean online games.

亞契很喜歡玩韓國的線上遊戲。

Practice

1

請用適當的「介系詞」填空，完成句子。

1. Looking for a job when you have experience is different _____ when you look for a job right after you graduate.

2. Only go for a job interview if you are seriously interested _____ the job with the company.

3. I'm capable _____ handling the customers' complaints, so I would be a good person for this job.

4. It is OK to be a little worried _____ what will happen if you leave your safe and secure job.

5. It was nice _____ you to ask for my advice on this matter.

6. I have never been keen _____ job hopping, but sometimes you have to do it.

7. I have been here so long that I'm practically married _____ my job.

8. I'm tired _____ making hundreds of phone calls every day.

9. It was kind _____ John to recommend me for the post, but I'm not looking for a new job at this time.

10. Louis is jealous _____ my being promoted.

11. I feel ashamed _____ what I've done to you.

12. His solution to this problem is different _____ yours.

2

請從圖片中選出適當的用語填空，完成句子。

try smoking	help the elderly	take a shortcut	yell at people

1. It was rude of you to _____.

2. It was kind of you to _____.

3. It was stupid of you to _____.

4. It was clever of you to _____.

Unit **147**

Nouns With Specific Prepositions (1)
名詞所搭配的特定介系詞（1）

answer to ……的答案
However, the answer to the problem is not buying more food from local restaurants. 然而，並不只是到本地市場多買一點食物就能解決問題。

attitude toward/ towards 對……的態度
Many people's feelings and attitudes towards bullfighting are ambivalent.

許多人對鬥牛的觀感和態度是好壞參半。

cause of ……的原因
The cause of the large-scale power outage is still unknown.

這次大規模的停電原因依舊不明。

decrease in
在……方面的減少
There was a decrease in the company's profit last year.

去年該公司的營收減少。

demand for
對……的要求
The demand for housing is increasing.

住屋的需求逐漸增加。

difference between
（兩者之間的）不同
In terms of taste, there is no difference between fructose and sugar.

說到吃起來的味道，果糖和砂糖並沒有什麼不同。

difficulty (in) V-ing
在……方面的困難
The young girl had difficulty (in) cooking for her family when her mom became sick.

媽媽生病期間，那位年輕的女孩要為家人做飯是有困難的。

have difficulty with sb./sth.
與某人相處或做某事有困難
A rebellious teenager has difficulty with people of authority.

叛逆的青少年不易與權威人士相處。

example of ……的範例
As an example of her cooking difficulties, the young girl said making seaweed salad was especially hard.

為了說明她做飯的困難，這位年輕女士舉例說，做海帶沙拉就特別困難。

fall in 在……方面的下降
There will be a fall in the price of bananas because of overproduction.

香蕉產量過剩的結果，造成售價下跌。

increase in
在……方面的增加
The elder women in the neighborhood have all noticed the increase in prices at the fruit stand.

這一帶年紀大一點的婦女都注意到水果攤的價格上升了。

Practice

1

請從框內選出適當的「介系詞」填空。

to

for

of

with

between

in

toward

1. There are many differences ＿＿＿＿＿＿ scooters and motorcycles.

2. There is a great demand ＿＿＿＿＿＿ employees with language skills.

3. My son has difficulty ＿＿＿＿＿ concentrating on his homework when the TV is blaring.

4. The new clerk in the accounting department has a bad attitude ＿＿＿＿＿ me.

5. One of the answers ＿＿＿＿＿ cheap and safe space travel is the building of space elevators.

6. I had difficulty ＿＿＿＿＿ the language when I moved to Japan three years ago, but I can communicate without any big problems now.

7. There has been a fall ＿＿＿＿＿ the country's industrial exports recently.

8. A recent policy allowed a small increase ＿＿＿＿＿ the taxi fare.

2

請依圖示，從框內選出適當的用語填空，完成句子。

difficulty in

demand for

example of

decrease in

causes of

1 The Pont du Gard is a good ＿＿＿＿＿＿ ＿＿＿＿＿＿ Roman architecture.

2 Toxic chemical substances are one of the ＿＿＿＿＿＿ water pollution.

3 In the market there is a growing ＿＿＿＿＿＿ ＿＿＿＿＿＿ fresh and organically grown vegetables.

4 There has been a ＿＿＿＿＿＿ the amount of ice in western Antarctica due to melting and the increased calving of icebergs.

5 Scientists are having ＿＿＿＿＿＿ accurately predicting when and where an earthquake will occur.

Nouns With Specific Prepositions (2)
名詞所搭配的特定介系詞（2）

invitation to
（到某活動的）邀請

Everyone in the office has received the invitation to her wedding.

辦公室裡的每一個人都收到她的喜帖。

need for 對……的需要

We have no need for a loan.

我們沒有貸款的需要。

picture/photograph of ……的圖片

I've uploaded the pictures of my trip to Malaysia to my web album.

我已經把我去馬來西亞旅遊的照片放上我的網路相簿了。

reaction to 對……的反應

What's their reaction to the new policy?

他們對新政策的反應如何？

reason for ……的理由

There is no reason for buying expensive clothing for kids when they outgrow their clothes so fast.

孩子們長那麼快，沒必要為他們買太貴的衣服。

relationship with
和……的關係

Elle has kept a close relationship with her college roommate.

艾兒一直和她的大學室友維持親近的關係。

relationship between
（兩者或以上之間的）關係

The relationship between the three sisters has become complicated after they all got married.

三位姐妹結婚後，她們之間的關係就變得複雜起來了。

reply to 對……的回覆

You haven't provided a reply to my question.

你還沒有回覆我所提的問題。

rise in 在……方面的上升

The rise in unemployment needs to be dealt with.

失業率的攀升問題需要解決。

solution to
……的解決方式

The government was unable to implement any solution to inflation.

政府對於通貨膨脹的問題始終無法提出解決方案。

Practice

1

請從框內選出適當的「介系詞」填空。

to
for
of
with
between
in

1. Recently, there has been a steep rise _____ gasoline prices.

2. Roscoe was surprised when he received a photograph _____ his ex-girlfriend.

3. Vivian suggested a solution _____ the scheduling problem.

4. Helen has a good relationship _____ her husband's parents.

5. The reason _____ quitting a job differs from person to person.

6. The relationship _____ Tom and me is awful.

7. There's no urgent need _____ more doctors.

8. I haven't received any replies _____ my job applications.

2

請選出正確的答案。

_____ 1. The _____ sea level is linked to global warming.

   Ⓐ reaction to   Ⓑ rise in   Ⓒ reason for   Ⓓ solution to

_____ 2. The _____ a man and his father-in-law should be positive.

   Ⓐ relationship with   Ⓑ reply to
   Ⓒ relationship between   Ⓓ invitation to

_____ 3. Sulfur trioxide's _____ contact with water can be violent.

   Ⓐ reaction to   Ⓑ reply to   Ⓒ need for   Ⓓ rise in

_____ 4. You need to carefully maintain good _____ your family members and friends.

   Ⓐ relationships with   Ⓑ solution to
   Ⓒ relationships in   Ⓓ pictures of

_____ 5. Did you get an _____ Sue's birthday party this weekend?

   Ⓐ reply to   Ⓑ need for   Ⓒ rise in   Ⓓ invitation to

_____ 6. His _____ our request was astonishing.

   Ⓐ apply for   Ⓑ need for
   Ⓒ reply to   Ⓓ relationship with

Verbs With Specific Prepositions
動詞所搭配的特定介系詞

「**動詞 + 介系詞**」的用法，其實屬於**片語動詞**的一種，在 Units 85、86 當中已經有詳細的範例。

在本單元裡，將把重點放在「**動詞 + 受詞 + 介系詞**」，甚至受詞之前還要加介系詞的習慣用法。

---

apologize to *sb.* for *sth.*
為了某事向某人道歉

Cody apologized to Miranda for being late.

寇帝為了遲到的事向米蘭達道歉。

---

accuse *sb.* of *sth.*
指控某人做了某事

Edgar claimed he didn't take Sophia's teddy bear, but Sophia accused him of not being honest.

艾加說他沒拿蘇菲亞的泰迪熊，但是蘇菲亞指控他不老實。

---

blame *sb.* for *sth.*
責怪某人做了某事

Don't blame me for losing that sale.

別因為失去那筆買賣而責怪我。

---

blame *sth.* on *sb.*
為某件事怪罪某人

Don't blame losing that sale on me.

別把失去那筆買賣算在我頭上。

---

borrow *sth.* from *sb.*
向某人借某物

George borrowed a truck from his brother to move our new furniture.

喬治向哥哥借了一輛卡車搬我們的新家具。

---

complain to *sb.* about *sth.*
向某人抱怨某事

My sister complained to me about her mother-in-law.

我妹妹對我抱怨她婆婆。

---

congratulate *sb.* on doing *sth.*
為了某件事恭喜某人

Trevor congratulated his neighbors on having a new baby.

崔弗恭喜鄰居誕育新生兒。

---

explain *sth.* to *sb.*
向某人解釋某事

Jeanette explained the city map to her son.

珍奈對兒子解說市區地圖。

---

invite *sb.* to *sth.*
邀請某人參加某活動

Malcolm is planning to invite his girlfriend's parents to dinner.

麥爾康打算邀請他女友的父母去吃晚餐。

---

remind *sb.* about *sth.*
提醒某人做某事

Miranda reminded Conrad about their plan to have dinner with the Harrisons.

米蘭達提醒康瑞德，他們要和哈里森一家人一起吃晚餐。

---

remind *sb.* of *sth.*
使某人回想起某事

Her story reminds me of a camping experience I once had.

她的故事讓我想起我曾有過的一次露營經驗。

---

tell *sb.* about *sth.*
告訴某人某事

Tell Oliver about the new manifests for shipping containers.

跟奧利佛說一下貨櫃箱的新貨單。

---

warn someone about _sth./sb._ 警告某人提防某事／某人

Tanya <u>warned</u> Chris <u>about</u> paying for their house insurance so it wouldn't lapse.

譚雅提醒克利斯要付房屋保險了，不然要過期限了。

Sandra <u>warned</u> me <u>about</u> Mr. Parker.

珊卓提醒我要提防帕克先生這個人。

Practice

1

請從框內選出適當的「介系詞」填空。

of
for
from
to
about
on

1. The victim accused the tall man _____ snatching her purse.
2. Don't blame the bride _____ the groom's foolishness in drinking too much.
3. I borrowed a tuxedo _____ my brother for a friend's wedding.
4. Jack congratulated his boss _____ getting a promotion.
5. Sue explained _____ her mother how to create an Instagram story.
6. My neighbor invited me _____ a graduation party for his son.
7. The mother reminded her son _____ packing his recorder on the day he had music class.
8. Did you tell your teacher _____ your doctor's appointment tomorrow?
9. Sandy apologized _____ her brother _____ having used his car without asking him.
10. I can't agree with you if you're going to blame all this _____ me.
11. Will you explain your project _____ Mr. Robertson, please?

2

請從框內選出適當的用語，搭配括弧內的詞彙填空，完成句子。

remind of
warn about
blame for
congratulate on
borrow from
complain to . . . about . . .

1. Travis _____*warned Marcia about the risk of buying stocks*_____
   (Marcia / the risk of buying stocks).
2. Warren _____
   (a food processor / his sister).
3. You shouldn't _____
   (her / spoil the children). You're the one who buys them new toys every week.
4. Andrea _____
   _____ (her husband / his overloading the washing machine).
5. We held a dinner party to _____
   _____ (Bernard / winning the award).
6. His story _____
   (me / my childhood).

Unit **150**

Prepositional Phrases
慣用的介系詞片語

on time
準時（正好落在正確時間）

Dina always gets her work done on time.

蒂娜總是準時完成工作。

Jerry rarely turns in his reports on time.

傑瑞很少在規定的時間內交報告。

in time
及時（在規定的時間內）

She arrived home just in time for the Christmas dinner.

她剛好及時到家吃聖誕晚餐。

by credit card / check
用信用卡／支票

Lindsay is going to pay for the clothes by credit card.

琳賽要用信用卡支付買衣服的錢。

in cash 付現金

Bennett paid for his meal in cash.

班內特吃飯以現金付款。

at the end of
最終（表示事情結束）

At the end of the track meet, the medals were awarded to the winners.

田徑賽結束後，獎牌便頒發給得獎者。

The washer was making so much noise at the end of its rinse cycle that I was not surprised when it broke down.

洗衣機最後漂洗運轉的聲音那麼吵，我一點也不訝異它會壞掉。

in the end
終於（一段時間之後）

In the end, we chose some traditional wood furniture despite our initial indecision.

儘管難以決定，到頭來我們還是選了傳統的木製家具。

At first my mom didn't like the furniture, but in the end she grew to love it.

剛開始我媽媽不喜歡這些家具，但是過一陣子她漸漸開始喜歡了。

in someone's opinion
就某人的看法

In Wally's opinion, people are inherently good, but eventually some become corrupt.

華利認為人性本善，不過也有些人會受後天影響學壞。

for example 例如

Let's eat some healthy food for lunch, for example, a fruit salad.

我們午餐吃健康一點的食物吧，例如水果沙拉。

(fall) in love with
愛上

Nick is falling in love with Nancy. 尼克愛上了南西。

by mistake 不小心

Alison sent you the file by mistake.

艾莉森不小心把檔案寄給了你。

by accident/chance
意外地

I ran into Lisa by accident this afternoon.

我今天下午巧遇莉莎。

by chance 無意間

I saw this advertisement by chance.

我無意間看到這則廣告。

Practice

1

請勾選正確的答案。

1. Did you get the ticket ☐ in time ☐ on time to attend the basketball game?

2. Since the tickets didn't arrive either early or late, I guess you could say they arrived ☐ in time ☐ on time.

3. The buses are always late, and they never arrive ☐ in time ☐ on time.

4. We didn't arrive ☐ in time ☐ on time to see the pre-game show.

5. Helen is very punctual, and she always comes ☐ in time ☐ on time.

6. I hope my thank-you present arrives ☐ in time ☐ on time for you to take it with you when you leave.

7. In the beginning I disliked living in Caracas, but ☐ in the end ☐ at the end I didn't want to leave.

8. We are moving to Kuala Lumpur in Malaysia ☐ in the end ☐ at the end of the month.

9. At first Oscar didn't want to give up smoking, but ☐ in the end ☐ at the end he decided to give it a try.

10. I called every bookstore in the city, and ☐ in the end ☐ at the end I found exactly the right edition of the play.

11. Vince is starring in his first lead role ☐ in the end ☐ at the end of September.

12. Tony was barely able to walk or even stand ☐ in the end ☐ at the end of the 26.5 mile marathon.

2

請從框內選出適當的「介系詞」填空。

by
for
in

1. I forgot who I was calling and dialed your extension _____ accident.

2. I think I will pay _____ cash.

3. Seaweed, _____ example, often smells bad but tastes delicious.

4. Martin and Angela fell _____ love and got married.

5. _____ my girlfriend's opinion, we should get married right away.

Unit **151**

Review of Prepositions
介系詞總複習

1

請以正確的「介系詞」填空，完成句子。如果不需要介系詞，
請在空格內劃上「/」。

1. The team is meeting _____ the gym _____ Green Street _____ 7:00 _____ tomorrow morning.

2. We are looking for an apartment _____ Fukuoka.

3. Bonnie went for a drive _____ the countryside _____ Sunday afternoon.

4. I decided to take a taxi so that I could arrive _____ time for Sue's birthday party.

5. Marie is thinking _____ going to the art museum _____ Saturday. Are you interested _____ joining her?

6. Claude has been working _____ the design firm _____ Dresden _____ the last five years.

7. Ian had some difficulty _____ finding a place to live _____ the south of France.

8. The Harper family lives _____ 21 Beach Street. They live _____ the third floor.

9. Roger went to the Van Gogh Museum _____ his visit _____ Amsterdam two years ago.

10. _____ my opinion, there are too many commercials on TV.

11. Julia went _____ a vacation _____ the end of last month.

12. My parents have been staying _____ the Marriott Hotel _____ Broadway since they arrived _____ New York.

13. Kim has suffered _____ knee problems since she started to play on the tennis team.

14. At first Lou wanted to go home, but _____ the end he decided to go with everybody else to the pub.

15. I am reading a novel _____ Margaret Atwood.

16. Last summer Erica worked _____ a photographer _____ Africa _____ two months.

17. Alfred found an old coin _____ the floor _____ the desk _____ his grandfather's room.

18. Robbie is not very good _____ driving a motorcycle.

19. Howard and Cathy arranged to meet _____ the café on Tenth Street for a drink _____ 4:00 _____ Saturday afternoon.

20. Brigit has a good relationship _____ her boss.

21. There is an urgent need _____ better education in developing countries, as it is expected to improve local people's lives.

22. Joyce is very different _____ her mother but quite similar _____ her father.

23. Mona is looking for a new apartment _____ three bedrooms, two bathrooms, a kitchen, and a big living room.

24. The district attorney accused the defendant _____ filing a civil lawsuit for the sole purpose of harassment.

25. Do you know _____ a drink called coconut jelly tea?

26. Chicago is located _____ the southwestern tip of Lake Michigan _____ the Midwest of the United States. It is an industrial city _____ a population of about 2.7 million.

27. Is there any significant difference _____ these two kinds of flour?

28. Brook has always wanted his wife to be proud _____ her accomplishments.

29. The employees are happy _____ the increase _____ their year-end bonuses.

30. Sue complained _____ her sister _____ the smell _____ the downstairs where the tenant is always frying fish.

31. Last summer Sue went _____ Rome _____ a tourist trip _____ her husband.

32. I am a little bored _____ the job sometimes, but I am deeply committed to it.

33. What did you have _____ breakfast this morning?

Unit 152

Yes/No Questions
Yes/No 疑問句

1 所謂的「Yes/No 問句」,是要以「Yes.」或「No.」作為回答的問句。「Yes/No 問句」的構成,是將句中的 **be** 動詞或助動詞移到句首。

Monty is reading. 蒙提正在讀書。

→ Is Monty reading? 蒙提正在讀書嗎?

Virginia has finished her book.

維吉妮亞已經把書看完了。

→ Has Virginia finished her book?

維吉妮亞看完書了嗎?

Shelby can read one book a week.

莎碧每星期可以看一本書。

→ Can Shelby read one book a week?

莎碧每星期可以看一本書嗎?

2 句中**沒有 be** 動詞或助動詞時,就在句首加上 do、does、did,此時主要動詞要用原形動詞。

Airplanes fly over here. 這裡有飛機經過。

→ Do airplanes fly over here?

飛機會從這邊經過嗎?

Joe enjoyed flying over the mountains.

喬很享受飛過山岳的感覺。

→ Did Josephine enjoy flying over the mountains? 喬很享受飛過山岳的感覺嗎?

3 「Yes/No 問句」經常以**簡答**作為回應:

Yes, 主詞 + be 動詞/助動詞

No, 主詞 + be 動詞/助動詞 + not

Sue: Are you going out for breakfast?
Ann: Yes, I am. / No, I am not.

蘇: 你要出去吃早餐嗎?

安: 對,我要出去吃。/不,我不出去吃。

4 「Yes/No 問句」若回答時沒有明確的答案,有時會用 think、hope、expect、suppose、imagine、be afraid 等字來簡答,表達自己的想法,這些字的後面可以用 so 來表示肯定的簡答。

Jane: Is your daughter drawing a picture?
Mary: I think so.
　　　(= Yes, I think she is drawing a picture.)

珍: 你的女兒在畫畫嗎?

瑪莉: 應該是吧。

　　（對,我想她應該是在畫畫。）

Jane: Do you think it will be a good picture?
Mary: I expect so.
　　　(= Yes, I expect it will be a good picture.)

珍: 你認為那會是一幅好畫嗎?

瑪莉: 希望如此囉。（我希望那會是一幅好畫。）

5 think/expect/suppose/imagine 若要做**否定簡答**,是在這些字「前面」加上 don't。

Pete: Are you going to buy whiteboard markers?
Rene: I don't think so.

比特: 你要去買白板筆嗎?

芮奈: 沒有。

- I don't think so.
- I don't expect so.
- I don't suppose so.
- I don't imagine so.

6 hope 和 be afraid 的**否定簡答**,則是在後面加上 not。

Are you going to the meeting with the boss?

你要跟老闆一起去開會嗎?

I hope not.

希望不要。

Did they cancel the meeting?

他們取消會議了嗎?

I am afraid not.

恐怕沒有。

Lena: Do you have any money on you?
Stan: Yes, I do. / No, I don't.

莉娜: 你身上有錢嗎?

史丹: 對,我有。/不,我沒有。

Practice

1

寫出與下列各回答對應的「Yes/No 問句」。

1. This is a seaside spa.
   → *Is this a seaside spa?*

2. You can soak in the hot tub in your room.
   →

3. They have reserved two adjacent rooms for us.
   →

4. The hotel has been expecting our arrival.
   →

5. Connie likes spas with not much sulfur in the water.
   →

6. Andrew enjoyed the Japanese restaurant at the resort.
   →

2

請用「簡答」填空，完成句子。

1. "Can you drive?" "Yes, _____."

2. "Are you ready to start?" "Yes, _____."

3. "Have you got all the photocopies?" "No, _____."

4. "Have you been working on it?" "Yes, _____."

5. "Did you get all the books?" "No, _____."

6. "Is Susan late?" "Yes, _____."

3

請用括弧內的提示字寫出「簡答句」。

1. Is that a drawing of a bunny rabbit? (yes / think)
   → *Yes, I think so.*

2. Does that bunny rabbit have two ears? (yes / hope)
   →

3. Is that cute little bunny rabbit carrying a machine gun? (yes / afraid)
   →

4. Are you going to the meeting on Saturday? (no / think)
   →

5. Will the boss make me go? (no / expect)
   →

6. Are you going to have the weekend off? (no / afraid)
   →

Unit 153

Wh- Questions

Wh- 疑問句

1　Wh- 疑問句以字首為 wh- 的疑問詞開頭（how 也屬於這種疑問詞），同時句中的 **be** 動詞或助動詞也要移到主詞前面。

- who
- what
- where
- when
- why
- how
- which
- whose

❶ Erica is thinking. 艾瑞卡正在思考。

What is Erica thinking about?

艾瑞卡正在思考什麼？

❷ Jerome has stopped. 傑洛米停下來了。

Why has Jerome stopped?

傑洛米為什麼停下來了？

2　如果原句中沒有 **be** 動詞或助動詞，就要在疑問詞的後面加上 do、does、did。

❶ Bill wants a new job.

比爾想要新的工作。

Why does Bill want a new job?

比爾為什麼想要新的工作？

❷ Tim needs a ride.

提姆需要人載他一程。

When does Tim need a ride?

提姆什麼時候需要人載他？

❸ Ruby bought a sandwich toaster.

露比買了一台壓吐司機。

Where did Ruby buy a sandwich toaster?

露比在哪裡買了一台壓吐司機？

3　who 和 what 常用來詢問**主詞**，也就是「行為者為何」，此時可以直接以 **who** 或 **what** 當作主詞，不需要改變直述句的語序，也不需要另外加 do、does 或 did。

❶ Stephanie loves Tom. 史黛芬妮很愛湯姆。

Who loves Tom? 誰愛湯姆？　↳ 語序不改

❷ Bobby phoned Amy. 鮑比打電話給愛咪。

Who phoned Amy? 誰打電話給愛咪？

❸ James is helping Stella.

詹姆斯正在幫史黛拉的忙。

Who is helping Stella?

誰正在幫史黛拉的忙？

4　who 和 what 也可以詢問**受詞**，也就是「動作的接受者為何」，此時 who 和 what 仍位於**句首**，但句子要使用**疑問句的語序**，並視情況加上 do、does 或 did。

❶ Ruby loves his grandmother.

露比很愛他祖母。

Who does Ruby love? ↳ 改疑問句語序

露比愛誰？

❷ Christine phoned her boyfriend just now.

克莉絲汀剛剛打電話給她男友。

Who did Christine phone just now?

克莉絲汀剛剛打電話給誰？

❸ Margaret is helping her father.

瑪格麗特正在幫她爸爸的忙。

Who is Margaret helping?

瑪格麗特正在幫誰的忙？

Practice

1

請依據提示的疑問詞，將右列各句子改寫為「疑問句」。

1. You are leaving.
   → When _are you leaving?_

2. Adrian will leave early.
   → Why _____

3. Woody can hide.
   → Where _____

4. Bryan is coming.
   → When _____

5. Rex has your hat.
   → Why _____

6. Susan has been taking photos.
   → Where _____

7. Mary wants to dance.
   → When _____

8. Herman went to an audition.
   → Why _____

2

請以 who 或 what 寫出詢問主詞或受詞的「疑問句」。

1. Ken likes somebody.
   → _Who does Ken like?_

2. Someone loves Buddy.
   → _____

3. Randy is playing something on his smartphone.
   → _____

4. Somebody called Lily.
   → _____

5. Bruce is cooking something.
   → _____

6. Something went wrong.
   → _____

7. Somebody is honking at Karla.
   → _____

8. Jack is waving at someone.
   → _____

Unit **154**

Question Words: What, Who, Which, Whose
疑問詞：**What**、**Who**、**Which**、**Whose**

what

1 疑問詞 what 可以指「人」也可以指「物」，經常可以搭配名詞使用。

What **channel** are you watching?
你在看哪一台？

What **time** does this show end?
這個節目幾點結束？

What **musicians** do you like?
你喜歡哪些音樂家？

2 what 也可以**單獨使用**，不接**名詞**。

What **is Jordan doing tonight?**
喬登今晚要做什麼？

What **would you like to do tomorrow?**
你明天想要做什麼？

who

3 疑問詞 who 用來指「人」，通常**單獨使用**，不接**名詞**。

Who **is going to be awarded a prize?**
誰將會獲獎？

Who **picks the winner from the finalists?**
是誰從參加決賽的名單中選出贏家？

which

4 which 用來詢問「**選擇**」，可以指「**人**」也可以指「**物**」。which 可以**單獨使用**，也可以接名詞。

Which **living ex-president should be sent to the ceremony?** 應該派哪一位仍健在的前總裁去參加典禮呢？

Which **restaurant in the food court at the mall do you prefer?**
你比較喜歡購物中心美食街的哪一家餐廳？

Which **one of these black suitcases is yours?** 這些黑皮箱哪一個是你的？

Which **is your favorite, Chinese food or Japanese food?** 你最愛哪一國料理？中華料理還是日本料理？

whose

5 疑問詞 whose 用來詢問「**所有權**」，可以**單獨使用**，也可以接名詞。

Whose **toothbrushes are these in my coffee cup?**
我咖啡杯裡的這些是誰的牙刷呀？

Whose **are these pajamas on my bed?**
我床上這些睡衣是誰的？

Practice

1 請從框內選出適當的「疑問詞」填空，完成句子。

what

who

whose

which

1. _____ is that you are holding in your hand?

2. _____ is your all-time favorite singer?

3. _____ do you prefer, black tea or milk tea?

4. _____ books did you borrow from the library?

5. _____ house is that next to the post office?

6. _____ newspaper are you going to buy today, the *Daily News* or the *New York Post*?

7. _____ choice do I have for lunch?

8. _____ will the runners-up get?

9. _____ do you want, a tomato salad or a chicken salad?

2 請從框內選出適當的名詞，搭配 what、which 或 whose 填空，完成句子。

kind of tea

burger

magazine

toys

shoes

Ⓐ _____ are these in front of the door?

Ⓑ Those are Jane's. He dropped by for a coffee.

Ⓐ _____ do you want today?

Ⓑ I want the fish burger.

Ⓐ _____ are you reading?

Ⓑ It's a financial weekly. Would you like to take a look?

Ⓐ _____ did you order? It smells good.

Ⓑ It's Earl Grey.

Ⓐ _____ are those on the floor?

Ⓑ Those are mine.

Unit **155**

Question Words: Where, When, Why, How
疑問詞：**Where**、**When**、**Why**、**How**

where

1 疑問詞 where 用來詢問「**地點**」，通常**單獨使用**，不接**名詞**。

Where **is your sister?** 你姐姐在哪裡？

Where **does Lee work?** 李在哪裡工作？

when

2 疑問詞 when 用來詢問「**時間**」，通常**單獨使用**，不接**名詞**。

When **is the application due?**
申請什麼時候截止？

When **are they interviewing?**
他們什麼時候要面談？

why

3 疑問詞 why 用來詢問「**原因**」和「**目的**」，通常**單獨使用**，不接**名詞**。

Why **can't I read your comic book?**
為什麼我不能看你的漫畫書？

Why **are you so mean to me?**
你為什麼對我那麼壞？

WHY?

how

4 疑問詞 how 用來詢問「**程序**」或「**方法**」，通常**單獨使用**，不接**名詞**。

How **do you make guacamole?**
你是如何製作鱷梨沙拉醬的？

How **can I chop onions without shedding tears?**
我要怎麼切洋蔥才不會流眼淚？

5 how 常用來「**打招呼**」、「**詢問對方健康狀況**」。

How **are you?** 你好嗎？

How **do you do? I'm Joseph. Nice to meet you.**
你好嗎？我是喬瑟夫，很高興認識你。

How **is your father doing? Is he still in the hospital?**
你父親現在好嗎？他還在住院嗎？

6 how 可以搭配形容詞或 many/much，來詢問「**程度**」。

How **tall are you?** 你多高？

How **often do you go to the library?**
你多常去圖書館？

How **many dance classes do you have each week?** 你每星期有幾堂舞蹈課？

How **much does a Nintendo Switch cost?**
任天堂 Switch 一台要多少錢？

Practice

1

請從框內選出適當的
「疑問詞」填空，完
成句子。

where

when

how

why

1. ＿＿＿＿＿ did you live when you were a child?

2. ＿＿＿＿＿ can you manage a team of 20 people so effectively?

3. ＿＿＿＿＿ did you decide to go after saying you wouldn't attend her wedding?

4. ＿＿＿＿＿ are you free to meet me for lunch?

5. ＿＿＿＿＿ are you taking the guitar class? Friday nights?

6. ＿＿＿＿＿ did you open that can? I gave up after I had tried five times.

7. ＿＿＿＿＿ are you saying this? It doesn't sound like you.

8. ＿＿＿＿＿ are you going scuba diving? I want to join you if I am free then.

2

請從框內選出適當的
「疑問詞」填空，完
成句子。

how often

how long

how early

how many

how much

＿＿＿＿＿ do you get a haircut?

＿＿＿＿＿ pairs of shoes do you have in your dressing room?

＿＿＿＿＿ have you been married?

＿＿＿＿＿ money did you pay for that wonderful two-piece suit?

＿＿＿＿＿ do you get up for school every morning?

Negative Questions
否定疑問句

Form 形式

1　否定疑問句是以帶有 n't 的 be 動詞或助動詞開頭。

Aren't **you ready to leave?**
你還沒準備好要離開嗎？

Can't **you sit still?** 你就不能靜靜坐著嗎？

Haven't **you been doing your homework?**
你不是一直在做功課嗎？

2　句中**沒有 be 動詞或助動詞**的時候，則使用 don't、doesn't、didn't 構成否定疑問句。

Don't **you know the time?**
你不知道現在幾點嗎？

Doesn't **your alarm clock work?**
你的鬧鐘不是停掉了嗎？

Didn't **you get up for school?**
你沒有起床去上學嗎？

Doesn't **she have a new car?**
她不是有一輛新車嗎？

3　否定疑問句也可以不用 n't 的縮寫形式，而在**主詞後面**加上 not，但這種用法過於正式，比較少用。

Aren't **you going?** = Are **you** not **going?**
你沒有要走嗎？

Why didn't **she return my calls?**
= Why did **she** not **return my calls?**
為什麼她沒有回我電話？

Use 用法

4　否定疑問句可以用來表達「**驚訝**」、「**失望**」或「**憤怒**」。

驚訝 Don't **you live here anymore?**
你已經不住在這裡了嗎？

失望 Haven't **we been planning on this outing for a long time?**
我們不是已經計畫這次出遊很久了嗎？

憤怒 Isn't **there something more important that you should be doing?**
你不是還有一些更重要的事該做嗎？

5　否定疑問句經常用於「**感嘆句**」。

Isn't **that a terrible waste of money?**
那不是太浪費錢了嗎？

Isn't **it an informative magazine?**
這雜誌的內容不是很豐富嗎？

6　否定疑問句常用來「**確認一件已知的事情**」。

Aren't **we meeting at 1:00 this afternoon?**
我們不是約今天下午一點見面嗎？

Isn't **this a departmental meeting everybody is supposed to attend?**
這次的部門會議，不是大家都得參加嗎？

Practice

請將括弧內的詞組以「n't 的縮寫形式」改寫為「否定疑問句」，完成句子。

1. I sent you an email. _Didn't you receive it?_ (did you receive it)

2. You are not wearing a jacket. _____
(are you getting cold)

3. Just a minute ago you were carrying an umbrella, and now you're not.
_____ (is that your umbrella)

4. I am talking to you, and you are looking out of the window.
_____ (are you paying
attention to me)

5. I thought you liked ballet, not modern dance. _____
_____ (do you like ballet)

6. You have been eating for over an hour. _____
_____ (have you finished eating yet)

7. When will we arrive at Grandma's house?
_____
(have we been driving on this road too long)

2

請從框內選出適當的「否定助動詞」或「否定 be 動詞」，搭配括弧內的主詞和動詞填空，完成句子。

isn't
aren't
don't
doesn't
didn't
haven't
hasn't
won't

1. _____ (you / run) ten times around the track already?

2. _____ (she) on business in New York right now?

3. _____ (you / go) to the beach with us tomorrow?

4. _____ (you / love) eating kiwi fruit?

5. _____ (he / graduate) from college yet?

6. _____ (this restaurant) the one you go for dinner every Saturday?

7. _____ (you / call) me last night?

8. _____ (she / play) the kind queen in the opera?

Part 20 Types of Sentences 句子的種類

Unit 157

Tag Questions
附加問句

1 附加問句是在一個句子的最後，加上一個
「簡短的疑問句」，形式為：
be 動詞／助動詞 + 人稱代名詞

That's a terrible TV show, **isn't it?**
那個電視節目真難看，不是嗎？

We can't catch the 7:55 train on time, **can we?**
我們趕不上 7 點 55 分的火車了，對吧？

That's about it, **isn't it?**
就這樣了，不是嗎？

You haven't taken a break, **have you?**
你到現在都還沒休息，對吧？

2 附加問句所使用的 be 動詞或助動詞，要與
主要句子的動詞相同。

It is 2:00, isn't it? 現在時間是 2 點，對嗎？

You can jump high, can't you?
你可以跳很高，不是嗎？

You don't have the time to help me, do you?
你沒有時間可以幫我，是嗎？

He hasn't finished his homework, has he?
他還沒有完成他的家庭作業，對吧？

3 如果句子裡沒有 be 動詞或助動詞，那麼
就要用 do、does、did 來構成附加問句。

You like cheese, don't you?
你喜歡起司，對吧？

He likes pizza, doesn't he?
他喜歡披薩，對吧？

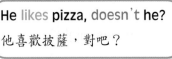

He ate the whole pie, didn't he?
他把整個派吃光了，是不是？

4 一般來說，肯定句要用否定的附加
問句；否定句要用肯定的附加問句。

It is hot today, isn't it?
今天好熱，不是嗎？

He can cook, can't he?
他會做菜，不是嗎？

It isn't cold today, is it?
今天不冷，對吧？

He can't drive a car, can he?
他不會開車，對嗎？

5 「否定句 + 肯定附加問句」的句
型，經常用來「提出要求」。

You don't know where my sunglasses
are, do you?
↳ 其實想問對方太陽眼鏡在哪裡
你不知道我的太陽眼鏡在
哪裡，對嗎？

6 附加問句的「語調」會影響意義：

1 若語調「上揚」，表示「不太確定」；
2 若語調「下降」，表示「非常肯定」，
只是做確認。

You haven't finished reading my
magazine, have you? →
↳ 詢問對方是否已經看完
我那本雜誌你還沒看完，對嗎？

You haven't finished reading today's
newspaper, have you? →
↳ 確定對方並沒有看完
你還沒看完今天的報紙，是吧？

Practice

1

請在空格內填上正確的「附加問句」。

1. You aren't cooking curry, _____?

2. Melanie hasn't left yet, _____?

3. Linda can find the right bus, _____?

4. Because of the pollution, it's hard to see the mountains today, _____?

5. Randy doesn't have a map, _____?

6. Jerry hasn't been lost for very long, _____?

7. You like Switzerland, _____?

8. Sarah couldn't go with Tammy, _____?

9. You are a professional gambler, _____?

10. Joseph can't repair the computer, _____?

11. Claudia has taken out the garbage, _____?

12. It isn't my dad on the phone, _____?

13. He couldn't have saved so much money, _____?

14. You don't happen to have a stapler with you, _____?

15. Sandy loves parasailing, _____?

16. Ramon sent us a memorandum about the meeting yesterday, _____?

2

請依據「附加問句」的形式,寫出「主要問句」裡的正確動詞形式。

1. Sally _____ (sketch) portraits of people, can't she?

2. It _____ (be) unbelievable news, isn't it?

3. Kent _____ (speak) Japanese, could he?

4. You _____ (talk) with the vice president last week, didn't you?

5. She _____ (write) editorials for the newspaper, doesn't she?

6. You _____ (ask) for money, are you?

7. They _____ (translate) hundreds of finance articles, haven't they?

8. You wife _____ (cook) on weekdays, does she?

9. Tony _____ (go) for a walk last night, didn't he?

10. Susan _____ (have) a sports car, does she?

Unit **158**

Tag Questions: Other Forms
特殊的附加問句形式

---

1 若**主要句子**以「I am」為首,附加問句要用「aren't I?」。

I am **going first,** aren't I?

我第一個出發,對吧?

I am **working the night shift today,** aren't I? 我今天上晚班,對嗎?

---

2 若**主要子句**為「祈使句」,附加問句要用 will you、would you、can you 或 can't you,這時帶有「**命令、要求**」的意味。

Call **your brother,** will you?

打電話給你哥哥,好嗎?

Give **my suggestion some thought,** would you? 對我的提議表示一些想法,好嗎?

Buddy, sit down, can't you?

巴弟,你坐下行不行?

OK. 好吧。

---

3 在表示「**邀約**」的祈使句中,會使用 won't you 作為附加問句。

Come and join **us,** won't you?

來加入我們吧,好不好?

---

4 若**主要子句**是 there be 句型,附加問句也要用 there。

There aren't **any napkins,** are there?

一點餐巾紙都沒有了,對吧?

---

5 若**主要句子**以 Let's 開頭,附加問句要用「shall we?」。

Let's **go to the hot spring every weekend,** shall we?

我們每個週末都來泡溫泉,好嗎?

---

6 若**主要子句**的主詞是 nothing,附加問句則用 it 代替。

Nothing **is happening,** is it?

沒有事發生,對吧?

Nothing **mattered,** did it?

沒什麼大不了的吧,是不是?

---

7 **1** 若**主要子句**的動詞 have 是「**行為動詞**」,表示「**做某事**」,那麼附加問句要用 do/does/did;

2 如果 have 表示「**擁有**」,則附加問句可以用 do/does/did 也可以用 have。

You just **had lunch,** didn't you?

你剛吃過午餐,是嗎?

She has **a lot of work to do,** doesn't she?

= She has **a lot of work to do,** hasn't she?

她有很多工作要做,不是嗎?

Practice

1

請在空格內填上正確的「附加問句」。

1. I am right about everything I said, _____?

2. Let's forget all about our misunderstanding, _____?

3. There won't be any problems buying the spices, _____?

4. I am washing the dishes tonight, _____?

5. Drop in some time and have a cup of tea, _____?

6. There isn't any shower gel in the bathroom, _____?

7. Nothing is more important than your own health, _____?

8. You had three cups of coffee, _____?

2

請勾選正確的答案。

1. It's a beautiful day, ☐ isn't it? ☐ isn't that?

2. ☐ Let's clean ☐ Clean the refrigerator this afternoon, shall we?

3. Turn off the computer and go to bed now, ☐ will you? ☐ don't you?

4. Let's take Ruby to the theme park this Sunday, ☐ don't we? ☐ shall we?

5. Say something constructive, ☐ won't you? ☐ can't you?

6. Move over a little, ☐ would you? ☐ aren't you?

7. There is some misunderstanding between us, ☐ isn't it? ☐ isn't there?

8. They don't have an elevator in their building, ☐ do they? ☐ don't they?

9. You just had an argument with your husband, ☐ haven't you? ☐ didn't you?

10. ☐ Put ☐ Let's put the bunny back on the shelf, would you?

11. ☐ Nothing ☐ No one matters anymore, does it?

Unit 159

Reply Questions
回應式疑問句

1 有時我們對於別人的陳述，會以**疑問句**來回應，這種回應式疑問句並不是真正的疑問句，反而是**感嘆句**，有時也暗示出**說話者的情緒**，例如感到有趣、同情、驚訝或憤怒。

> I'm living in Soho now.
> 我現在住在蘇活區。

> Are you? That is nice.
> 是嗎？那真不錯。

> I moved last month.
> 我上個月搬家了。

> Did you? I didn't hear about it.
> 是嗎？我沒聽說。

2 回應式疑問句的句型：
be 動詞／助動詞 + 人稱代名詞
這裡的 be 動詞和助動詞都要跟**原句一樣**。

Annie:	I am registering to vote.
Brad:	Are you? This is a big step for you.

安妮：　我正要登記去投票。
布萊德：是嗎？這可是你的一大步。

Celine:	David has finished his painting.
Samuel:	Has he? Let's go and take a look at it.

席琳：　大衛的畫已經完成了。
山謬：　是嗎？我們去看看。

Vivian:	Roger isn't cutting the grass as you asked.
Laura:	Isn't he? Well, then, I need to have a word with him.

薇薇安：羅傑沒有照你說的去剪草。
蘿拉：　沒有嗎？那我得和他談一談。

3 如果原句中**沒有 be** 動詞或助動詞，那麼回應式疑問句就要用 do、does 或 did。

Kelly:	I like buying lottery tickets.
Sue:	Do you? I never knew you liked gambling.

凱莉：　我喜歡買樂透彩券。
蘇：　　是嗎？我都不知道你愛賭博。

Rita:	Morton bets on horses and plays cards.
Liz:	Does he? What does his wife say about that?

麗塔：　莫頓賭馬又打牌。
麗茲：　是嗎？那他的太太怎麼說？

Craig:	Jill won a jackpot the very first time she bought a lottery ticket.
Nick:	Did she? I am amazed. The odds of that happening are very small.

克雷格：潔兒第一次買樂透彩券就中獎了。
尼克：　真的嗎？我太驚訝了，中獎的機率實在是很低。

4 原句是**肯定句**時，要以肯定疑問句回覆；原句是**否定句**時，就以否定疑問句回覆。

> Grace can dance.
> 葛蕾絲會跳舞。

> Can she? I never knew she could dance.
> 是嗎？我都不知道她會跳舞。

> Helen doesn't like to drink alcohol.
> 海倫不喜歡喝酒。

> Doesn't she? What does she drink when she goes to a pub?
> 是嗎？那她去酒吧都喝什麼？

5 唯有對原**肯定句**表達「強烈同意」時，會採用否定疑問句。

Tim:	It was a romantic restaurant.
Gill:	Wasn't it? It's a good place for a date.

提姆：那是一間很浪漫的餐廳。
吉兒：可不是嗎？那是個約會的好地方。

Practice

1   請以適當的「疑問句」填空，回應下列各句。

1. I'm leaving tomorrow for two weeks.

   →   _Are you?_   Where are you going?

2. Pat can't remember his home address.

   →   _____ That's unbelievable.

3. Daphne has just announced her engagement.

   →   _____ That's good news.

4. Charles is tired of playing video games.

   →   _____ I thought he enjoyed video games very much.

5. I have been raking the leaves in the yard.

   →   _____ Mom will be pleased to hear that.

6. Bernard likes seaweed salad.

   →   _____ I never knew he liked salad.

7. Yvonne went fishing with her brothers.

   →   _____ That must have been fun.

8. Paula has a new hairdo.

   →   _____ Does it look good?

2   連連看：請將 A 欄的「陳述句」與 B 欄的「回應式疑問句」組合成完整的句子。

A   **B**

_____ 1.   I went to a fortune teller last night.   Ⓐ Did you? I thought you don't believe in fate.

_____ 2.   Johnny didn't win the match.   Ⓑ Didn't he? But he plays so well.

_____ 3.   I haven't been home for two years.   Ⓒ Did she? She doesn't look like a political radical.

_____ 4.   Connie joined the demonstration.   Ⓓ Haven't you? You must miss your family.

Unit 160

Indirect Questions
間接問句

1 間接問句是在句子裡使用了「疑問詞所引導的附屬子句」。間接問句的主要子句，通常以下列句型開頭：

- Could you tell me . . . ?
- Do you know . . . ?
- Can you tell me . . . ?
- I know . . . .
- He asked . . . .

1 Where **is** Bourbon Street?
  ↳ 疑問句

  波本街在哪裡？

  Could you tell me **where** Bourbon Street is?
  ↳ 間接引述了 where 引導的疑問句，成為間接問句。

  你能告訴我波本街在哪裡嗎？

2 When **will** the restaurant open?
  ↳ 疑問句

  餐廳什麼時候開始營業？

  Do you know **when** the restaurant will open?
  ↳ 間接引述了 when 引導的疑問句，成為間接問句。

  你知不知道餐廳什麼時候開始營業？

2 間接問句裡頭，「疑問詞所引導的附屬子句」要使用**直述句**的語序，不用疑問句的語序。

Do you know **what** the time is?
  ↳ 不是用 what is the time。

你知不知道現在幾點？

I can't remember **what** the name of the restaurant is.
  ↳ 不是用 what is the name of the restaurant。

我不記得那間餐廳的名字了。

3 間接問句裡，不可使用**助動詞 do**、**does 或 did**，都要改成**直述句**。

1 What **do** you need?

  你需要什麼？

  Could you tell me **what** you need?

  你能告訴我你需要什麼嗎？

2 When **did** Thomas arrive?

  湯瑪士是什麼時候到的？

  Do you know **when** Thomas arrived?

  你知道湯瑪士是什麼時候到的嗎？

3 What **did** she say her name was?

  她說她叫什麼名字？

  Can you remember **what** she said her name was?

  你記得她說她叫什麼名字嗎？

4 如果原疑問句沒有 **what**、**where** 等**疑問詞**，那麼間接問句就要用 if 或 whether。

1 Is Jenny free for lunch?

  珍妮現在有空去吃午餐嗎？

  Do you know **if** Jenny is free for lunch?

  你知道珍妮現在是否有空去吃午餐嗎？

2 Did Hillary say she would meet us at the café?

  希拉蕊說她要跟我們在咖啡館碰面嗎？

  Could you tell me **whether** Hillary said she would meet us at the café?

  你可不可以告訴我，希拉蕊是不是說她要跟我們在咖啡館碰面？

Practice

1   請將句子改寫為「間接問句」。

1. Where are the water boilers located?
   → Could you tell me *where the water boilers are located?*

2. How many liters can this water boiler hold?
   → Do you know _____
   _____

3. What other floor lamps do you have?
   → Could you show me _____
   _____

4. Where are programmable rice cookers sold?
   → Do you remember _____
   _____

5. Why can't this rice cooker be used to steam food?
   → Can you explain to me _____
   _____

6. When did the new rice cookers arrive?
   → Do you happen to know _____
   _____

7. Is this the only low-suds laundry soap you have in stock?
   → Do you know _____
   _____

8. Can I get this washing machine delivered tonight?
   → Do you have any idea _____
   _____

9. He asked, "Can I move to a small tropical island and go on with my writing?"
   → Did he ask _____
   _____

Unit 161

Short Replies With "So Do I," "Neither Do I," etc.
So Do I、Neither Do I 等簡答句型

1 「so + 助動詞 + 主詞」的倒裝句型，用來表示「某人也……」。

If you are having a drink, then so am I.
如果你要喝杯飲料，那我也要。

You can cook German food, and so can I.
你會做德國菜，我也會。

2 「neither + 助動詞 + 主詞」的倒裝句型，用來表示「某人也不……」。

If you are not drinking cocoa, then neither am I.
如果你不喝可可，那我也不要。

這種句型裡的 **neither** 也可以用 nor 取代。

Mia: **We aren't ready to start.**
Lou: Nor are we.
米雅：我們還沒準備好要開始。
盧： 我們也還沒。

You don't like pigs' knuckles, and neither do I.
你不喜歡豬腳，我也是。

3 上述兩種 so 和 neither 的**倒裝句**，經常用來做「**簡答**」。如果原句是**肯定句**，就用 so 的倒裝句簡答；如果原句是**否定句**，就用 neither 的倒裝句簡答。

Fay: I haven't eaten. 費：我還沒吃東西。
Kay: Neither have I. 凱：我也還沒。

Tony: I already ate. 東尼：我已經吃過了。
Tommy: So did I. 湯米：我也是。

4 so 和 neither 的倒裝句裡，使用的 **be** 動詞和助動詞要和原問句對應。

Helen: **Hal** is **ready to go dancing.**
Marie: So am I.
↳ 原句用 be 動詞，簡答句也用 be 動詞。
海倫： 哈爾已經準備好要去跳舞了。
瑪麗： 我也是。

Larry: **Jenny** will not play **volleyball this afternoon.**
Sammi: Neither will I.
↳ 原句用助動詞 will，簡答也用 will。
賴瑞： 珍妮今天下午不會去打排球。
珊米： 我也不會。

Sally: **Penny** has got **a new yellow highlighter.**
Daniel: So have I.
↳ 原句用助動詞 has，簡答句也用 have。
莎莉： 潘妮有一支新的黃色螢光筆。
丹尼爾：我也有。

5 如果原句裡**沒有 be 動詞或助動詞**，so 和 neither 的簡答句就要用 do、does、did。

Albert likes **jogging.**
亞伯特喜歡慢跑。
So do I.
我也是。

Pan doesn't eat **shellfish.**
潘不吃帶殼海鮮。
Neither does Ron.
榮恩也不吃。

Penelope loved **the book.**
潘妮洛普很愛這本書。
So did I.
我也是。

6 neither 或 nor 的句型，也可以用「not … either」取代，此時就**不必倒裝**。

Yvonne: **I'm not sleeping in that dirty old hotel.**
Marian: I'm not either.
         (= Neither am I. = Nor am I.)
伊芳： 我不要睡在那間又髒又舊的旅館。
瑪麗安：我也不要。

Practice

1

請用「so . . . I」和「neither . . . I」句型簡答，並在句中加上適當的 be 動詞或助動詞。

1. I am not interested in motorcycles.
   → *Neither am I.*

2. I like listening to early swing music.
   →

3. Roger has never been to Madagascar.
   →

4. Tina is a healthy and happy person.
   →

5. I don't like noisy bars and restaurants.
   →

6. George has been studying different Asian languages.
   →

7. My brother doesn't like to eat vegetables.
   →

8. I climbed Mount Jade last year.
   →

9. I don't believe in "happily ever after."
   →

2

請將括弧內的動詞以正確的形式填空，完成句子。

1. Sarah _____ (know) how to cook seafood, and so do I.

2. If Elvis _____ (join) the summer camp, then so am I.

3. If Luis _____ (agree) on the camping site, then neither do I.

4. Ashley _____ (play) tennis yesterday, and neither did I.

5. Michael _____ (skydive), and neither could I.

6. Kelly _____ (do) her part, and so have I.

7. Wendy _____ (finish) her meal, and neither have I.

8. Lindsay _____ (like) her job, nor do I.

9. Brad _____ (be) a baker, and so am I.

Unit 162

The Passive: Forms
被動語態的形式

1 英語可分為主動語態（active voice）與被動語態（passive voice）。當主詞是「**動作的執行者**」時，就用主動語態；當主詞是「**動作的接受者**」時，就用被動語態。

主動語態 Johnny turned off the air conditioner.
強尼關掉了冷氣。

被動語態 The air conditioner was turned off.
冷氣被關掉了。

2 被動語態的句型，是「be 動詞 + 過去分詞」。各種時態都可以用被動語態。

現在式 The coffee is brewed fresh every morning. 咖啡都是每天早上現煮的。

過去式 The café was cleaned from top to bottom yesterday.
昨天咖啡廳被徹底打掃得乾乾淨淨。

未來式 The performance will be held in the National Theater.
這場表演將於國家戲劇院登場。

3 被動語態也有「**進行式**」，句型是：「be + being + 過去分詞」。

The staff was being helped by the owner's wife.
工作人員當時一直受到老闆娘的幫助。

Cinnamon rolls are being baked in the oven.
肉桂捲現在正在烤箱中烘烤著。

4 被動語態也有「**完成式**」，句型是：「has/have/had + been + 過去分詞」。

His café has been expanded.
他的咖啡廳已經擴大營業了。

但是被動語態並沒有「**完成進行式**」。

✗ have/has/had + being been + 過去分詞

5 被動語態也有「不定詞」形式：「(to) be + 過去分詞」。在情態動詞 can、will 等或**特定動詞**的後面，都需要使用被動語態的不定詞。

The rabbit in the garden must be caught.
一定要捉到花園裡的兔子。

The carrots shouldn't be pulled up until they are bigger.
要等到紅蘿蔔再大一點才能採收。

The rice will be harvested next week.
稻米將於下週收成。

The rice field is going to be enlarged next month. 下個月起稻田將擴大範圍。

The irrigation system will have to be expanded. 灌溉系統將必須擴充。

That farmer wants to be phoned when his truck is repaired.
農人希望卡車修好時能電話通知他。

6 被動語態也有「**動名詞**」，也就是「being + 過去分詞」。當句子需要動名詞要做受詞，或任何需要使用動名詞的時候，就要用「being + 過去分詞」。

The line judges like being shown the instant replay.
↳ being shown 是被動式，當作動詞 like 的受詞，要用動名詞。

線審希望立刻觀看重播鏡頭。

Practice

1

請勾選正確的答案。
同時，若句子是「主
動語態」，請在空格
內填上 A（active），
若是「被動語態」，
請填上 P（passive）。

1. The construction company ☐ dug ☐ has been dug the hole for the foundation. → _____

2. The hole for the foundation ☐ dug ☐ has been dug by the construction company. → _____

3. The workers ☐ set up ☐ are set up the forms for the cement. → _____

4. The rebar ☐ has been wired ☐ wired together. → _____

5. The cement truck ☐ has been arrived ☐ has arrived. → _____

6. The cement ☐ is being poured ☐ poured. → _____

7. The masons ☐ have been working ☐ were being worked on the brick walls. → _____

8. The plumbers ☐ had told ☐ have been told to start to work next week. → _____

9. The sewer pipe ☐ was connecting ☐ was being connected. → _____

10. The carpenters ☐ are arriving ☐ have been arrived at the job site at this moment. → _____

2

請將右列主動語態句
子改寫為「被動語
態」。

1. That clerk ground those coffee beans.
   → *Those coffee beans were ground by that clerk.*

2. Father polished the leather shoes.
   → _____

3. Ariel is painting the house.
   → _____

4. Paul must have found the boar.
   → _____

5. We're going to close the shop.
   → _____

6. The boss is encouraging Ian.
   → _____

7. The scientists have discovered a supernova.
   → _____

8. Freddie planted a cactus in the garden.
   → _____

Unit 163

The Passive: General Use
被動語態的一般用法

1 當我們要強調動作的「**接受者**」時，就可以用被動語態。

主動語態要改寫為**被動語態**時，只要將原本的受詞變成主詞。

Dad cooks dinner **almost every night.**
爸爸幾乎每天做晚餐。

Dinner is cooked **almost every night by Dad.** 每天的晚餐幾乎都是爸爸做的。

Most Canadians speak English.
大多數的加拿大人是說英語的。

English is spoken **by most Canadians.**
大多數的加拿大人都說英語。

2 當「**動作的肇始者不明**」，我們通常會用被動語態。

That library book was stolen.
↳ 主動語態是「Somebody stole that library book.」，我們不知道是誰偷了書的，通常用被動語態。

那本圖書館的書被偷了。

3 當「**事件發生的原因不重要**」時，也會用被動語態。

This library book has been damaged.
↳ 用被動語態比較不追究責任，表示對書被弄破的原因沒興趣，只強調「書已經破了」這樣一個事實。

這本圖書館的書被弄破了。

4 當「**我們不想追究事件的責任是誰的**」，通常可以用被動語態，巧妙地避免提到動作的執行者。

My son ripped **a page out of the book.**
↳ 用主動語態，提到了撕書的人。

我兒子把書撕了一頁下來。

A page has been ripped **out of the book.**
↳ 用被動語態，巧妙地不提是誰撕的。

書裡其中一頁被撕了下來。

5 另外還有一種比較不正式的被動語態，是以 get 代替 be 動詞，句型是「get + 過去分詞」。這種用法通常用於討論「**預料之外的偶發事件**」。

For some reason, the cat didn't get fed **yesterday.**

因為某個原因，
昨天沒有餵貓咪。

Even though Maureen was raising her hand, she didn't get chosen **by the coach.**
雖然瑪琳舉起了手，但是教練並沒有選她。

The thread in the sewing machine got stuck **in the bobbin.**
縫紉機上的線卡在捲軸上了。

Doug asked for a 7 a.m. wake-up call but he got called **at 7 p.m.**
道格要求上午 7 點打電話叫他起床，卻在晚上 7 點接到電話。

Practice

1　請將下列句子改寫為「被動語態」。

1. Someone must call the newspaper.
   → _The newspaper must be called._

2. The TV station will send a cameraman and a reporter.
   → ⋯⋯⋯⋯⋯⋯⋯⋯⋯⋯⋯⋯⋯⋯⋯⋯⋯⋯⋯⋯⋯⋯

3. The reporter is going to interview the store owner.
   → ⋯⋯⋯⋯⋯⋯⋯⋯⋯⋯⋯⋯⋯⋯⋯⋯⋯⋯⋯⋯⋯⋯

4. The gang may have involved the store owner in their criminal activity.
   → ⋯⋯⋯⋯⋯⋯⋯⋯⋯⋯⋯⋯⋯⋯⋯⋯⋯⋯⋯⋯⋯⋯

5. Someone should have called the reporter earlier.
   → ⋯⋯⋯⋯⋯⋯⋯⋯⋯⋯⋯⋯⋯⋯⋯⋯⋯⋯⋯⋯⋯⋯

6. The store owner doesn't like the cameraman to videotape him.
   → ⋯⋯⋯⋯⋯⋯⋯⋯⋯⋯⋯⋯⋯⋯⋯⋯⋯⋯⋯⋯⋯⋯

2　請用 **get** 與括號中的單字組成「過去被動式」，填空完成句子。

1. Mike said his pants ⋯⋯⋯⋯⋯⋯⋯⋯⋯ (tear) while he was climbing over a fence.

2. When Paul was playing in the garden, he ⋯⋯⋯⋯⋯⋯⋯⋯⋯ (sting) by a bee.

3. Allen tried to save some money, but it all ⋯⋯⋯⋯⋯⋯⋯⋯⋯ (spend) quickly.

4. Bessie ⋯⋯⋯⋯⋯⋯⋯⋯⋯ (lose) while looking for her friend's beach house.

5. Doris said she ⋯⋯⋯⋯⋯⋯⋯⋯⋯ (hurt) when she was moving a heavy bookcase.

6. Curtis ⋯⋯⋯⋯⋯⋯⋯⋯⋯ (elect) president of his class.

7. Little Kate ⋯⋯⋯⋯⋯⋯⋯⋯⋯ (kidnap) on her way to school.

8. The kidnapper ⋯⋯⋯⋯⋯⋯⋯⋯⋯ (catch) by the police when he was buying a beer at the grocery store.

Unit 164

Verbs With Two Objects and the Use of "By" and "With" in the Passive

雙受詞的動詞以及 By 與 With 在被動句裡的用法

1 擁有「**雙受詞**」的動詞，任一受詞都可於被動語態中扮演主詞的角色，因此有**兩種被動句型**。

The groom's parents bought *the new couple* a house.

↳ 句中的兩個受詞分別是 the new couple 和 a house。

新郎的父母幫這對新人買了一棟房子。

The new couple was bought a house by

↳ the new couple 當主詞。

the groom's parents.

這對新人的房子是新郎的父母買給他們的。

A house was bought *for the new couple*

↳ a house 當主詞。

by the groom's parents.

房子是新郎的父母買給這對新人的。

2 擁有「**雙受詞**」的動詞改寫為被動語態，以「**人**」當主詞的用法比較常見。

Tony offered *me* a sandwich.

湯尼給了我一個三明治。

常見 I was offered a sandwich by Tony.

罕見 A sandwich was offered *to me* by Tony.

3 這類經常接「**雙受詞**」的動詞有：

Lillian was sent a registered letter by her insurance carrier. 莉莉安收到一封保險公司寄給她的掛號信。

Theresa was shown a notice by the salesman that said she had to exchange the defective memory card.

泰瑞莎被業務員通知，她需要更換壞掉的記憶卡。

4 如果要在被動句裡提及**動作的執行者**，可以用 by，表明「**這件事是誰做的**」。

Sir Isaac Newton formulated the law of gravity. 艾薩克・牛頓爵士算出了地心引力。

↳ 主動句：動作的執行者 Sir Isaac Newton 是主詞。

The law of gravity was formulated by Sir Isaac Newton.

↳ 被動句：用 by 點出動作的執行者 Sir Isaac Newton。

地心引力是艾薩克・牛頓爵士算出來的。

Newton also created the branch of mathematics called calculus.

↳ 主動句

牛頓還發明數學的其中一個分支——微積分。

The branch of mathematics called calculus was also created by Newton.

↳ 被動句

數學的其中一個分支——微積分——也是牛頓發明的。

5 如果被動句裡面需要交代「**動作執行者所使用的工具**」，則可以用 with。

The garden is watered with an automated sprinkler system.
花園是用自動灑水系統澆水的。

The bulbs were planted with a trowel and the sweat of my brow. 這些球莖是用一個小鏟子和我額頭上的汗水所種出來的。

6 被動句裡，也可以用 with 來說明「**材料和成分**」。

The bread is made with flour, sugar, oranges, raisins, and walnuts. 這個麵包是用麵粉、糖、柳橙、葡萄乾和核桃做成的。

The bus was filled with peasants and chickens. 這輛巴士上載滿了農人與雞隻。

- send
- pay
- tell
- offer
- teach
- show
- promise

Practice

1

請用提示的主詞，及「過去簡單式的被動語態」改寫句子。

1. The thankful client sent Richard two ballet tickets.
   Richard *was sent two ballet tickets by the thankful client*.

2. The sales representative offered Lauren a discount tour package.
   Lauren _____
   _____.

3. The real estate agent showed Lucy the model home.
   Lucy _____.

4. The advertising agency paid the baseball player about $1,000,000.
   The baseball player _____
   _____.

5. The instructor taught the class four nights a week.
   The class _____
   _____.

6. The sailor promised the woman a letter a day.
   The woman _____.

7. Hazel bought me a digital watch.
   A digital watch _____.

2

請用 by 或 with 填空，完成句子。

1. Brenda and Ronny were married _____ a priest.

2. The bowls are glazed _____ lead-free paint and varnish.

3. The hole for the swimming pool was dug _____ a backhoe.

4. The clouds on the ceiling were painted _____ Mike.

5. Christopher's house was purchased _____ his mother.

6. The tall fluted vases are made _____ a potter's wheel.

7. The windows in the car are tinted _____ a reflective silver coating.

8. Joan's teeth were examined _____ a dentist.

Unit 165

Some Common Passive Sentence Structures
常見的被動句型

1 被動句型經常用來「轉述他人的話」、「轉述他人認定的事情」。其中一種便是「It is said that . . .」的句型,表示「據說……」。

主動語態 People say that Gloria has perfect pitch.
人家說葛洛莉亞的音準奇佳。

被動語態 It is said that Gloria has perfect pitch.
據說葛洛莉亞的音準奇佳。

2 上述句型也可以用「人或物」當主詞,句型是:

somebody/something is said + 加 to 的不定詞

Gloria is said to have perfect pitch.
據說葛洛莉亞的音準奇佳。

Cheetahs are said to run faster than any other animal in the world.
據說獵豹是全世界跑得最快的動物。

3 這種被動句型常見於正式對話或寫作中,常用這種句型的動詞有:

It is expected that the Prime Minister is going to veto the resolution.
= The Prime Minister is expected to veto the resolution.
眾人預期總理將對該決議運用否決權。

It is believed that our department head will start the new program on August 1st.
= Our department head is believed to start the new program on August 1st.
大家相信,系主任將從 8 月 1 日起推行新課程。

- say
- think
- believe
- consider
- understand
- know
- report
- expect
- claim
- acknowledge

4 如果這裡所談論的事件是發生於「過去」,則「加 to 的不定詞」要使用完成式。

It is widely known that the XY9 computer virus wreaked havoc on the internet last week.
= The XY9 computer virus is widely known to have wreaked havoc on the internet last week.
大家都知道上星期的 XY9 電腦病毒造成網路一片混亂。

5 be supposed to 也常有「據說」的意味。

This cell phone is supposed to be pretty good for such a low price.
↳ 據說這是一支很不錯的手機。
以這麼低的價格來說,這應該算是一支很不錯的手機。

That smartphone was supposed to have been on sale.
↳ 用過去式,表示「據說手機有特價,但其實沒有。」
這支智慧型手機應該有特價才對。

6 be supposed to 也可以用來「提出質疑」。

Carrot cake is supposed to be healthy, but I doubt it.
紅蘿蔔蛋糕應該對健康有益,不過我很懷疑。

Practice

1

請分別用「it is said that . . .」和「. . . is said to . . .」改寫句子。

1. People believe that the number of school-age children will drop again this year.
   → *It is believed that the number of school-age children will drop again this year.*
   → *The number of school-age children is believed to drop again this year.*

2. People know that the secret negotiations started last week.
   → ....
   ....
   → ....
   ....

3. People think the sailors have been rescued.
   → ....
   ....
   → ....
   ....

4. People say that the pandemic completely changed how the world works.
   → ....
   ....
   → ....
   ....

2

請用 be supposed to 改寫句子。

1. People say that sitting too long is bad for your health.
   → *Sitting too long is supposed to be bad for your health.*

2. People say that watching TV is bad for kids.
   → ....

3. People say that drinking two liters of water a day is healthy.
   → ....

4. People say that quitting smoking is simply a matter of will power.
   → ....

5. People say that Doraemon is the most popular cat in the world.
   → ....

Unit 166

Have Something Done
Have Something Done 的用法

1 have 後面如果接的是「**事物**」，經常會用「have + 某物 + 過去分詞」的句型，表示「**讓某物接受某個動作**」，通常指「**安排他人完成某事**」，屬於被動用法的一種。

主動語態 **Ben is cutting his own hair.**
班正在幫自己剪頭髮。

被動語態 **Ben is having his hair cut.**
別人在幫班剪頭髮。

Martin is installing a hard drive in his
↳ 主動語態：馬丁自己安裝。
computer.
馬丁正在為他的電腦安裝硬碟。

Martin is having a hard drive installed in
↳ 被動語態：安排他人安裝。
his computer.
馬丁正在請人幫他安裝電腦硬碟。

Beverly had the battery in her watch replaced. 貝佛莉讓人給她的手錶換了電池。

How often do you have your car tuned up? 你多久保養一次車？

Are you going to have your eyes examined before you get new glasses?
你去配新眼鏡之前，會先去檢查眼睛嗎？

2 「have + 某物 + 過去分詞」也可以表達「**某人為某物做了某事**」。

Russell is having his sofa reupholstered.
羅素正在幫他的沙發換坐墊。

Sam has just had the oil changed in his car.
山姆剛剛才為他的車子換了機油。

Helen is having her legs waxed at the moment. 海倫此刻正在做腿部蜜蠟除毛。

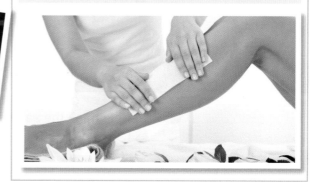

3 當某物發生「**始料未及、不愉快的事**」，或者是「**事情沒有安排好**」，也可以用這種句型。

Adrian had her glasses broken over the weekend. 雅德恩的眼鏡在週末時弄壞了。

Laura had her vacation cancelled because her replacement got sick.
蘿拉把假期取消了，因為她的職務代理人生病。

4 在非正式的對話中，可以用 get something done 取代 **have something done**。

Max needs to get his tickets reserved today. 麥斯今天一定得訂到票。

Gordon must get his son's birthday party set up right away.
戈登必須馬上把他兒子的生日派對準備好。

Practice

1   請用括號中的單字搭配 have something done 的句型填空，完成句子。

1. Janice must _____ *have her shoes repaired* _____ (her shoes / repair).

2. Paul is going to _____ (his shoes / shine).

3. Where are you going to _____ (your skirt / dry clean)?

4. Are you going to _____ (that dress / alter)?

5. Last month the proud parents _____ (their daughter's baby shoes / bronze).

6. Last night Angela _____ (her dress / rip) when getting out of her car.

7. Bonnie _____ (the heel on her left shoe / break) early this morning.

8. Roger _____ (his briefcase / steal) on the train on his way to work this morning.

2   請將下列句子以 have something done 的句型改寫。

1. Ed is cutting the grass in his yard.
   → _____

2. Dennis is fixing the toilet.
   → _____

3. Rick just replaced three light bulbs.
   → _____

4. Wayne will change the sheets later.
   → _____

5. Eleanor is frying a steak on the stove.
   → _____

6. Claudia has ironed all the shirts.
   → _____

7. Ashley could switch a propane tank easily with this device.
   → _____

Unit **167**

"Wish" and "If Only"
Wish 與 If Only 的用法

假設句型中，過去式的 be 動詞不分人稱都要用 were，不用 **was**。

- I wish Mike were here so I could congratulate him.

  我希望邁克人在這裡，我就可以當面恭喜他。

- If I were you, I wouldn't do that.

  如果我是你的話，我不會那麼做。

1 假設語氣用來表示「**假設、願望**」等，常使用假設語氣的用語有：wish、if only、if 等。

Tonya wishes she could fire her boss.

唐雅真希望她能開除老闆。

If only I hadn't sold my lovely dog. I miss him so much. 要是我沒把我的可愛狗狗賣掉就好了，我好想牠。

If I had been there, I would have stopped it. 如果我當時在場的話，我就能阻止這件事。

2 「wish + 過去式動詞」用來表示「**與現在或未來事實相反的願望**」、「**目前的悔恨**」，希望可以有不同的處理方式。

Tom wishes he had a job repairing cars.
↳ 用了假設語氣，表示他現在並沒有做修車工作。

湯姆希望可以做修車工作。

Ralph wishes he weren't working 50 hours a week. ↳ 但是他得一週工作 50 小時。

雷夫希望他不用一週工作 50 個小時。

3 「wish + 過去完成式動詞（had + 過去分詞）」則表示「**與過去事實相反的願望**」、「**過去的遺憾**」。

I wish I had saved the business card Grace gave me. ↳ 事實是：我並沒有把名片留下來。

真希望我當初有把葛麗絲給我的名片留下來。

I wish I hadn't given my tennis racquet to my brother. ↳ 事實是：我已經把網球拍送給弟弟了。

真希望我當初沒有把我的網球拍送給我弟弟。

4 if only 也用來表示「**願望**」，並且更強調個人感受。「if only + 過去式動詞」表示「**與現在或未來事實相反的願望**」。

If only Serena spoke Japanese, then she could sell more notebook computers. 要是瑟琳娜會說日語，她就能多賣幾台筆記型電腦了。

If only the committee were to decide, then we could write the amendment. 如果委員會做出決定，我們就可以撰寫修正案。

5 「if only + 過去完成式動詞（had + 過去分詞）」表示「**與過去事實相反的願望**」。

If only Ken hadn't closed that last sale, then Sylvia would have received a sales bonus.

要是肯沒有結束最後的拍賣，施薇亞就能拿到銷售紅利。

If only you had told me those were rare books before I sold them. 要是你在我賣書之前，有跟我說那些書很稀有就好了。

6 wish 和 if only 也可以接「would + 不加 to 的不定詞」，表示「**希望某事發生或不要發生**」。

Maybe Julia will sing. I wish she would.

說不定茉莉亞會唱歌，我希望她唱。

I wish you wouldn't feed the healthy food I made for you to your dog. 我希望你別把我為你準備的健康食物拿來餵你的狗。

If only he would come home soon.

希望他早日返家。

Practice

1 請從框內選出適當的動詞，依據提示搭配 wish 或 if only 填空，完成下列表示「假設」或「願望」的句子。

jog

lower

be watching

leave home

speak

bring

save

lock

come

1. Rick is out of breath while jogging.
   He said, "____I wish I jogged____ more often." (wish)

2. Doug is going to be late for his dentist's appointment.
   He said, "_____ earlier." (wish)

3. Cynthia was scared while watching a horror movie in the movie theater.
   She messaged her mom, "_____ a comedy instead." (if only)

4. Sandy does not qualify for the job because she doesn't speak English.
   She said, "_____ English." (if only)

5. Harriet saw an expensive house for sale.
   She said, "_____ enough money to buy it." (wish)

6. Peggy wanted to bring her little brother to see the dinosaur bones, but the museum was closed.
   Her brother said, "_____ earlier." (wish)

7. Lorna and her boyfriend got soaking wet in a thunder storm. She said, "_____ our matching red raincoats." (if only)

8. Ron's scooter was stolen. He said, "_____ it with my U-bolt lock." (if only)

9. Mandy burned the pancakes.
   She said, "_____ the heat." (if only)

2 請從框內選出適當的動詞，依據提示搭配 wish 或 if only，以 would 或 wouldn't 的句型填空，完成句子。

talk

swim

sing

take off

1. Danny went to hear a female jazz singer.
   He said, "_____ more of her own songs." (wish)

2. Clay and his wife went to their son's graduation party.
   His wife said, "_____ to those young girls so much." (wish)

3. The warden put a new lock on the gate to keep the kids out.
   He said, "_____ in the reservoir." (if only)

4. Candy complained to her sister about the man next door.
   She said, "_____ his shoes when he brings us flowers." (if only)

Unit 168

"If" Sentences:
Real Present or Future Conditionals
If 子句：現在或未來可能發生的真實假設

1 if 子句是**條件子句**的一種，它可以放在**句首**或是**句尾**。當 if 子句位於句首時，要加逗號，與主要子句分開。

If you don't water your plants, they will wither and die.
= Your plants will wither and die if you don't water them.
你要是不幫植物澆水，它們會枯萎死亡。

2 當表示「**現在或未來有可能發生的事**」，不會使用假設語氣。此時，if 子句裡會使用現在簡單式，而主要子句要用未來簡單式 will。這種條件句被稱為**第一條件句**。

If Henry talks to Violet, he will learn about the photos.
↳ if 子句使用現在簡單式 talks；後面是主要子句，使用未來式 will learn。
如果亨利和薇麗交談，他就會得知照片的事。

If Eva leaves now, she will beat the rush hour traffic.
↳ 「現在」可能發生的事。
如果依芙現在出發，正好會碰上交通尖峰時刻。

If Frankie uses all his vacation days, he will go for almost a month.
↳ 「未來」可能發生的事。
如果法蘭基把假期一次休完，就可以去度假近一個月。

3 主要子句除了 will，也可以用 shall、can 或 may。

If we lose the case, we shall appeal.
要是我們輸了這場官司，我們將再上訴。

If we finish early, we can take a break.
如果我們早點完成，就可以休息一下。

If you're hungry, you may take some cookies from the plate.
如果你餓了，可以從盤子裡拿一些餅乾去吃。

4 主要子句也可以直接用祈使句。

If you are ready, let's go.
要是你已經準備好了，我們就出發吧！

If you don't want to quit, do the best you can. 如果你不想放棄，就盡力去做吧。

5 除了現在簡單式，if 子句也可以用其他現在式，如現在完成式或現在進行式。

If Herman has remembered to buy some pizzas, cheesecake, and ice cream, I would like you to dine with us tonight.
如果賀曼有記得去買一些披薩、起司蛋糕和冰淇淋的話，我今晚想請你過來和我們一起吃飯。

If Trudy is cooking dinner, would you join us as our guest? 如果楚蒂在準備晚餐，你願意加入我們，做我們的貴客嗎？

Practice

1

請將括弧內的動詞以正確形式填空，並從框內選出適當的用語填入第二個空格，完成句子。

will buy

can ride

will cool

will load

will be

will tell

tell her

will run

1. If I _____ (go) to the grocery store, I _____ paper towels for you.

2. If Tom _____ (go) jogging, I _____ with him.

3. If Archie _____ (have) enough space in his car, I _____ with him.

4. If Jan _____ (call), _____ I'm still waiting for her.

5. If Veronica _____ (have packed) all her boxes, I _____ them on the truck.

6. If Johanna _____ (be making) dinner, I _____ happy to come over.

7. If Willie _____ (turn) on the air conditioner, it _____ down the room.

8. If Sara _____ (call), I _____ her you are sick.

2

請依圖示，從框內選出適當的用語填空，完成句子。

go shopping

grow higher

keep eating

will make pudding

isn't working

doesn't rain

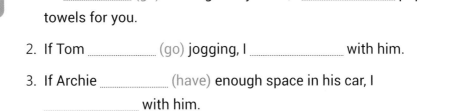

If the waves _____, we can go surfing.

We'll camp by the woods if it _____ tomorrow.

You'll get fat if you _____ like that.

If Emma is free this afternoon, she _____ for us.

If you can take this afternoon off, let's _____!

We'll go crazy if the air conditioner _____.

Unit **169**

General Conditionals:
Repeated Events or Truth
表示「習慣」或「真理」的條件句

1 在含有 if 子句的句子裡，**主要子句**如果描述的是「**習慣性**」的行為，會用現在簡單式。

If **Nick tells me something**, I always believe **him.**
↳ 一直都是這樣
只要尼克告訴我什麼，我都會相信。

If **I have a little free time**, I take a coffee break.
只要我一有點空，我就會喝咖啡小憩一下。

If **Gerry works hard in the morning**, he naps **on the sofa after lunch.**
如果傑瑞早上很認真工作，他午飯後會在沙發上睡一下。

2 在這種句型裡，if 相當於 **whenever**。

If / Whenever **Walter goes drinking with his friends at night**, the following day he sleeps all morning.
華特只要晚上和朋友一起出去喝一杯，第二天一定睡一整個上午。

If / Whenever **it's the weekend**, I always spent time watching sports on TV.
只要一到週末，我就會看電視上的運動比賽。

3 如果是 when 所引導的條件子句，也是屬於「某種條件下的習慣行為」，此時，**when** 子句和主要子句都會用現在簡單式。

When **it's sunny**, I ride **my motorcycle to work.** 晴天的時候我都騎摩托車上班。

When **it's rainy**, I take **the subway to my office.** 下雨的時候我會搭地鐵去公司。

4 主要子句如果描述的是「**必然會發生的事**」或「**不變的真理**」，則可以用現在簡單式，也可以用未來簡單式。

Egg yolks solidify when **the temperature reaches 65 °C.**
當溫度到達攝氏 65 度，蛋黃就開始凝固。

Oil will wash **away** if **you use soap and hot water.**
用肥皂和熱水沖洗，油汙就會洗掉了。

Practice

1

請用 if 或 when 填空，完成對話。

Son: Mom, ❶_____ I invite my friend Charley over, can he stay overnight?

Mom: Have you talked to Charley or Charley's mom?

Son: Not yet. ❷_____ I ask him, he will probably want to come.

Mom: ❸_____ you want to invite friends over, you always have to make plans ahead of time.

Son: ❹_____ you say it that way, I always know the answer.

Mom: ❺_____ you are so smart, tell me what I am going to say.

Son: You always say the same thing. ❻_____ you want to invite your friends over, you always have to make sure we call their parents.

Mom: ❼_____ we call Charley's mom right now, will she be home?

Son: I don't know. I will call.

Mom: ❽_____ you call to make plans, you always have to let me speak to the mom or dad.

Son: I know. Can I call now?

Mom: ❾_____ you know what to say, you can call.

2

請將括弧內的動詞以正確的形式填空，並從框內選出搭配的主要子句，連接起來。

> he dresses up in his sharkskin suit
>
> he takes Monday off
>
> I give him the silent treatment
>
> she knocks on wood three times
>
> she listens to jazz music
>
> we have to walk up to our 12th floor apartment

1. When Raymond _____ (work) on the weekend, _____.

2. When Sabrina _____ (see) a black cat, _____.

3. When the elevator _____ (not work), _____.

4. When Darren _____ (go) on a date, _____.

5. When my boyfriend _____ (not take) me out on Friday night, _____.

6. When Jess _____ (relax) at home, _____.

Unit **170**

"If" Sentences:
Unreal Present or Future Conditionals
If 子句：與現在或未來事實相反的條件句

1 如果要表示「**與現在或未來事實相反
的假設**」，就會使用假設語氣。此時
if 子句裡會使用過去式，而**主要子句**
要用「**would/could/might/should +
不加 to 的不定詞**」，我們稱之為**第二
條件句**。

If **Nancy** had **some extra money,** she'd
(= would) go **traveling in Europe.**
↳ 事實是南西沒有閒錢去旅遊。

如果南西有閒錢，她就會
去歐洲旅遊。

If **his travel agent** offered **tourist trips to
the moon,** Jim would book **tickets right
away.**
↳ 但是月球之旅目前是不可能的。

如果旅行社有提供月球之旅，吉姆一定會立刻
訂票。

If **Antonia** spoke **Korean,** she would travel
to Seoul.
↳ 可是她並不會說韓語。

如果安東妮雅會說韓語，
她就會去首爾旅遊了。

2 如果談論的事情，雖然有可能發生，但
是機會「微乎其微」，屬於「**現在或未
來不太可能發生的事**」，也可使用假設語氣。

If **basketball players** were **all short,** I would
be playing **in the NBA.**
↳ 但是籃球選手幾乎都很高，而我卻很矮。

要是打籃球的運動員都很矮，我就可以去
NBA 打籃球了。

If **Amy** went **to Patagonia next year,** she
would see **some real penguins.**
↳ 但是她或許根本不會去。

如果艾咪明年前往巴塔哥尼亞，她就會看到真
正的企鵝。

3 **假設語氣**裡，如果是「**非口語**」、「**正
式用語**」，那麼 be 動詞不分人稱，都
要使用 were，而不用 **was**。

If **Tonya** were **married,** she would move to
the suburbs.

要是唐雅結婚，她就會搬到郊區。

Dean would propose marriage to Tonya if
he were **more established in his career.**

要是迪恩的事業更穩定一點，他就會開口向唐
雅求婚。

4 但是如果所談論的事情，是「**現在或未
來有可能發生，只是機會微乎其微**」，
那我們會在 if 子句裡用 should，在**主要子句**
裡用未來簡單式 will。也就是不使用**假設語
氣**，因為仍有發生的機會。

If **I** should hear **anything,** I will tell **you.**
↳ 我非常不確定會聽到。

要是我能聽到任何事，我就會告訴你。

Should **I** talk **to Tom,** I will explain **why you
are angry with him.**
↳ should 用倒裝句型，更強調「可能性不高」。

要是我真能和湯姆談話，我就會向他解釋你為
什麼生他的氣了。

Practice

1 請從框內選出適當的動詞組合，並以「假設語氣」填空，完成下列「現在或未來不可能發生或不太可能發生的事」的描述。

give / have
call / donate
hold / attend
change / inherit
be / give

1. If I _____ *were* _____ independently wealthy, I _____ *would give* _____ money to an art museum.

2. If my university _____, I _____ some stock.

3. If a fundraiser for starting a colony on Mars _____, I _____ the event.

4. What _____ in your life if you _____ a ton of money?

5. Who _____ you _____ money to if you _____ lots of money?

2 請勾選正確的答案。

1. When Nelson graduates, he ☐ will need ☐ would have needed a job.

2. If Nelson doesn't get a job, he ☐ wouldn't feel ☐ won't feel like an adult.

3. If Nelson wanted a job at the company where I work, I ☐ would ask ☐ always ask about openings for him.

4. If Nelson called me about his job hunting, I ☐ will discuss ☐ would discuss the possibilities with him.

5. If Nelson inquires about the job opening, I ☐ would be ☐ will be happy to tell him about it.

6. When Nelson contacts me at my office, I ☐ usually take ☐ would usually take his call.

7. If Nelson wanted advice about getting a job, I ☐ would have found ☐ would find time to talk to him.

8. If Nelson ☐ job-hunts ☐ job-hunted diligently, he will soon find the right job for him.

Unit 171

"If" Sentences: Unreal Past Conditionals
If 子句：與過去事實相反的條件句

1 如果要表示「**與過去事實相反的假設**」，也會使用假設語氣。此時 if 子句裡會使用過去完成式，而**主要子句**要用「would/could/might/should + have + 過去分詞」，我們稱之為**第三條件句**。

If I had cut the grass, it would have been easy to find the ant hills.
↳ 事實是我當時沒有除草，不容易找到蟻丘。
如果我當時除了草，要找到蟻丘就很容易了。

If the traffic hadn't been so bad, the trip wouldn't have taken so long.
↳ 事實是當時交通很塞，旅程花了很長時間。
要不是交通那麼塞，這趟旅程也不用花那麼長的時間。

If Dave had made a higher offer on the house, he would have gotten it.
↳ 但是他出的價太低了。
要是當初戴維出更高價，他早就買到那棟房子了。

If our air conditioner had worked properly, we wouldn't have bought a new one.
↳ 但是它已經壞了，而且我們也已經又買了一台。
如果我們的冷氣還能正常運轉的話，我們也就不用再買一台新的了。

If Willie had contacted his office, he might have heard about the meeting.
↳ 事實是他沒有聯絡辦公室，錯過了會議。
如果威利當初有聯絡辦公室，他也許就會得知開會的事。

2 had 和 would 的縮寫都是「'd」，因此要仔細判斷句中的縮寫是哪一種。

If I'd (= had) called the store, I'd (= would) have discovered that it was closed.
如果我有先打電話去店裡，我就會知道他們已經關門了。

3 再來比較一次各種 if 假設句的用法：

現在或未來可能發生的事

If you find the time, I will meet you for lunch.
如果你能挪出時間，我會去找你吃午餐。
If you give me your shirts, I will iron them for you. 如果你把襯衫拿給我，我會幫你燙好。

與現在或未來事實相反，或不太可能發生的事

If you could find the time, I would meet you for lunch. 如果你挪得出時間，我就去找你吃午餐。
If you gave me your shirts, I would iron them for you. 如果你把襯衫拿給我，我會幫你燙好。

與過去事實相反的事

If you had found the time, I would have met you for lunch. 要是你當時有時間的話，我就會去找你吃午餐了。
If you had given me your shirts, I would have ironed them for you. 要是你之前把襯衫拿給我的話，我就會幫你燙好了。

Practice

1

請將括弧裡的動詞以正確的形式填空，完成右列「與過去事實相反」的句子。

1. If Donnie _____ (behave) properly, he _____ (not / embarrass) his family.

2. If Tara _____ (read) her horoscope, she _____ (know) Martin wasn't her celestial soul mate.

3. If Sharon _____ (buy) that dress, she _____ (not / worry) about what to wear to the wedding.

4. If Gary _____ (pay) his parking ticket, the police _____ (not / impound) his car.

5. If Michelle _____ (accept) Gordo's marriage proposal, she _____ (not / stay) single so long.

6. If Jeri _____ (mail) in the rebate form, she _____ (not / pay) full price.

2

請依據「if 子句」的形式，將主要子句括弧內的動詞以正確的形式填空，完成句子。

1. If you look by the TV, you _____ (find) your magazine.

2. If you finish the milk, I _____ (buy) more tonight.

3. If you had some time for a movie, I _____ (meet) you at the multiplex.

4. If I were going to meet you, I _____ (leave) around 6 p.m.

5. If you had called, I _____ (know) all about it.

6. If my boss had told me she needed the report by noon, I _____ (finish) it this morning.

3

請依據主要子句的形式，將「if 子句」括弧內的動詞以正確的形式填空，完成句子。

1. If Tammy _____ (want) me to go to see her, I will go right over.

2. If Sherry _____ (like) comic books, I would give her my old ones.

3. If Rhonda _____ (inquire) about the room, I would have rented it to her.

4. If Peter _____ (need) a ride, I will drive him to school.

5. If Matt _____ (study) a life saving course, he would improve his chances of getting a job at the swimming pool.

6. If Nelly _____ (wash) the lunch dishes earlier, she would have saved time in preparing dinner.

7. When Ned _____ (go) to the jazz club, he always invites me along.

Unit 172

Conditional Clauses Without "If"
不使用 If 的條件子句

1 unless 可構成條件子句，它的意義接近「**if . . . not**」（除非⋯⋯否則）。

Unless you win the lottery, you can't quit your job. 除非你中了樂透，否則不能辭職。

I won't marry you unless you get down on one knee and propose.

除非你跪下來向我求婚，否則我不會嫁給你。

2 unless 常用來表示「**威脅**」和「**警告**」。

Unless you turn yourself in to the police, I will present evidence of your misconduct to the newspapers. 你要是不自己向警察自首，我就把你行為不當的證據交給報社。

Unless Tom names his source for this story, the owner of the newspaper is going to fire him.

除非湯姆能說出這篇報導來源，否則報社老闆就要開除他。

3 unless 和 if 都可以用來表示「**條件**」，但是 if 具有**正面意義**，unless 具有**負面意義**。

If you buy a ticket, then you can go in.
如果你買了票，就可以進去。

Unless you buy a ticket, then you can't go in.
除非你買票，否則不能進去。

The store will be closed if you get there after 9 p.m. 如果你晚上 9 點以後才到，店就打烊了。

The store will be closed unless you get there before 9 p.m.

除非你晚上 9 點以前到，不然店就打烊了。

4 as long as 和 so long as 可以用於條件子句，意義為「只要」（**so long as** 不太常用）。

You can go camping with your friends as long as you finish your homework.

只要你把功課做完，就可以和朋友一起去露營。

You can borrow my tent as long as you clean and dry it before you put it back with my outdoor gear.

我可以把帳篷借給你，只要你把它清理晾乾，和其他露營用具一起放回原處就好。

5 provided that 和 providing that 可用於條件子句，意義也是「只要」。

Amber says she will go on the camping trip provided that she doesn't have to climb any mountains.

安柏說只要不爬山，她就願意去參加露營。

Providing that John can bring his dog, he will come along. 只要約翰能帶他的狗，他就會來。

6 在表示「**與事實相反的假設**」時，suppose 和 supposing 也可以用於條件子句，取代 **if** 的位置。

Suppose/Supposing you were offered a promotion, but it involved moving to Malaysia, would you take the offer?
↳ 假設子句裡使用過去式 were offered 和 involved，主要子句使用「would + 不加 to 的不定詞」，是假設語氣的用法

假設你升職了，但是得到馬來西亞工作，你會接受嗎？

Suppose I gave you some plant fertilizer, would you use it?

假如我給你一些肥料，你會用嗎？

Practice

1

請勾選正確的用語。

1. ☐ **Unless** ☐ **Providing** you call now, it will be too late to call tonight.

2. ☐ **Supposing** ☐ **As long as** you call her before her birthday, it doesn't matter whether it's tonight or tomorrow.

3. ☐ **Providing that** ☐ **Unless** the gift you sent her gets there in time, you can call a little later.

4. You don't have to call your aunt ☐ **so long as** ☐ **suppose** you send her a birthday card.

5. Unless Nelson spends less time on the sofa, he ☐ **would have turned** ☐ **will turn** into a couch potato.

6. ☐ **Suppose** ☐ **As long as** you gave your mother a trip to Bali as a gift, would she take it?

7. ☐ **Unless** ☐ **If** you put your potted plants inside your house, you will have to cover them with blankets because it's going to freeze tonight.

8. As long as Paul keeps looking for a job, his father ☐ **gave** ☐ **will give** him an allowance.

9. Suppose Bob didn't need a job, what ☐ **would have he done** ☐ **would he do**?

2

請用括弧裡的詞語改寫句子。

1. You must pass the driving test before you can drive on the road. (unless)
   → *Unless you pass the driving test, you can't drive on the road.*

2. You can improve your reading comprehension by reading every day. (unless)
   → ....

3. I will forgive you if you apologize sincerely. (as long as)
   → ....

4. He will come to the dinner, but you must not mention his divorce. (provided that)
   → ....

5. I can write a recommendation for you. Will it help? (suppose)
   → ....

Part
22
假設語氣與條件句

172
不使用 **If** 的條件子句

357

"It's Time" in Subjunctive Mood and "And/Or" in Conditionals

It's Time 的假設用法與 **And/Or** 表示「條件」的用法

it's time

1 「it's time + 加 to 的不定詞」的句型，常用來「叫某人做某事」。

It's time to eat **your dinner.**
你該吃晚餐了。

It's time **for you** to buy **a new car.**
你該換一輛新車了。

2 但如果是「暗示某人去做某事」，經常用「it's time + (that) 子句」，that 子句用**過去式動詞**。

這是假設語氣，並不是在講過去的事，而是「現在或未來該做的事」。

Don't you think it's time Marian fixed **the crack in the living room wall?**
你不認為瑪麗安現在應該把客廳牆上的裂縫補一補了嗎？

It's time **you** cleaned **your ears.**
你該清清耳朵了。

3 it's about time 和 it's high time 的用法，和 **it's time** 相同。

It's about time to pick up **Katie.**
差不多到時間去接凱蒂了。

Don't you think it's about time to return **the books to your aunt?**
你不覺得現在差不多該還你阿姨書了嗎？

It's high time **you** called **your mother.**
你真該打電話給你母親了。

and/or

4 and 常用來連結兩個「**互為條件、因果**」的句子，雖不是假設語氣或條件子句的用法，但意義相同。

Get there early and you will avoid the line.
↳ 只要早點到那裡，你就能避開排隊的人潮。
早點到那兒，才能避開排隊的人潮。

Work hard and you will succeed.
↳ 如果你努力，你就會成功。
努力就能成功。

5 or (else) 也可用來連結兩個「**互為條件、因果**」的句子，表示「**不然、否則**」。

它也不是假設語氣或條件子句的用法，但意義類似。

Be there before 7:00 p.m. when the first act starts or (else) you won't get a seat.
↳ 你要是 7 點以前沒到，就會沒有位子坐。
你得在晚上 7 點鐘第一幕開演前抵達，不然會沒有位子。

Practice

1

請將括弧內的動詞以「it's time + somebody + did something」的句型填空，完成句子。

1. Let's go get Jimmy. We need to go now. School gets out at 12:00. It's 11:55. __It's time we left__ (leave) to get Jimmy.

2. You said you were going to fix the air conditioner last month. Now it's the middle of the summer. It's so hot in here. _____ (fix) the air conditioner.

3. Keith should have picked up his package at the post office last week. This attempted delivery notice says he has ten days to claim it. Today is the last day. _____ (pick up) his package.

4. Penny wants Tom to design a new ad campaign. Penny has asked him several times to talk about the new ads. The plan for the new ads needs to be made right away. _____ (design) the new advertisements.

2

請從框內選出適當的子句，完成句子。

| her feelings will get hurt | you'll get sun burned |
| swallow the cough medicine | listen to the expert |

1

You need to wish her happy birthday or else
_____.

2

You should put on sunblock or else
_____.

3

_____
and you'll stop coughing in a few minutes.

4

_____
and you will learn how to do it right.

359

Direct and Reported Speech
直接引述與間接引述

1 引述他人說過的話有兩種方法，分別是**直接引述**和**間接引述**。

直接引述是**一字不改地說出某人說過的話**，這種句型裡，引述句要放在引號（ "..." ）裡。

Billy said, "Let's get a little wild tonight."
比利說：「我們今晚瘋狂一下吧！」
Mia reminded Billy, "Let's not get too wild. Last time you got 'a little wild,' I had to get you out jail."
米雅提醒比利：「也別太瘋狂了。上回你不過『瘋狂一下』，我就得把你從警局保出來。」

2 而**間接引述句**是**將別人講過的話，透過我們自己的口吻、釋義來轉述出來**。這種句型裡，不需要加**引號**。

I have Jason on the phone and he says he can't go out with us tonight.
我在和傑森講電話，他說今晚不能跟我們一起出去了。
I asked if he was sure. He said not tonight.
我問他確定不去了嗎，他說今晚不行。

3 引導引述句的動詞，稱為**引述動詞**，常見的引述動詞有：

Glenn said he would be busy next week.
葛倫說他下個星期會很忙。
He stated that he did not do anything wrong.
他說他沒有做錯任何事。

- say
- tell
- state
- report

4 **引述動詞**和**間接引述句**之間，可以加 that 也可以省略，加了 that 較為正式。

Victor said (that) he was being called to testify before the commission.
維克多說他正被召至委員會前作證。
Margery told me (that) she was attending a board meeting.
瑪格莉對我說，她要去參加董事會議。

5 say 和 tell 是常見的引述動詞。在**間接引述**中，say 後面可以直接加「**一件事**」，或者先加上「to somebody」，再接要講的事。

I said I was going to take a break.
我說我要休息一下。
Margo says she wants to take a day off.
瑪歌說她想休息一天。
I said to Jacob that we were all going to the break room.
我對雅各說我們全都要去休息室。

6 tell 要先接「人」當作受詞，再接所要講的事。

I told Roger I was going to take a break.
我跟羅傑說我要休息一下。
Margo tells us she wants to take a day off. 瑪歌跟我們說她想休息一天。

7 tell 和某些詞連用時，可以不需要加「人」做受詞。

tell a story 說故事
tell the time 說出時間
tell the truth 說實話
tell a lie 說謊
tell a tale 說故事
tell a joke 說笑話
tell a secret 說祕密
tell the answer 說出答案

Practice

1

在「直接引述句」前面寫上 D（**direct**），「間接引述句」前面寫上 R（**reported**）。

.... 1. Ruth says, "I want to go to the science museum."

.... 2. Ruth says she wants to go to the science museum.

.... 3. Julius said he preferred to see the aquarium.

.... 4. Last week Angela said, "I have to work tomorrow."

.... 5. Lillie says that she wishes she could go with you.

.... 6. Yesterday Ted said, "I already went there."

.... 7. Last night Philip said, "I want to visit to the planetarium."

.... 8. Janet said she had been to Mexico three times.

.... 9. This morning Susan told me she's going to quit the job.

2

請用 **say** 或 **tell** 的正確形式填空，完成句子。

1. Yesterday Robert _____, "Let's go to a pub on Friday night."

2. Last night Bernie _____ me he was going out with Robert to a pub.

3. Have you _____ Julie we are going out tonight?

4. Last week Julie _____ she would be working late on Friday.

5. Just now Alice _____ to me that it is a dark and dirty pub.

6. Johnny _____, "I don't think Jade would lie to me."

7. Sandy _____ to her boss, "Why not try the new technology to achieve better efficiency?"

8. Could you _____ me the name and phone number of the piano teacher?

3

tell 常和哪些非「人」的受詞連用？請勾選出正確用法。

☐ tell tales   ☐ tell a dream

☐ tell love   ☐ tell the truth

☐ tell a joke   ☐ tell a report

☐ tell a fortune   ☐ tell a news

☐ tell the year   ☐ tell a lie

☐ tell the time   ☐ tell a book

Unit **175**

Reported Speech: Verb Forms
間接引述的一般動詞時態

1 要將**直接引述句**改為**間接引述句**時，需要注意句子的「**時態**」。

如果**引述動詞**是現在式或未來式，那麼**間接引述句**的時態就和**直接引述句**相同，不需要改變。

Rene says, "I'm in a mood to go dancing tonight."

= Rene says she is in a mood to go dancing tonight. 芮奈說她今晚想去跳舞。

↳ 引述動詞 says 是現在式，直接引述句是**現在式**，則間接引述也用**現在式**。

2 **引述動詞**是過去式時，那麼**直接引述句**改為**間接引述句**，就需要改變動詞時態。

如果**直接引述句**是現在式，**間接引述句**就要改為過去式。

❶ Zane said, "I love surfing the Internet."

贊恩說：「我喜歡上網。」
Zane said he loved surfing the Internet.
                    ↳ 現在式要變成過去式。
贊恩說他喜歡上網。

❷ Dorothy said, "I don't like online games."

桃樂絲說：「我不喜歡線上遊戲。」
Dorothy said she didn't like online games.

桃樂絲說她不喜歡線上遊戲。

❸ Michelle said, "I'm going to an Internet café." 蜜雪兒說：「我要去網咖。」
Michelle said she was going to an Internet
現在進行式要變成過去進行式。↵
café. 蜜雪兒說她要去網咖。

❹ Bruce said, "Louise has downloaded hundreds of songs."

布魯斯說：「露意絲下載了數百首歌曲。」
Bruce said Louise had downloaded
            現在完成式要變成過去完成式。↵
hundreds of songs.

布魯斯說露意絲下載了數百首歌曲。

3 **引述動詞**是過去式時，如果**直接引述句**是過去式，**間接引述句**就要改為過去完成式。但有時也可以維持過去式。

❶ Bob said, "I bought a wireless LAN for my house."

鮑伯說：「我在家裡裝了無線網路。」
Bob said he had bought a wireless LAN for his house.

= Bob said he bought a wireless LAN for his house.

鮑伯說他在家裡裝了無線網路。

❷ Francine said, "Bob bought more computer gizmos."

法蘭辛說：「鮑伯買了更多電腦零件。」
Francine said Bob had bought more computer gizmos.

= Francine said Bob bought more computer gizmos.

法蘭辛說鮑伯買了更多電腦零件。

4 如果**直接引述句**是過去完成式，**間接引述句**仍然維持過去完成式。

Amy said, "Bob had forgotten to buy a USB cable until I reminded him with a message."

愛咪說：「我發訊息提醒鮑伯，他才想起要買 USB 線。」
Amy said Bob had forgotten to buy a USB cable until she reminded him with a message.

愛咪說她發訊息提醒鮑伯，他才想起要買 USB 線。

Practice

1

請將右列句子改寫為「間接引述句」。

1. Kathy said, "I am going out to dinner."
   → ....

2. Abby said, "I spoke to the Director."
   → ....

3. Sam said, "I saw a car accident on my way to the store."
   → ....

4. Scott said, "I have listened to that song thousands of times."
   → ....

5. Sarah said, "I am in a taxi with my mom."
   → ....

6. Tina said, "I had finished my homework long before my mom came back home."
   → ....

2

請依圖示，從框內選出適當的詞語填空，完成右列「間接引述句」。

| had bought him the watch | everyone has gone to work |
| wanted to enjoy the sea breeze | the pizza had already arrived |

1

Liz said Huck ....
.... for twenty more minutes.

2

Puca says ....
.... and he is so bored.

3

Anna said ....
....

4

Steve said Lisa ....
.... as his birthday gift.

Unit **176**

Reported Speech: Modal Verb Forms
間接引述的情態動詞時態

1 如果**引述動詞**是過去式，**間接引述句**要改變動詞時態，情態動詞也一樣。當**直接引述句**裡面使用了現在式的情態動詞，改寫為**間接引述句**時要改為過去式的情態動詞。

will → would	
can → could	
shall → should	
may → might	

❶ Bob said, "I can upgrade my computer myself." 鮑伯說：「我自己會升級電腦。」
Bob said he could upgrade his computer himself. 鮑伯說他自己會升級電腦。

❷ Tony said, "Bob will install a Linux operating system."
湯尼說：「鮑伯要安裝 Linux 作業系統。」
Tony said Bob would install a Linux operating system.
湯尼說鮑伯要安裝 Linux 作業系統。

2 但如果**直接引述句**中的情態動詞是過去式，則**間接引述句**仍然沿用過去式，不需要改變。直接引述句中的情態動詞 should，在間接引述句中也不用改變。

❶ Howard said, "Bob should use a firewall on his PC at home." 霍華說：「鮑伯應該在他家裡的電腦上設置防火牆。」
Howard said Bob should use a firewall on his PC at home. 霍華說鮑伯應該在他家裡的電腦上設置防火牆。

❷ Eleanor said, "I might buy an iPhone someday." 愛麗諾說：「有一天或許我會買 iPhone。」
Eleanor said she might buy an iPhone someday. 愛麗諾說有一天或許她會買 iPhone。

3 如果**直接引述句**中使用的情態動詞是 must，則在**間接引述句**裡可以用 must 或 had to。

Sam said, "I must learn Python in my MIS class." 山姆說：「我在資訊管理系統課，得學 Python 程式語言。」
Sam said he must learn Python in his MIS class.
= Sam said he had to learn Python in his MIS class.
山姆說他在資訊管理系統課上，得學 Python 程式語言。

4 如果「**引述內容從過去到現在都是事實**」，那麼即使引述動詞是過去式，**直接引述句**改寫為**間接引述句**時，通常**不改變**原本的動詞時態，但如果為了強調時態一致，也**可以**改變。

❶ Mia said, "Linux is a free operating system."
麥雅說：「Linux 是一種免費的作業系統。」
Mia said Linux is a free operating system.
= Mia said Linux was a free operating system.
麥雅說 Linux 是一種免費的作業系統。

❷ Joe said, "Many versions of Linux are free to download from the internet."
喬說：「Linux 有很多版本都可以從網路上免費下載。」
Joe said many versions of Linux are free to download from the internet.
= Joe said many versions of Linux were free to download from the internet.
喬說 Linux 有很多版本都可以從網路上免費下載。

當然如果當初所說的事實，到了現在已經改變，那麼動詞時態還是要改變。

• Elle said, "All versions of Linux are free."
艾兒說：「Linux 系統的所有版本都是免費的。」

• Elle said all versions of Linux were free, but in fact many companies sell their own versions of Linux.
艾兒說 Linux 系統的所有版本都是免費的，但實際上許多公司都有販售他們自己的 Linux 版本。

Practice

1　請將粗體動詞改以正確的時態填空，完成改寫的句子。

1. Dina said, "I **can handle** the job."
   → Dina said she ＿＿＿＿＿＿＿＿＿ the job.

2. Ivan said, "I **must get** home before 9:00."
   → Ivan said he ＿＿＿＿＿＿＿＿＿ home before 9:00.

3. Gwen said, "Mount Everest **is** the tallest mountain in the world."
   → Gwen said Mount Everest ＿＿＿＿＿＿ the tallest mountain in the world.

4. Jake said, "Taipei 101 **is** the tallest building in the world."
   → Jake said Taipei 101 ＿＿＿＿＿＿ the tallest building in the world, but it has been surpassed by Burj Khalifa.

5. Ann said, "We **shall arrive** in a minute."
   → Ann said they ＿＿＿＿＿＿＿＿＿ in a minute.

6. Anita said, "Uncle Bob **may drop by** some time."
   → Anita said Uncle Bob ＿＿＿＿＿＿＿＿ some time.

7. Rudolph said, "You **should come** and see it."
   → Rudolph said I ＿＿＿＿＿＿＿＿＿ and see it.

8. Father said, "I **must cook** dinner before your mom gets home."
   → Father said he ＿＿＿＿＿＿＿＿ dinner before Mom got home.

9. Larry said, "Pirating a book **is** illegal."
   → Larry said pirating a book ＿＿＿＿＿＿ illegal.

10. The weather forecast said, "It **will rain** tomorrow."
    → The weather forecast said it ＿＿＿＿＿＿＿＿ tomorrow.

11. Johnny said, "The teacher **is going to punish** us."
    → John said the teacher ＿＿＿＿＿＿＿＿＿＿ us, but in fact, the teacher has forgiven us.

12. Frances said, "I **can speak** three languages."
    → Frances said she ＿＿＿＿＿＿＿＿＿ three languages.

Unit **177**

Reported Speech: Changes of Pronouns, Adjectives, and Adverbs
間接引述的代名詞、形容詞與副詞的變化

1 直接敘述句中的代名詞和所有格形容詞，到了引述句中要改變人稱，例如 **I** 可能要改成 **he/she**，而 **my** 可能要改成 **his/her**。

Norman said he was at the zoo with his daughter, and they were looking at the baby elephant.

諾曼說他和他女兒在動物園，他們在看大象寶寶。

Norman said, "I am at the zoo with my daughter, and we are looking at the baby elephant."

諾曼說：「我和我女兒在動物園，我們在看大象寶寶。」

2 直接引述句中的時間副詞或地方副詞到了間接引述句中也往往需要改變。

here → there
now → then
right now → right away
today → that day
tonight → that night
tomorrow → the next day / the following day
yesterday → the day before / the previous day
next Friday → the following Friday
last Sunday → the previous Sunday

Tom said, "I'm here." 湯姆說：「我在這裡」。

Tom said he was there. 湯姆說他在那裡。

Jane said, "I will visit Mr. Lee tomorrow."

珍說：「我明天會去拜訪李先生。」

Jane said she would visit Mr. Lee the next day.

珍說她隔天會去拜訪李先生。

3 另外有些動詞和指示詞，也會視需要改變。

come → go
this → that/the

Peter said, "I want you to come to my birthday party."

彼德說：「我希望你來參加我的慶生會。」

Peter said he wanted me to go to his birthday party.

彼德說他希望我去參加他的慶生會。

引述別人說的話時，到底要對原句做哪些改變，**視情況而定**。

例如在不同日期使用 tomorrow 這個字，就代表不同的時間。

如果你在昨天用 tomorrow 這個字，時間其實是今天（today）；如果 tomorrow 是你在一星期前提的，那麼那時候的「明天」早就已經過了。

tomorrow 這個字是指說話當時的明天，因此在引述句中是否要修改，其實要視該敘述句是何時說出而定。

1　請將下列「直接引述句」改寫為「間接引述句」。

1. Yesterday Elmore said, "I will call you tomorrow."
   → ....

2. Hans said, "You should wash your hands before meals."
   → ....

3. Ann said, "I want you to come here right now."
   → ....

4. Bruce said, "I bought this watch from a vendor in the night market."
   → ....
   ....

5. Bernie said, "I'm going to have tuna for lunch today."
   → ....
   ....

6. Kayla said, "I'll stay here until noon."
   → ....

7. Charlotte said, "My brother went camping yesterday."
   → ....
   ....

8. Amy said, "I don't know where Tom was last week."
   → ....
   ....

9. Steve said, "I'll be out of town for a couple of days."
   → ....
   ....

10. Bella said, "I'll go to your place this afternoon," but she never showed up.
    → ....
    ....

Reported Questions
間接引述疑問句

1 當**引述動詞**是「**提問**」的動詞，如 ask、inquire 等，就可以構成引述疑問句。

在間接引述疑問句中，要用**直述句**的語序，而不用疑問句的語序。句末也不用問號而用「**句號**」。

| 直接引述疑問句 | **1** My friend asked me, "What are you listening to?"

我朋友問：「你在聽什麼？」

| 間接引述疑問句 | My friend asked me what I was listening to.

↳ 不用疑問句的語序 what was I listening to，而用直述句的語序 what I was listening to；句尾用句號。

我朋友問我在聽什麼。

| 直接引述疑問句 | **2** My sister asked me, "When is the concert?"

我妹妹問我：「音樂會是什麼時候？」

| 間接引述疑問句 | My sister asked me when the concert was.

我妹妹問我音樂會是什麼時候。

2 間接引述疑問句中，也不能使用**助動詞 do/does/did**。

1 I asked him, "What do you think of this song?"

我問他：「你覺得這首歌如何？」

I asked him what he thought of this song.

↳ 原本句子裡使用了助動詞 do，但間接引述疑問句裡要用直述句的語序，因此不需要助動詞。

我問我朋友他覺得這首歌如何。

2 I asked, "Where did you get the ticket?

我問：「你從哪裡得到這張門票的？」

I asked where he got the ticket.

我問他從哪裡得到這這張門票的。

3 如果**直接引述疑問句**裡並沒有使用到 what、why 等 wh 開頭的疑問詞，是一般的 **Yes/No** 問句，那麼改寫成間接引述疑問句時，就要加上 if 或 whether。

1 I asked my girlfriend, "Do you like reggae and ska?" 我問我的女友：「你喜歡聽雷鬼和斯卡音樂嗎？」

I asked my girlfriend if she liked reggae and ska.

↳ 原句是 Yes/No 問句，改寫成間接引述句時，須使用 if 或 whether。

我問我女友是否喜歡雷鬼斯卡音樂。

2 I asked my boyfriend, "Can you dance and hold your soda at the same time?"

我問我男友：「你能夠拿著汽水跳舞嗎？」

I asked my boyfriend whether he could dance and hold his soda at the same time.

↳ 原句是 Yes/No 問句，改寫成間接引述句時，須使用 if 或 whether。

我問我男友是否能夠拿著汽水跳舞。

4 有些間接引述疑問句，如果引述動詞 ask 後面直接加 wh- 疑問詞的話，可以接「加 to 的不定詞」。

1 Rene asked, "How do I use the video chat on the cell phone?"

芮奈問：「這支手機的視訊功能要怎麼用？」

Rene asked how to use the video chat on the cell phone.

芮奈問這支手機的視訊功能要怎麼用。

2 Sunny asked, "What should we do next?"

桑尼問：「我們接下來要做什麼？」

Sunny asked what to do next.

桑尼問接下來要做什麼。

Practice

1

請從框內找出與各題目人物吻合的問句，並改為「間接引述疑問句」填空，完成句子。

> Do you like ballet?
>
> Do you have an affordable health insurance plan?
>
> How do you get enough protein and calcium?
>
> What type of music do you play?
>
> Have you ever felt nervous when flying?
>
> How many cows do you have?

1. I asked the dancer *if he/she liked ballet.*

2. I asked the vegetarian ....

3. I asked the musician ....

4. I asked the dairy farmer ....

5. I asked the airline pilot ....

   ....

6. I asked the insurance sales representative ....

   ....

2

請將右列各「直接引述疑問句」改寫為「間接引述疑問句」。

1. Pete asked his boss Annie, "Would you like to see the file?"

   → ....

2. Annie asked Pete, "What kind of file is it?"

   → ....

3. Pete asked, "Where shall I put the file?"

   → ....

4. Pete asked Annie, "Can I get a pay raise?"

   → ....

5. Annie asked Pete, "Why should I give you a pay raise?"

   → ....

6. Pete asked, "Aren't I working hard enough?"

   → ....

7. Annie asked Pete, "Do you want a pay raise or a nicer office?"

   → ....

Unit **179**

Reported Speech Using the "To Infinitive"
使用不定詞的間接引述句

1 引述「**命令、要求、警告、建議和邀請**」的句子，經常使用「引述動詞 + 受詞 + 加 to 的不定詞」的句型。
這類的**引述動詞**有：

- tell
- request
- invite
- ask
- warn
- beg
- order
- advise

❶ The brother ordered, "Put the Hello Kitty magnet back on the shelf right now." 哥哥命令說：「現在就把凱蒂貓的磁鐵放回架子上。」
The brother ordered his sister to put the Hello Kitty magnet back on the shelf right away. 哥哥命令妹妹現在就把凱蒂貓的磁鐵放回架子上。

❷ Amy requested, "Tom, could you pick up the marbles?" 愛咪要求說：「湯姆，請把彈珠撿起來好嗎？」
Amy requested Tom to pick up the marbles. 愛咪要求湯姆把彈珠撿起來。

❸ My mom warned me, "Avoid walking on the kitchen floor."
母親警告我說：「別踩廚房的地板。」
My mom warned me to avoid walking on the kitchen floor.
母親警告我別踩廚房的地板。

❹ He advised, "Lily, you should tell your dad about what happened."
他建議：「莉莉，你應該告訴你爸爸發生了什麼事。」
He advised Lily to tell her dad about what had happened.
他建議莉莉告訴她爸爸發生了什麼事。

2 引述「**提供幫助或物品、承諾和威脅**」的句子，則不加**受詞**，會使用「引述動詞 + 加 to 的不定詞」句型。
這類的**動詞**常用：

- offer
- promise
- threaten

❶ Mom asked, "Can I get you some milk?"
媽媽說：「我倒點牛奶給你喝好嗎？」
Mom offered to get me some milk.
媽媽說要倒點牛奶給我喝。

❷ Her son promised, "I will take my vitamin pill." 她兒子答應說：「我會吃維他命。」
Her son promised to take his vitamin pill.
她兒子答應要吃維他命。

❸ His father threatened, "I will take away your robot."
他父親威脅道：「我要把你的機器人沒收。」
His father threatened to take away the robot. 他父親威脅要把機器人沒收。

3 上述兩種**間接引述句型**，如果是**否定句**，句型是：
引述動詞（+ 受詞）+ not + 加 to 的不定詞

❶ My mother warned, "Don't throw the ball in the house."
我媽媽警告說：「不准在家裡玩球。」
My mother warned me not to throw the ball in the house.
我媽媽警告我不准在家裡玩球。

❷ He promised, "I won't climb on the furniture."
他保證說：「我不會爬到家具上」。
He promised not to climb on the furniture. 他保證不會爬到家具上。

Practice

1

請使用「不定詞」，將右列的「直接引述句」改寫為「間接引述句」。

1. Dan offered, "I will do the dishes."
   → *Dan offered to do the dishes.*

2. Mom ordered me, "Get your feet off the coffee table."
   → ....

3. My neighbor warned me, "Stay away from that dog."
   → ....

4. Tom asked me, "Would you like to go to a karaoke with us?"
   → ....

5. My husband offered, "Can I help you move the sofa?"
   → ....

6. The painter promised, "I will be careful up on the ladder."
   → ....

2

右列為一名求職者記錄他與餐廳老闆的對話。請將這些「直接引述句」改寫為「間接引述句」，描述他們的對話。

1. "I want a new job," I told him.
   → *I told him (that) I wanted a new job.*

2. "Are you a chef?" he asked me.
   → ....

3. "I have a job opening," he told me.
   → ....

4. "Don't touch the mushrooms," he warned me.
   → ....

5. "I was in the south digging truffles," he told me.
   → ....

6. "Maybe you can cook truffles for me." he said.
   → ....

7. "I have never cooked truffles before," I said.
   → ....

8. "You should never overcook truffles," he told me.
   → ....

9. "I won't overcook the truffles," I promised.
   → ....

10. "Can you start working here on Monday?" he asked me.
    → ....

Unit **180**

Restrictive and Non-restrictive Relative Clauses
「限定關係子句」與「非限定關係子句」

1 關係子句是以關係代名詞 what、who、
that、which 等引導的附屬子句。多用來
修飾**名詞**或**代名詞**，因此屬於形容詞子句。

Do you know the guy who is dressed in blue?
　　　　　↳ 關係子句，修飾名詞 the
　　　　　　guy。

你認識那個穿藍衣服的人嗎？

I think this is the bag which Jay was looking for.
　　　　　↳ 關係子句，修飾名詞 the
　　　　　　bag。

我認為這就是杰在找的袋子。

2 限定關係子句用於**界定名詞**，說明人物、
地點或事物。它是句中**不可或缺**的部分，
也就是說，刪除它之後，語意會不完整。

That is the man who started this company.
　　　　　↳ 用來界定那個人是什麼人，如
　　　　　　果刪除後，句子將不知所云。

那位就是創辦這間公司的人。

The coin which I found yesterday is about
150 years old.　↳ 用於界定硬幣是「我找到的硬
　　　　　　幣」，如果刪除，讀者將不知道
　　　　　　是哪個硬幣。

我昨天找到的硬幣將近有一百五十年的歷史。

3 非限定關係子句不是用來「指定」人事
物，而是**對已知的人物、地點或事物「提
供更多相關訊息」**，就算刪除，語意還是完整。

Barbie's boyfriend, who is a licensed pilot,
owns two aircraft.　↳ 並非用來界定是何人，因為
　　　　　　我們已知句中提到的是芭比
　　　　　　男朋友，只是用來補充說明
　　　　　　芭比男朋友是一位機師。

芭比的男朋友是位執照機師，他有兩架飛機。

4 非限定關係子句可以位於
句中，也可以位於**句尾**，
通常會用逗號和**主要子句**隔開，
傳達附屬的訊息。

> 限定子句則不
> 需要加**逗號**。

My mother sent me a box,
which still hasn't arrived.

我媽媽寄了一個包裹給我，但是還沒送達。

My wife, who loves kids, has decided to
open a daycare center.

我太太很愛小孩，所以決定要開一家托兒所。

5 **that** 不能用於非限定關係子句。

✗ Betty has a really inexpensive
apartment, that is an illegal rooftop
structure.

✓ Betty has a really inexpensive
apartment, which is an illegal rooftop
structure.

貝蒂有一間非常便宜的公寓，是一棟違建
的屋頂建築物。

6 在非限定關係子句中，「**不能省略**」關
係代名詞 who(m) 或 which。（關係代名
詞在限定關係子句的省略，請見 Unit 182。）

✗ Carey, I met in France, speaks excellent
French.

✓ Carey, whom I met in France, speaks
excellent French.

我在法國認識凱瑞，她說得一口流利法文。

✗ Jacob bought me a fountain pen, I carry
all the time.

✓ Jacob bought me a fountain pen, which
I carry all the time.

雅各買了一支鋼筆給我，我隨時都帶著。

The house on the corner, which has been empty
for years, is said to be haunted.

↳ 並沒有界定是哪一棟房子，因為我們已經知道是位在角落
的房子。

位於轉角的房子已經空在那兒好多年了，聽說鬧鬼。

Practice

1

請判斷下列句子中的關係子句是「限定子句」還是「非限定子句」。
請在「限定子句」前面寫上 R，「非限定子句」前面寫上 N。

.... 1. My sister, who is 16 years old, is a pest.

.... 2. The sale, which started today, will continue for two weeks.

.... 3. The girl who is sniffling has a cold.

.... 4. The used car, which I bought yesterday, runs pretty well.

.... 5. I spoke to the mechanic that fixed my car.

.... 6. The flu medicine, which I always buy, is on sale.

2

請從框內的「關係子句」中，選出與圖片呼應的用語填入空格中，完成句子。

Ⓐ who is tasting the wine?

Ⓑ who is holding a cup of coffee in his hand.

Ⓒ which I've been carrying with me for years.

Ⓓ that has mud around its nose

Ⓔ who is sitting on the bench and using a laptop?

Ⓕ which leads to my house.

Ⓖ that serves organic salads?

Do you know the woman
...A...

This is the pocket watch
....

Do you know the woman
....

Look at the guy ....

Have you been to the
restaurant ....

Don't you think the pig
.... is adorable?

This is the shortcut ....

Part 24 Relative Clauses 關係子句

Unit 181

Restrictive Relative Clauses With "Who," "Which," and "That"

以 Who、Which、That 引導的限定關係子句

who

1　who 指「人」，常用於限定關係子句。如果拆成兩個句子，who 就相當於代名詞的地位。

Robin called the person. He placed the ad in the newspaper.
↳ 第一個句子不是完整句子。
→ Robin called the person who placed the ad in the newspaper.
羅賓打電話給在報紙上登廣告的人。

I talked to the man. He owns the house.
→ I talked to the man who owns the house.
我跟這房子的屋主談過。

The man is talking to the agent. She is showing the house.
→ The man is talking to the agent who is showing the house.
那個男人跟正在展示這間房子的仲介說話。

which

2　which 指「事物」，常用於限定關係子句。

Did you see the phone bill? I paid it yesterday.
→ Did you see the phone bill which I paid yesterday?
你有看到我昨天付的電話帳單嗎？

The money is for your school lunches. I put it on the table.
→ The money which I put on the table is for your school lunches.
我放在桌上的錢是給你到學校吃午餐的。

Shirley wants to see the apartment. It is being advertised in the newspaper.
→ Shirley wants to see the apartment which is being advertised in the newspaper.
雪莉想要看看報紙廣告上的那間公寓。

that

3　that 可以在限定關係子句中指「人」，也可以指「物」。

I like the bag. I bought it in Tokyo.
→ I like the bag that I bought in Tokyo.
我喜歡那個我在東京買的包包。

Did you see the picture frame? It was on top of the TV.
→ Did you see the picture frame that was on top of the TV?
你有沒有看到電視機上面的相框？

Try the cherry tomatoes. They are on the table.
→ Try the cherry tomatoes that are on the table.
吃吃看那些放在桌上的小番茄。

4　關係代名詞和人稱代名詞不可並用。

✗ Janet asked the man who he was standing in the middle of the path to step aside.
✓ Janet asked the man who was standing in the middle of the path to step aside.
珍妮特要那擋在路中央的人靠邊一點。

✗ I took some boxes that they were on the shelf.
✓ I took some boxes that were on the shelf.
我從架子上拿了一些盒子。

Practice

1

請用「關係代名詞 who、that」連接各題的兩個句子，改寫為帶有「限定關係子句」的句型。

1. I called the woman with a German accent. She had left a message on my answering machine.

   → *I called the woman with a German accent who/that had left a message on my answering machine.*

2. Did you see the woman? She was sitting by me on the bus.

   →

3. The guy was cool. He talked to me while I was having my iced tea.

   →

4. Have you seen the water bottle? It was by the door.

   →

5. I tripped over the slippers. They were in the hallway.

   →

6. The hat was on the coat tree when I left home this morning. It is now on the floor.

   →

2

請將右列錯誤的句子改寫為正確的句子。

1. Did you see the blue backpack who I bought yesterday?

   → *Did you see the blue backpack which/that I bought yesterday?*

2. Could you please pass me the pepper who is on the counter?

   →

3. I called the history teacher who I met him at the party last night.

   →

4. I went to the new restaurant which it opened last Sunday.

   →

5. I didn't recognize the tall woman which talked to me at the bank yesterday.

   →

6. Jack said the woman, that he had dinner with last night, was his ex-wife.

   →

Unit 182

Leaving out Objective Relative Pronouns in Restrictive Relative Clauses
限定關係子句中受詞關係代名詞的省略

1 在限定關係子句中，關係代名詞 who、which、that 可以當作**主詞**，也可以當作**受詞**。

Amy is the waitress. She served us at the restaurant yesterday.
→ Amy is the waitress who served us at the restaurant yesterday. ↳ who 是主詞。
愛咪就是昨天餐廳為我們服務的服務生。

Emily is the woman. We talked with her at the restaurant last night.
→ Emily is the woman who we talked with at the restaurant last night.
↳ who 是 talked with 的受詞。
艾蜜莉就是昨晚我們在餐廳講話的那位女子。

2 當 who、which、that 在限定關係子句中當作**主詞**的時候，**不可以省略**。

✗ Colin is the accountant called about your tax refund.
✓ Colin is the accountant who called about your tax refund.
柯林就是打電話通知你退稅的那位會計師。

✗ Have you paid the electricity bill is due today?
✓ Have you paid the electricity bill which is due today?
你付了今天到期的電費帳單嗎？

3 當 who、which、that 在限定關係子句中當作**受詞**的時候，**可以省略**。

Barcelona is the city we went to on our last vacation.
= Barcelona is the city that we went to on our last vacation. ↳ that 是 went to 的受詞，可以省略。
巴塞隆納就是我們上次度假去的那個城市。

I really liked the laptop I saw in the computer shop last Sunday.
= I really liked the laptop which I saw in the computer shop last Sunday.
↳ which 是 saw 的受詞，可以省略。
我很喜歡我上星期日在電腦店看到的那台筆電。

4 who 當作受詞時，正式的用法是用 whom。但是 whom 聽起來太過正式，現在多用 who 或 that。

Stefan met an old friend whom he knew from college. ↳ 較正式
→ Stefan met an old friend (who) he knew from college.
→ Stefan met an old friend (that) he knew from college.
史蒂芬遇到了一位大學時期的老朋友。

Practice

1

請以 who 指「人」、that 指「物」做適當的填空，並將可以省略的「關係代名詞」加上括弧。

1. Mr. Roberts is the guy _____ sold us the painting.

2. Mrs. Stevens is the woman _____ we talked to about the auction.

3. Have you seen the auction house catalog _____ I received in the mail?

4. Check the reference number _____ was marked on the side.

5. I saw a large bronze statue of a ballet dancer _____ I liked.

6. Mr. Stone introduced me to a Russian woman _____ said she knew you.

2

請將下列句子以「省略關係代名詞的關係子句」句型改寫，合併為一個句子。

1

Guam is the island. We went to Guam for our honeymoon.

→ _____

_____

2

Sophia is the student. I mentioned her yesterday.

→ _____

_____

3

The roast duck was the dish. Patricia recommended the dish in this restaurant.

→ _____

_____

4

This is the house. Janet sold the house in two days.

→ _____

_____

Unit **183**

Restrictive Relative Clauses With "Whose," "Where," "When," and "Why/That"

以 **Whose**、**Where**、**When**、**Why/That** 引導的限定關係子句

whose

1 whose 表示「**所有權**」，可以用於限定關係子句，相當於**所有格代名詞 his**、**her** 等。

I have an uncle. His daughter is getting married.
→ I have an uncle whose daughter is getting married.

我有一個即將嫁女兒的叔叔。

That is the family. Their neighbor is a famous general.
→ That is the family whose neighbor is a famous general.

他們是那個鄰居為知名將軍的家庭。

2 whose 和 who's 很容易混淆，whose 是**所有格**，而 who's 則是 **who is** 或 **who has** 的縮寫，不是所有格。

✗ My brother is married to a woman who's family comes from Russia.
✓ My brother is married to a woman whose family comes from Russia.

我哥哥娶了一名來自俄國的女子。

where

3 where 指「**地點**」，可以用於限定關係子句。

The city in Russia where Natasha comes from is Vladivostok.

娜塔莎來自的城市是俄國的海參威。

4 where 在限定關係子句當中通常**不能省略**，但如果先行詞是 somewhere、anywhere、everywhere、nowhere、place 等字，通常**可以省略**。

The place (where) I learned to dive is said to have sharks around.

我以前學潛水的地方，現在據說有鯊魚出沒。

Last summer the hotel where we stayed was very noisy.

我們去年夏天住的飯店非常吵。

when

5 when 指「**時間**」，可以用於限定關係子句，也**可以省略**。

Lena didn't speak any other language other than Russian. She arrived in America on that day.
→ Lena didn't speak any other language other than Russian the day (when) she arrived in America.

莉娜剛來美國的時候，除了俄語，不會說別的語言。

Can you set a time? We can meet at that time.
→ Can you set a time (when) we can meet?

你可以定一個我們會面的時間嗎？

Is there a good time (when) we can play ping pong on Sunday?　↳ when 可以省略。

我們星期日有合適的時間打乒乓球嗎？

why that

6 why 表示「**理由**」，可以引導限定關係子句，但只搭配先行詞 reason 使用。這種句型也可以用 that。why 和 that 在這裡都**可以省略**。

What is the reason (why) she left Russia?

她離開俄國的原因是什麼？

Having no chance of promoting is the reason (that) he left the company.

缺乏升遷管道是他離開這間公司的原因。

Practice

1

whose

where

when

why/that

請從框內選出適當的「關係代名詞」填空，並將可以省略的加上括弧。

1. What is the reason ___(why/that)___ Terry wants to buy such an old house?

2. Joseph is the man _____ brother just returned from Patagonia.

3. This is the bakery _____ I always buy rye bread.

4. This meeting is as boring as yesterday's meeting _____ the boss fell asleep.

5. I knew he was my true love at the moment _____ I met him.

6. The bus stops next to a waterfall _____ you can take pictures.

7. Is there a reason _____ you want to put your money into gold?

8. Judy and Frank are the couple _____ picture was in yesterday's newspaper.

2

請用適當的「關係代名詞」合併各題的兩個句子。

1. I remember the day. We first met on that day.
   → ___I remember the day when we first met.___

2. We go to the city for a shopping trip every year. The city is Bangkok.
   → _____

3. I know a guy. His father owns a company with two thousand employees.
   → _____

4. He hasn't spoken to me for a week. I don't know the reason.
   → _____

5. I need the address. I can send this parcel to the address.
   → _____

6. The rain came at a time. The peasants needed it most.
   → _____

Unit 184

Non-restrictive Relative Clauses
非限定關係子句

唯有 *that* 不可用於非限定關係子句。

1 who 可以引導非限定關係子句,用來指「人」。

I called the police, who arrived at my apartment in five minutes. 我打電話報警,警察五分鐘後來到我的公寓。

The tall man with gray hair, who is wearing a pair of sunglasses, must be Professor Jones. 那個頭髮灰白、戴著墨鏡的高個子男人,一定是瓊斯教授。

2 which 可以引導非限定關係子句,用來指「物」。

I am going to sell this watch, which has increased in value.
這支錶已經增值了,我打算出售它。

3 which 可以用來代替「前面的句子」。

Mr. Brown grows his fruit completely without pesticides, which means it is organic. ↳ which 用來代替前面整個句子
布朗先生種水果完全不用農藥,意味著是有機栽培。

4 whom 可以引導非限定關係子句,用來指「人」,但只能在關係子句裡當受詞。當受詞時,whom 也可以用 who 代替。

Senator John Brown, who(m) we met at the fundraiser, has called to ask for a donation. 我們在募款會上遇到的約翰·布朗參議員,打電話來要求募捐。

5 whose 可以引導非限定關係子句,補充說明「所有權」。

The woman at the bakery, whose dog weighed 25 kilograms, was buying a birthday cake for her daughter.
麵包店裡那位女士有一隻重 25 公斤的狗,她那時正在為她的女兒買生日蛋糕。

The woman at the coffee shop, whose hair is gray, has a cute dog with white fur.
咖啡店那位灰白頭髮的女士,有一隻全身白毛、非常可愛的狗。

6 where 可以引導非限定關係子句,表示「地點」。

The bakery at the corner of Park Street and Vine Avenue, where I saw the woman with the cute dog, sells organic snacks.
在公園街和藤蔓大道轉角那家烘焙坊有賣有機點心,我在那裡看到過一位女士帶著一隻可愛的狗。

7 when 可以引導非限定關係子句,表示「時間」。

Today is my 18th birthday, when I am finally eligible to take the test for my driver's license.
今天是我 18 歲的生日,我終於有資格去考駕照了。

Practice

1

請從框內選出適當的
詞彙填空，完成句子。

who

which

whose

where

when

1. Lindsay, _____ brother is a friend of mine, wants to come with us.

2. My son, _____ you just met, wants me to drive him to baseball practice.

3. The bus stopped in front of the junior college, _____ I once took a welding course.

4. That awful bus accident happened in the fall, right before my birthday, _____ the leaves were changing colors.

5. We are going to the water park, _____ we held our wedding last year.

6. That is the school my son attends, and it's _____ I bring him every morning.

7. This is my son, _____ you met when he was little, is now a pilot.

2

請依圖示，從框內選
出適當的描述用語，
搭配正確的 who、
which、whose、
where 填空，完成句
子。

| car has a flat fire | lies in the South America |
| is sitting here reading a newspaper | the Emperor Penguins live |

The Amazon, _____
_____, is the
largest river in the world.

Jennifer, _____
_____, always enjoys her
morning break with a cup of coffee.

The Antarctica, _____
_____, is
mostly covered by ice.

I think we should help the woman
over there, _____
_____.

Unit 185

Relative Clauses With Prepositions
搭配介系詞的關係子句

---

1 關係代名詞可在**關係子句中當作介系詞的受詞**。當關係代名詞是 which 或 whom 時，介系詞可放在 which 或 whom 的**前面**。

That is the building. Daniel works <u>in it</u>.
→ That is the building <u>in which</u> Daniel works.
　　　　　　　↳ which 代替 it，是介系詞 in 的受詞。
那就是丹尼爾工作的大樓。

The application is from the Indian with a big beard. We know very little <u>about him</u>.
→ The application is from the Indian man with a big beard <u>about whom</u> we know very little.
　　　　　　↳ whom 代替 him，是介系詞 about 的受詞。
這張申請表，是來自那位我們不太熟悉、留著大鬍子的印度人。

---

2 在**非正式的用法**裡，介系詞可位於**子句動詞的後面**，不和關係代名詞連在一起。這種情況下，關係代名詞可以是 who、which、whom 或 that，並且**可以省略**。

That is the pot <u>(which)</u> I put the soup <u>in</u>.
那個就是我用來盛湯的鍋子。

The people <u>(who)</u> I work <u>with</u> are very nice. 和我一起工作的人都非常好。

This is the corkscrew <u>(that)</u> I open wine bottles <u>with</u>. 這是我用來開酒瓶的開瓶器。

---

3 因此，當關係代名詞是 which 或 whom 時，介系詞可以有兩種位置，意義都相同。

That is the company I <u>own stock in</u>.
→ That is the company <u>in which</u> I own stock.
那就是我擁有股票的公司。

Mr. Tanner is the man I <u>work for</u>.
→ Mr. Tanner is the man <u>for whom</u> I work.
坦納先生就是我老闆。

---

4 在正式的非限定關係子句裡，介系詞一樣可以放在 **which** 或 **whom** 的前面，這種用法很常見。

This is my pet mouse's favorite book, <u>at which</u> she can look for hours.
這是我的寵物鼠最愛的書，她可以盯著看好幾個小時。

This necklace was purchased by my wife, <u>on whom</u> it looks splendid.
這副項鍊是我太太買的，她戴上時光彩奪目。

---

5 在非正式的非限定關係子句裡，介系詞比較常放在**動詞後面**，不與關係代名詞連用。同時，多以 who 代替 **whom**。

Those are the songs from the early 1900s, <u>which</u> I listened <u>to</u> a lot as I grew up. 這是 1900 年代早期的歌曲，我在成長時期聽了很多。

Max and Lily, <u>who</u> I just talked <u>with</u>, are old friends of mine. 剛剛跟我講話的麥斯和莉莉，都是我的老朋友了。

---

6 在非限定關係子句裡，可以用一些 of 的詞組來表達「**數量**」。

• some of	• much of	• all of
• many of	• none of	• two of

Cliff owns three houses, <u>all of which</u> cost big bucks.
克里夫擁有三棟房子，全都價值不菲。

Miffy has three sisters, <u>none of whom</u> are married. 米菲有三個姐妹，全都未婚。

Practice

1

請用括弧裡提示的介系詞，搭配適當的「關係代名詞」填空，完成句子。

1. That is the university _____ (in) Dave is enrolled.

2. Wendy, _____ (with) you can speak privately, is our top attorney in this field of law.

3. The band _____ (in) I used to play is now on tour in Europe.

4. That is the armchair _____ (in) she was sitting half an hour ago.

5. Mary is an interior designer, _____ (about) I know very little.

2

請依圖示，從框內選出適當的用語填空，完成句子；再用「介系詞放在動詞後面的句型」，將各個句子改寫成另一種關係子句。

about whom

in which

for whom

with which

This is Mia's favorite toy, _with which_ she can play for hours.

= _This is Mia's favorite toy, which she can play with for hours._

That woman is our new manager, _____ I've heard a lot.

= _____

This is Lulu's favorite pool, _____ she often swims for a long time.

= _____

That pretty woman is my wife, _____ I make a cup of rooibos tea every day.

= _____

彩圖

Grammar Growth Curve

中級英文文法

Let's See! 四版

作　　者　Alex Rath Ph.D.
審　　訂　Dennis Le Boeuf / Liming Jing
譯　　者　羅竹君／丁宥榆
校　　對　梁立芳／樊志虹／吳佳芬
編　　輯　張盛傑／丁宥榆
主　　編　丁宥暄
內文設計　洪伊珊／林書玉
內文排版　洪伊珊／蔡怡柔
封面設計　林書玉
圖片協力　周演音
製程管理　洪巧玲
出 版 者　寂天文化事業股份有限公司
發 行 人　周均亮
電　　話　+886-(0)2-2365-9739
傳　　真　+886-(0)2-2365-9835
網　　址　www.icosmos.com.tw
讀者服務　onlineservice@icosmos.com.tw
出版日期　2021 年 4 月 四版一刷

郵撥帳號 1998620-0 寂天文化事業股份有限公司
劃撥金額 600 元（含）以上者，郵資免費。
訂購金額 600 元以下者，請外加郵資 65 元。
〔若有破損，請寄回更換，謝謝。〕

國家圖書館出版品預行編目 (CIP) 資料

彩圖中級英文文法 Let's see!/Alex Rath 著 . -- 四版 . -- 臺北市：寂天文化事業股份有限公司，2021.04
面；　公分

ISBN 978-986-318-986-2(平裝)
1. 英語　2. 語法
805.16　　110002443

Grammar Growth Curve

彩圖 中級英文文法 Let's See! 四版

Answers to Practice Questions

Unit 1 p. 9

1 1. frogs 2. dishes 3. heroes 4. factories
5. knives 6. galleys 7. safes
8. loaves, cartons 9. spies 10. plays

2 1. churches 2. wives 3. toothbrushes
4. matches 5. stomachs 6. babies, months
7. keys 8. boxes

3 1. **-es:** heroes, potatoes, tomatoes
-s: memos, kilos, solos
-s/-es: mangos/mangoes, zeros/zeroes,
cargos/cargoes
2. **-ves:** knives, halves, calves
-s: puffs, briefs, roofs, gulfs, chiefs, tariffs

Unit 2 p. 11

1 1. teeth 2. children 3. species 4. sheep
5. reindeer 6. lice 7. Bison
8. fungus（此處當作形容詞修飾 family〔科〕，
以單數形態呈現）
9. phenomena 10. series 11. crisis

2 1. Salmon 2. Cod 3. carp 4. shellfish

Unit 3 p. 13

1 1. soda, (U/C)（soda 原本是不可數名詞，但如
果在餐館裡點餐，指「一杯汽水」時，可以當
可數名詞使用）
2. sugar, (U) 3. cherry, (C) 4. typhoon, (C)
5. soup, (U) 6. block, (C) 7. anger, (U)
8. lamp, (C)

2 1. Sandy went to ~~store~~ a store to buy . . .
2. Sandy bought ~~sofa~~ a sofa, four dining ~~chair~~
chairs, and a ~~nightstands~~ nightstand for . . .
3. Trent isn't satisfied with the sofa. The sofa
~~are~~ is too dark.
4. There ~~is~~ are not enough . . .
5. The nightstand ~~do~~ does not fit their
bedroom . . .

6. They had ~~argument~~ an argument over the
newly bought ~~furnitures~~ furniture.
7. Trent thought Sandy should take ~~an advice
or two~~ some advice from him.
8. But Sandy doesn't like any of Trent's
~~opinion~~ opinions.
9. Now, Trent has convinced himself that the
dark sofa ~~are~~ is easy to maintain.

Unit 4 p. 15

1 1. wheat 2. cheese 3. jewelry 4. mud
5. hail 6. perfume 7. copper 8. pepper

2 1. Chinese, French 2. water, oxygen
3. intelligence 4. bacon, toast, chocolate
5. biology, chemistry 6. gas, smoke
7. confidence 8. copper

Unit 5 p. 17

1 1. is, is 2. sunglasses, They are 3. a pair of
4. is 5. indicate
6. is（billiards〔撞球〕為複數形態，但意義為
「單數」，搭配單數動詞使用）
7. are（earnings〔薪水〕為固定複數形態，沒
有單數形態 *earning）
8. thanks（thanks〔謝意〕為固定複數形態，
thank 則為動詞）

2 1. ruins 2. shears 3. gymnastics
4. pajamas 5. shoes 6. tights

Unit 6 p. 19

1 1. a jar of mustard 2. three slices of cheese
3. two pieces of luggage 4. a slice of melon
5. two pieces of toast 6. a can of mussels
7. two bars of soap 8. a glass of liquor
9. a bowl of bath salt 10. a jar of cookies
11. a pot of tea 12. four jars of spices
13. a bottle of shower gel
14. a tube of peach lotion

Unit 7   p. 21

1 1. is 2. is 3. need 4. are 5. Beijing
6. was 7. a large audience 8. was 9. is
10. has 11. they were

2 1. My <u>class</u> (C) elected <u>Mark</u> (P) to be the
class leader.
2. An <u>army</u> (C) of five thousand men
assembled at the border of <u>India</u> (P).
3. The criminal ran into the <u>crowd</u> (C) in
<u>Federation Square</u> (P).
4. <u>*La Traviata*</u> (P) attracted an <u>audience</u> (C) of
thousands to the <u>City Theater</u> (P).
5. Half of the <u>staff</u> (C) of <u>KPMG International
Limited</u> (P) got a pay raise.
6. The <u>mob</u> (C) occupied hospitals and
airports, causing chaos and wreaking
havoc.
7. Football <u>teams</u> (C) from 32 countries
gathered in <u>Russia</u> (P) to compete for the
<u>2018 World Cup</u> (P).
8. The <u>government</u> (C) has come up
with several solutions to prevent the
unemployment level from getting worse.

Unit 8   p. 23

1 1. fax machine 2. cotton field
3. coffee grinder 4. screwdriver
5. drug abuse 6. starfruit / star fruit
7. campfire

2 1. tissue paper 2. animal rights
3. rock music 4. football 5. brothers-in-law
6. passers-by 7. tool boxes 8. coffee milk

Unit 9   p. 25

1 1. deer's antlers 2. dog's paw
3. parrots' cage 4. bass's scales
5. lion's roar

2 1. John and Amy's apartment
2. Edward and Betty's kitchen
3. Selina's and Christine's teddy bears
4. Ken's and Lynn's laptops

Unit 10   p. 27

1 1. the hairdresser's 2. the barber's
3. the doctor's 4. the dentist's
5. the baker's

2 1. Paul's car 2. someone's keys
3. dog's bone 4. company's office
5. today's newspaper 6. week's vacation
7. grandparents' bicycles
8. Mick and Jeri's wedding photos
9. driver's license

Unit 11   p. 29

1 1. Nelly's school 2. name of the ballet
3. Nancy's dance teacher
4. address of the theater
5. price of the tickets 6. Norma's part
7. jury's judgment 8. workers' movement
9. Veasna's VIP card
10. facade of the building

2 1. The cap of the lotion is missing.
2. The vice president of the United Electric
Company will visit our new factory next
week.
3. The grocery store of Audrey and Lucas is
going to open next month.
4. The waiters of the Empire Hotel's Chinese
restaurant are well trained.
5. The birthday of my mother-in-law is
coming soon.

Unit 12   p. 31

1 1. a whale 2. an eagle 3. a volleyball
4. a first-aid kit 5. a meatball 6. an onion
7. a one-way road 8. an idea 9. an SUV
10. a UFO 11. an astronaut 12. an heir

2 1. a 2. a 3. a 4. an 5. a 6. a 7. an
8. an 9. an

Unit 13   p. 33

1 1. a 2. the 3. the 4. the 5. the 6. a
7. an 8. The 9. an 10. The 11. the
12. the 13. the 14. the 15. the 16. a

Unit 14   p. 35

1 1. / 2. the 3. / 4. / 5. / 6. the 7. /
8. The 9. The 10. The 11. The 12. /
13. the 14. the

2 1. The poor need national health insurance
more than the middle class and the rich.
2. The city council has approved several
proposals for the welfare of the elderly.
3. The excavation of these sites has revealed
the life and culture of the Maya.
4. Opportunities go to the strong, not the
weak.

Unit 15   p. 37

1 1. the countryside, the city 2. the cello
3. The mayor 4. the beach 5. The king
6. the Moon 7. The President
8. the airplane 9. The lion 10. the stars

2 1. Bill is climbing the mountain.
2. Lee commutes between his downtown
office and his home in the suburbs.

3. Larry is working for the Ministry of Education.
4. In 1990, NASA launched the Hubble Telescope into orbit.
5. John is swimming laps in the pool.
6. Caterina learned to play the flute when she was 12.

Unit 16   p. 39

1 1. a   2. the   3. an, *the*
4. the   5. The   6. the   7. a/the   8. a
9. The   10. the   11. an   12. the   13. the

2 1. Snow   2. Tornadoes   3. the rain
4. the circus, the performance
5. the evening   6. the wind
7. *the Taipei Times*

Unit 17   p. 41

1 1. The Dragon Boat Festival
2. summer, autumn
3. The Songkran Festival   4. June
5. Father's Day   6. noon   7. Valentine's Day
8. Saturday, Sunday   9. night

Unit 18   p. 43

1 1. /   2. /   3. /   4. the   5. /, /   6. /, /
7. the   8. the   9. /   10. /   11. the   12. /
13. /, /   14. the   15. /   16. /   17. the   18. /
19. the   20. the

Unit 19   p. 47

1 1. Europe   2. the United Kingdom
3. the Philippines   4. the Nile
5. The Colosseum
6. The Metropolitan Museum of Art
7. Ridge Street

2 1. /, /, /   2. /, /   3. the   4. /   5. the, /
6. the

Unit 20   p. 49

1 1. the   2. /   3. /   4. /   5. The   6. a
7. a   8. /   9. a

2 1. /   2. the   3. the   4. a   5. /   6. the
7. the   8. /

Unit 21   p. 51

1 1. he   2. her   3. them   4. They   5. we
6. She   7. me   8. her   9. her   10. I am
11. I can't   12. we

2 1. She   2. He   3. she   4. me   5. It   6. he
7. them   8. us   9. him   10. you

Unit 22   p. 53

1 1. it   2. we   3. We   4. It   5. you   6. They
7. They

2 1. It was cold outside   2. It was 10 p.m.
3. It is going to rain
4. It is 200 meters from here

3 1. It is exciting to go down a water slide.
2. It is good for your health to drink soy milk every day.
3. It is important that we follow the traffic rules.

Unit 23   p. 55

1 1. her   2. his   3. my   4. their   5. Our
6. mine   7. ours   8. my own   9. her own
10. on my own   11. my   12. hers
13. of my own   14. his own   15. my
16. on his own

2 1. theirs   2. hers   3. Mine, yours
4. his   5. ours   6. yours

Unit 24   p. 57

1 1. himself   2. himself   3. ourselves
4. by myself   5. all by yourself   6. by
7. yourself   8. himself   9. herself

2 1. myself   2. herself   3. yourself/yourselves
4. himself   5. herself   6. themselves

Unit 25   p. 59

1 1. me   2. by herself   3. /   4. ourselves
5. each other   6. one another   7. /   8. /
9. /   10. himself   11. /   12. each other

2 1. each other   2. one another   3. themselves
4. herself

Unit 26   p. 61

1 1. plenty of   2. Plenty of, was   3. are
4. people   5. a great deal of   6. planning
7. was   8. time   9. The number of, is
10. A number of, have   11. problems
12. a number of   13. lots of   14. sand
15. sand castles   16. are

Unit 27   p. 63

1 1. some   2. Both   3. A few of   4. neither
5. All / All of   6. a few   7. some
8 half / half of   9. some of   10. Most of
11. Many of

2 1. I need some crayons. Do you have any ~~crayons~~?
2. I bought some soy milk. Would you like to drink some ~~soy milk~~?

3

3. I ate some cherries, but not all of ~~the cherries~~ them.

4. I borrowed some books from the library, but not very many ~~books~~.

5. I've read a few articles in the newspaper, but not all of ~~the articles~~ them.

6. I've run out of printing paper. I need more ~~printing paper~~.

7. I dropped the spoon. Please give me another ~~spoon~~ one.

8. There're five singers in the band. Each ~~singer~~ has his or her own fans.

9. I can't decide which shirt to buy. I think I'll take both ~~shirts~~.

10. I took the whole box of grapes out of the fridge and found out half ~~of the grapes~~ had gone bad.

11. I can't lend you much money. I have only a little ~~money~~.

12. Over two hundred students joined our dance club. Most of ~~the students~~ them are college students.

Unit 28 p. 65

1 1. are 2. are 3. are swimming 4. has
5. are 6. works
2 1. Does 2. was 3. was 4. his or her
5. their 6. isn't 7. it 8. cost

Unit 29 p. 67

1 1. some 2. any 3. any 4. any
5. some/any 6. any 7. any 8. Some
9. some
2 1. → We can't take any grapes from the box.
→ Can we take any grapes from the box?
2. → I don't have any lip balm.
→ Do you have any lip balm?
3. → She didn't make any strawberry milkshake in the morning.
→ Did she make any strawberry milkshake in the morning?
3 1. Sue never buys any diamonds.
2. Tanya rarely plays any online games.
3. Sunny hardly cooks any fish.
4. We seldom watch any horror movies.

Unit 30 p. 69

1 1. many 2. a lot of 3. much 4. plenty of
5. many 6. much 7. much 8. a lot of
9. too much 10. many
2 1. much 2. too much 3. as many
4. too many / plenty of 5. plenty of
6. many

Unit 31 p. 71

1 1. few 2. little 3. a little 4. A few
5. Few of the 6. a little 7. a little 8. a little
9. A few of
2 1. is poured 2. have solved 3. are 4. is
5. penetrates 6. survive

Unit 32 p. 73

1 1. both of 2. both 3. are both
4. are athletes 5. Both of you
6. Both / Both of 7. Both concerts 8. and
9. Both / Both of 10. them both
2 1. both love fishing 2. are both violinists
3. are both Russian Blue cats
4. have both passed the exam
5. can both do the freestyle
6. are both the best friends of human beings

Unit 33 p. 75

1 1. neither of 2. either 3. either of
4. Either 5. Neither of 6. Either 7. Neither
2 1. is flying（正式）；are flying（非正式）
2. is 3. are
4. has made（正式）；have made（非正式）
5. is 6. can make 7. is

Unit 34 p. 77

1 1. love 2. Do 3. them all 4. All 5. is
6. should all 7. All / All of 8. is
9. that was 10. was all 11. is 12. it all
2 1. I've sold all I had.
2. This lamb chop is all that is left.
3. Do you have all the books I requested?
4. All you've done right is marrying that woman.
5. You will find all you need in this outlet.
6. Did you eat all that was in the refrigerator?
7. I looked up all the words I didn't know in the dictionary.
8. All I read last week was *The Stolen Bicycle*.

Unit 35 p. 79

1 1. Every 2. all 3. Everybody 4. all
5. the whole 6. all the 7. all 8. every
9. Every one of
2 1. every 2. whole 3. All 4. every
5. every 6. whole 7. whole
8. every, all 9. whole 10. all

Unit 36 p. 81

1 1. no 2. None 3. no 4. none 5. no
2 1. no 2. none 3. None of the plates
4. is 5. is/are 6. was/were 7. wants

8. No Smoking　9. was/were

3 1. There is no milk in the refrigerator.

2. She trusts no one but her sister.

3. I have no money with me.

4. There are no rooms available today in this hotel.

5. There is no room for negotiation.

Unit 37　　　　　　　　　　p. 83

1 1. one　2. ones　3. ones　4. one　5. one
6. ones　7. ones　8. one

Unit 38　　　　　　　　　　p. 85

1 1. anywhere　2. somewhere　3. anybody
4. nobody　5. something　6. anything
7. everybody　8. nothing　9. nothing
10. everything

2 1. to drink　2. to read　3. to eat
4. to talk to　5. to play with　6. to go

Unit 40　　　　　　　　　　p. 89

1 1. Do, shave, shave　2. Does, open, opens
3. Do, migrate, migrate
4. Does, come, comes
5. does, return, returns
6. Does, eat, doesn't eat　7. do, drive, drive
8. does, feel, feels　9. does, depart, departs
10. do, check out, check out

2 1. likes　2. prepare　3. lives　4. don't raise
5. Does, study　6. takes　7. finishes　8. pays
9. rises

Unit 41　　　　　　　　　　p. 91

1 1. is getting　2. am sending
3. Are, practicing　4. is applying for
5. is carrying out　6. is selling　7. is going
8. is waiting
9. is bringing（who 當主詞時，視為第三人稱單數，故用 is）
10. is having　11. am flying　12. are enjoying
13. is rocking　14. am writing
15. is growing, am not working

2 1. is always jumping　2. is always working
3. is always messing　4. is always losing

Unit 42　　　　　　　　　　p. 93

1 1. are burning　2. bloom　3. am eating
4. am hiding　5. Is Lonny reading
6. often watch　7. Do you play　8. travel

2 1. is weeding, weeds　2. is raining, rains
3. is checking, receives　4. are taking, take

3 1. consists, (A)　2. am taking, (D)

3. don't eat, (A)　4. is changing, (F)
5. am playing, (C)　6. am attending, (E)
7. orbits, (A)　8. is getting, (F)
9. sits, enjoys, (B)　10. am teaching, (D)

Unit 43　　　　　　　　　　p. 95

1 1. recognize　2. does not like　3. have
4. am thinking　5. Do you believe　6. heard
7. am listening　8. deserves

2 1. doesn't exist　2. cost　3. forgets
4. includes　5. knows　6. owns
7. do, prefer　8. weigh

Unit 44　　　　　　　　　　p. 97

1 1. sounds　2. cannot see　3. looks　4. feels
5. is　6. is having　7. is looking after
8. can't smell

2 1. is looking, looks　2. are tasting, taste
3. is smelling, smell　4. is feeling, feel
5. is weighing, weighs　6. is having, has

Unit 45　　　　　　　　　　p. 99

1 1. was　2. gave　3. hoped　4. worked
5. played　6. composed　7. earned　8. lost
9. wrote　10. died

2 1. called　2. went　3. Did, spend　4. saw
5. Did, get　6. did, buy　7. Did, pick up
8. bought　9. Did, need　10. needed
11. did, pay　12. got　13. Did, buy
14. bargained　15. got

Unit 47　　　　　　　　　　p. 103

1 1. She was hanging the drape.
2. They were inspecting the bike.
3. He was installing the tiles.
4. He was fixing the pipe.
5. He was washing the car.
6. They were putting up wallpaper.

2 1. was taking　2. was changing
3. was studying
4. was eating, squeezing（前面的 eating 已有 be 動詞，因此 squeezing 不須再加 be 動詞）

Unit 48　　　　　　　　　　p. 105

1 1. was walking　2. was minding　3. was going
4. passed　5. was leaning　6. felt　7. looked
8. was staring　9. raised　10. said　11. walked
12. ran　13. sprinted　14. stopped　15. looked
16. slowed

2 1. I was playing football when I sprained my ankle.
2. I was fighting with my sister when Mom came home.

3. I was buying a wedding present when I heard you were getting married.
4. I lost my passport when I was vacationing in Italy.
5. I was sleeping soundly when the alarm clock rang.
6. I was cranking the volume when I blew out the speakers.

Unit 49   p. 107

1 1. was always dripping   2. was always jumping
3. was always crashing   4. is always watching
5. was always complaining ·
6. is always playing   7. are always telling
2 1. is always piling up   2. is always scattering
3. is always storing up   4. is always drinking
5. is always crying   6. is always leaving

Unit 50   p. 109

1 1. have read   2. have not been   3. Have, seen
4. have never seen   5. have been
2 1. Have, used   2. Have, tried   3. Have, seen
4. have seen   5. have heard   6. have, seen

Unit 51   p. 111

1 1. have planned   2. have invited
3. has not started   4. has arrived
5. has left   6. has dried   7. Have, missed
8. have, thrown
2 1. Lawrence ~~is working~~ has worked at Flying Tomato Pizzeria for six months.
2. Iris ~~stars~~ has starred in a soap opera since last year.
3. Tom ~~is owning~~ has owned this car for several months.
4. How long ~~are you working~~ have you worked on this proposal?
3 1. has gone   2. has been   3. have gone
4. have been

Unit 52   p. 113

1 1. We have already eaten dinner.
2. We haven't finished our coffee yet.
3. We have just received her phone call.
4. The singer has just gotten her first single on the top ten chart.
5. Have you already thrown away your old books?
6. I haven't discussed the problem with my doctor yet.
7. I have never bought anything online.
8. Have you ever run in a marathon?
9. I haven't been to Russia before.
10. This is the most splendid view I have ever seen.

2 1. for   2. since   3. for   4. since   5. for
6. since

Unit 53   p. 115

1 1. have searched, has left   2. found
3. has changed   4. hit, caused / has caused
2 1. have adopted   2. was abandoned
3. wandered   4. was brought   5. was
6. has become
3 1. went to bed at 1:00, has slept since 1:00, has slept for four hours
2. moved in here on July 3rd, have lived here since July 3rd, have lived here for a week

Unit 54   p. 117

1 1. did, arrive   2. arrived   3. Have, been
4. have been   5. did, buy   6. gave
7. Have, started   8. have started
2 1. have played   2. Have you ever been injured
3. have had   4. you played   5. played
6. did you hurt   7. hurt
8. Have you ever played   9. played
10. Did you like   11. loved
12. Have you ever been recruited
13. has received   14. have said

Unit 55   p. 119

1 1. It has been raining.
2. We have been drinking.
3. Those people have been chatting.
4. Camille has been wearing high heels.
5. People have been boarding the plane.
6. Have you been practicing your Spanish?
7. Have you been redecorating your house?
2 1. have been arguing   2. has been raining
3. have been washing   4. has been reeling

Unit 56   p. 121

1 1. have you eaten, (D)   2. has been sitting, (C)
3. has cleaned, (C/F)   4. have you realized, (G)
5. have been chatting, (C)
6. has been sending, (B/E)
7. have been working, (E)   8. have finished, (A)
9. have imagined, (G)   10. has traveled, (A)

Unit 57   p. 123

1 1. I ~~have been~~ was out for dinner last night.
2. Roy ~~has held~~ held a party yesterday afternoon.
3. Sandra ~~wrote~~ has been writing her essay since this morning.
4. Larry ~~hasn't gone~~ didn't go home until his boss left the office.

2 1. Jessica and her kids have decorated the Christmas tree for three hours.
   = Jessica and her kids have been decorating the Christmas tree for three hours.
   2. Emma has taken photos for *National Geographic*.
   = Emma has been taking photos for *National Geographic*.
   3. Daniel has made trips with a hot air balloon across America since 2019.
   = Daniel has been making trips with a hot air balloon across America since 2019.
   4. Nicky has stood by the window since 2 p.m.
   = Nicky has been standing by the window since 2 p.m.

Unit 58   p. 125

1 1. called, had ended
   2. arrived, had already started
   3. had proposed, was   4. wanted, had told
   5. accepted, took
2 1. talked, had seen
   2. hadn't practiced, dropped
   3. looked at, had already passed
   4. left, was finished   5. had given
   6. did not dawn, needed   7. opened, dashed
   8. had taken   9. had built

Unit 59   p. 127

1 1. had been playing   2. hadn't been trying
   3. had Charlie been cracking
   4. had been eating   5. had been smiling
   6. had been trading   7. hadn't been living
   8. Louise had been planning
2 1. had been eating   2. had been washing
   3. had been talking   4. had been preparing

Unit 60   p. 129

1 1. will recognize   2. won't be   3. will sell
   4. will serve   5. will have   6. will arrive
   7. won't be   8. will, do   9. will be
2 1. won't find   2. will hear   3. Will, finish
   4. won't go   5. will buy   6. will eat

Unit 61   p. 131

1 1. am going to rewrite   2. am going to work
   3. are going to have   4. are, going to get
   5. Is, going to lend   6. am going to buy
   7. are going to smash   8. am going to quit
   9. are, going to buy   10. are going to win

Unit 62   p. 133

1 1. will leave   2. am going to take / will take
   3. will start / am going to start
   4. I'll have / I'm going to have   5. will do
   6. will come   7. will begin / is going to begin
   8. will grab
2 1. Edmond will apply for a new job.
   2. He is going to apply for a job at a cookie factory.
   3. He said, "I'll be the best cookie tester in the world!"
   4. He said, "I am going to pass the exam with flying colors."
   5. He said, "First, I'll practice testing some cookies."
   6. Lou asked, "Are you going to bake cookies as well?"
   7. Lou claimed, "You'll burn those cookies."
   8. Edmond retorted, "I'll bake some cookies right away!"

Unit 63   p. 135

1 1. is performing   2. is cutting
   3. is transferring   4. is closing
   5. is inspecting   6. is planning
2 1. is going to leave / is leaving
   2. is going to tank   3. is going to fix
   4. is going to run out
   5. is paying / is going to pay
   6. is graduating / is going to graduate
   7. is going to have
   8. is going to bankrupt / is bankrupting

Unit 64   p. 137

1 1. makes   2. washes, leaves   3. picks up
   4. does, open   5. opens   6. serves
   7. are closed   8. starts
2 1. will go, goes   2. will sneak out, is
   3. will enlist, graduates   4. will tour, visit
   5. will stay up, turn in   6. will stay, bring
   7. will appear, performs   8. will be, accepts
   9. will sing, plays   10. will eat, have put

Unit 65   p. 139

1 1. Dr. Edwards will be meeting the committee members at 9:00.
   2. Dr. Edwards will be watching the demonstration of sterilization equipment at 10:30.
   3. Dr. Edwards will be eating lunch at 12:00.
   4. Dr. Edwards will be listening to a panel discussion about childhood disease at 15:00.

5. Dr. Edwards will be presenting a paper about disease treatment plans at 16:30.

6. Dr. Edwards will be touring the city at 19:30.

2 1. won't be cooking, Can you buy us a pizza?

2. won't be driving, Could I get a ride from you?

3. will be leaving, Would you like to use my computer this afternoon?

4. will be returning, Are you planning to watch it again?

5. will, be walking, Can I walk with you on the Nature Trail?

6. Will, be playing, Can I come to listen to you play?

Unit 66   p. 141

1 1. will have moved   2. will have settled
3. will have climbed   4. will have started
5. will have finished   6. will have begun

2 1. How long will he have been swimming in the ocean by sunset? /
He will have been swimming in the ocean for four hours by sunset.

2. How long will he have been traveling by the time he gets to Buenos Aires? /
He will have been traveling for four months by the time he gets to Buenos Aires.

Unit 67   p. 143

1 1. Have you got   2. have got
3. does not have   4. does not have
5. Does she have

2 1. have / have got   2. have   3. have
4. don't

Unit 68   p. 145

1 1. had a fight   2. having a baby
3. have a glass of orange juice
4. has a bowl of soup   5. have a bubble bath
6. have a look

2 1. (C)   2. (A)   3. (B)   4. (A)   5. (A)

Unit 69   p. 147

1 1. is   2. was just being   3. was being
4. was / was being   5. was   6. is
7. was / was being   8. is   9. was   10. was
11. was   12. was / was being   13. am

Unit 70   p. 149

1 1. fruity   2. like raspberry   3. the aroma
4. graceful   5. the most beautiful lady

6. at me   7. my Mapo tofu   8. spicy
9. like a dish   10. cool and hairy
11. my finger   12. red   13. better   14. bigger
15. worse   16. to him   17. the medicine
18. normal

Unit 71   p. 151

1 1. (B)   2. (D)   3. (D)   4. (A)   5. (D)   6. (D)

2 1. make her go away   2. make the baby cry
3. get him to move over a little
4. get the coffee cup washed
5. have her write an article
6. have the pillowcase changed

Unit 72   p. 153

1 1. Please don't fire us. ~~Let's~~ Let us stay . . .
2. Let's not ~~to have~~ have . . .
3. Sarah lets her daughter ~~to go~~ go . . .
4. Let's build another sand castle, ~~don't~~ shall we?
5. Let's ~~don't~~ not cry.
6. ~~Let's~~ Let me hang up your coat . . .
7. Father won't ~~let's~~ let us / let me come . . .
8. ~~Let's do~~ Let's make a . . .
9. Let us race to the bridge, ~~do~~ shall we?
10. Let's not ~~entering~~ enter that house . . .
11. Let me ~~to have~~ have a talk with him . . .
12. ~~Don't let's~~ Let's not go to that beach. . . .

Unit 73   p. 155

1 1. (A)   2. (B)   3. (A)   4. (B/C)   5. (C)

2 1. Driving   2. to roast   3. to compete
4. Stretching   5. Enjoying

Unit 74   p. 157

1 1. to attend   2. to find   3. to tell
4. to be able   5. to use   6. to play

2 1. how to contact   2. where to find
3. what to wear   4. when to arrive
5. what to watch

Unit 75   p. 159

1 1. to have   2. to help   3. going   4. to join
5. to go   6. ordered Melvin to attend
7. to calibrate

2 1. Colleen to knit   2. Dolly to accept
3. me not to exceed   4. to drop by
5. the airport to close   6. us to finish

3 1. We were instructed how to key in the code to open the gate (by them).
2. Simon was encouraged to take part in the speech contest by Mr. White.

3. Hal was advised to wear a suit for the press conference (by them).

Unit 76   p. 161

1 1. eating   2. cooking   3. shopping
4. offending   5. inviting   6. vacuuming
7. reading   8. smoking
2 1. not delivering   2. not watching
3. not using   4. not listening   5. not having
3 1. go fishing   2. does some reading
3. do the painting   4. goes swimming
5. doing the washing

Unit 77   p. 163

1 1. barbequing / to barbeque
2. heating / to heat   3. to fast   4. to join
5. exercising / to exercise   6. participate
7. to read, play   8. to feel   9. to realize
10. feeling / to feel
2 1. to help   2. to buy   3. to spend
4. to reduce
3 1. ride a banana boat
2. climbing a mountain
3. to relax on a tropical island

Unit 78   p. 165

1 1. to bring   2. lending   3. running
4. to send   5. jogging   6. to rest
2 1. to put   2. finishing   3. taking   4. to pay
5. to talk   6. to stay   7. hanging
8. to drink

Unit 79   p. 167

1 1. playing   2. to become   3. withdrawing
4. canceling
2 1. to discuss   2. to discuss   3. taking
4. feeding, playing, loving, abandoning
5. walking   6. to lie   7. moving   8. to tell
9. not joining   10. recommending

Unit 80   p. 169

1 1. to drink   2. to help
3. We are happy to hear   4. to ask
5. clever of you to open
6. polite of you to knock on   7. to mail
8. to play
2 1. to buy   2. to help   3. to celebrate
4. to check   5. to see   6. to update
3 1. visit her daughter   2. keep fit
3. reduce paper waste
4. cure his eye disease

Unit 81   p. 171

1 1. on paying（plan on V-ing/V 表示「打算做……」）2. about getting
3. for parking   4. before driving
5. of listening   6. at finding
7. in collecting   8. to traveling
2 1. to hopping   2. to ride   3. to own
4. to fighting   5. to navigating
6. to moving

Unit 82   p. 173

1 1. need to set   2. need to buy
3. needs fixing（英式）/
needs to be fixed（美式）
4. need washing（英式）/
need to be washed（美式）
5. needs cleaning（英式）/
needs to be cleaned（美式）
6. need picking up
2 1. watching   2. announce/announcing
3. leave   4. walking   5. floating   6. rushing
7. running

Unit 83   p. 175

1 1. brushing her hair
2. looking at himself in the mirror
3. shopping at the department store
4. Thinking about buying a pair of news shoes
5. Having purchased a three-piece suit
6. Having bought a new dress
7. Knowing she had to look sharp for her presentation
8. Having an attractive new hair style
2 1. While eating the glazed strawberries on a stick, Howard bit his tongue.
2. Irene lay on the bed, thinking about the next day's presentation. /
Lying on the bed, Irene thought about the next day's presentation.
3. Who is that woman talking on a cell phone?
4. Having taken some medicine, Mary started to feel better. /
After taking some medicine, Mary started to feel better.
5. Having the ambition to win the championship, John practiced extremely hard.
6. Wanting to have a bubble bath after work, Trudy bought a cedar bathtub last week.

Unit 84 — p. 179

1 1. turn off   2. put away   3. try on   4. look up
5. think over   6. talk it over
2 1. pick her up   2. called it off   3. figure it out
4. bring it in   5. write it down
6. hung them up   7. turn it down
8. made it up

Unit 85 — p. 181

1 1. look after Puffy   2. keep off the grass
3. waiting on Table 2
4. takes after her twin sister
5. came across a stray dog
6. applied for a scholarship
2 1. get over   2. pull for   3. is made from
4. are made of

Unit 86 — p. 183

1 1. for   2. in   3. to   4. about   5. over   6. in
7. on   8. at   9. from   10. of
11. of/about（這句用 of 和 about 都正確，
「was thinking of」指「正在考慮」，「was
thinking about」指「此刻腦海裡正浮現的
事」）
12. of   13. for   14. of   15. on   16. into
17. at   18. of

Unit 87 — p. 185

1 1. The wolf came out from behind the tree
and blocked the path of Little Red Riding
Hood.
2. Gin is staying up to watch *Emily in Paris*.
3. I feel like throwing up. I'll go to the
bathroom.
4. The fire broke out in the middle of the
night and spread very quickly.
5. I've come up with an idea. Let's start over.
6. My sister is dressing up for the
masquerade.
2 1. The fire broke out at 2:00 a.m.
2. The smoke alarm went off.
3. The fire department showed up.
4. The police shouted, "Come out of the
building."
5. I fell down while running out.
6. After I got out, I started to shake and then
threw up.

Unit 88 — p. 189

1 1. fed up with   2. Keep away from
3. looking forward to   4. stand up for

5. keep up with   6. come up with
2 1. Watch out for the banana peel!
2. We will set off for Venice on Friday.
3. Why are you moving out of the apartment?
4. Have you signed up for the bus tour yet?
5. We are running out of tissue paper.
6. Hang on to the buoy! I'll pull you up.
7. Please come over to my office to sign the
contract.
8. I don't want you to drop out of the team.
We really need you.

Unit 89 — p. 191

1 1. calmed down   2. blew up   3. blew up
4. woke up   5. Cheer up   6. cheer, up
7. blew out   8. cheered up   9. calm, down
10. Calm down   11. working out
12. work out   13. blow, out   14. woke, up
15. woke up   16. blew out

Unit 90 — p. 193

1 1. be able to play   2. had to leave   3. can
4. will   5. ought to   6. shouldn't   7. Could
8. have to   9. can do
2 1. He could drink ten bowls of miso soup.
2. Jeffery will explain everything.
3. Dad must quit smoking and drinking.
4. Alison should file the documents.
5. We might get lost without a GPS system.
6. You ought to take off your dirty shoes and
socks.
7. Denis can speak five languages.

Unit 91 — p. 195

1 1. should go   2. Can Megan run   3. must go
4. may have left   5. should not
6. will not win   7. Shall I   8. should not
9. Could you have thrown
2 1. Karl can ride his snowboard all day.
2. Audrey will observe the lunar eclipse.
3. Elwood may have fallen off his horse.
4. Can Julio play the accordion?
5. Jasper must be feeding pigeons in the
park.

Unit 92 — p. 197

1 1. Can   2. be able to   3. be able to   4. can
5. be able to   6. be able to   7. can
8. be able to
2 1. can do bike tricks   2. can't swim

3. can maintain her balance   4. can't skate
5. can paint with watercolors

Unit 93 p. 199

1 1. could   2. was able to   3. could have
4. could have   5. being able to   6. could
7. could

2 1. I could see the sunrise over the ocean from my hotel window.
2. I couldn't read English newspapers before I was twelve.
3. I was not able to get out of the bed by myself. My mom helped me.
4. I managed to walk to the bathroom while holding the IV bottle above my head.
5. I could remember those crazy summers when we were hanging out together at the beach all the time.

Unit 94 p. 201

1 1. Can   2. was allowed to   3. May
4. was allowed to   5. can't   6. may

2 1. can't, can/may   2. can't   3. can't   4. may
5. can   6. may not   7. can't, are allowed
8. was not able

Unit 95 p. 203

1 1. must / have to   2. must / have to
3. have to   4. having to   5. had to
6. Must   7. have to

2 1. must have   2. must take   3. must show

3 1. have to apply   2. have to take
3. have to process

Unit 96 p. 205

1 1. have got to hurry   2. have got to eat
3. have got to give

2 1. have to   2. have got to   3. had to
4. Do you always have to   5. will have to
6. Does Nancy have to   7. have got to
8. Will you have to   9. had to

Unit 97 p. 207

1 1. mustn't   2. don't have to   3. haven't
4. needn't   5. mustn't   6. didn't have to
7. have to   8. don't have to
9. don't have to   10. must   11. don't have to

2 1. didn't need to bring
2. didn't need to go back / needn't have gone back
3. didn't need to buy / needn't have bought

4. didn't need to call / needn't have called
5. didn't need to get up / needn't have gotten up
6. didn't need to work

Unit 98 p. 209

1 1. I think you should go to the auction.
2. I think you ought to bid on the small statue.
3. I think you should offer $2,000 for the statue.
4. I think you ought to use an online auction company.
5. Shall I give the statue to my mother?

2 1. You should have brought in the laundry before it started to rain.
2. You should have simmered the sauce for five more minutes.
3. Angus shouldn't have poured too much soy sauce on the fried noodles.
4. You shouldn't have thrown away the receipt.

3 1. ought to have told
2. ought to have known

Unit 99 p. 211

1 1. had better   2. had better not   3. leave
4. Are you supposed to
5. are not supposed to
6. wasn't supposed to   7. was supposed to

2 1. I think you had better clean the house before the guests arrive.
2. You are supposed to take a number and wait for your turn.
3. You had better not invite your motorcycle club to the party.
4. You are not supposed to cut in the line.
5. I think you had better vacuum the rug.
6. You are supposed to fill out your deposit ticket while you are waiting.
7. You had better not let the dog into the house.
8. You are supposed to hand the passbook and the cash to the clerk.

Unit 100 p. 213

1 1. Bonnie may go out with us tomorrow night.
2. The plane might be delayed because of the fog.
3. The movie star could have arrived by now.
4. The police think Carl may have stolen a Ming dynasty vase.
5. The chocolate-flavored pastry might have sold out.

11

6. You could have sprained your ankle.

2 1. could have gotten up

2. could have presented   3. may have spent

Unit 101 p. 215

1 1. can scan   2. can connect   3. can locate

4. can sell   5. can make

2 1. should be   2. could

3. ought to have arrived

4. should have received   5. may

6. ought to contact   7. ought to hear

8. should know   9. can

Unit 102 p. 217

1 1. must   2. can't   3. can't   4. must

5. must   6. couldn't   7. couldn't   8. can

9. Could

2 1. bought this villa   2. talking with

3. made a fortune   4. drinking in the bar

Unit 103 p. 219

1 1. Can I have a cup of coffee?

2. Would you please answer the phone for me?

3. Will you turn off the air conditioner?

4. May I use the bench press when you are finished?

5. Could I take a nap on the sofa if you are not going to watch TV?

6. Can you go jogging with me tomorrow morning at 5:30?

2 1. borrow this book   2. get off the phone

3. a copy of the application form

4. open the gift   5. pass me a tissue

6. turned the light on   7. to fix the fence

Unit 104 p. 221

1 1. Will you sew this button back on my pajamas?

2. Shall I carry that big heavy suitcase for you?

3. Can I help you change that light bulb?

4. May I have your daughter's hand in marriage?

5. Would you like to go out to a French restaurant for dinner this evening?

6. Will you try a glass of white wine with the meal?

2 1. Shall I pay the phone bill at the convenience store?

2. Can I take out the garbage you put by the door?

3. Will you please have another cookie?

4. I could fry an egg for your breakfast.

5. Would you like to hear my explanation?

6. I can walk the dog for you tonight.

Unit 105 p. 223

1 1. shall we   2. Let's   3. Why don't we

4. Shall we   5. How about   6. We can

7. could   8. we could

2 1. visiting the wine factory

2. waiting for five more minutes

3. make dumplings   4. go bicycling

5. take a coffee break   6. join the health club

Unit 106 p. 225

1 1. used to   2. spend   3. work   4. used to

5. used to go   6. loves to

2 1. She used to drink a cup of black tea when reading a book.

2. He is used to sipping a glass of wine before going to bed.

3. Kristine used to watch horror movies.

4. Did Karl use to stay in his office overnight to work?

5. Sam used to be naive, but now he is a mature young man.

6. Where did you use to go bowling?

7. I am used to writing a journal every day.

8. Are you used to reading a newspaper before going to work?

Unit 107 p. 227

1 1. will   2. would   3. used to   4. will

2 1. will often sneak onto the bed

2. will always go to the beach

3. will always sing loudly

4. will always spread a lot of peanut butter

3 1. would often chat with friends

2. would often sit by Grandpa

3. would always eat her breakfast

4. would always doze off

Unit 108 p. 229

1 1. Kathy won't change her opinion.

2. Kenny won't come out of his room.

3. Yesterday I invited Lionel to the party, but he won't/wouldn't go.

4. I suggested Yvonne get a new suit for the interview, but she won't/wouldn't buy one.

5. The washing machine won't work properly.

2 1. If you don't stay out of my room, I will tell Mom.

2. If you let me use your computer, I will be careful with it.

3. If you tell Dad what I did, I won't forget and you'll regret it.

4. I took your favorite doll. Unless you stop kicking my sheep, I won't tell you where your doll is.

5. If you tell me where Mom hid the cookies, I will buy you snacks next time.

Unit 109   p. 231

1 1. would rather drink
2. would rather not jump
3. would rather not hunt
4. would rather, continued

2 1. She would rather Lisa did the dishes.
2. Joe would rather Mary didn't revise too much of his paper.
3. I would rather you went to the play with me.
4. I would rather you didn't cook chicken for dinner every day.

3 1. may as well go   2. may as well order
3. may as well read   4. might as well ride
5. might as well have   6. might as well wash

Unit 110   p. 233

1 1. that I (should) consult the doctor about the bump on my leg
2. that the meat (should) be fried quickly with high heat
3. that I (should) walk around by the lavatory
4. that you (should) finish your homework every night
5. that he (should) pack the sunscreen
6. that you (should) watch the movie and not talk

2 1. They say it is important that you drive without talking on your phone.
2. The mayor ordered that free food be distributed to the poor.

Unit 111   p. 235

1 1. The old man sat on the bench.
2. This tea tasted delicious.
3. The woman is 160 cm tall.
4. The large blue coat is mine.
5. We have had three weeks of hot weather.
6. The shelter has sleeping quarters on the second floor.

2 1. The rope is ~~long~~ 45 cm long.
2. We had a ~~two-hours~~ two-hour walk after dinner.
3. It was a lovely crystal lamp.

4. Did you see my blue Japanese silk dress?
5. I'm going to visit my ~~ill~~ sick Grandpa tomorrow.
6. Is your bird still ~~living~~ alive?
7. I fell ~~sleeping~~ asleep.
8. We have a tight schedule.

Unit 112   p. 237

1 1. bigger   2. youngest   3. most delicious
4. sunnier   5. farther   6. longer

2 1. Mount Everest is the highest mountain in the world.
2. The Louvre is one of the most famous museums in the world.
3. The Mariana Trench is the deepest place in the ocean.
4. Shakespeare is considered to be one of the greatest poets and dramatists.
5. Solar energy is one of the most important sources of energy.
6. Cirque du Soleil is the most innovative contemporary circus.

Unit 113   p. 239

1 1. shorter   2. happiest   3. more honest
4. most careful   5. worst   6. cheaper
7. hotter and hotter   8. more   9. she is

2 1. more important than
2. the more expensive   3. the sourest
4. as hot   5. closer (and closer)
6. the most boring   7. more specific

3 1. as hip   2. as smart as   3. as frugal as
4. as fast as   5. as neat as   6. as high as

Unit 114   p. 241

1 1. graceful   2. efficiently   3. absurd
4. inspiring   5. in a silly way   6. impressively
7. tentatively   8. in an ugly way   9. quickly

2 1. as high（high 也可以當副詞，意為「（高度上的）高地」，與 highly 表「（程度上的）高地」、「非常」不同。此處指的是「跳得高」，故用 high）
2. beautifully   3. better than
4. the latest   5. as far as   6. carefully
7. more intelligently   8. sooner than
9. heavily   10. emotionlessly

3 1. in a friendly way   2. in a lovely way

Unit 115   p. 243

1 1. the food hungrily
2. works in this office
3. casually at 2:30 in the afternoon

4. quickly in the office last week
5. hard at the champion last night
6. watched the fight excitedly
7. in the south this afternoon
8. at his brother angrily

2 1. Trent put the box here.
2. Sally just poured some milk into her coffee.
3. Sonia left the library at 10 a.m.
4. I will buy some books at the bookstore tomorrow.
5. Mom still won't let me go to the party.
6. Jacky jumped off the tree quickly. / Jacky quickly jumped off the tree.

Unit 116 — p. 245

1 1. Trisha usually gets up at 6:30 in the morning.
2. Ester is never late for work.
3. Vanessa will bring a box of donuts for her co-workers sometimes. / Sometimes Vanessa will bring a box of donuts for her co-workers. / Vanessa will sometimes bring a box of donuts for her co-workers.
4. Does Brigit take time off work often? / Does Brigit often take time off work?
5. Felix goes to a client's office once a week.
6. Irvin writes up his sales report daily.

2 1. goes biking every weekend
2. have a sandwich for breakfast every day
3. goes to a yoga class once a week
4. have Thai food monthly
5. has his car maintained every three months

Unit 117 — p. 247

1 1. definitely knows   2. certainly won't
3. obviously not   4. Perhaps Stanley will
5. is probably   6. Maybe Jill

2 1. Beryl will probably run in the 100 meter race.
2. Amy certainly swims faster than anybody I know.
3. Luke is definitely in the running for a medal.
4. Jenna obviously won't continue dancing after her injury.
5. Kathleen certainly isn't the best teacher, but she is well loved.
6. Mort is probably not going to get promoted this year.
7. Maybe Shirley can fill in for you while you're gone.
8. Perhaps Rod will play his guitar in a concert for the earthquake survivors.

Unit 118 — p. 249

1 1. quite   2. fairly   3. quite   4. rather
5. rather   6. quite   7. extremely cold
8. rather   9. quite   10. almost there
11. rather   12. is quite

2 1. Antone is quite a famous chef.
2. Meg was rather satisfied with the result.
3. I feel fairly depressed.
4. Louis drove rather faster than usual.
5. Tim simply pushed the "Start" button.
6. Larry is a pretty smart person.
7. Mom's roast beef is really delicious.

Unit 119 — p. 251

1 1. Not yet   2. still knits   3. is still   4. can still
5. I have already weeded
6. have already warmed up
7. already cooked   8. yet   9. yet
10. haven't gone to bed yet

2 1. already   2. yet   3. still   4. still   5. yet
6. already   7. still   8. still   9. already
10. already   11. still

Unit 120 — p. 253

1 1. too   2. enough   3. too many
4. too much   5. enough
6. too small for him   7. too early to look
8. much too high   9. enough coins

2 1. enough   2. too many   3. too
4. too many / enough   5. much

Unit 121 — p. 255

1 1. such   2. so   3. so   4. so   5. such
6. such   7. so   8. so

2 1. Victoria doesn't wear glasses anymore.
2. Matthew no longer watches auto racing on TV.
3. Laurie doesn't read comic books anymore.
4. Sandy is very tired. She can't drive any longer today.
5. Andy will no longer play in the Asian Cup.

Unit 122 — p. 257

1 1. When   2. When   3. as soon as
4. until, before   5. as soon as   6. while

2 1. I counted the steps when I was walking home from the MRT station.
2. Do not speak when you have food in your mouth.
3. I got grains of instant coffee all over the table while I was making a cup of cappuccino.

4. The baby fell asleep while Mom was humming a lullaby.

5. The light went out as we were playing cards.

6. I lost eight pounds after I quit eating hamburgers and French fries.

7. Dad checked on the electricity, gas, and windows before we set off for our vacation.

8. I ran to my computer and checked the email as soon as I got home.

Unit 123   p. 259

1 1. Although Kathy likes toy dinosaurs, she doesn't like dinosaur movies.

2. Despite the silly plot, we enjoyed the movie.（despite 後面接名詞，所以須將形容詞 silly 放到名詞 plot 前面，變成「the silly plot」）

3. Though the movie was a little long, it was great.

4. Though we planned to have dinner in the Italian restaurant before the movie, we didn't have time.

5. In spite of the movie's bad reviews, we went to see it anyway.（in spite of 後面接名詞，所以須將句子「the movie received bad news」改成名詞「the movie's bad news」）

6. Even though Hank planned to stay up for the late movie, he fell asleep before it started.

7. Alan looks very conservative, while his wife is totally wild and artistic.

8. Jerry likes to get up at dawn, whereas his wife likes to sleep until noon.

Unit 124   p. 261

1 1. because   2. Since   3. because of
   4. due to the fact that   5. As   6. Because

2 1. Because of his miserliness, I won't ask him for help.（形容詞 miserly → 名詞 miserliness）

2. We had to stay home because of the rain. / Because of the rain, we had to stay home.

3. Because he was generous, we survived the hard times.（名詞 generosity → 形容詞 generous）

4. Since they had security concerns, they decided to close the front gate after sunset.

5. Cherries are good for our health due to their richness in vitamins.（形容詞 rich → 名詞 richness，後面都須加 in）

6. As he has an ankle injury, he can't play tennis as well as before.

7. As he didn't play fair in the final, he was deprived of the title two days after the match.

Unit 125   p. 263

1 1. As   2. as a result   3. so   4. As a result
   5. such   6. so

2 1. Grandma was sick. As a result, we had to put off our trip. /
Grandma was sick. We had to put off our trip as a result.

2. We didn't have vegetables at home. Therefore, we went out for dinner. /
We didn't have vegetables at home. We, therefore, went out for dinner.

3. I left home late this morning. As a result, I was caught in the traffic. /
I left home late this morning. I was caught in the traffic as a result.

3 1. Those were such sweet peaches that I ate three of them.

2. The scenery was so splendid that we took hundreds of pictures.

3. It was such an amazing show that the audience applauded the performers for three minutes.

Unit 126   p. 265

1 1. William brought his own bag to carry his groceries.

2. The dog wants to go for a walk so as to go to the bathroom.

3. Lauren got to the store early in order to avoid the rush.

4. Kevin often eats dinner out so as not to mess up his kitchen.

5. Paulina bought some shrimp for lunch.

6. Lawrence has a knife with a serrated edge for cutting bread.

7. Nadia will give you some money so that you can buy a new dress.

8. Tamara closed the window so that it wouldn't get too cold.

Unit 127   p. 267

1 1. in case   2. in case   3. in case   4. in case
   5. if   6. in case

2 1. Take your purse with you in case you want to buy anything while walking the dog.

2. Give me your phone number in case I need to reach you.

3. Call him later in case he hasn't arrived at the office.

15

4. Lock your cell phone keypad in case you accidentally make a call.

5. Give Mary a call in case she's forgotten about her promise to buy some frozen pizzas for tonight.

6. Back up your files every day in case your computer crashes.

Unit 128 p. 269
1 1. at 2. on 3. at 4. in 5. on 6. on
2 1. on 2. in 3. at 4. on 5. at

Unit 129 p. 271
1 1. in/at 2. in 3. on 4. in 5. in 6. in
   7. at 8. on
2 1. on 2. at/in 3. at 4. in 5. in

Unit 130 p. 273
1 1. under 2. over 3. under 4. above
   5. over 6. below
2 1. over 2. under 3. above 4. below
   5. under 6. under

Unit 131 p. 275
1 1. in front of 2. among 3. between
   4. behind
2 1. in front of 2. opposite 3. behind
   4. between 5. among

Unit 132 p. 277
1 1. outside 2. by 3. outside 4. against
   5. near 6. next to 7. outside 8. beside

Unit 133 p. 279
1 1. into/in 2. out of 3. in 4. on 5. on
   6. off 7. in 8. on
2 1. on 2. out of 3. in 4. off 5. into
   6. onto 7. out of

Unit 134 p. 281
1 1. up 2. down 3. down 4. from
2 1. up, to 2. toward 3. from 4. down, at
   5. toward, to 6. to

Unit 135 p. 283
1 1. in front of 2. behind 3. opposite
   4. between 5. close to 6. next to 7. by
   8. stroll along 9. across 10. through
   11. over 12. across 13. to 14. around
   15. past 16. over 17. from, to 18. near
   19. arrive at 20. at 21. around 22. across

Unit 136 p. 285
1 1. in/into 2. by 3. on 4. by 5. by 6. in
   7. by 8. by, on 9. on
2 1. in 2. on 3. on 4. get on 5. got off

Unit 137 p. 287
1 1. at 2. in 3. in 4. on 5. in 6. in 7. on
   8. at 9. on 10. in, in 11. at
   12. on（winter solstice〔冬至〕為「日子」，故用 on） 13. on
2 1. at the Mid-Autumn Festival
   2. at/on Christmas 3. on Halloween
   4. on New Year's Eve
   5. at Chinese New Year

Unit 138 p. 289
1 1. in 2. on 3. / 4. in 5. in 6. in 7. /
   8. / 9. / 10. / 11. in 12. in 13. / 14. /
   15. / 16. /（或者 at any time），/ 17. /

Unit 139 p. 291
1 1. for 2. since 3. ago 4. ago 5. for
   6. for 7. since 8. ago 9. since 10. since
2 1. I have been playing the piano for fifteen years.
   2. I have studied the history of art since 2005.
   3. I started my YouTube channel three years ago.
   4. I will stay in Toronto for six months.
   5. I arrived four hours ago.
   6. I have been selling fried chicken in the night market since last year.

Unit 140 p. 293
1 1. during 2. for 3. During 4. during
   5. for 6. during 7. while 8. for
2 1. I burned my fingers in the cooking class.
   2. I had to go to the bank during my lunch break.
   3. I watched a basketball game while my wife was taking a shower and getting ready to go.
   4. I ate a lot of ramen and pork chops during my vacation in Tokyo.
   5. I've been busy with the bank merger for the whole week.

Unit 141 p. 295
1 1. From, to/until 2. until 3. by/before
   4. from, to/until 5. before 6. by/before
   7. before/after 8. before 9. until 10. after

2 1. by/before   2. before   3. from, to/until
4. until   5. After   6. after

Unit 142   p. 297

1 1. with   2. in   3. with   4. with   5. in   6. by
7. with
2 1. in pen   2. on (a) vacation
3. by Andrew Lloyd Webber
4. with two garage doors
5. with the soap   6. in a gray scarf

Unit 143   p. 299

1 1. like   2. as   3. like   4. as   5. like   6. as if
7. as if   8. as if   9. like
2 1. as   2. as   3. like   4. as   5. as if
6. had happened   7. as though   8. like
9. like   10. as if

Unit 144   p. 301

1 1. Bella will give Trevor the letter.
2. Phil will forward Dave the email.
3. John is going to buy Mindy a coat.
4. Mark bought Rita the teapot.
5. Can you read Grandpa the news?
6. I will show you the ingredients.
7. I am going to build my parents a house.
2 1. Morris is going to bring the paint to/for
Gabriel.
2. Gerald is going to pay the money to Kate.
3. Suzanne is going to read a book to her
son.
4. Larry will recommend a restaurant to Gail.
5. I'll buy lunch for you.

Unit 145   p. 303

1 1. about   2. at   3. at/by   4. for   5. with
6. at   7. about   8. at   9. for
2 1. amazed by the dolphin show
2. bored with our teacher's long and
uninformative speech
3. satisfied with our son's English exam score
4. good at solving a Rubik's cube
5. nervous about having dinner with my
girlfriend's parents

Unit 146   p. 305

1 1. from/to   2. in   3. of   4. about   5. of
6. on   7. to   8. of   9. of   10. of
11. of   12. from/to
2 1. yell at people   2. help the elderly
3. try smoking   4. take a shortcut

Unit 147   p. 307

1 1. between   2. for   3. in   4. toward   5. to
6. with   7. in   8. in
2 1. example of   2. causes of   3. demand for
4. decrease in   5. difficulty in

Unit 148   p. 309

1 1. in   2. of   3. to   4. with   5. for
6. between   7. for   8. to
2 1. (B)   2. (C)   3. (A)   4. (A)   5. (D)   6. (C)

Unit 149   p. 311

1 1. of   2. for   3. from   4. on   5. to   6. to
7. about   8. about   9. to, for   10. on   11. to
2 1. warned Marcia about the risk of buying
stocks
2. borrowed a food processor from his sister
3. blame her for spoiling the children
4. complained to her husband about his
overloading the washing machine
5. congratulate Bernard on winning the
award
6. reminds me of my childhood

Unit 150   p. 313

1 1. in time   2. on time   3. on time   4. in time
5. on time   6. in time   7. in the end
8. at the end   9. in the end   10. in the end
11. at the end   12. at the end
2 1. by   2. in   3. for   4. in   5. In

Unit 151   p. 314

1 1. at, on, at, /   2. in   3. in, on   4. in
5. about, on, in   6. at, in, for   7. in, in
8. at, on   9. during, to   10. In   11. on, at
12. at, on, in   13. from   14. in   15. by
16. as, in, for   17. on, under, in   18. at
19. at, at, on   20. with   21. for
22. from/to, to   23. with   24. of
25. about   26. at, in, with
27. between   28. of   29. with, in
30. to, about, from   31. to, on, with   32. with
33. for

Unit 152   p. 317

1 1. Is this a seaside spa?
2. Can I soak in the hot tub in my room?
3. Have they reserved two adjacent rooms for
us?
4. Has the hotel been expecting our arrival?
5. Does Connie like spas with not much sulfur
in the water?

6. Did Andrew enjoy the Japanese restaurant at the resort?

2 1. I can 2. I am 3. I haven't 4. I have
5. I didn't 6. she is

3 1. Yes, I think so. 2. Yes, I hope so.
3. Yes, I'm afraid so. 4. No, I don't think so.
5. No, I don't expect so.
6. No, I'm afraid not.

Unit 153 p. 319

1 1. are you leaving? 2. will Adrian leave early?
3. can Woody hide? 4. is Bryan coming?
5. does Rex have my hat?
6. has Susan been taking photos?
7. does Mary want to dance?
8. did Herman go to an audition?

2 1. Who does Ken like? 2. Who loves Buddy?
3. What is Randy playing on his smartphone?
4. Who called Lily?
5. What is Bruce cooking?
6. What went wrong?
7. Who is honking at Karla?
8. Who is Jack waving at?

Unit 154 p. 321

1 1. What 2. Who 3. Which 4. What
5. Whose 6. Which 7. What 8. What
9. Which

2 1. Whose shoes 2. Which burger
3. What magazine 4. What kind of tea
5. Whose toys

Unit 155 p. 323

1 1. Where 2. How 3. Why 4. When
5. When 6. How 7. Why 8. When

2 1. How often 2. How many 3. How long
4. How much 5. How early

Unit 156 p. 325

1 1. Didn't you receive it?
2. Aren't you getting cold?
3. Isn't that your umbrella?
4. Aren't you paying attention to me?
5. Don't you like ballet?
6. Haven't you finished eating yet?
7. Haven't we been driving on this road too long?

2 1. Haven't you run 2. Isn't she
3. Won't you go / Aren't you going
4. Don't you love 5. Hasn't he graduated
6. Isn't this restaurant 7. Didn't you call
8. Doesn't she play / Isn't she playing / Didn't she play

Unit 157 p. 327

1 1. are you 2. has she 3. can't she
4. isn't it 5. does he 6. has he
7. don't you 8. could she 9. aren't you
10. can he 11. hasn't she 12. is it
13. could he 14. do you 15. doesn't she
16. didn't he

2 1. can sketch 2. is 3. couldn't speak
4. talked 5. writes 6. aren't asking
7. have translated 8. doesn't cook 9. went
10. doesn't have

Unit 158 p. 329

1 1. aren't I 2. shall we 3. will there
4. aren't I 5. won't you 6. is there 7. is it
8. didn't you

2 1. isn't it? 2. Let's clean 3. will you?
4. shall we? 5. can't you? 6. would you?
7. isn't there? 8. do they? 9. didn't you?
10. Put 11. Nothing

Unit 159 p. 331

1 1. Are you? 2. Can't he? 3. Has she?
4. Is he? 5. Have you? 6. Does he?
7. Did she? 8. Does she?

2 1. (A) 2. (B) 3. (D) 4. (C)

Unit 160 p. 333

1 1. where the water boilers are located?
2. how many liters this water boiler can hold?
3. what other floor lamps you have?
4. where programmable rice cookers are sold?
5. why this rice cooker can't be used to steam food?
6. when the new rice cookers arrived?
7. if/whether this is the only low-suds laundry soap you have in stock?
8. if/whether I can get this washing machine delivered tonight?
9. if/whether he could move to a small tropical island and go on with his writing?

Unit 161 p. 335

1 1. Neither am I. 2. So do I. 3. Neither have I.
4. So am I. 5. Neither do I. 6. So have I.
7. Neither do I. 8. So did I. 9. Neither do I.

2 1. knows 2. is going to join
3. doesn't agree 4. didn't play
5. couldn't skydive 6. has done
7. hasn't finished 8. doesn't like 9. is

Unit 162   p. 337

1 1. dug, (A)   2. has been dug, (P)
  3. set up, (A)   4. has been wired, (P)
  5. has arrived, (A)   6. is being poured, (P)
  7. have been working, (A)
  8. have been told, (P)
  9. was being connected, (P)
  10. are arriving, (A)

2 1. Those coffee beans were ground by the clerk.
  2. The leather shoes were polished by Father.
  3. The house is being painted by Ariel.
  4. The boar must have been found by Paul.
  5. The shop is going to be closed by us.
  6. Ian is being encouraged by the boss.
  7. A supernova has been discovered by the scientists.
  8. A cactus was planted in the garden by Freddie.

Unit 163   p. 339

1 1. The newspaper must be called.
  2. A cameraman and a reporter will be sent by the TV station.
  3. The store owner is going to be interviewed by the reporter.
  4. The store owner may have been involved with the gang in their criminal activity.
  5. The reporter should have been called earlier.
  6. The store owner doesn't like to be videotaped by the cameraman.

2 1. got torn   2. got stung   3. got spent
  4. got lost   5. got hurt   6. got elected
  7. got kidnapped   8. got caught

Unit 164   p. 341

1 1. was sent two ballet tickets by the thankful client
  2. was offered a discount tour package by the sales representative
  3. was shown the model home by the real estate agent
  4. was paid about $1,000,000 by the advertising agency
  5. was taught four nights a week by the instructor
  6. was promised a letter a day by the sailor
  7. was bought for me by Hazel

2 1. by   2. with   3. with   4. by   5. by
  6. with   7. with   8. by

Unit 165   p. 343

1 1. → It is believed that the number of school-age children will drop again this year.
  → The number of school-age children is believed to drop again this year.
  2. → It is widely known that the secret negotiations started last week.
  → The secret negotiations are widely known to have started last week.
  3. → It is thought that the sailors have been rescued.
  → The sailors are thought to have been rescued.
  4. → It is said that the pandemic completely changed how the world works.
  → The pandemic is said to have completely changed how the world works.

2 1. Sitting too long is supposed to be bad for your health.
  2. Watching TV is supposed to be bad for kids.
  3. Drinking two liters of water a day is supposed to be healthy.
  4. Quitting smoking is supposed to be simply a matter of will power.
  5. Doraemon is supposed to be the most popular cat in the world.

Unit 166   p. 345

1 1. have her shoes repaired
  2. have his shoes shined（「擦亮」的三態為 shine, shined, shined，注意不要寫成「發光」：shine, shone, shone）
  3. have your skirt dry cleaned
  4. have that dress altered
  5. had their daughter's baby shoes bronzed
  6. had her dress ripped
  7. had the heel on her left shoe broken
  8. had his briefcase stolen

2 1. Ed is having the grass in his yard cut.
  2. Dennis is having the toilet fixed.
  3. Rick just had three light bulbs replaced.
  4. Wayne will have the sheets changed later.
  5. Eleanor is having a steak fried on the stove.
  6. Claudia has had all the shirts ironed.
  7. Ashley could have a propane tank switched easily with this device.

Unit 167   p. 347

1 1. I wish I jogged   2. I wish I had left home
  3. If only I were watching   4. If only I spoke
  5. I wish I had saved   6. I wish we had come
  7. If only we had brought

8. If only I had locked
9. If only I had lowered
2 1. I wish she would sing
2. I wish he wouldn't talk
3. If only the kids wouldn't swim
4. If only he would take off

Unit 168 p. 349

1 1. go, will buy   2. goes, will run
3. has, can ride   4. calls, tell her
5. has packed, will load   6. is making, will be
7. turns, will cool   8. calls, will tell
2 1. grow higher   2. doesn't rain
3. keep eating   4. will make pudding
5. go shopping   6. isn't working

Unit 169 p. 351

1 1. if   2. If   3. When   4. When   5. If
6. When   7. If   8. When   9. If
2 1. works, he takes Monday off
2. sees, she knocks on wood three times
3. does not work, we have to walk up to our
12th floor apartment
4. goes, he dresses up in his sharkskin suit
5. does not take, I give him the silent
treatment
6. relaxes, she listens to jazz music

Unit 170 p. 353

1 1. were, would give   2. called, would donate
3. were held, would attend
4. would change, inherited
5. would, give, had
2 1. will need   2. won't feel   3. would ask
4. would discuss   5. will be
6. usually take   7. would find
8. job-hunts

Unit 171 p. 355

1 1. had behaved, wouldn't have embarrassed
2. had read, would have known
3. had bought, wouldn't have worried
4. had paid, wouldn't have impounded
5. had accepted, wouldn't have stayed
6. had mailed, wouldn't have paid
2 1. will find   2. will buy   3. would meet
4. would leave   5. would have known
6. would have finished
3 1. wants   2. liked   3. had inquired   4. needs
5. studied   6. had washed   7. goes

Unit 172 p. 357

1 1. Unless   2. As long as   3. Providing that
4. so long as   5. will turn   6. Suppose
7. Unless   8. will give   9. would he do
2 1. Unless you pass the driving test, you can't
drive on the road.
2. Unless you read every day, you can't
improve your reading comprehension.
3. As long as you apologize sincerely, I will
forgive you.
4. He will come to the dinner provided that
you don't mention his divorce.
5. Suppose I wrote a recommendation for
you, would it help?

Unit 173 p. 359

1 1. It's time we left   2. It's time you fixed
3. It's time he picked up
4. It's time he designed
2 1. her feelings will get hurt
2. you'll get sun burned
3. Swallow the cough medicine
4. Listen to the expert

Unit 174 p. 361

1 1. (D)   2. (R)   3. (R)   4. (D)   5. (R)   6. (D)
7. (D)   8. (R)   9. (R)
2 1. said   2. told   3. told   4. said   5. said
6. said   7. said   8. tell
3 1. tell tales   2. tell a joke   3. tell a fortune
4. tell the time   5. tell the truth   6. tell a lie

Unit 175 p. 363

1 1. Kathy said she was going out to dinner.
2. Abby said she had spoken / spoke to the
director.
3. Sam said he had seen / saw a car accident
on his way to the store.
4. Scott said he had listened to that song
thousands of times.
5. Sarah said she was in a taxi with her mom.
6. Tina said she had finished her homework
long before her mom came back home.
2 1. wanted to enjoy the sea breeze
2. everyone has gone to work
3. the pizza had already arrived
4. had bought him the watch

Unit 176 p. 365

1 1. could handle   2. must get / had to get
3. is   4. was   5. should arrive

6. might drop by   7. should go
8. must cook / had to cook   9. is/was
10. would rain   11. was going to punish
12. can speak / could speak

Unit 177   p. 367

1 1. Yesterday Elmore said he would call me today.
2. Hans said I should wash my hands before meals.
3. Ann said she wanted me to go there right away.
4. Bruce said he <u>had bought</u> / <u>bought</u> the watch from a vendor in the night market.
5. Bernie said he was going to have tuna for lunch that day. /
Bernie said he is going to have tuna for lunch today.（轉述時還在今天）
6. Kayla said she would stay there until noon.
7. Charlotte said her brother had gone camping the previous day. /
Charlotte said her brother went camping yesterday.（轉述時還在今天）
8. Amy said she didn't know where Tom had been the previous week. /
Amy said she didn't know where Tom was last week.（轉述時還在這週）
9. Stevie said he would be out of town for a couple of days.
10. Bella said she would come to my place that afternoon, but she never showed up.

Unit 178   p. 369

1 1. if he/she liked ballet.
2. how he/she got enough protein and calcium.
3. what type of music he/she played.
4. how many cows he/she had.
5. if/whether he/she had ever felt nervous when flying.
6. if he/she had an affordable health insurance plan.
2 1. Pete asked his boss Annie if/whether she would like to see the file.
2. Annie asked Pete what kind of file it was.
3. Pete asked <u>where he should put the file</u> / <u>where to put the file</u>.
4. Pete asked Annie if/whether he could get a pay raise.
5. Annie asked Pete why she should give him a pay raise.
6. Pete asked if/whether he wasn't working hard enough.

7. Annie asked Pete if/whether he wanted a pay raise or a nicer office.

Unit 179   p. 371

1 1. Dan offered to do the dishes.
2. Mom ordered me to get my feet off the coffee table.
3. My neighbor warned me to stay away from that dog.
4. Tom asked/invited me to go to a karaoke with them.
5. My husband offered to help me move the sofa.
6. The painter promised to be careful up on the ladder.
2 1. I told him (that) I wanted a new job.
2. He asked me if/whether I was a chef.
3. He told me (that) he had a job opening.
4. He warned me not to touch the mushrooms.
5. He told me (that) he <u>had been</u> / <u>was</u> in the south digging truffles.
6. He said (that) maybe I could cook truffles for him.
7. I said (that) I had never cooked truffles before.
8. He told me (that) I should never overcook truffles.
9. I promised not to overcook the truffles.
10. He asked me if/whether I could start working there on Monday.

Unit 180   p. 373

1 1. (N)   2. (N)   3. (R)   4. (N)   5. (R)   6. (N)
2 1. (A)   2. (C)   3. (E)   4. (B)   5. (G)   6. (D)
7. (F)

Unit 181   p. 375

1 1. I called the woman who/that had left a message on my answering machine.
2. Did you see the woman who/that was sitting by me on the bus?
3. The guy who/that talked to me while I was having my iced tea was cool.
4. Have you seen the water bottle which/that was by the door?
5. I tripped over the slippers which/that were in the hallway.
6. The hat which/that is now on the floor was on the coat tree when I left home this morning.
2 1. Did you see the blue backpack ~~who~~ which/that I bought yesterday?
2. Could you please pass me the pepper ~~who~~ which/that is on the counter?

3. I called the history teacher who I met ~~him~~ at the party last night.
4. I went to the new restaurant which ~~it~~ opened last Sunday.
5. I didn't recognize the tall woman ~~which~~ who/that talked to me at the bank yesterday.
6. Jack said the woman, ~~that~~ who he had dinner with last night, was his ex-wife.

Unit 182   p. 377

1 1. who   2. (who)   3. (that)   4. that   5. (who)
6. who
2 1. Guam is the island we went to for our honeymoon.
2. Sophia is the student I mentioned yesterday.
3. The roast duck was the dish Patricia recommended in this restaurant.
4. This is the house Janet sold in two days.

Unit 183   p. 379

1 1. (why/that)   2. whose   3. where   4. where
5. (when)   6. where   7. (why/that)
8. whose
2 1. I remember the day when we first met.
2. Bangkok is the city where we go for a shopping trip every year.
3. I know a guy whose father owns a company with two thousand employees.
4. I don't know the reason why/that he hasn't spoken to me for a week.
5. I need the address where I can send this parcel.
6. The rain came at a time when the peasants needed it most.

Unit 184   p. 381

1 1. whose   2. who   3. where   4. when
5. where   6. where   7. who
2 1. which lies in the South America
2. who is sitting here reading a newspaper
3. where the Emperor Penguins live
4. whose car has a flat tire

Unit 185   p. 383

1 1. in which   2. with whom   3. in which
4. in which   5. about whom
2 1. with which, This is Mia's favorite toy, which she can play with for hours.
2. about whom, That woman is our new manager, who/whom I've heard a lot about.
3. in which, This is Lulu's favorite pool, which she often swims for a long time in.
4. for whom, That pretty woman is my wife, who/whom I make a cup of rooibos tea for every day.